THE MAN
I LOVE

SUANNE LAQUEUR

CATHEDRAL ROCK PRESS

NEW YORK

2014

Suanne Laqueur/Cathedral Rock Press
Somers, New York
www.suannelaqueur.com

Book Design by Write Dream Repeat Book Design LLC

Cover Design by Tracy Kopsachilis

The Man I Love/ Suanne Laqueur. — 1st ed.

ISBN 978-1499715606

To my favorite

"Dancers live in light as fish live in water."
—Jean Rosenthal

Part One: Erik

A GUARDED BOY

SOME SEEK THE LIMELIGHT and some hold the light in place.

Erik Fiskare didn't like being the center of attention, but he liked situations where he had to keep the attention centered.

He was the son of a builder and a musician. He grew up around his father's workbench, watching how things were made, or around his mother's piano, listening to how things were composed. The smoky smell of cut wood and the dizzy odor of turpentine wreathed his childhood days, along with the strains of Bach and Mozart. He played with scrap wood on the saw-dusty floor, pattering along to the ring of hammer on nail and the dissonant squeal of a power saw. Or he lay on the rug beneath the piano, listening to hammers striking strings, nattering to himself as his mother gave lessons to neighborhood kids.

"Erik is happiest when he's underfoot," she always said.

In the dark of a night when he was eight years old, Erik awoke to the sound of wheels crunching over gravel in the driveway. From his bedroom window he stared as his father's pickup truck backed out. It gleamed white in the moonlight, the blue letters crisp on the driver's side door—*FISKARE CONSTRUCTION* arching over a fleet of blue fish. Fiskare was Swedish for "fisherman."

Erik watched the red tail lights pull further and further down the street, then turn a corner and disappear.

He never saw his father again.

It was a cruel and unexplained desertion which left in its wake a little boy soothed by routine and structure, calmed when things went to according plan. He grew into a teenager with an insatiable need to know how things worked and why. He took everything apart and put it back together, usually successfully. Anything refusing to reassemble was jerry-rigged, and anything that wouldn't jerry-rig was recycled. Any guy with half a brain knew to have a plan B. Erik had a plan C and D, minimum.

In youth sports he was continually elected captain, for not only was he a natural athlete, but also a natural rallying point. He knew just enough about all his teammates' personalities to figure out how the team worked best. The team had its superstars, its weak links and its filler. And the self-effacing guy who had his finger on the pulse of it all, the oil keeping the gears in motion, the unifying force making the many into one—that was Erik.

Basketball was his passion and he'd been a talented, scrappy point guard on the junior varsity team until he was benched with an ankle injury his sophomore year. Christine Fiskare allowed her oldest son a three-day pity party. It was all she could afford. She'd sold the piano and now worked two jobs while pursuing a nursing degree. The bulk of her worry was allocated to her younger son, Peter, who was profoundly deaf after a childhood illness and stubbornly uncommunicative since his father had left.

Three days was also the limit of her patience. Even before the desertion, Christine had never coddled either of her sons. Nor had public hand-wringing ever been in her nature. Her pain as an abandoned wife was suffered in private, far from the boys' eyes. As a single mother, she set the past aside and made plans. Shrewdness and self-sufficiency were the bedrock beneath her little family. Once Erik was in a walking cast and maneuvering easily on his crutches, she challenged him to find a new hobby, something to fill up the hours between dismissal and five-thirty.

"Something accountable, Mister," Christine said. "I need to know where you are. And no hanging around street corners, or I'll find you a job."

She ruffled his short blond hair, teasing. Erik wasn't a troublemaker. He'd been making his own pocket money since he was eleven, when he became familiar with such terms as "willful desertion" and "child support," and the need to check the "divorced" box on forms. He knew his Fiskare grandparents contributed to his and Pete's upbringing. They lived far upstate near the Canadian border, a modest and self-sufficient couple full of Scandinavian reserve. They pledged support to their two grandsons, but it was a stoic assurance. Erik could never tell if they helped out of love, obligation or shame.

Erik became his mother's apt pupil. He earned his degree in shrewdness, stayed out of trouble and always let Christine know where he was. He knew how hard she worked, knew the basics were covered, and knew Peter's needs took priority. If he wanted luxuries, either material or spiritual, he had to get them himself. With sports out of the equation, though, Erik had no idea what to do with his time. His soul was lost, and his inner compass whirled in a desperate search for another True North he could align to.

He had a creative streak, an inherent desire for expression, one not easily channeled into the obvious mediums. He already played piano and a little guitar, taking lessons at the local Y for the former and banging away by ear on the latter. But neither of those were for public consumption. He played for himself, or in a small jamming group at most. His voice was legitimate, but he didn't like to sing in front of people, and he most definitely didn't dance. Truth was he was a much better tinkerer than creator, although it all felt like the same thing to him.

"Why don't you come by play rehearsal," said Mrs. Jerome, wisest in the school's cadre of wise teachers and faculty adviser to the drama club. "I know you're not an actor but we have plenty to do behind the scenes."

Erik liked the sound of behind the scenes. It seemed the defense of the performing arts team. And he also liked Mindy Meredith, one of the drama club starlets. Curious, he loped into the auditorium, took a good look around at the pandemonium and immediately dialed into the current of purposeful action beneath it, and the big picture around it. Things had to get done here. The show was on the stage, true, but a second show was going on backstage, in front of the stage, even over the stage. And without *those* shows, there was no show.

He started low on the totem pole: manning a follow spotlight, keeping its powerful beam centered on Mindy. He caught the technical theater bug like a chronic flu. Wiring up the lanterns and organizing their light into cues was satisfying work. Building sets—immersed in the cacophony of hammering, sawing drilling—reminded him of childhood days at the legs of his father's workbench, but not enough to hurt. Later musical theater productions appealed to both his eyes and ears. Everything about being a stagehand felt right to him.

By his junior year, Mrs. Jerome had entrusted him with the keys to the auditorium and he had the run of the place. Until he graduated, he owned the same bit of square inch real estate in every program of every school production: *Erik Fiskare, stage manager*. The greatest tree houses of the world had nothing on the small concrete bunker built into the balcony, his command central, his crows' nest, his throne. From this perch he ran the lights and called the shows. With his privileged keys he let himself in during off hours. He hung there alone. He hung there with friends. He even got laid there once, with Mindy. And though it wasn't anything close to true love, or even false love, the encounter seemed to fix the coordinates for Erik's place in the universe.

His relationships with girls weren't meaningless, yet they were always brief, and none left him deeply hurt or changed. Like most his age, he was rabidly curious about sex and sought it out in the juvenile way of boys who yearn to find what it means for them, rather than thinking of themselves as lovers intent on someone else's pleasure. He was usually taken on as the pet project of older girls who were feeling their own wings. Nice girls, all of them, but not one moved him to make plans. He wasn't sure why. Whether out of shyness or idealized romanticism, he didn't get scrappy with love, and rarely applied any of his mechanical curiosity to the inner workings of women. Some in the know would say this was the inevitable result of his father's abandonment, impressing love's cruel nature upon the young Erik Fiskare. Giving your heart only made you more vulnerable to pain. Anyone you loved could and would only hurt you in the end, likely without explanation. It was best you figured out an escape plan from the get-go, and always eject first.

Erik was indeed a guarded boy, struggling to grow into a guarded man. His father had scarred him. He pushed the experience into a far corner of his heart and made every attempt to forget about it. Still, he was young, with his moments of uncontrollable rage, inconsolable despair and forsaken agony.

Young, but not jaded. He was neither cagey, nor unapproachable, but what he gave forth was carefully chosen to give, and what he kept back was off limits. Girls were drawn to his good looks and his sunny nature. They grew quickly frustrated with him because he always seemed slightly aloof, holding back some essential key to the workings of his heart.

Yet Erik Fiskare's heart was good, and it secretly yearned to be told so. He thought a lot about love, dissected and deconstructed it as a concept to the best of his abilities. And with these dismantled parts he tinkered, constructing dreams of a girl for him. Only dreams. No plans. Watching a performance of *Guys and Dolls*, he rather agreed with Sky Masterson—he would leave things to chance and chemistry, and when the girl came along, he would simply know.

Until then, he would wait.

THE GIRL WITH THE WRONG NAME

ERIK HAD NEVER ENTERTAINED big college dreams. His record was good, his grades were impressive. Money was the killer. He assumed he'd attend community college at least, or one of the state universities at most. But his grandfather Fiskare had died during Erik's junior year of high school, leaving an unexpected inheritance for Erik and his brother. The windfall allowed Erik to look beyond the borders of New York to a fine arts university outside Philadelphia. An academic scholarship won through his community service at the Y brought the tuition down to an even more manageable level. And a letter of recommendation from Mrs. Jerome clinched it: fall of 1989, Erik was a business major at Lancaster University, and a technical theater minor in their prestigious conservatory program.

Low on the totem pole again, he was enrolled in Stagecraft 100, Professor Leo Graham's required introductory course. Leo was a paradox: while he looked and acted like a stoner—some swore he was Jerry Garcia's twin brother—he ran his shop and his productions with almost military zeal. He was laconic and laid-back, rarely raising his voice unless he was directing someone in the catwalk, yet his soft-spoken words were law. He built manpower from the bottom up and let knowledge cascade from the top down. He shepherded his students through a four-year program that took them from servitude to artist. Freshmen toiled for him, their resentment quickly turning to respect. Sophomores would follow him anywhere. Juniors revered him. Seniors would kill for him.

The first half of the semester, Erik built sets for the one-act plays in the black box theater. Leo believed in a small task force—you worked harder, but you learned faster. Erik and three other underclassmen took direction from two seniors, for whom the one-acts were a last hurrah, their graduating project. Leo provided guidance from a distance and divine intervention when necessary. Subjects of this unholy trinity, Erik and his mates worked like sled dogs, soon with Erik as their unspoken lead musher.

Erik thrived within the wartime camaraderie in the warm, window-less shops beneath Mallory Hall. Long hours spent in philosophical con-versation as the stagehands painted sets and backdrops. Raucous bond-ing as they hammered and sawed. And punchy horseplay while sinking countless numbers of screws into crossbeams and struts. Erik drove one comrade to the campus health center for stitches after a slight mishap with the power saw, and another who tripped over a poorly-taped light-ing cable and broke his wrist.

When performance week arrived, the sets were brought to the black box via the service elevator. Load-in started at seven in the morning with coffee and bagels, and went into the wee hours with pizza and beers. In the wee-est of those hours, a red-haired ingénue lured Erik into one of the dressing rooms and showed him the meaning of "casting couch." She never called afterward.

He never had so much fun in his life.

Now, on a Sunday in November, he walked into the vast main audito-rium of Mallory Hall, taking on his second assignment for the semester: running lights for the conservatory's fall dance concert.

He wasn't sure what to expect. Leo told him the dance division of the conservatory was one of the top programs on the East Coast, but Erik had no frame of reference. Other than musical theater numbers, dance was utterly foreign to him, though he had enough brains to figure out "Born to Hand Jive" from *Grease* wasn't what was going down today.

Nice scenery here, however, especially if one was a leg man. Erik moved aside as a trio of girls in leotards chattered their way up the aisle. They smiled at him in passing, six eyes sweeping him head to toe in a frank once-over. A definitive leg man, he smiled back, but politely counted ten before he glanced over his shoulder and ran appreciative eyes over those six perfect limbs.

He found Leo coiling cables at the side of the stage with a dark-haired boy in a flannel button-down shirt. Leo tossed Erik a hank of cable without preamble and made introductions. "This is David Alto, he'll be running lights for the concert, consider him the sorcerer. David, this is Erik. Consider him the apprentice. Finish these up and take him back in the booth, show him the boards. You got about twenty minutes before the madness."

David and Erik shook hands and after dealing with the cables, headed back up the aisle to the glassed-in booth at the back of the auditorium. It was four feet wide by eight feet long, with lighting consoles along two-thirds of the raised counter. Two captains' chairs sat before the consoles, each with a headset hooked over one arm. Clipboards holding design schematics and cue sheets hung on the back wall. Mason jars of pencils, all sharpened, perched on the counter. Wires and cables, neatly taped, snaked overhead and underfoot, turning precise corners around and through things.

It was a tighter, cleaner ship than Erik had been on in high school. Clearly childish things had been put away and no one would be getting laid here.

"Equipment's kind of kludgy," David said. "You work boards like these before?"

"Looks sort of the same. You write out the cue sheets or is it computerized?"

"Nothing in this place is computerized, but they're going to bat for us in the next budget, I hear. I worked a sweet system at SUNY Purchase over the summer, all computers. Coming back here is like working with candles."

Through the glass booth Erik watched Leo Graham direct a band of techs in bringing out the boom stands—long poles with crossbars, to be hung with fixtures and set in each of the stage's four wings. "I've never rigged booms."

"Booms are key when you're lighting dance. In fact if it came down to a choice between four lanterns on booms and forty overhead, Leo would take the four on booms."

"Really?"

"The booms are the bitches, my friend," David said. "It's one of the sayings around here."

The noise level in the theater was rising as more and more dancers arrived. Erik hadn't encountered them much within Mallory, for the studios were all on the third floor while the tech theater students roamed like rats in the building's basement. Bumping occasional shoulders in the student lounge had been the extent of his contact with the dance students. Leaning elbows on the console, he watched the full gathered company. They stretched in the aisles, limbered up at the edge of the stage or hanging on the grand piano. Girls in leotards, long-legged and sleek, their hair pulled up revealing slender necks and sculpted shoulders. The boys were just as sleek, some prettier than the girls, loud and flamboyant, indiscriminately touchy-feely. Two of them sauntered up the aisle past the booth, loud and animated as they headed out the lobby doors. They were back thirty seconds later, camping down to the stage, shoving and laughing.

"Quite the fabulous crowd," Erik said.

"Congrats, dude. You just got a fly-by."

Erik turned in his chair, eyebrows raised. "Say what?"

A half smile twisted around David's mouth. "Think they were walking past the booth to stretch their legs? I'm shocked they waited this long to come check you out."

Erik sank in his seat, crossing his arms. "Great."

"Eh, don't worry. They talk a big game but they keep their hands to themselves. Except for Will Kaeger. He'll definitely grab your ass."

Erik wasn't exactly worried, just out of his comfort zone. Coming from an insular small town in upstate New York, he had little to no contact with gay men. Even with all his involvement in the drama club productions, nobody openly discussed their sexual orientation. There were veiled hints, vague implications. Looks askance, rolled eyes, muttered jeers out of sheer self-protection. Being gay was an accusation, not a lifestyle, and Erik didn't know anyone who was definitively *out*.

Here, half the male student body of the conservatory was out. Not just out but confidently out and accepted. Erik was still getting used to it. It evoked in him a confusing blend of fascination and defensiveness, which he approached the way he would anything unfamiliar: he hung back and observed until he could figure out how to take it apart and put it back together in some way that made sense.

"How long is this show?" he asked.

"Concert," David said. "It's a concert. They'll fine you a dollar if you call it a show or a recital."

"Concert," Erik said, pretending to write it on the palm of his hand.

"It's two acts. First act is for the ballet company, second for the contemporary dance theater." David swiveled in his chair, looking out at the activity in the theater. "All right, a few faces you should know. Guy standing on the apron with Leo is Michael Kantz, the director of the whole department. He's God. Woman in the long purple sweater, standing in that group over there—Marie Del'Amici. She heads the ballet division. She's from Milan, you can barely understand a word she says but she's a ton of fun. Then see the tall, black guy with the bald head? That's Cornelis Justi, he runs the contemporary dance division. He's from Amsterdam. And he's crazy..."

Erik's eyes had been flicking around the auditorium, following David's brisk narrative, recording names and quick impressions on mental index cards. But then a wind was blowing through his mind, scattering the cards, drowning out David's patter. A girl in black tights and a navy Lancaster hoodie, the neck cut into a deep V, was coming up the aisle. Her hair was pulled up loosely, a couple of thin, spiral curls dangled across one eye. She carried a paper bag in one hand and a Coke in the other.

"Who's she?" Erik said.

David looked. "That's Daisy."

Daisy, Erik thought. *Seriously?* A daisy was a sunny little flower. A girl named Daisy should be pert and blonde, shades of yellow and white and pink. A girl named Daisy was a cheerleader, athletic and peppy. Daisy was the screwed-up chick in *The Great Gatsby*. Daisy was a stupid cartoon duck, for crying out loud.

The girl coming up the aisle, however, was none of those things. She was dark-haired and exuded a cool sexiness, moving along with the lithe grace of a cat. Waving to the left. Smiling at someone to the right. Nothing was sunny or pert about her errant curls, her dangling earrings or dark lipstick. This was not a screwed-up cartoon. Whoever this girl was, she was coming up the aisle and coming, it seemed, right toward the lighting booth.

"She your girlfriend?" Erik asked, dry-mouthed.

"I wish," David said. "Took her on a couple dates but—" He threw out an arm, palm flat to Erik. "—she gave me the Heisman. If I'm nice she brings me lunch sometimes." He got up from his chair and patted Erik on the shoulder. "Try not to look her in the eye. We got a lot of work to do today. Yo, baby, what's up?"

Erik spun in his own chair, too far and banged his elbow against the console. The girl with the wrong name was in the door of the booth. He should get up. He couldn't move. She'd come in and was standing by him. He smelled her skin, a light, clean candied scent, like sugared soap. If you tasted her she would be sweet.

He abruptly spun his chair the other way, as if trying to reverse something, direction, polarity. Now his mouth was watering, imagining the sweetness of this girl so vividly, he felt his face flare with heated blood.

Daisy was handing the bag and soda over to David. "They didn't have the chicken parm. I got you a meatball sub."

"What are you doing walking around barefoot? Marie will kill you."

Erik glanced down. Her tights were rolled up and her feet were indeed bare, every single toe encased neatly in what looked like surgical tape. Guiltily, she hooked one foot behind the other calf. Her legs were thin, but lusciously curved, a strong saber of quadriceps in front, and a smaller arc of hamstring opposite, both lines disappearing up under the hem of her sweatshirt. Erik swallowed and looked away, looked up at her face. Too late he remembered David's warning.

Jesus.

Her eyes were astonishing. No other word sufficed. A blue he'd never seen in eyes before. A blue iris shot through with green and rimmed with an even darker blue. Her lashes were a black fringe, her eyebrows two chiseled bows. Eyes like those were impossible, they just didn't happen in real life.

Yet there they were. There she was. She was looking at him. As if she knew him.

"This is Daisy Bianco," David said. "Rising star and bringer of sustenance. Dais, this is Erik. He's running your follow spot so be nice to him."

Daisy looked at David, then took the bag and the soda from his hands and handed them to Erik.

"Shit," David said.

Clutching his prize, Erik felt his face widen. She smiled back at him. Neither of them had said so much as hello yet she was looking at him with those eyes. Deep in the cathedral of his young being, Erik felt a bell toll, a peal of recognition. And for the rest of his life, he would swear, he would swear to anyone who asked, although nothing was said aloud, he heard Daisy Bianco speak to him. She said it with her eyes, he heard it clearly in his head, and it wasn't hello.

It was, "Well, here you are."

Here I am, he thought.

Her expression grew expansive. The green in her eyes deepened.

David cleared his throat. "Go put some shoes on, honey. Nails are all over the damn place."

"See ya," she said, looking at Erik. Her voice was soft, a secret meant only for his ears.

"Bye." His mouth formed the word with barely a sound. It rose like a shimmering bubble and followed Daisy out the door.

Pointedly David retrieved his lunch. Erik surrendered it, and through the glass of the lighting booth he watched Daisy walk back down the aisle of the auditorium. Sat and watched her as the atoms in his body slowly rearranged themselves.

THE MODERN NEANDERTHAL

"GOOD MORNING, ladies and gentlemen."

The glass of the lighting booth was no match for the vocal power of Michael Kantz. Straight through it came, clear and resonant.

"He's got some set of pipes," Erik said.

"Double degree dance and voice," David said around a mouthful of sandwich.

"With the usual opening festivities concluded," Michael said, "let's get this show on the road."

"Foul," someone yelled, at the same time the bald-headed Cornelis Justi stood up and bellowed, "Illegal."

Erik looked at David, eyebrows wrinkled.

David chewed and swallowed. "I told you," he said. "It's a concert, not a show."

The theater had erupted in hoots and catcalls, shouts of "Dollar, that's a dollar..."

"I didn't realize they were so touchy about it," Erik said.

"You learn to carry a lot of singles during Tech Week."

Michael tucked his clipboard under his arm and reached for his wallet, extricating a dollar. He waved it about until one of the dancers plucked it from his fingers.

"Buy yourself a Snickers. All right, all right, indentured servants to the stage, please, let's get this concert on the road."

His voice was laced with humor and courtesy, yet it demanded instant action, and the dancers promptly took themselves to the stage, shedding sweaters and sweatshirts and other extra layers of clothes. When finally gathered, thirty or so strong, they were silent, standing in tableau, straight, proud, attentive. Erik crammed his eyes with girls—he'd never seen so many great bodies in one place in his life.

David bundled up the rest of his sub and stuffed it back into the paper bag. "Come on," he said, belching behind a fist.

Erik followed David down the aisle and slipped into the center fifth row, sitting down behind Leo Graham. In the row ahead of Leo were Cornelis Justi, the contemporary dance director, and Marie Del'Amici, the ballet director.

"What do we do?" Erik asked quietly.

"Listen, observe, take notes," David said. He'd taken two clipboards from the lighting booth and now passed one to Erik. "Write down whatever Leo tells you to, or if you hear him mutter something under his breath. If you have impressions of your own, jot those down. Michael wants everyone included in the design aspects. You'll see."

"Hello everyone, I'm Michael."

The dancers sang back in unison. "Hi, Michael."

Michael turned back to his crew with a closed-mouth grin. "Aren't they adorable? All right, my children, we have a week to turn water into wine."

"First step is admitting we have a problem," Cornelis said.

"For the benefit of our esteemed tech director, Sir Leo von Graham—" Wild applause from the dancers. Leo raised a fist to the ceiling. "—and his accolades, we'll go through the program as we understand it to be."

Erik twirled his pencil and scanned the cluster of dancers on the stage, looking for Daisy and finally locating her, stage left. She'd pinned back those stray curls and donned a blue headband around her hairline. Her earrings were off, as was the sweatshirt. In a purple leotard with the black tights pulled over, she stood with her arms crossed, one foot poised up on the hard block of her shoe. Erik knew ballerinas danced on their toes, but he'd never seen it in action. He leaned forward a little in his seat, squinting at the footwear and wondering how it was made.

"We have a ballet program set entirely to Johann Sebastian Bach. We'll be using seven pieces in all. In order, they are..."

Erik noticed David was writing. He started writing too, listening and scribbling a rough outline:

> *Bourée from Suite in E Minor. Ensemble.*
> *Prelude from Cello Suite. Sr male solo.*
> *Prelude in C #. Sr female solo.*
> *Prelude in F Minor. 5 girls.*
> *Gavotte in E Major. 5 boys.*
> *Siciliano from Sonata #2. Dance for Sr couple*
> *Brandenberg Concerto. Finale, feature Sr couple.*

He flexed his fingers and reread it all. His piano teacher had him play a lot of Bach, back in the day. Back in the long day. His allegiance switched to guitar and he hadn't sat down at the keys in years.

He frowned at his list and drew a question mark by the Siciliano. Michael used some other term but Erik didn't know how to spell it so he put "dance." His eyes flicked to the stage. Daisy had moved next to a tall boy, tallest of all the male dancers, with dark hair pulled back in a ponytail. Daisy's hand was on his shoulder and she was up on her toes, shifting her weight from foot to foot. Her leotard had elaborate criss-cross straps in the back. Her shoulders were defined, as were her arms.

And dear God, those legs.

"All right then. Let's start from the top," Michael said. "Marie, any last requests?"

Marie Del'Amici stood up, a black shawl swathed around her purple sweater, salt-and-pepper hair in a rumpled braid down her back. Her speech spilled out in bubbles, a thick Italian accent garbling a third of it. "Don't go crazy with the spacing, darlings, I'm not giving any notes or corrections. Just dance. We want to let Leo here know how this tastes."

"No notes, my ass," David said under his breath.

Erik smiled. He expected Marie would be out of her seat in two minutes, going crazy with the spacing.

The dancers took up positions onstage and the Bourée started. Sure enough, Marie was already down by the apron, jumping around and waving her hands, yelling directions. Leo kept calling her back to talk to him about the design. She would come back, effusive with apology. After engaging with Leo for barely a minute, the dancers would distract her and she would wander off again.

This happened several times, and Erik found it more entertaining than watching the dancing. Cornelis was no help. He made a thing of holding Marie's hands behind her back, seeing if she could talk without moving them.

"David, my love," he said, after setting Marie free. "Introduce me to your disciple?"

"Erik Fiskare, chick magnet," David said. "Cornelis Justi, gypsy queen."

"Call me Case," the black man said, shaking Erik's hand.

Erik wrote *Cornelis—Case* in a corner of his notes.

"No," David said. "K-e-e-s. Kees."

"Rhymes with lace," Kees said. "Or you could use Keesja, but only if we're dating."

"Don't scare the child," David said.

In the midst of all this clowning, Leo was muttering either to himself or over his shoulder, and Erik was scribbling anything he could pick up, making more lists:

Both low and mid shins.

Blue cyc on opening.

Cut new gels for bars.

Pink wash for first transition, poppy red for first male solo, maybe. Definitely maybe?

Remind Leo to inventory Fresnels.

Remind Leo to fix lens on follow spot.

The dancers gulped water and ran the Bourée again. This time Marie stayed by Leo, keeping only a token knee on the seat of a chair, but at least she held still. Leo had less to say, so Erik was able to watch.

Despite the invitation for artistic input, he had nothing. He wasn't entirely sure what he was looking at or for, except Daisy. It took some time to be able to pick her out of the group, but during the third run-through, he'd gotten a general feel for when and where she was on the stage. Even then, he only watched her out of pure attraction. He had no true interest in or appreciation for what she was doing. He simply liked how she looked doing it.

Ironically, it was during the section of the Bourée which featured all the male dancers when Erik was finally moved to speak up. He leaned into David. "The tall guy with the ponytail. Front row, far right. Who's he?"

"That's Will Kaeger. He got the Brighton last year."

"The what?"

"Brighton scholarship. Full free ride for two incoming conservatory freshman. Daisy's got one of them this year. Not that she needs it—little rich girl from Gladwyne."

"Don't be a bitch, David," Kees said.

"What? It's true. Her father made a killing laying pipe along the Main Line, now he owns a zillion-acre farm out in Amish country."

"It's an orchard, dumbass. And her father working hard is not her character flaw."

With half a mind, Erik recorded all these details about Daisy. But he was still looking at Will, squinting beneath wrinkled eyebrows. Will had the moves. Erik didn't even know the moves but at a rudimentary level he could still grasp Will's talent. Observing the other boys dance, Erik felt a prickling defensiveness, some primal affront to his own masculinity. He watched as though a pane of glass were between him and the stage. *Fine, I'll look at you, but it doesn't mean I'm enjoying it.*

With Will, the barrier dissolved. He was approachable. He didn't demand your attention, but he made looking somewhere else not as interesting. Something about his style was distinctive, powerful, yet controlled and percussive—he cleverly caught little accents in the music, making Erik wonder if he were a drummer. An adjective dangled just beyond the edge of Erik's mind, a proper metaphor to capture this way of moving. He tried to pin it down, along with all these other impressions, feeling a little puzzled Will Kaeger was the one to provoke them.

The Bourée rehearsal finished. Leo passed a few dollars over his shoulder and dispatched Erik to the soda machine in the lounge. He came back to find Kees and David having a heated discussion in another language.

Benignly excluded, Erik sipped his soda and observed the two men. David was olive-skinned, good-looking in a scruffy way with long sideburns. He wasn't much taller than Erik, but he took up far more space.

Not fat, but a bulky weight slapped in chunks on his frame. Kees, on the other hand, was tall and lean, broad-shouldered, distinctive with his bald pate and single diamond earring. His deep voice slid gracefully around the guttural lingo Erik was trying to identify. German, maybe?

A rustle behind him, a waft of sugar, and Daisy Bianco sat down, leaning her elbows on the back of the empty seat between Erik and David. With the blue headband drawing her hair back, her face was a palette of soap-and-water loveliness, her eyes two splashes of aquamarine. Erik wanted to dive into them, plunge like a dolphin through their warm, salty depths and surface somewhere inside, shaking her from his wet head in spraying arcs of—

"Can I have a sip?" she said.

He blinked and passed her the soda. "What are they speaking," he whispered, leaning his head toward her, motioning to David and Kees with his chin.

"Dutch," she said, capping the bottle and returning it. "Kees is from Amsterdam. David was born in Belgium."

It got worse. Will Kaeger passed by, saying something to Daisy in yet another language, possibly French, and Daisy was answering him. And then, gee whiz, David and Kees jumped right in, switching tongues with ease. Will said something as he walked away and they all laughed. Erik sank in his seat and moodily drank his soda, feeling like a slice of white bread in a basket of croissants.

Leo Graham, who had been quietly sitting and sketching, turned around in his seat. "Enjoying the United Nations conference?"

The cross-talk dwindled away, almost guiltily.

"Where you from, Erik?" Kees said.

Erik looked up, reached for the memory of his Swedish grandfather's dry reserve and replied, "Shanghai."

He got a laugh and Daisy touched his shoulder. He passed her the soda again and their fingertips brushed. He watched the pull of her mouth at the bottle. The rise and fall of her throat. Her tongue quickly brushing her lips. The flash of her straight, even teeth as she laughed at something Kees said. She gave the bottle back to Erik and smiled.

"Thanks," he said, wanting to kiss her. He thought about sliding his palm along her smooth neck and smelling the skin of her face. The first touch of her mouth on his. The edges of her teeth against his tongue. The last drops of Coke lingering sweetly there.

The intense vision sideswiped him, left him mute, stupid and staring as Daisy got up and went back to the stage to rehearse the Prelude in F Minor. Unfortunately, Leo chose that moment to send Erik and Alison Pierce on a thousand errands. When they returned to the auditorium, the male quintet was finishing up.

Erik sat down by David and watched Will again, trying to take apart his distinctive style. Such disciplined mastery of his body, and yet effortless at the same time, jumps and turns coming out of nowhere. The energized fluidity reminded Erik of something, what the hell was it?

"He's good," he said to David.

"Right? The thing with Will is when he's not in the dance studio, he's in martial arts class. And it shows."

Erik put a palm to his forehead. "That's what I've been seeing," he said.

"Yeah, you don't want to fuck with him. He'll double pirouette and break your nose."

"Where's he from, how does he speak fluent French?"

"He's a Canuck," David said. "Montreal or somewhere."

Kees turned around. "Will's from New Brunswick, dumbass. He went to school in Montreal."

"Excusez-moi. Why in hell they speak French in a place called New Brunswick is beyond me."

"Well, you're in college, David," Kees said. "Four libraries on campus, why don't you go look it up? Learn something?"

David responded in Dutch. Kees laughed and turned back to face the stage. Erik wanted to know how Daisy was fluent in French but decided he'd ask someone other than David.

The boys' quintet was finished. Kathy Curran and Matt Lombardi, the senior graduating couple, returned to the stage for the Siciliano.

Erik looked back at his notes and the question mark he'd put down. Shyly he leaned forward to tap Kees's shoulder. "What do you call a duet like this, pah de something?"

"Pas de deux. It's French, means dance for two." He took Erik's clipboard and wrote the words down. "You should come to my class."

Erik swallowed a slight panic. He wasn't sure if it was an order or an invitation, but no way in hell was he going to dance class.

But David laughed. "Kees's most popular course is called 'Dance Appreciation for the Modern Neanderthal.'"

"There's a waiting list," Kees said.

Erik wrote it down.

Interestingly, while the seniors rehearsed front and center, Daisy and Will were upstage, dancing the same choreography. Kees explained they were understudying, and would get to dance one matinee performance.

The arrangement was for strings, flute and oboe, and against the slightly mournful melody, the pas de deux was decidedly romantic, full of longing. The partnering looked difficult, yet Will didn't seem to give much thought to what his hands were doing. They lifted, threw and caught Daisy with unconscious confidence, allowing his touch to be both supportive and tender. His fingers lingered on her limbs. He crushed her against his chest as if he loved her. At times, he seemed to be whispering to her. Daisy trusted him implicitly, jumping backward or turning blind without hesitation, her hand reaching for a precise spot where she knew he would be.

At an especially emotional swell in the music, Daisy fell backward in the circle of Will's arms and he laid his head down at the base of her throat. His mouth opened a little and Erik's eyes narrowed in fascinated jealousy. Will wasn't kissing her neck, he was just inhaling there, resting, as Daisy's hand came up behind his head. Downstage, Kathy made the same exact gesture to Matt's head. Clearly it was part of the choreography, but Kathy's motion seemed a throwaway while Daisy's was a definitive human caress. The hair at the back of Erik's own neck stirred, wanting to feel what Will felt.

When Will brought Daisy back up, the look they exchanged was smoldering. Their faces seemed to twitch with the suppressed laughter of a private joke. As Daisy moved forward into the next phrase, her smile back over her shoulder at Will was laced with affection. Erik felt a crushing despair sweep through his bones.

Beside him, David was chuckling low in his chest. "I swear sometimes I hate the man's guts," he said.

"Are they together?"

"Depends. What day is it, Sunday? Yeah, Sunday is Will's straight day, they could be together."

Kees looked back, chuckling. "And you tell *me* not to scare the child?"

Erik was starting to feel slightly overwhelmed. He didn't know what the hell David was talking about, but he was more than a little sure Will and Daisy were together offstage. Dancing the way they did, looking at each other the way they did, how could they not?

Shit...

And yet, throughout the rest of the rehearsal, whenever she wasn't dancing, Daisy kept coming back to their rows of seats. Coming, it seemed, to sit somewhere in Erik's general vicinity.

"Well, now, Keesja," David said after one such visit. "We know Daisy never comes to sit with me."

"We know she's not after me," Kees said, grinning. "Sunday's my gay day."

In unison, they turned eyes to Erik.

"She must like you," David said with a sigh.

COAX ANOTHER REVOLUTION

"ABANDON ALL HOPE, ye who enter here," David said to Erik as they arrived at the theater Monday afternoon.

Leo gathered his crew for a short meeting. "What do you see before you?" he asked Erik and Allison Pierce, the two freshmen. They exchanged confused glances, looking for a trick question within the obvious.

"A stage?" Allison said.

"Wrong. David?"

"A fish tank," David said, sighing and cleaning his fingernails with the tip of a screw.

"Exactly. 'Dancers live in light as fish live in water.' Jean Rosenthal, *The Magic of Light*. If you haven't read it, read it, and if you've already read it, read it again. Erik, stop writing things on your hand. Learn to trust your memory."

Erik sheepishly put his pen and his hand down.

The normally laid-back Leo was pacing briskly. "If you've never lit a dance concert before, forget everything you thought you knew. This is all different. It will take us half an hour to hang all the instruments on the booms. To focus them? If we're lucky, we'll get out of here at midnight. In fact, if you have pressing business at the DMV or a root canal scheduled, I'd go now and have a better time. This will be tedious, boring work and the dancers are going to be grouchy. Stay out of their way because they kick high, they kick fast and they kick hard. Any questions?"

None.

The stage techs rose. Unless perching on a bar or crawling on your stomach on the catwalk qualified as sitting, nobody sat again for three hours.

"On a lighting boom," Leo said, working with Erik and Allison, "the lantern lowest to the floor is called the shin buster. Which is self-explanatory. An inexperienced dancer will bump into them. And they will blame you when they do. We just knock them back into line."

"The dancers?" Allison asked, wide-eyed.

"The lanterns," Erik murmured.

"Booms can have a low- and mid-shin buster," Leo said. "As you can see we're wiring a mid-lantern for all eight." He went on explaining how these two lowest fixtures were the most crucial. They kept the light on the moving bodies without reflecting off the floor, allowing the dancers to appear floating in space, not unlike fish in an aquarium.

True to Leo's prediction, the booms were hung in no time and hoisted to attention in the wings when the dancers arrived. They were all somewhat sloppily dressed. None of the girls had their pointe shoes on and a lot of them wore their hair down.

"Business casual," David said.

Indeed, the company exuded more the air of a pajama party than a rehearsal. As the lights were being designed and focused and the cues recorded, the dancers had little to do but stand in the generalized areas of each piece's choreography and be bored.

Erik quickly learned dancers hated nothing more than standing still and being bored.

Meanwhile, eight boom stands divvied among six techs and two ladders meant a constant do-si-do backstage and across the stage. The potential to trip over something or someone was a constant threat. Multiplied by the seven Bach Variations over two hours, and Erik began to wish he'd eaten a more substantial lunch.

He was paired up with Allison, who had a maddening habit of saying "okey-dokey" to everything and a tendency to zone out when she was holding the ladder. Plus they always seemed to end up with the ladder with the uneven feet.

Up the ladder, down the ladder, move the ladder. Wait for the dancers to move. Wait while Leo brought lights up, brought lights down. Wait for Marie to make an agonizing decision and for Leo to translate her decision into focus. Swivel the lights into place. Wait for Marie to look and decide if she liked it. Shutter the lenses, bolt everything down. Keep the lights off the floor. Keep the lights off the curtains. Erik swore if he heard "Move it a quarter inch" one more time, he would stick a screwdriver in his eye.

"You're on the floor, move it a quarter inch up. Now you're on the curtain, take it quarter inch down. No, too much. Back it up. Just a hair. A tad. A smidgen. Just kiss it to the left. No, come back. Now hold it. Don't move. Perfect. No, you moved it."

They toiled and trudged on through each of the variations. Through it all, the dancers stood around. Most of them talked. Incessantly. If they had nothing of substance to say, they went for volume. One boy's braying laugh made Erik wince and suppress a desire to throw a wrench in his general direction. He was getting decidedly punchy.

The non-talkers read books—Daisy was in this group—or sat and stretched, retreating into private universes. One girl was knitting, deftly stuffing needles and yarn down her shirt whenever she needed to move. A few kids actually looked like they were sleeping in five-minute increments, magically coming back to life whenever it was time to migrate. Will simply sat still, staring, in a Zen-like trance. Any moment Erik expected him to levitate right off the stage floor, but then Will would break out and stand on his head or do one-armed push-ups or something equally enviable.

As the lights were focused for the Siciliano pas de deux, Will and Daisy sat around together. Several times Erik walked by them, lugging the ladder and grudging their companionable chatter in French. At one point Will knelt beside Daisy, one arm curved around her chest, supporting her slumped weight, while with the other hand he pressed and kneaded all up and down the length of her spine. Daisy's head lolled, eyes closed, a faint smile around her lips. Then Erik wanted to throw a slightly larger, considerably heavier object.

Like Allison.

Finally the ordeal wound down and Marie gave her flock twenty minutes. No such privilege was awarded the techs. They stayed up on the boom stands, tightening C-clamps, threading safety cables through the instrument yokes and securing them around the bar. A soft hand settled on Erik's calf as he was working. He nearly flicked it off, thinking it was Allison but it was Daisy.

"Do you want me to bring you something to eat?" she asked.

"No, thanks," he said automatically, and then felt the growling bite of his stomach. "Actually, yes, that would be great."

"A sandwich all right?"

"Perfect. Anything." Juggling wrench and cables he reached for his wallet but she waved him off.

"We can square up later." She turned to go and smacked into David.

"Can I get a cheese steak, Marge?" he said. He said it sweetly but something in his manner was challenging. Erik had heard him refer to Daisy as Marge several times, but didn't know why.

Daisy held out her hand, calmly locking eyes with David until he took out his wallet and gave her a twenty.

"Bring back the change this time," he called after her, and then tossed a roll of gaffer tape up to Erik. "Chick thinks I'm made of money," he said.

They hit the deck, dealing with the cables. Five snaked down from every boom stand and they had to be precisely lined up at the base and thoroughly taped to the Marley floor. "If a dancer trips on a loose cable," Leo said, "I will blame you."

Threatened, hungry and manic, Erik and David got progressively obsessive about the job, arguing about the best and least circuitous routes from the bases to the circuit panel. Yet for all their grouchiness, they worked well together. They chatted as they taped, about music, basketball and theater. Will passed by and pretended to peel up an edge of their sweated-over labors. David leapt up and gave ferocious chase through the wings, threatening to strangle Will with a safety cable.

And Daisy brought Erik the world's most perfect turkey sandwich, a bag of potato chips and a brownie.

"LOOK HOW JESSICA DOES this phrase," Kees spoke lowly, leaning on the back of the seat beside Erik's.

"All right," Erik said, his eyes on the stage, one ear on Kees and the other taking notes from Leo.

"See how she comes out of the turn. Now look how Daisy does it. Watch. Did you see?"

"It looked smoother, I guess? I don't know."

"Don't worry if you can't say what it was. I just care if you noticed something different."

They were watching the girls' quintet. Daisy was good, no question, but Erik hadn't the means to articulate why. Like a benevolent Svengali, Kees was giving Erik a crash course in dance appreciation. Erik might have resisted had Kees not been such an excellent teacher, and had Daisy not been so relentlessly compelling. He needed help if he was going to speak this girl's language.

During the alternating runs of the Siciliano pas de deux, Erik strove to take apart the mechanics of partnering and peppered Kees with questions. "How much is the girl balancing and how much is the guy holding her? How does he spin her? Or is she spinning herself?"

Kees was delighted. "He supports her. Watch their hands. She nearly always takes his, not the other way around. He'll throw her off balance if he grabs her. No, she's turning herself. He's there to make the turn come to an attractive finish and possibly coax another revolution out. If he's any good, that is."

Then the lifts fascinated Erik, provoking more questions about how much these girls weighed and if the male dancers did any weight training.

"All of them do," Kees said. "Mandatory."

"And handstand push-ups after every class," David said. "Sets of fifty."

"Still, how much is lift and how much is the girl jumping?" Erik asked. "They are jumping, right? They can't just give dead weight to be hoisted."

"The trick is all in the plié," Kees said. "How she bends her knees before the lift. It's the springboard."

"But they're dancing slow," Erik said, a corner of his mouth twisting up in doubt. "How do you get spring without speed?"

"Lot of power in a plié if you do it right," Kees said. "And anyway, with lifts it's not the going up that's so hard. It's the coming down."

"Will makes it look easy."

"Watch him in the weight room some time. He doesn't bench press heavy but he presses it slow. Lot of slow reps and slow resistance—that's how he can set a girl down like she's a pillow."

"But enough about his sex life," David muttered.

Kees laughed. "You know, man, I'm starting to think you *want* him."

"Who doesn't?"

On a break, Daisy came and sat down in the aisle by Erik's seat. She took off her pointe shoes to rest her feet. Erik picked one up.

"Careful, those are pretty gross," she said.

"I just want to see how they work. Is there wood in here?"

Just as patiently as Kees, she showed him how the shoes were made, with layers of canvas, satin and glue. More terms for him to absorb: box, shank, vamp and binding. He watched her re-tape the toes on her right foot. Most girls wore full-footed tights or socks, but Daisy went barefoot in her shoes, saying she could feel the floor better. She did put a gel spacer between her big and first toes to take the pressure off the bunion joint. Re-shod now, she stood up and rolled through her strong, bare feet, onto her pointes. He watched, mechanical curiosity satisfied.

The more dire interest in her legs, however, had yet to be assuaged.

ENTRE NOUS

ERIK GOT TO WATCH the dancing from several vantage points: the stage catwalk, the ceiling catwalk, the balcony, the wings. It was here he found himself watching the Prelude and keeping a low profile, trying to disguise how for once, he wasn't doing much of anything.

He noticed Will was standing by him, watching as well. They both raised chins in silent acknowledgment but said nothing. Erik had been slouching against a boom stand, but now he stood up straight, slightly envious of Will's height. Not breaking the six-foot ceiling was one of Erik's sore spots: an early growth spurt had him at a promising five-eleven by the start of junior high, but later adolescence only granted him another measly three-quarters of an inch. He *just* missed it.

When the dancers reached a passage Erik particularly liked, he stepped closer to Will and asked, "The step they just did, when their leg whipped around, what's it called?"

"Renversé," Will said. "I love this part, they repeat the same phrase but in a round, and when they do the renversé, here it is, look. One leg after the other. Looks like a windmill."

"It does."

"We met but we didn't. I'm Will."

"Erik." They shook hands and Erik noticed both Will's arms sported a number of tattoos.

"David calls you Fish."

"It's what my last name means."

"Ah." Will gestured to the theater at large. "First time at the rodeo?"

"Yeah. In between Leo running me ragged, I think Kees is trying to graduate me from Neanderthal 101 in one week."

"It's a good course. Chicks like going to the ballet, you can't go wrong if you know how to talk a little shop at intermission." Will's accent was interesting. His English was natural and slangy, but some of the words seemed to shimmy through his nose or get breathily stuck in the corners of his mouth.

Erik turned to the stage again, watching Daisy in her solo passage. She did a step facing the wings and her eyes caught his, held him for an electric blue moment. The air grew thick in his chest. She smiled, her body pulling away but her gaze fixed on him. He smiled back, filled with an impulse to follow.

Then she was gone, circling the stage in a rush of turns. Her leotard was pale green today, again with the black tights pulled over. She also wore a short black skirt, thin as a tissue. It flew up and floated down against the high, tight curve where the back of her thigh met her—

"Dude," Will said. "Is that not the sweetest ass you ever saw in your life?"

Thrown by hearing his thoughts voiced aloud, Erik flicked his eyes to Will, but Will wasn't looking at the stage. He was looking off in the wings to a girl with crazy spirals of blonde hair, a little compact body in jeans and a T-shirt, the clothes clinging to hourglass curves, full breasts, full hips, tiny waist.

"Who's she?"

"She's called Lucky Dare," Will said. His eyes were intent, a little smile played around his mouth.

"Seriously? That's her name?"

"Her name's Lucia, they call her Lucky. She's Daisy's roommate."

Erik squinted, interested. "She's not a dancer though, and she's not tech. What does she do around here?"

"She's a sports medicine major, studying to be a physical therapist. They all have to do a dance rotation at some point. God, would you look at that body. And her hair, Jesus. A hundred years ago she'd be burned as a witch."

"You go out with her?"

"You kidding, I go *in...*"

Erik laughed.

"Dude, she gave me a toe-curling blow job last night."

Erik's eyes widened. "Thanks for the visual."

His eyes not leaving Lucky, Will put up a hand and slowly ruffled Erik's hair. "Entre nous."

Erik looked again to the stage, his mind a jumble. Growing up fatherless, his mother's brothers had taken it upon themselves to offer their nephew advice on sexual etiquette. One valuable tip was you neither bitched about what a girl didn't do in the sack, nor bragged about what she *did* do.

He watched Daisy, thinking about toe-curling blow jobs and feeling Will's palm print lingering on him. Two things Erik didn't necessarily want connected in his mind. But the sense memory loitering on the crown of his head was benign and unthreatening. It had been a brotherly touch. Masculine and friendly. Almost like a secret handshake.

Michael called fifteen minutes for everyone. Will turned back to Erik. "I'm going to have a smoke, come with."

Erik didn't smoke but he went. As they passed by Lucky, Will tugged one of her spiral curls and she grabbed his ass in return.

"Funny, I thought you and Daisy were a thing," Erik said, once they were clear of the auditorium

"Everyone does," Will said, sounding bored.

"You can't blame them. You guys have sick chemistry onstage."

"Onstage, sure. Offstage? Not happening."

"Why not?"

They'd reached the lounge with its cracked leather furniture, mismatched tables and chairs. Will sat down on a couch and lit up. "I love Daisy. Don't get me wrong, I love her to pieces. And I was born to partner her. End of story."

Erik chewed the inside of his lip, unsatisfied. He needed the beginning of the story. He needed a lot more story about this girl.

Exhaling a ribbon of smoke and setting his slippered feet on the ottoman, Will looked relaxed and expansive. Erik decided to probe a little.

"How long have you partnered her?" he asked.

"Two months. Back in September she came into auditions, which are a brutal freshman ordeal, especially for the girls. You know anything about the world of ballet?"

"Zero."

"It is the most competitive, catty universe you'll ever encounter. The upperclassmen girls scrutinize the new kids like a pack of bitches. And Daisy's good, which they hate—freshman talent is a threat to their existence. So anyway, Marie wants to see some partnering work so she points to me and Dais, you and you, together. All right. Hi. How are you?"

"What was she like?" Shy and nervous, he imagined, paired with Will's confidence while being stared at and sized up by the other girls.

"Dude, she was the most poised person I'd ever met in my life." Will's eyes squinted against the smoke. "You know she's still seventeen, she won't turn eighteen until December. I'd just turned twenty so you know, I'm feeling my decade. She definitely seemed young to me but there was this incredible stillness to her. Anyway, we were practicing the steps and finding a groove, but always when you pair up with someone new, it's awkward. Hands go the wrong way, you bump into each other, you topple. It takes time to figure each other out, it's like any relationship. But she had this quiet confidence. She made jokes but she wasn't giggly or apologetic. She was calm and...it was no time at all. We started going to class together. Marie paired us up to understudy the Siciliano—for a freshman to cover a senior duet, dude, that just doesn't happen. And we turned into something. I don't like dancing with anyone else now. I can. Sometimes I don't have a choice. But it's the best with Daisy. She speaks my language."

"French."

"French?" Will picked a piece of tobacco off his tongue with his thumb and ring finger and flicked it away. "French has nothing to do with anything. I can shoot the shit with David or Kees if I'm homesick. With Dais, I'm talking about a language that doesn't even have words."

"All your chemistry onstage... None of it's real?"

"Of course it's real. Look, I know what you're asking, let's be honest: Dais is beautiful. She has an amazing body. I'm a mortal male. It doesn't suck to look at her. But at the same time, I know we're not alike and we wouldn't work as a couple. If I started something it would crash and burn, then it would be sad and awkward, and I'd be out of a partner. And I want her as my partner. I'm not fucking with it. I couldn't bear to lose it."

Erik chewed on that, with no small amount of relief, while Will smoked. He rolled "Dais" around his mind a few times and found he liked the shortened version with its hard S. It was a more evocative sound. Intimate. It fit her better. Dais.

"You like her?" Will said.

Erik looked at him a long moment, trying to formulate an answer to encapsulate everything he'd been thinking, feeling and contemplating since meeting this girl. Only two days ago.

Will cocked his head. "You looked her in the eye, didn't you?"

Erik smiled, feeling the heat rise up in his face as he nodded.

"See, it's weird, everyone has a thing about her eyes. Her eyes freak me out."

"Her eyes are beautiful," Erik said.

"I don't know. Something about them isn't right. It took me like two weeks to be comfortable looking at her when we were partnering."

Erik had to laugh. "Why?"

Will blew a few smoke rings. "Dais doesn't talk a lot but she watches everything. She comes off aloof at first, but when you get to know her, it's... She's insanely passionate but it's all behind this thoughtful exterior. She doesn't miss anything with those eyes. They look through you. It was like she was going to put the juju on me, I don't know. I'd be, like, 'Bianco, cut it out. You're looking at my *soul.*'"

Which may have been the most accurate description of what Erik had experienced when Daisy first put eyes on him in the lighting booth. Still, he said nothing, firmly in his home base mode, which was watching, taking apart and figuring out.

Will formed another ring in the air. "You want me to say something to her?"

Erik shook his head. He'd never been particularly bold with girls but he hadn't ever felt the need to work with a wingman.

"No. I mean, I just met her. I'm still feeling it out."

"You got a funny look on your face, my friend."

"When I met her yesterday? It felt like finding something I didn't know I was looking for. I can't even explain... Never mind. My head's kind of spinning so I think I'll keep going about this in my own inept way."

Will stubbed out his cigarette and stood up. "Well for all your ineptness you've definitely made an impression. Bunch of the guys already asking me who the fresh meat is in the lighting booth. It's always the guys. The girls are more discreet."

"Shut up."

"Hand to God." Will stretched, cracking his neck and grinning. "Wait, how did Matt Lombardi put it, it was funny... Oh yeah, he said you were the love child of Bryan Adams and Sting. Not bad for a first conquest." Will wrinkled his eyebrows and touched Erik's shoulder. "It is your first conquest, right?"

"Please stop talking."

Will laughed and gave Erik a shove. As they left the lounge, his touch lingered, easy and fraternal. Like fragrant smoke from a tobacco pipe.

Halfway up the stairs Will stopped. "Oh. Word to the wise. Entre nous? David Alto set rather a large cap for Dais in the beginning of the year. And he took it rather badly when she rejected him."

"I kind of picked up on that."

"She wasn't mean to him. She doesn't have a mean bone in her body. But he took it hard and the way he deals with it is by teasing her."

"Teasing her."

"Sometimes it can be just short of nasty. She can handle it, but I didn't want you to see it and feel you had to come to the rescue. Really he's just licking his wounds."

"He's an interesting guy," Erik said carefully.

Will shrugged and started up the stairs again. "I can only take him in small doses. You don't get many genuine moments with Dave and the sad thing is he only wants what he can't have. If Dais had accepted him, he'd have chewed her up and spit her out."

"You think?"

"I'm positive. She's a novelty to him. I think he just wanted to bust her cherry for the experience."

Erik winced and stopped walking. "What?"

Will turned around and for once, looked sheepish. "Nothing."

Erik looked at him a long moment. "What does entre nous mean?"

"Between you and me."

He nodded. "I'm glad we had this little chat."

"Welcome to the jungle."

AFTER ONE MORE RUN-THROUGH, the ballet dancers were excused. The contemporary dancers had arrived and were getting ready for their focus session, the whole mess to repeat all over again. Erik was exhausted, sitting in the back row yawning and rubbing his face. The rest of the evening stretched before him like a desert, parched and barren without the entertainment of Daisy's presence. He was getting hungry again. And a ton of homework was waiting for him later.

A hand brushed his shoulder. Daisy smiled at him as she passed, trim and pretty in a silver-grey down jacket. "Night, Fish. See you tomorrow."

"Night, Dais," he said, turning in his seat, watching her walk out the auditorium doors. Pleased she'd learned and used his nickname. Bereft she was gone.

He turned back in his seat, and now David was coming up the aisle. "Fishy, fishy in the brook," he sang to the ceiling, "into Fish, she put her hook."

An hour later, Erik was up on the ladder rearranging one of the booms, when, once again, a soft touch settled on his calf, but this time she called his name. He twisted around and from the foot of the ladder she gazed up at him, holding a paper bag.

"I brought you a snack."

"I still owe you for the sandwich," he said, his heart splashing against the wall of his chest.

"Oh, and coffee, do you drink coffee?"

He was actually a tea drinker but he would've gladly accepted a cup of warm piss from her.

"Thank you," he said.

Her eyes and nose crinkled, then she set the bag at the base of the boom. "Don't tell David."

"Entre nous," he said.

EVERY GOOD BOY DOES FINE

TUESDAY, HE WAS DUE at the theater at four. His accounting class let out at three, and he decided to just grab something at the campus center and kill time at the theater. Possibly he could sit in a back row and power nap for twenty minutes.

He was at one of the condiment stations, getting napkins and packets of mustard when someone nudged him in the ribs. He looked left, as the trickster ducked around to his right, but by then he'd already smelled her sugar-soap perfume.

"Hey," he said happily. In her grey jacket and purple scarf, Daisy looked criminally pretty. Her hair was down, something he'd not seen before today. It fell down her back in rippling waves, a bit of it caught beneath the straps of her dance bag.

"Going over to Mallory?" she asked.

"I am. Come with?"

They were the only ones there. The auditorium was quiet and dim with a hallowed feeling, like an empty church. Erik went to the circuit panel in the wings and flicked on a few of the stage lights. Daisy plopped down by the leg of the grand piano and from her capacious bag drew a pair of pointe shoes and a sewing kit. It seemed the ballet girls were always working on their shoes, sewing or re-sewing ribbons, bending them in half, banging them on the floor. And then lamenting they wore out too quickly.

Hopping down from the apron of the stage, Erik did a double-take as Daisy threaded a needle. "You sew them with dental floss?"

Breaking off a length with her teeth, she smiled up at him. "It's stronger than thread, and you only need a few stitches per ribbon. Goes faster."

"I am learning something new every day from you dancers." Impulsively he opened the piano bench to see if there was any sheet music. There was, including a book of Bach.

He closed the bench and sat, thumbing through the pages. *Let's see how big an ass I can make of myself.*

"You play?" Daisy said.

"I used to. You might want to back up a little, this could get ugly." He settled on the Prelude in C Major, the friendliest key. He shook out his suddenly cold fingers. "Let's see, every good boy does fine..."

She laughed. "It's more than I know."

He dug deep, shrugged off his nerves. He was a good sight reader. At least, he'd been told he was a good sight reader way back when. And he knew how the Prelude was supposed to sound, which made it easier. Still, he was clumsy, and stopped after a few plunking measures, embarrassed. "God, I haven't used this part of my brain in years."

"Try again. And go slower, it's a lullaby."

He started over, played slower. Upstairs his brain finally realized he was serious about this, and quickly sorted out the staffs. Bass clef, treble clef, the notes began to tell him their names. Little by little it came back to him, came together. His shoulders relaxed, his foot sought out the pedal. He stopped, flexed his fingers.

"Don't stop," Daisy murmured, bent over her work.

"No, I got it now, I got it." He went back to the beginning and played it straight through with only a couple clunkers.

"Nice," she said, as he made the last notes of the arpeggio die away. Her sewing done, she was wiggling one foot into her shoe then wrapping the ribbons around her ankle, her hands deft and sure. "Play another." Something about her quiet composure gave him confidence. If she'd been gushing praise and batting her eyes at him, he would've known she was full of shit, and he would have stopped.

He shuffled the sheet music around and picked through a couple Mozart minuets, then movements of the Beethoven sonatas he'd learned years ago. Daisy warmed up, first stretching on the floor, then getting up and using the piano as a barre. Realizing she was timing her movements to his playing, he slowed down or sped up, following her, trying to keep a steady tempo. She smiled at him, her face growing pinker, a fine mist of sweat across her throat and chest.

"All right," he said, flattening the spine of the Bach book with his fist. "Here's the real test. Prelude in F Minor."

"My prelude, really?"

"Don't get too excited. F minor is...four flats, Jesus." He tried a few measures and then abruptly bailed, making a mosh on the keys with his fists.

"You're doing fine," Daisy said. "Keep going."

"No, forget it." He went back to the Prelude in C, now the old friend. Daisy stretched, holding onto the piano, the other hand holding her long leg straight to twelve o'clock high. With difficulty Erik kept his eyes on the music.

"Who else is musical in your family," she asked, breathing into the stretch.

"My mom played most of her life," he said. "And she used to give lessons in our house. She'd put me in the playpen next to the piano, and then my brother, too."

"How old is your brother?"

"Sixteen. He's deaf. I mean, he's a lot of things but, incidentally, he's deaf."

"Was he born deaf?" She was holding her extended leg behind her now, slowly inclining forward.

"No, he had meningitis when he was a baby."

"Oh." Her head and shoulders disappeared from view as she pitched enough to put her hands on the floor. Just her foot in its pointe shoe left in the air. Her voice floated up. "It must have been hard on your parents."

"Well, for my mother it was. My father left us and she had to go back to work."

"What does she do?"

"She's a nurse. And now she's getting her Master's in speech pathology."

She resurfaced, ponytail askew, face flushed from being upside-down. "I see."

"Anyway, my father leaving was the end of her giving music lessons, and we were so broke, she ended up selling the piano."

"So how did you play, who gave you lessons then?"

"I went to the Y after school until sixth grade. A woman there worked with me, and I could play every day. Then I would just hang around the school music rooms and bang on the piano any chance I got. I kept up with it until maybe sophomore year, then I got more into guitar."

Daisy put her foot onto the piano and extended her torso over her leg. "Your father left you?" she asked, forehead on her knee.

He nodded. "Went out one night and never came back."

She looked up. "After a fight with your mother, you mean?"

"No. He just left."

Slowly she took her leg down and put both hands on the piano lid. "How old were you?"

"Eight."

"You haven't seen your father since you were eight?"

He shook his head.

"No word. No contact. No nothing?"

"Nothing."

Daisy's eyes flicked right and left before coming back to his. "Is he alive?"

Erik looked away and turned a page. He was surprised he'd revealed this to someone he barely knew. Normally this was the card he kept closest to his chest. He turned back to the blue-green gaze studying him. Something about her expression—calm and interested, sympathetic but not pitying, tactfully curious—seemed to be reaching into the tangle of emotions comprising the experience of being so cruelly deserted, and gently drawing out a thread.

"My mom still gets child support payments for my brother," he said. "But they come through a lawyer's office. I suppose if they're still coming then he's still alive. But I really have no idea."

"He doesn't send money for you?"

"Not anymore, I'm nineteen."

Her delicate eyebrows wrinkled. "That is," she said slowly, "such a violent thing. For a parent to disappear. Emotionally violent. It just stops a story dead in the middle. Like you turn the page and there are no more pages. What do you do with the story?"

He shrugged one shoulder. "It becomes a different story."

She nodded. "Your story."

He had stopped playing, and a hush fell over them. For a long moment, while she was leaning her chin on her hand atop the piano lid, and his hands rested lightly on the keys, they stared at each other. The stage, the wings, the maw of the theater and its rows of seats and ornamental moldings, all receded. The air about them shimmered, drew in, coalesced into a bubble. They looked at each other, breathing together, long past a socially acceptable interval. It was far beyond the border where Erik normally would have dropped his gaze, cracked a joke or at least a smile.

She's peaceful, he thought, and her eyes widened slightly, as if she'd heard him. He leaned a little further into her stillness, found he trusted it. And the trust coaxed from him yet another secret:

"My real name's Byron," he said. "It's his name, too. My father's. Byron Erik."

"You probably didn't want to be his junior anymore."

"No."

She smiled, and the blue of her gaze deepened. "My real name is Marguerite."

"Is that why David calls you Marge?"

She nodded, then held up a warning finger.

He put his palms up, indicating he wouldn't dare. "Where does Daisy come from?"

"Marguerite means daisy in French. It's what they call the flowers."

"Your family's from France?"

"Both my parents. I was born here."

"Brothers? Sisters?"

"Only me."

"Only you," he said. He wanted to kiss her.

She put a foot up on the piano. "Try the Prelude again," she said. And she kept stretching her long limbs as he picked his way through it once more. Not perfectly. But a good boy doing fine.

THE FOURTH WALL

LATER IN THE EVENING, during the run-through, Erik was in the balcony changing the lenses on the follow spotlights. The house lights were down and the stage was awash in pink and gold light. Erik had always found it a particularly magic moment: turning out the house and crossing the bridge between rehearsal and production. The theater seemed to stretch and preen like it was wearing a new ball gown. People moved about more quietly, recognizing their steps and voices were now an intrusive disruption.

Kees came down the wide stairs and slid into a seat. "Nice to have all these vantage points, right?"

Erik finished his chore just as the Siciliano began. From the balcony's front row, they watched together.

"Wat denk je, mijn vriend?" Such was Kees's customary opening remark, and the one thing Erik now understood in Dutch: "What do you think, my friend?"

Under Kees's brief but vigorous tutelage, Erik was far more comfortable with formulating observations and articulating them than just three days ago. "I like this part," he said.

Kathy Curran was up in the air, her pliant back draped over Matt Lombardi's shoulder, legs unfolding in an upside-down split. Matt brought her down a few steps and turned her under his arm. She turned him under hers and they revolved around each other. Then, out of nowhere,

Kathy was back over his shoulder, going up and the sequence repeated. Three times in all.

Upstage, Daisy and Will mirrored.

"Theirs is so much smoother," Erik said, trying hard to be objective. "Not the steps but how the steps connect."

"Steps are words and the choreography is sentences. The sentences have to flow with the music."

"Right. And I see what you mean about the coming down being harder than going up."

"Most difficult thing about lifts. Up in the air Kathy is beautiful. Beautiful line."

"What's line?"

"The picture the body makes in the air, the shape. The lift is gorgeous but now watch as he puts her down. See how the flow breaks as she gets her feet on the ground? She doesn't quite have the knack of sustaining the flow. Now watch Daisy. She goes up. Beautiful line, look how she uses her head, there's a little modulation in the music and she turns her head against his arm, did you see it?"

"No."

"Watch next time. Now he's bringing her down, down, down but her head is still back, her head is the last thing to come up which sustains the downward flow. And right into the next phrase without a break. Gorgeous."

"They make long sentences."

"One more time, watch her head against his arm. Right now. I love how she tells a whole story with just a little turn of her head. And the way she keeps it thrown back tells a story, too."

"She doesn't want to come down."

"Exactly."

Erik twisted his mouth, debating how to phrase a question. "Can I just throw something out there and you can call me an idiot if it's warranted?"

"Fire away."

"Does the difference in how they partner women have anything to do with Matt being gay and Will being straight?"

Kees laughed, low and deep in his chest, his teeth flashing in the dark.

Erik felt slightly foolish. "Never mind," he said.

"No, no, man, it's a fair question."

"But does it hold any weight?"

"Look, no gay man is oblivious to a beautiful woman. I'm gay, I've partnered women and believe me, you feel it going on. Beauty is beauty. And straight or gay, you are immersed in this intense, artistic chemistry which is both sensual and sensory. Chemistry is chemistry. It just isn't rooted in sexual attraction."

"But still, it seems Matt and Kathy dance out here." Erik gestured around them. "They're looking out here to the audience, breaking the fourth wall."

Kees reared back, corners of his mouth turned down in mock surprise. "Fourth wall, check out the theater fag."

"Tuesday's my gay day," Erik said, smiling, which got him a swat upside the head. "But their focus is out here while Will and Daisy only look at each other. They're not dancing for us. It's like we're not even here. It's more their private moment and we're just invited into it. Or we stumbled on it. Matt and Kathy are performing but Will and Daisy tell a story."

"Exactly. And it tends to give all their dancing a romantic feel. Which is fine for a program like this. Be interesting to see them dance something a little more abstract and edgier. Something angry."

"Is that how you'd choreograph for them?"

"It would certainly be a challenge," Kees said, with some relish. "Daisy's adagio is so mesmerizing. I'm itching to see what kind of speed she has. Take that sleek race car out on the straightaway and open it up, make her dance fast."

Sitting with his arms crossed on the ledge, Erik was indeed mesmerized. He looked at Kees. "Do you think she's good?"

Kees nodded slowly. "She's unquestionably talented in her own right. Her technique is superb. But what she has with Will is extraordinary."

"Why? What makes it extraordinary?"

Kees was quiet a while, watching. "One thing I notice is Daisy seems more interested in making something beautiful together with Will than being adored as the prima ballerina. She is a much more forgiving partner than Kathy."

"Forgiving."

"You have to understand in ballet, there's an unspoken code of chivalry for the danseur noble."

"What's that?"

"The male dancer. Same way you'd use prima ballerina for a woman. Anyway, he's expected to always present the woman in the best light. So you can see this little flicker of annoyance on Kathy's face if Matt bobbles something. But Daisy, she's conscious of Will as a dancer, not just someone propping her up. She doesn't betray his mistakes."

Squinting at the couple on the stage, Erik made a quantum leap. "She partners him. As much as he does her."

"Exactly. If he's not where she needs him to be, she covers and she moves on. She doesn't stop and blame. She incorporates the rough spots into the whole. Strikes me as interesting."

"Why?"

"She's a generous dancer. Makes me wonder if she treats all the people she loves the same way."

"Oh."

Kees smiled. "You like her?"

Erik glanced at him, then back to the stage. "I do."

"She's a lovely girl."

"It's weird, Kees, at first I just liked how she looked. Now I'm starting to like who she is. And a lot of it, maybe even all of it, is coming from watching her dance."

"Like I said, my friend, she seems the type who likes to make something beautiful with her partner, rather than just be carried around and adored in the spotlight." He patted Erik' shoulder and got up. "So I imagine she's generous and forgiving in the dark."

He left then, and Erik looked back at the stage, rolling the words "in the dark" around his mouth like hard candies. He watched Daisy dance, illuminated and suspended in the sidelight coming from the booms.

In the dark.

What are you like in the dark?

NATURAL SPIN

WEDNESDAY AFTERNOON, they came to the theater together again, communing in the quiet of the empty auditorium. Daisy sewed her shoes and Erik played the piano. He played more confidently today, and when his hands coaxed from the keys a competent version of the F minor Prelude, Daisy began to dance parts of it.

"Do the last part of your solo, with all the turns." He stopped playing as she first circled the stage, then headed down the diagonal in a blur of turns, moving fast, foot-to-foot, up on her toes, into a double pirouette to end the phrase.

"Keesja dared me to do a triple here."

"Can you?"

Daisy backed up a few feet, moved into the chain of quick turns, then into the final spin, one revolution, then two and a third. She finished soft, her arms the last to melt down, a small smile on her face.

"Nice," Erik said.

She did it again and flubbed, falling off balance after the second turn. "See, I'm turning to the right, and it's not my strong side. My natural spin is to the left."

"Can't you just change it, then?"

She smiled at him, shaking her head. "I have to do it the way it's choreographed."

She tried another, again wobbling off the final revolution. "I don't trust myself. If I'm turning right then a triple happens by luck, rather than me controlling it. Two and a half turns with a fudged ending looks like shit. I'd rather just do the double."

It was the first dress rehearsal, and after warming up she disappeared into the depths of the backstage world: down in the dressing rooms beneath the stage and into the strict governance of wardrobe and makeup. Starting tonight, it was performance mode and the dancers weren't allowed out in the auditorium during the run-through.

David and Erik were going into their world as well. The cues designed on the temporary board were now programmed into the main boards in the lighting booth. They would be running lights from there, David in charge, in direct contact with the stage manager, and Erik second-in-command. They had their own dress orders, anything as long as it was black.

Last-minute adjustments and tweaks were needed all around the theater, including backstage. Passing through the controlled chaos in the wings, Erik made the interesting discovery that the contemporary girls had to be taped into their short little trunks. Intrigued, he stopped, drew back behind a curtain and stared as the wardrobe techs worked with double-sided tape to secure the edges along all those nether regions. And the dancers, either bent over double, or lying on the floor with their legs thrown over their heads, just chatted away, as if nothing out of the ordinary were happening.

Naturally he couldn't ogle in peace—David came along and whacked him between the shoulder blades, breaking the trance.

"Dude, close your mouth."

"Sorry," Erik muttered.

"What are you, twelve?"

"No, it's just my first time walking through a troupe of girls with their cooches waving in the breeze."

"Yeah, well don't ruin it for the rest of us, all right?"

Now holding the ladder for David, Erik glanced more covertly at Daisy being secured into her costume. The wardrobe tech was kneeling, closing the seam from the bottom up with a more civilized needle and thread. The entire back of the dress was open and Erik could see the top of Daisy's tights and the whole, smooth expanse of her skin, the bumps of her spine and the wings of her shoulder blades

Over his head, David was singing softly. "Fishy, fishy in the brook, will she ever turn and look?"

The wardrobe tech made a cut with her scissors, then sat back on her knees to inspect. Daisy went up onto her toes, her hands reaching over her head. Out of the flowing skirt her waist rose up, tight and slender. The soft grey material hugged her small breasts, draped her back. Her neck was long and sleek, framed by the curves of her arms.

She is, Erik thought, *the most beautiful girl I've ever seen.*

David came down the ladder, jumping the last few rungs. He retrieved the cup of soda he'd left at the base and took a long, sucking slurp from its straw.

"You can fold it up," he said to Erik, indicating the ladder, and walked off.

"Say please," Erik said under his breath, peeved. He watched as David passed the free-standing barres where Daisy was up on one foot, deep in concentration as she held a balance. Without breaking stride, David's hand darted out and back. Daisy let out a yell and came off her pointes.

"David, you little shit," she cried, seizing a towel and lobbing it as he stepped up his pace and disappeared further backstage. Shaking her head, she reached her hand down between her shoulder blades, worrying at the back of her dress.

Erik walked over to her. "What did he do?"

"Dropped a fucking ice cube down my back," she said, twisting and reaching.

He could see the lump and the spreading dark spot where the ice was starting to melt.

"Hold still," he said. He pulled the material away, just enough for him to get his fingers in and retrieve the cube, and trying not to linger longer than was necessary.

"How bad does it look?" she asked, peering back over her shoulder.

"It'll dry, don't worry." And entirely without his brain's permission, he blurted out, "You look beautiful."

Her eyes lifted up to his. "Thank you."

"Do a triple," he said.

She laughed then, and shook her head. "Not to the right."

He watched her walk away, then popped the ice cube into his mouth.

SAINT BIRGITTA

THE COGS AND GEARS of the concert were turning ever more smoothly and faster. Two run-throughs seemed to take no time at all. Notes were given swiftly. Leo had only minor changes to make. With some ceremony he blessed the final cue sheets and gave them to David and Erik to transpose. "Lock it down, boys. And make copies."

"Let's go kick back, hookers," Will said. And the five of them—Will, Erik, David, Lucky and Daisy—headed over to the campus center to eat.

They unloaded jackets and clobber at a large booth, then dispersed in search of their dinners. After dealing with long lines at the deli counter, Erik arrived back at the table in the middle of a conversation, sitting down just as David was saying, "Oh yeah, Madame Virgo von Intacta over here."

Daisy blew her straw wrapper at him. "Bite me," she said.

"Hey, Fish," David said. "Remember I told you Daisy's old man owns an orchard out in Amish land? Guess what the name of the town is."

"Bird-In-Hand," Daisy and Will said, their voices unified in abject boredom.

"I thought you were from Gladwyne?" Erik said to Daisy.

"I am. But after I graduated my parents moved full time out to the country."

"To Bird-In-Hand," David said, nudging Erik's side. "It's just southwest of Intercourse."

"Gee, I haven't heard this joke in an hour," Will muttered.

"Don't forget you have to go through Intercourse to get to Paradise," Daisy said as she tore open a salad dressing packet with her teeth. Erik's eyes followed the banter like a tennis match.

"And stop by Mount Joy," Will said.

"I've only been to Blue Ball," David said, looking intently at Daisy.

"How frustrating." Daisy got up, leaving just the men at the table.

"Why are you such an ass to her, Dave," Will said around a mouthful.

"What?"

"For starters, you have this weird fascination with Daisy being a virgin. It's just southwest of perverted."

Chewing his sandwich, Erik tracked Daisy through the maze of tables and chairs, watched her stop and chat with someone. He studied how her V-neck shirt clung to the shallow curve of her waist and out over her hip, and wondered how that curve would feel under his hand.

God, she was beautiful.

And she was a virgin.

He took another reflective bite, recalling what Will had said: *He just wanted to bust her cherry for the experience.*

Bust her cherry. It was a crass expression.

So why was it turning him on?

This was weird. He crossed one leg over the other and kept eating, lost in horny thoughtfulness.

"It's hot being the first," David said, squeezing ketchup on his fries. "You belong to a girl's history forever."

"Technical penetration doesn't mean shit," Will said. "Half the time it sucks for her. I'd rather be the guy who makes her come the first time. That's the better pantheon. He's the one she'll remember forever."

Erik crunched a few potato chips, nibbling on the image of Daisy under him, her hair spread out on a pillow and all her curves in his hands. Her eyes full of blue-green fire. Opening her knees to him. Raising her hips up and letting him be the first to slide into her warm, wet...

He squirmed and casually hitched closer to the table. Great. He was stuck here now. Served him right.

"Hey, Lucia," David said as Lucky arrived at the table and sat next to Will. "When were you deflowered? Wait, let me guess. Fifteen? Sixteen, tops."

"You know, Dave, you're really unattractive when you're coked up," Lucky said.

Erik had been mentally reciting states and capitals—a trick which usually deflected blood away from an unwanted erection back to his brain. He lifted his head at Lucky's remark. He glanced at Will, who rolled his eyes as he bit into his burger.

David was unperturbed. "Willy, you had to have been what, twelve?"

Will chewed and swallowed, took a sip of his drink and replied, "Male or female?"

Lucky gave a little catcall under her breath.

"I always knew you batted for both sides," David said.

"Sure," Will said, looking around the table. "I'll fuck any one of you."

"Not in front of the children," David said, as Daisy returned to the table.

"Not what in front of the children," she said, sliding in next to Lucky, across from Erik.

"Talking about Will's bisexual tendencies."

"He's double the lay," Daisy said.

"Thank you, darling." Will kissed the air at her.

David laughed. "Look at Fish's face, he's about to shit."

Fighting the heat rising up his neck, Erik looked coolly around the table. "Clearly I'm not in Kansas anymore."

"So," David said. "Marge is the only one keeping herself pure for marriage."

"Dave, give it a rest," Will said.

"I'm not waiting for marriage," Daisy said. Both her body language and her expression were smolderingly serene, despite David having thrown her virginity onto the table like an order of onion rings to be shared.

She was calm and gorgeous. Unapologetic. Erik knew he was staring but he couldn't look away. He was imagining her stillness transforming in his arms. The poise turning wild. Watching her unfold, melt and crumble underneath him in the dark.

What are you like in the dark?

What do you look like when you come?

His mind reared back in awe while his stupid erection gave a standing ovation.

"What are you waiting for then? True love?"

David's tone took on an edge of cruelness. This teasing was just short of nasty. It actually seemed irrational. Erik caught Will's eye, silently asking if this was what he meant yesterday. Will lifted his chin in confirmation.

Daisy wasn't taking any of his bait. "I'm just waiting for the one."

"The one?"

"The One," she said again, and then slowly began to sing, "singular sensation...every little step he—"

The table erupted in moans and fries being pelted at Daisy.

"Let me know how that goes, honey," David said.

"For that, honey, you'll be the first," Daisy said. She looked over at Will, who was offering her his pack of cigarettes. She reached for one, glanced quickly at Erik, then took her hand back. "No, I'm good."

"You have a girlfriend, Erik?" Lucky asked casually, shaking the ice cubes in her cup.

He looked up, shook his head.

"Fishy, fishy, in the brook," David said, "at what young age were you took?"

Silence at the table. Unnerved, Erik looked sideways at David, then across the table. "Ask Will."

They all laughed and threw more fries. Will held his palm out to Erik, who smacked his against it.

Thankfully the subject then turned to the concert and shop talk. Erik went back to states and capitals. After another ten minutes, David departed, leaving his tray of trash on the table and the cue sheets for Erik to transpose. Daisy had gotten herself a cup of tea and taken a book out of her bag.

His pup-tent safely dismantled, Erik went and got a cup of his own. Back at the table, he worked slowly, harboring the hope Daisy was hanging around because of him, and the greater hope Will and Lucky might take off soon and give him a few minutes alone with her.

Miracle of miracles, they did. "You'll see my partner home?" Will said, shrugging on his jacket. Erik glanced at Daisy who smiled. Erik looked back at Will and nodded.

Lucky was pulling on her gloves. She bent and put her cheek next to Daisy's. "Don't wait up, dear," she said.

Daisy kissed the air. "I never do, dear." She watched them walk away, then looked back to Erik, giving him a quick smile before returning to her book.

Erik looked left and right before speaking. "Was David coked up?"

Daisy looked up. Her eyes flared bright blue for a split second, then mellowed. "Probably," she said slowly. "I know he does it. But I'm not good at detecting that kind of thing. Lucky knows better."

"She was the one who said."

"Then he probably was. Poor David."

"Poor?"

"Sometimes I think he's homesick," she said. "For Belgium, I mean."

Erik knew the story. David's parents had died in a car accident when he was eleven, leaving him with only elderly grandparents who could not care for him. His mother's sister, Helen, had flown to Brussels and collected her nephew, bringing him to her home in New York and becoming his legal guardian.

"He wears his father's wedding band," she said. "On his index finger. Funny. It just occurred to me you're both fatherless."

And we both want you, Erik thought. He flipped his pencil around a few times, and then tried to sound nonchalant as he asked, "Is Will really bisexual?"

Daisy put her tea down and leaned toward him a little. "I don't know," she mouthed, as if confessing.

"You don't know?" he mouthed back with exaggeration.

Her smile was infectious. "I certainly couldn't go to court with anything on him. I hear it plenty, but I've never seen it in action. And he sleeps with my roommate, so..."

"Huh," Erik said thoughtfully, staring at the faint lipstick mark on the rim of Daisy's cup. She was staring at his cup as well, which was bothersome because he already took a lot of shit for drinking tea. Apparently it wasn't the manly thing to do. But he'd never liked coffee and tea had sentimental roots in his heart: growing up, his mother had brewed tea every night, making cups for her sons while they did homework. Erik's first independent act in the kitchen was learning to light the burner under the kettle. And he liked how it tasted, especially when it was brewed strong. He used two bags and barely any sugar.

Daisy said nothing about his beverage of choice, though, and opened her book again. Erik went back to work, and a pleasant interlude passed where he was busy and she was reading, yet the space they shared was companionable. The silence between them shimmered warm and inviting, like a campfire. He settled into it contentedly. A cat on the hearth.

"I like your necklace," she said.

"This?"

"Can I see?"

He put his pencil down, reached behind his neck and unclasped it. He put it in a coiled heap in her waiting palm. She stretched it carefully across her long fingers. It was a gold chain with squared, faceted links. The squares gave it a unique, masculine silhouette, heavy but streamlined. Off the chain hung three small charms. Erik watched as Daisy examined each one: a boat, a fish and a saint's medal, which was also square.

"Who is this?"

"Birgitta. She's the patron saint of Sweden."

Her fingers, with their unpolished oval nails, played with the charms which, like the chain, were old gold, weathered. They had a dull, wise brightness. Many fingers had rubbed, contemplated and worried over them.

"This is beautiful," Daisy said. "Actually it's handsome. I don't want to say macho, but it's strong-looking."

"I like the weight of it," he said. "It's solid."

"Is it old?"

He reached and turned the medal over, to show her the engraving on the back: *B.K.E.F. 1865.*

"Bjorn Kennet Erik Fiskare. My great-great-grandfather."

"Wow. This is like your history right here."

"I'm told the boat and the fish are even older but nobody knows really. See. Here." Erik turned the boat over and showed her *Fiskare* engraved into its bottom. "Fiskare means fisherman in Swedish."

She looked at him sheepishly. "I thought it meant scissors. You know, the ones with the orange handles."

He laughed. "I get that all the time."

"Do you know the word for scissors?"

"No idea."

"You're Swedish but your eyes are brown," she said, gazing intently at him.

"You're French but your eyes are impossible."

"I get that all the time."

He looked away. "My mother's Italian. So I get blond hair and brown eyes. Makes for a weird combination."

"Not weird at all. I like it." She studied the necklace again, holding it up. "So this has come down through the generations?"

He nodded. She wasn't the first girl to ask him about his father's side of the family. But other girls' questions always felt like birds pecking at him, wearing him down or tearing him open. Daisy's curiosity was soft on his skin. She was a beautiful china cup on a table, quietly asking to be filled. And little by little, Erik was tipping over and pouring out.

"Do you remember your father wearing this?"

"Sure. All the time. If I was sitting on his lap I'd like, you know, play with it. I had a little story in my head, this is the pretty lady and this is her boat and she goes sailing in the boat and catches this beautiful fish..."

She held the chain back out to him and he took it, their fingertips touching. "When did he give it to you? You said you were eight when he left."

He fastened the chain behind his neck again. "The story I know," he said, "is my mom saw him one more time after he left. To sign divorce papers."

He glanced down. Daisy had put her hand out, palm up on the table between them. "And sometime during the meeting—" he put his hand on hers. "—he gave this to her. To give to me. And she didn't for a long time, she kept it put away. I was too young." His other hand joined the first, holding Daisy's, rolling it between his palms, running his fingertips along the edges of her nails. "Then when I was about sixteen, she gave it to me."

"Did you want it?"

"I hadn't seen it in years so at first it was like, 'Oh wow, I remember this, the lady and the boat.' But then I had to be sixteen about it, you know, prove he was no big deal to me. I told her I didn't want it, I didn't want anything of his. Screw him. All that shit."

Under the table their ankles had cozied up together. It felt intimate and close there in the booth, holding her hands and feet, telling her secret things.

"What did she say?"

"She didn't push it. Just reminded me it had been my grandfather's too, and his father's before, and back on through the generations. It was mine now, to give to my son if I ever had one. She said, 'It's an heirloom, it belongs to your name. Don't let one asshole ruin it for you.'"

"Don't let one weak link break the chain."

"Right. I kept in a little box in my dresser for a while, and then my great-uncle died, my grandfather's brother. And he was the last Fiskare brother, the last of his generation and... I don't know. I was just moved to start wearing it."

She leaned forward again, touched the chain, then put her chin on the heel of her hand. "For the record, you know what my favorite candy is?"

Which seemed a random question but then it hit him. "Swedish Fish?"

She nodded, smiling, and looked away, the color rising up in her face a little. He laughed. She looked back. And then they were staring again. And it happened again, just as it had in the theater yesterday. Time slowed, atoms and particles separating and recombining into a secret sphere around them.

"I like you," he said.

Her hand out on the table again, between them, and he put his on it. "I like you," she said, almost soundless.

They stared on through another timeless moment, after which she went back to her book, and he bent his head over his work again. They held hands on the table, held feet beneath. Erik had never been so relaxed with a girl, never known such comfort with another human being. He had no desire to leave this space, and yet within it, he was free. He could sit with her and feel what he was feeling, with no need to explain it, dismiss it or joke it away. Every time he looked up at her and thought, *I love this,* she looked up too, and her eyes seemed to nod at him.

LOVE WILL DO THAT

FINAL DRESS REHEARSAL. The atmosphere backstage was significantly calmer, but still carried a buzzing pulse of energy. Erik threaded his way through dancers and techs, looking for Daisy, not even bothering with the pretense of an errand or task.

She was being sewn up. David was standing by her, with the sole of one foot against the wall. His arms were crossed and he looked both calm and content. A rare stance for David, who was one moody son of a bitch. He always kept you guessing. His compliments were backhanded, his humor dark and sardonic. He joked everything away, constantly pushing buttons and boundaries. And just when you had him pegged as an asshole, he showed his softer side: he sat still for a serious conversation, or showed sympathy for someone in a bind, offering a fix or a favor without the "you owe me one" implication. Once you relaxed into this kinder, gentler David, he abruptly turned into an asshole again.

Erik felt a stab of jealousy at the sight of David and Daisy chatting, smiling and laughing with ease. Probably in French. He didn't feel right barging in on the conversation so he was forced to invent business after all. He fussed with cables that didn't need fussing with, shielded his eyes and gazed up at the catwalk as if in contact with someone up there. When at last he saw David pat Daisy's shoulder and walk away, he counted to thirty before casually putting himself in her sight.

She smiled at him and held out her hands. He went to her and took them in his. His skin seemed to peel away like a dry husk, leaving him a core of pure joy. They stood in silence, fingers clasped, staring in a way that felt like kissing. Her gravity was so strong, his attraction to her so complex and layered, he felt he was drifting in another dimension. Turning over and over like a satellite broken free of its mother planet, re-orienting itself to the center of a new universe. He ached to touch more of her, longed to pull her against him as he'd never longed for anything before in his life.

"Do a triple tonight," he said.

She looked a long moment back, then smiled. "Are you daring me?"

"I'm asking." Her beauty turned him inside-out. He had to touch her. He reached with shy fingertips and brushed her small diamond earring and then trailed down her jawline. Her eyes followed his hand and closed as he touched her, her chin lifting a little. She opened them again, put her own fingertips on his necklace charms.

"All right. I'll do one for you."

But she didn't.

Erik watched her in the Prelude, feeling the pull of her across the rows of seats and through the glass of the lighting booth. She was dancing well—a heightened energy in her movements, a palpable transcendence of all thought and calculation. She was on her game, in her element. This was everything she was, everything she was born to do.

The end of her solo passage now, the circle of turns, the dizzying rush down the diagonal of the stage. The controlled preparation onto her right foot, the step onto the pointe of her left, followed by blind speed turning into spin.

"Dave, watch this," Erik whispered.

One turn. Two turns. Three.

Four.

"Holy fuck, Marge," David said, a hand on his head.

Marie Del'Amici was sitting just outside the lighting booth. They could hear her bubbling laugh. "O mio dio, Margarita. You naughty thing..."

Me, Erik thought, as triumphant as if he'd pulled it off. *She did it for me. That was mine.*

He sat through the Siciliano, mesmerized by Daisy, yet connected to Will. It was a strange bond, but through the medium of Will's body, Erik could *feel* Daisy. Her weight and warmth and closeness. Her arms here, her leg there, her waist in his hands, her back arching against his chest.

Will took Daisy back in his arms, laid his cheek at the base of her throat. Erik's own cheek grew warmer, feeling her damp skin and the elevated beat of her heart. Her hand came up to Will's head and Erik felt it caress his hair. She was fifty feet away, yet she was touching Erik. She was moving him. He felt his heart swell in his chest, his entire being condensing down to one truth: *I'm falling in love with her.*

He was grateful for the dark of the booth and the simplicity of the Siciliano's lighting cues, which left him free and alone to savor this moment, hold it in his hands and press it into his memory.

I'm falling in love.

This was the first time he felt powerfully and instinctively connected to a girl without yet possessing any intimate physical knowledge of her. This was the profound realization that sex was the fruit of an emotional bond, not the dirt in which it grew. How limited his experience was in this realm of human affinity. He was a baby. As much a virgin as Daisy. At least she was waiting to make love.

He wanted to make love with her, to partner her and create something together, to find their own dance.

And he wanted it badly enough to wait for it.

So rapt was his attention he missed his cue at the end of the pas de deux. David reached over him to slide the levers, bringing the lights down. Erik snapped back to the present, his face burning. "My bad," he mumbled.

David gazed at him, smiling, his expression neither reproachful nor teasing. "Love will do that to a guy," he whispered.

Erik nodded, not looking away, caught between making a stand for love and apologizing for it. He had such a strong urge to tell David he was sorry. But for what?

Love did what it did.

David looked away then, still smiling. Chin on his hand, staring at the stage. It was dimmed down to the lowest beams on the boom stands, illuminating the hushed interval between pieces.

"Fishy, fishy in the brook," he said under his breath, "many things, but not a crook."

SAX

A BAG OF SWEDISH FISH was no problem, but Friday night, Erik had to go to three different convenience stores and a gas station before he could find a bouquet of daisies. He separated two from the bunch and taped them to the candy, leaned paper and pen against the wall backstage and wrote a note:

The library had a Swedish-English dictionary.
Sax = scissors.

He almost wrote "good luck," then remembered it was bad luck to say it in the theater.

He stopped Aisha Johnson, one of the contemporary girls. "You wouldn't say 'break a leg' to a dancer," he said. "How do you wish good luck before a show?"

Aisha raised her eyebrows and held out an expectant palm.

"Goddammit," he muttered, reaching for his wallet and the dollar he now owed.

"I'm teasing," she said, laughing. "No, no, I don't want your money. You say 'merde.'"

"Merde."

She spelled it for him. "It's French for shit."

He went to sign his name, then decided not to. He took the note and his gifts to the row of little wooden cubbies, which served as mailboxes for the performers and stagehands, and slid the offering into the one marked Bianco. Checking his own cubby, he found a short note of appreciation from Leo, and a longer one from Allison Pierce, heavy with exclamation points and smiley faces. He put it politely in his pocket, then nervously checked his offering to Daisy hadn't inexplicably fallen out of her box in the last sixty seconds.

The dancers performed to a full and enthusiastic house. Daisy behaved in the Prelude and did a double pirouette at the end of her solo, and the audience still gave her a small, spontaneous ovation. Erik didn't miss any cues, but he watched the ballet program filled with distracted anticipation. He wondered if Daisy had found the gift in her mailbox, worried she wouldn't know it was from him, then both wondered and worried how he could see her after the concert when he had the whole second act to run and she could just leave.

She did leave. After the curtain came down, and Erik and David closed up shop, he searched backstage, but she was gone. He stood in the wings a few confused moments, not knowing what to do. He needed a cue here.

He saw Will crossing the stage, his arm wrapped around Lucky Dare's curvy body. Erik had never worked with a wingman but maybe now was the time. He started walking over, passing by the wooden cubbies, and a flicker of yellow in his own slot made him stop short. He reached in and retrieved the now-empty wrapper from the Swedish Fish. His face filled with swift heat, then it went numb, as if he'd been slapped. He didn't understand. He turned the wrapper over and over, not understanding. Then he looked and saw his own note to Daisy folded inside the plastic bag.

She'd eaten the candy, but given the rest back.

She didn't want him.

With shaking fingers he drew out the paper and unfolded it, re-reading what he'd written. Where had he gone wrong? Ten simple, almost stupid words, and she'd changed her mind?

He turned the paper over.

A pile of penned lines on the back of his note. Words jumped out at him. *Heart. Happiness. Want. Hands. Whisper.* Shaking, Erik pulled back into the privacy of the curtains to read:

I don't know what to do since I met you. I don't know how to be since you showed me your necklace and told me about your father. You let me touch some of the sadness you carry in your heart and now your happiness is something I need. I'm looking for you all the time. I want to talk to you about everything.

Who are you? I feel like I already know. Like I always knew. I want to be near you. I was born to be near you. I want to know you in the dark. I want you to look at me with your hands. To talk to me with your body. To show me without words. To trust me with your most secret self while I trust you with mine. I want to feel your smile against my mouth when I tell you things and hear you whisper, "I know. Me too."

I didn't know love would be like this. I didn't know I would love like this. And I want to see you seeing me love you. Like this.

I'm in my room.

If you don't feel the same, please be kind.

But if you are thinking right now, "Me too," then please come here, come talk to me.

I need to talk to you.

Right now.

God, I can't breathe...

Erik lifted up his head and let go the breath he'd been holding.

But if you are thinking right now, "Me too," then please come...

He left the wings, jumped off the apron and ran up the aisle to the booth. Seizing his jacket, he bolted out the lobby doors, out of Mallory and into the icy November night. He ran. Ran for his life. Ran to start his life. Across campus to the south quad, to Daisy's dorm.

Heart pounding in his heaving chest, he knocked on her door.

It opened.

Daisy in the doorway, backlit and beautiful. Sweats and her Lancaster hoodie, her hair down, the makeup scrubbed off her face. Her hand reached out to touch him. Her brimming eyes glowed blue-green.

"Me too," he said.

Daisy drew him in, closing the door behind.

The room was dark except for a reading lamp clipped onto one of the beds, and a string of Christmas lights around the window. She slid her arms around his neck. Her head settled on his chest and he exhaled. *Thank you*, he thought, rubbing his cheek against her hair.

For a long time they held each other.

"I can feel your heart," she whispered.

"I can feel everything," he said. A thudding pulse in his ears, the hum and roar of his own blood coursing through his body. Daisy unzipped his jacket and peeled it down his back and off his arms. She laid it on the bed and switched off the reading lamp. They stood together, her hands lightly touching his chest. His fingers traced her eyebrows, pushed her hair behind her ears. He felt himself expanding, swollen with emotion, unfolding for her like a map.

"Have you ever felt this way," she said, beautiful in the Christmas lights.

"Never," he said, his voice squeezed tight through his throat. He thought about maps, roads taken and untaken. The twists and turns of life, choices and their consequences sending a person in a certain direction. He could have chosen a different school. He could've come to this school but not gone with the tech theater minor. Anything could've thrown him off course. He could've missed her. He might have gone his whole life not knowing who or where she was.

"See, I don't think I can explain," she said slowly, "what this week has been like for me."

"Dais, I—"

"No, wait," she said, a finger at his mouth. "Just listen. Let me say this. You have to understand something. I'm such a practical person. To a fault. A lot of people think I'm cold but it's just... I don't like drama. I don't like ooey-gooey sentimental shit. I don't coo over babies or cry at movies. And I never believed in love at first sight. I don't write love notes, either. I mean, I don't bleed my feelings on paper. Especially for someone I just met. But I swear, Erik, I wrote to you tonight and I... I just breathed it. Breathed myself onto the paper. It was so easy and it was like seeing myself for the first time. Who I really am. I should be thinking

'This isn't me. This isn't what I'm about.' But it is. This is me. I just didn't know it until I met you."

Erik couldn't speak. He'd made her become herself. What else could love be? How could he have imagined love was anything but a force which made you your most authentic being?

"God, I love looking at you," she said, putting her palm on his face. Her thumb ran along his bottom lip and desire smacked him hard in the chest. He closed his eyes, leaned out over the edge of the abyss behind his lids. He opened them, kept them open as he brought his mouth to hers.

"Keep looking at me," he whispered.

They kissed, staring at each other, breathing each other's air, her fingertips grazing his lips. He'd never kissed with his eyes open like this. Never known a girl who made her fingers part of a kiss. He would never want it any other way now. Already he was changed.

Long, magic, elastic stretches of time, holding each other, kissing. He gave her a little of his tongue and her throat let loose a tiny sigh. Then her tongue against his, their kisses blooming like flowers and her arms twining up around his neck.

I want to be inside you, he thought, following the aching, physical concept into another dimension of need. He wanted to be conjoined, his atoms and cells combined with hers. Their perceptions melded so he could see the world through her eyes.

His soul cried out for her. How different this was from being fifteen and consumed with desperate, hormonal curiosity. Willing to take it from anyone, just for the sake of getting it. His brain now swirled in a mature and masculine revelation as his mouth found her neck, sweet with her sugar-soap scent. He tilted her head back, set his tongue in the hollow of her throat and tasted what was there. Carefully. Selectively. He didn't want just any experience. He wanted hers.

"Kiss me," she said. The bite of her fingernails was in his skin as he worked his mouth up her neck, over her chin, and then onto and into her mouth again. Finally their eyes closed and they fell into each other, kissing deep, kissing like lovers, sighing, clinging, drowning in each other.

"I want you so bad," he said against her mouth.

"You know I've never—"

"I know," he said. "You said you were waiting for the one."

"I think I was waiting for you."

He slid all ten fingers into the hair at the nape of her neck. "What is happening," he said. "I only met you a week ago."

"Do you feel it's going too fast?"

"I'm feeling a lot of things. But doubt isn't one of them."

"I'm feeling so much. I don't even have names for what I feel."

Out of words, he wrapped his arms around her slender body and pulled her closer. Her body lined up with his. The crown of her head grazed the bottom of his chin. She fit him perfectly.

"I swear, Erik. I've never wanted someone so bad."

"I'll wait. Whenever you're ready, I'll wait, I don't care how long."

She put her hands on his face, her eyes wide and shining, a cluster of Christmas tree twinkles pooled in each iris. "I'm so happy."

He stared down at her, transfixed and transformed. "I love seeing you happy."

She was all up in him again, her mouth wonderful. She kissed like a dream, kissed him like she was born to.

Born to, he thought. *I would move in her like I was born to.*

He drew her tight against him, sliding his hands up the back of her shirt. He was hard, and he let her feel it. Let her feel his want while his hands stayed soft and patient on her bare skin. Let her know he couldn't wait. And yet he would gladly wait. It was all there for the taking. Time was plentiful, a spilling basket of golden minutes and hours. Time was a gift from this girl who had waited for him to find her.

YOUR CLOTHES AGAINST MY SKIN

"DO YOU HAVE good memories of your father?" Daisy asked. She was lying on Erik's chest, playing with the little gold fish on his necklace. His hand moved slowly up and down her back underneath her shirt. His, rather: she'd taken to buttoning herself into his clothes at night, wearing one of his flannel shirts and her underwear and nothing else.

It was a sweet look.

"All my memories of him are good," he said. "That's what made it so bad when he left."

"What did he do, what was his job?"

"He owned a construction company, did some carpentry on the side. He built my and Pete's bedroom. It's a good memory."

"Tell me."

"He knocked down the wall between our rooms, made one big space for us. Then he built these beds—mine was a loft, and he cut tree shapes out of plywood, screwed them onto the front, so it looked like a forest. I had a swing, an actual rope swing hanging down from the bed. Pete was young so his bed was down low, but it had the trees all around it, and a little hammock for him."

"Sounds like something you'd see in a magazine," she said. She was making the boat charm sail in and out of the hollow of his throat.

"He built it all one summer. I remember watching for hours. Watching him work."

"So he was a set designer."

"Huh." Erik smiled. "Didn't occur to me. You're right."

"Do you remember his voice?"

"Sort of. He said *Prosit* when I sneezed. *Skål* for a toast. Those were the only Swedish words he used. I can hear them in my head. In his voice."

"What did he look like?"

Relaxed and warm, Erik thought about how to answer. He loved lying in bed with Daisy, in the gold haze of the Christmas tree lights, talking. She asked him the funniest things. Unexpected questions often startling him into thoughtfulness. He found himself opening up in a way he never had before, telling her everything, answering anything she asked.

"Like me," he finally said, laughing a little. "I don't know how else to describe him. He looked like me. But with blue eyes. Dark blue."

"Was he tall?"

"I was a kid. Everyone was tall." He gathered her hair up in his hands, then slowly let it fall. "If you come to my house someday I'll show you his picture. I have a few I kept."

"I'd like that." She dropped the charms and pulled herself up and onto him. "And I like you."

"I can't keep my hands off you..."

It was their honeymoon.

With the rigors of the fall dance concert behind them, and no other stage productions on the docket, life had downshifted into a more relaxed pace. Only classes and homework demanded their attention, and a heady surplus of free time was available to be together and evolve into a couple.

They went out often with Will and Lucky. The four of them laughed and carried on, all around Philadelphia, ambling through museums and galleries, going out to dinner or the movies. Sometimes David came along, sometimes with a date. But usually it was the four of them on the town, young, crazy, high on life and each other.

The nights passed in slower, quieter hours. Being alone. Falling in love.

And fooling around.

Spoiled by Lucky's regular sleepovers at Will's place, Erik and Daisy had the room to themselves, and together they were constructing a sexual fortress. She was still a virgin, spoon-feeding Erik her body. He ate what she offered, relishing it. He knew the pace wasn't set out of mistrust or teasing, but from her own desire not to throw any of the journey away.

"It's not that I'm totally inexperienced," she said, the first time he spent the night with her.

He tucked her hair behind her ears. "I'm stunned you're not with someone. And I'd be more stunned if there never had been anyone."

"I've had boyfriends," she said, gazing off over his shoulder. "But this is the first time everything I feel about a boy and everything I want from a boy, I want to feel inside me." She looked at him. "David's such an ass. I have no delusions about sex and marriage. I just wanted to wait until I knew. And I figured I would know when my mind stopped debating and my body said 'Him. All of him. Inside me.'"

It wasn't the first time Erik heard a girl say she wanted to wait, but he'd never heard a girl articulate why so clearly. She was so self-aware and fearlessly true to herself and it made his heart peel open to its most tender core. She was beautiful in his arms, a mermaid in jeans and a silvery-grey bra, her long hair spilling down her back. He made to gather her to him but she hung back, touching his face.

"You've done it," she said.

"I have," he said, hestitating to admit the particulars of who and when. Not because he was considering lying, but because his gallery of sexual encounters, so thrillingly delicious at the time, were now revealed as being so void of emotional connection he regarded them not sadly, but the same way a parent would indulge a child's mediocre artwork—*oh yes, lovely, dear*—and then secretly chuck it.

Daisy touched his face, bringing him back. "What were you going to say?"

"I've done it. But what I'm doing with you is totally different."

He had more experience yet he was following her in this dance of slow, intense exploration. Daisy wasn't meek or passive. Not prudish or shy. She knew her body, knew what turned her on and what got her off and she trusted Erik with the knowledge. He didn't take it lightly. He was on his own journey—learning what it meant to be a lover. A good one. To take pleasure in pleasing her. To make love instead of assuming its perpetual existence.

In her bed they devoured the nights. More often than not when he slept over, they woke up naked, tangled in each other's arms. She was ardently curious about his body and what she could do to it. Not a square inch of him went untouched. She wanted to know him down to the electrons. And for a young man naturally averse to being scrutinized, Erik was becoming addicted to her attention. The more he let her look and let her in, the more open and responsive she became to him. And the more she gave, the more he wanted.

He wanted all of this girl, all of the time. By day, he wanted her thoughts, her words, her silences and her stillness. By night, he wanted her skin, her smell, her taste and her noises. He loved making her come, could not get enough of the sound she made when he was bringing her around. Or rather, it was the absence of sound. Other girls he'd been with seemed to explode when they came, but Daisy would implode, pulling everything into her—light, air, sound, even her own voice.

He would never forget the first time it happened. Locked up in her room one night, they were making out, making in, making time stop. Erik was half-sitting, half-leaning on her desk, holding her in front of him. Kissing her mouth, unclipping her bra and then kissing her breasts, filling himself with her scent and her skin. And then, in an astonishing move, Daisy took her hands off his shoulders and unsnapped her jeans. Started pushing them down. Herself. Never had a girl loosened her own clothing with an unabashed invitation for him to come in. He held her steady even as he was exploding with stunned arousal.

Graceful and confident, she stepped out of her clothes and kicked them aside. Slid her arms around his neck, pulling up tight to him. "I like this. Being naked while you're dressed."

He swallowed hard, running his hands up and down her back.

"I love feeling your clothes against my skin," she said.

He moved more of his forearms along her spine, then down around her waist, letting her feel the material of his shirt bunching up around his elbows then smoothing out again. He slid his leg between her calf, then drew her closer so he could feel on his thigh where she was softest and warmest. His hands curved around her ass and the air in his chest thickened as her hips rocked back, then forward, pressing down on his leg, rubbing as she pushed deeper into his kiss.

He started to draw her over to the bed but she resisted. "Stay here, stay like this," she whispered.

Kissing, he slid his palm down her soft stomach, then further down one hard, sculpted quadriceps muscle. Up the tender, smooth skin of her inner thigh until he reached the damp heat between her legs. Her breath shook by his ear as he slid his fingers into her.

"God," she said.

"There?"

She swallowed hard. "Oh yeah."

There. No awkward, hit-or-miss fumbling, trying to guess where things might be. It was right *there*, that little bright pearl of flesh, right where he knew it would be, cozying up against his fingertips.

"Feels so good," she said against his mouth. Little hitches of air on his lips. His own trembling breaths back to her.

"Like that?"

"Yes. Just slide on it. Like that." Her hand at the back of his head, the other's nails biting into his arm. A click in her throat as she swallowed. "Little harder. Just press, like... Yeah." Her voice got thinner, with no breath behind it, and her forehead ground down on his. "That's gonna make me come."

"Show me." His hand pressed flat on the small of her back while the other slid along her and into her. His eyes fixed on her face. If a rock came through the window, he wouldn't have looked away.

"Erik," she whispered.

"Let it come," he said. "Show me..."

She said his name again but it fell apart in her mouth. She was squeezing hot and wet all around his fingers as he felt it rise up and bring her around. Her hips bucked hard against his hand. Her head flew back, taking the wave of her hair with it. A vein flickered at her temple and she came. No noise, just a keening rush of air through her throat. Her chin dropped down, and as it did, her teeth chattered.

Holy shit. His mouth shaped the words with no sound. That little rattle was an arrow to the core of his maleness. It hijacked his breath, thoroughly did him in.

I made her come...

She softened into his arms, her head lolling on his shoulder. He gathered her limp weight against his chest, running his hands along her back as her body quieted.

"That was crazy," he said.

She laughed, twitching one more time. Her head lifted and she touched his shirt. "I totally drooled on you..."

He glanced at the damp spot on his shoulder, laughing with her. "Oh my God, your teeth chattered."

Her breaths were slowing down. "I know. It happens when I come really hard like that."

He took her face and kissed her, tongue going deep, running along the edges of her teeth, wanting them to clatter together again, wanting to make her come even harder. But the kiss was turning around now. She had his head in her hands, her mouth taking the lead. Her touch pressed on him, her naked presence growing heavier and intentional.

It was his turn.

That first night, it took some effort for him to take his hands off her and not engage. To scale the walls of vulnerability instead of taking refuge behind them. He stood still. Tried to expand instead of contract under her touch. He was utterly exposed with no way to divert the attention or diffuse it by adding his own actions. It wasn't his home base. But he let her at him. He breathed through it as her fingers unbuttoned his shirt, opening his skin to the Christmas light. He breathed as her lips nudged his apart and her fingers trailed down his chest and stomach. He kept still and slowly he came out the other side into a new place of electric arousal, his entire body taut and coiled and wanting.

Her mouth drew silken lines up and down his neck. Her fingernails in his chest hair. The tightening and release of his belt, the metallic whisper of the zipper on his jeans. She pushed them down, helped him out as he had for her. Then he was naked in front of her and he was hard, so hard, closed up tight in her warm, eager hands. She reached for the lotion bottle on her night table, pumped it twice, then her slippery palms coaxed him up high against his stomach, long strokes, her thumb circling beneath the ridge, finding that little sweet spot. A moan escaped his chest, knuckles tightening white on the desk top.

"There?" Her mouth curled on his lower lip, drawing his tongue in. He tasted something rich and alive in her kiss that hadn't been there before.

"Yeah," he whispered. "Right like that."

"I want to see you come," she said.

"Dais."

"Just let me..."

He let her. And she got him. She was good at him. As nights gathered into weeks, she made both his teeth chatter and his toes curl. She could make him come like a freight train, or come in slow motion. Climax laced with emotional intensity made him lose his mind, and in the divine insanity, he became expressively fearless. Verbally uninhibited. Things he'd never imagined saying to a girl came tumbling forth unchecked.

"I want to kiss you until I die." Which was the truth.

"Your mouth feels amazing." She was going down on him, the warm wet of her tongue and throat advancing and reatreating like the tide, her head dipping and bobbing under his hand. The words floated out of him into the dark, she responded with a fierce sigh deep in her chest, then she sucked him down hard and finished off him and the rest of his words.

"I love watching you come." Another one—in his head and right out his mouth. She took his hand, slid it due south down her stomach, her hips yearning up and her knees swooning open, and she whispered, "Then do it again."

"God, you taste so good." He groaned it one trembling night when he was up to his chin in her sweetness, a tart rush along the roof of his mouth and the back of his tongue. Her palm lay heavy on his crown, her fingers threaded in his hair. Her shoulder blades plowed furrows in the mattress and her calves glided warm and smooth on his shoulders. He practically hummed with contentment as he drank her in, feeling her unfold and shiver, closing his eyes as she came against his mouth.

"Let me get this straight," she said a little while later. "I'm supposed to leave this room, dance thirty hours a week, earn a BFA and get an education... All the while knowing you can do *that* to me?"

"Mm-hm." Her body limp in his arms and her taste lingering on his tongue, Erik was swaying in a hammock of perfect contentment. "Any time you want."

Daisy rose up on her elbow, eyebrows wrinkled. "I'm so fucked."

Staring up at her, he felt his face widen in a grin of wicked delight. He reached his hand into her tangled hair and pulled her face to his.

"Me too," he said.

PRINCE HENRY THE NAVIGATOR

THE MONTH OF DECEMBER brought what Will called Nutcracker Mercenary Season. Private ballet schools around Philadelphia were getting their *Nutcracker*s ready, and they needed experienced dancers for the more difficult roles in the second act—always Sugarplum and Cavalier, sometimes a Dewdrop for the iconic flower waltz. They came scouting around the conservatory, looking for hired guns.

"It's a stupid easy gig," Will said. "One or two rehearsals a week, a few on weekends. The choreography is never complicated and you're only doing the second act anyway. In and out. It's good exposure and you earn a couple hundred bucks. Win-win all around."

Daisy and Will landed Sugarplum and Cavalier at a school in Ardmore. The whole entourage—Erik, Lucky, David, Marie and Kees—turned out to watch the Saturday evening performance, which happened to coincide with Daisy's eighteenth birthday.

Daisy's parents came, too. They all stood around the lobby at intermission, talking and chatting easily. This was Erik's second time seeing them, the first back at the fall dance concert. Tonight Francine Bianco hugged and kissed him, which was an encouraging sign.

Francine had once danced with the Paris Opera. She now ran the orchard, raising chickens, ducks and organic produce, but she still looked and carried herself like a dancer. Her posture was impeccable. Her black hair, elegantly threaded with silver, was drawn up in a bun, showing her long neck. Standing with turned out feet, she was talking vigorous shop with Kees and Marie, switching effortlessly between French and English.

Erik and David stood apart with Daisy's father, Joe.

"My mother kisses everybody," Daisy had said. "But with Pop, approval is all in the handshake. First time meeting, it's single hand." She shook Erik's hand, demonstrating. "But if he likes you, you graduate to a shake with the other hand on top, or better, on your upper arm. This is acceptance. If the other hand comes up like this—" She patted Erik's face gently but heartily with her palm. "—you're family. But here's the carte blanche: handshake, palm pat and tug on the earlobe." Her fingers gave Erik's ear a single, brisk tug.

"Then I'm in?"

"Then you're behind the velvet rope."

Erik's ears had gone untouched tonight but he'd received the single handshake with upper arm grasp. He was satisfied.

Joseph Bianco had gained American citizenship by joining the Army and doing two tours in Vietnam as a combat engineer. Poised and observant, with a dry humor, Joe didn't say much, yet he was fully present. His reticence wasn't awkward or exclusionary. Rather he put out a companionable sort of silence, much like Daisy's. Erik was instinctively drawn to it. And he couldn't help but appreciate a man who could dismantle land mines. He suspected Joe Bianco had a plan K, minimum.

"Is it true sappers are the only ones in the army who can wear beards?" David asked.

"In the French Foreign Legion, yes," Joe said. "And they're allowed to carry an axe, too."

"What did you carry in Vietnam?"

"An axe." Joe winked at the boys. His bright blue eyes didn't have Daisy's green overtones, but the same dark rim was around the iris.

"Well, she's clearly not the milkman's child," David mumbled to Erik, as they filed back into the theater for the second act.

It was the first tutu role Erik had ever seen Daisy dance. A role firmly entrenched in the classical vocabulary. Her technique was clean, polished, precise. She sparkled. He noticed her feet were especially controlled, defying gravity whenever she came down off her pointes.

Will dismissed the role of the Cavalier, calling it a mindless, hands-and-arms role. "It's a snore. I never string two steps together, I just stand where she needs me to be and make her look good."

But it was still Will and Daisy dancing, and they still put their own interpretation into the conventional partnering, making eye contact and smiling at each other. Real smiles. They didn't make it romantic, they maintained a certain regal, storybook air, yet their natural human connection transformed them from an insipid dessert to a textured couple who ruled this make-believe land together.

"This is the first time I've seen a Sugar-Cavi couple who actually looked like a couple," Kees said afterward.

"It's pure Daisy and Will," Marie said.

It's generous partnering, Erik thought.

Joe and Francine took him and Daisy out for a late supper, where the wait staff brought Daisy a piece of cake with a candle. Back in her room, she unwrapped Erik's present, a set of Russian nesting dolls. Matryoshka. Daisy had been collecting them since she was a child.

They locked the door, unfolded the night and spread it out like a blanket. They tumbled onto its softness, kissing, touching and undressing.

"Don't move," Erik said.

"What?"

"Don't move. Stay still. This."

"This?"

"This. This right here is like the greatest moment of my life."

He was standing behind her, looking over her shoulder down the full length of her body, its curves and contours and shadows. One of his arms across her collar bones, above the swell of her breasts in the silver-grey bra he loved. His other forearm, darker against the skin of her stomach, and his hand slid halfway into her underwear, just on the verge of easing them down. He held still. Took a mental picture and framed it.

"This," he said. He touched the heat coming off her, the heat he'd created.

She pulled her breath in. He slid his hand under her bra, fingers curving around her breast. Opening the clasp, she tilted her head to look up at him.

"I love you," she whispered.

"I love you."

"And I'm ready if you are."

He turned her, held her head in his hands, their eyebrows together. "You're supposed to get presents today, not give them."

She smiled. "It is my present." She slid her arms out of the bra straps and brought them up around his neck, her hands gliding on his bare skin. Beneath them he trembled, hard and aching with the need to be inside her. He was pure, mouth-watering want. Dying to seize it all and swallow it whole and curbing himself to let the taste linger.

"You're sure?" He felt compelled to ask one last time.

She kissed him. Her fingers curled around his earlobe and pulled slowly. "You're in," she said.

HER SKIN WAS AMAZING: burnished gold under twinkling light garlands. She was sitting on her bed, her long legs stretched out in the tangle they had made of the covers. They had kissed and touched and caressed and licked and explored each other until the sheets were a twisted and rumpled mess beneath their sweating, trembling bodies. Now Erik was kneeling between her calves and together, with shaking fingers, they were tearing open the condom packet and rolling it on him.

The air in the little room was close and warm, redolent with anticipation, sweat, sex, the faint smell of latex overlaid with Daisy's perfume. She lay back and pulled him along with her. He gathered the covers up around them, tucking them into a cocoon. Her hand was tender at the back of his neck, her knees inching up his hips.

"Come inside me," she whispered.

Cradled in her thighs, he had to take a split-second to absorb what this meant. She'd never told another boy, *Come inside me.* He was the first. He would belong to her history after tonight. And in an instant of reflection, he grasped man's need to walk where none had walked before. He understood Columbus and Neil Armstrong and Hillary and Peary when she put her arms around his neck and his hands drew her hips up.

"This is the best thing I've ever done," he said. And he pushed into her, hungry to take the step for his own mankind.

Daisy sucked in her breath and her back arched so suddenly, Erik froze, no longer Prince Henry the Navigator but just an amateur lover, a nineteen-year-old emotional virgin.

"I'll stop," he said.

"No, don't."

"I don't want to hurt you."

"You're not." Her damp hands held his head. "You're not hurting me. It's just really tight."

It was. All of her body was an incredible squeezing pressure around him. He was in some primitive place, the first, the only, the one, sliding into the gripping heat, the sensual effort to get inch by delicious inch inside her nearly undoing him.

"Is it all right?" he whispered, barely holding it together.

"Yes," she said, her voice filled with laughing wonder. "It's good. God it's... It's good."

Then he was on his elbows, stretched full out on top of her. In. *Inside.* His hips snugged up tight to hers, unable to go any further. She wound her legs around him and they held still, breathing hard, kissing harder, feeling their bodies joined.

"I love you so much," he said.

"I love you," she murmured beneath him, her hands sliding over his skin. "You feel so good in me." She ran her shaking mouth up his neck. "I knew you would."

"You're so tight." He was trying to move in her, trying to make love, make it more, make it *something.* "I don't know if I can... God, Dais."

"It's so good," she said. She was beautiful and exhilarated under him. Too beautiful. And he was too young, too excited, too inexperienced with making love and being in love. He tried to hang on to his desire, rearing and pawing like an untamed colt at the stable doors. But she kept whispering in his ear, responding to every move he made inside her and it was too much.

"Go then," she said. "We have all night. Let it go. Let me feel you come..."

He was already gone. The colt busted free and ran for the pastures, dragging Erik behind. He turned inside-out and ground down hard into her heat, bucking and writhing as he poured into her. She hung onto him with arms and legs, stuck to his body like a starfish on a rock, riding out the tremors. Interminable minutes passed. The colt slowed to a walk. Erik's heartbeat grew softer in his ears. The mist of sweat on his body felt cooler. Finally he lifted up his head to look at her.

She smiled at him, but tears were dripping from the corners of her eyes, running diagonally along her cheeks. Erik's thumbs smudged them away.

"Don't cry," he whispered through a throat of iron.

"I'm just happy."

The minutes passed in kissing, and he felt the muscles in Daisy's body quiver and relax. First one leg, then the other dropped off his hips. Then her head fell back on the pillow. Finally her arms released, which he took as a signal, and rolled off her.

"Oh," she said, looking down between them. He looked, and saw the condom was smeared scarlet.

"Yikes," he said. "You sure I didn't hurt you?"

"No, not at all..." Her confidence seemed rattled. "Sorry," she said, a little meekly, which he found odd.

"Don't be," he said. "It's just blood." He touched it, a little mesmerized, rubbing the warm tackiness. Now he could see Daisy's thighs were smudged with it. A small, bright rose had bloomed on the mattress beneath her.

"Can you get me a towel?" she asked.

"Yeah. One sec." He pushed up on an elbow, dipped a finger and began to trace letters on her leg, just above her bent knee. E. Then R.

"What are you doing?" But she was laughing, and her hand caressed his head.

He smiled, not sure himself, but into it, carefully making the crossbars of the I. Boldly, he slid his finger into her, and then finished with a strong K. And there, on her leg, his name, in her blood.

"Now you're mine," he said. She looked down at her leg, up at him, and her eyes turned wicked. Her hand, which had been soft in his hair, seized the nape of his neck and pulled him on her again, all of his body along hers. She opened her mouth under his, wound her limbs around him like vines.

Caught up in her savage and greedy grip, he kissed her, crushed her down into the bed even as the joy in him spiraled up through the roof and burst into the sky. He'd always known the one was out there and he'd found her.

And he'd marked her in blood.

PART TWO: JAMES

THE ALPHA MALE

JAMES DOW CAME TO Lancaster the fall of Erik's junior year.

Erik heard about him first through Daisy, who spoke of a talented transfer from Juilliard who was wowing the tights off the conservatory. "Marie's having him partner me a lot," she said. "I think he's being groomed as the heir apparent." She still danced with Will, but Will was a senior now, and clearly Marie was keeping a shrewd eye on the future.

"Is he any good?" Erik asked.

"He's a good dancer," Daisy said. "But he's kind of erratic. Good days are phenomenal, bad days are horrendous and it's either one or the other. No middle ground."

"Perfect or useless."

"Right, which makes it hard to partner with him. He's strong, his timing is good. But he's not consistent."

"He's not Will," Erik said.

"Nobody is Will. But I can't ignore he's graduating. That would be stupid."

"And no stupid girls are in ballet." It was something Daisy's old ballet teacher used to say, and one of Daisy's personal credos.

"James isn't stupid," she said. "He's got a phenomenal memory. He's just unpredictable. And I have to think so much when we dance together, which is exhausting."

Erik followed the gossip with interest, wondering if a rivalry would erupt between the newcomer and Will. They sounded intensely competitive in the studio. But then Will started bringing James around to hang socially and Erik's interest quickly morphed into concern. While James was a dynamic and likeable guy, something about the new friendship seemed odd to Erik. Troubling in a way he couldn't quite articulate.

James Dow came from a small town outside Pittsburgh. His face had a dark, devilish handsomeness punctuated by stormy grey eyes. He was twenty-one but already losing his hair. "I got crap genes. None of the men in my family can keep a head of hair to save their lives." He gave in gracefully by sporting an eighth-inch buzz cut and a slick goatee. Gold hoops hung from both his ears. These, the beard and his olive skin gave him the look of a pirate, Erik thought. Or a conquistador. "You look like Vasco da Gama," he said.

"You, you look like freakin' Adonis," James said. He turned to Will. "How do you concentrate with this guy around?"

"With great difficulty," Will said.

"Jesus, with a face like his I could've conquered half of Greenwich Village. Must be a pussy market around your place. What, does he just stand in bars and take numbers?"

"Fishy, fishy in the brook," David said, "doesn't have a little black book."

"He's Bianco's boy," Will said.

"Oh." James gave Erik an appraising look.

"He could be the Olympic champ of getting laid," Will said. "But where is he on Saturday night? Pushing up daisies."

"Can you blame him?" David asked.

"I'm standing right here, guys," Erik said.

"We know," Will said.

James shushed him. "Don't speak, Fish. Just stand there, look cute and let us talk about you, okay?" His tone and cadence were an uncanny mimicry of Will. He even captured the little French-Canadian inflection on "okay," drawing the word tight up against the roof of his mouth. Erik was puzzled by the tactic. Trying to emulate Will was one thing—imitation, sincere flattery and so forth—but James seemed to be taking it to extreme levels. Making himself into a Kaeger Klone. It made Erik feel strangely defensive.

Maintaining a healthy social life did require some effort on Erik's part. Given his way, he would only be with Daisy. He was happiest with her. But he pragmatically sensed this wasn't a healthy way to go through college, and so when the boys went out, he went along. His circle of friends within the conservatory was diverse and casual. Then he had a smaller exclusive circle with David, with whom he spent most his time, and Will, with whom he shared most his thoughts.

Against the fixed constant of Daisy, Erik found it odd he'd ended up with two wild cards like Will and David as mates. Odd because a third of the time he couldn't even stand David. Erik's friendship with Will, on the other hand, had only strengthened over the past two years.

He often wondered if he and Will would have been as close, had they not been involved with Daisy and Lucky. Erik didn't think the bond was born solely out of the convenience of two roommates banging two roommates, but he wasn't positive Will's company was something he would have sought out on his own. Despite the strong affinity, they were nothing alike.

"You can't pick human connection apart, honey," Daisy said. "Sometimes the affinity just exists without a reason. Or in spite of the reasons not to exist."

Erik shrugged, not entirely convinced.

"Anyway, I think you're a lot alike," Daisy said. "You and Will seek out the same things in life, you just use different tactics. Will tries everything until he arrives at what he wants. Process of elimination. You get what you want all worked out in your head first, then you make a plan to go get it. But at the end of the day, what you're both after is essentially the same thing."

"Which is?"

"Creativity," Daisy said thoughtfully. "Mastery of a skill. Athleticism. And connection. Mostly connection."

"We just want to be loved?"

"By women, no doubt. But maybe you're looking for a male kindred spirit."

"Maybe." He and Will hadn't sliced palms and mingled blood, but it had been a mindless decision to room up sophomore year, and to continue the living arrangements this year. They lived well together—neither was a slob, in fact, both gravitated toward order, liking things to be in their place. They never lacked for conversation. And as Daisy had said, each had skills the other was curious to master. Some of them quite useful.

"What's with you and the pineapple juice?" Erik asked Will once, noting never less than a gallon of it was in their fridge.

"Il donne le coup un bon goût," Will said, twisting the cap off a new bottle.

"English, please."

Will did a high pour into two glasses, handed one over. "It makes your jiz taste good."

"Jesus," Erik muttered. But naturally he started drinking it, too. Such a sexual tidbit coming from David could be immediately dismissed as a mind-fuck. From Will, however, it required serious consideration. ("And it doesn't exactly make it taste good," Daisy said later. "It just makes it not taste.")

On the less-useful but more refined front, Will was learning to play credible guitar under Erik's tutelage. He was also a born-again tea drinker. Erik had taken two semesters of Taekwondo. They worked out together several times a week. Will hated to run, but he ran if Erik wanted to, and eventually hated it less. Will's cross-training routine left Erik winded and wounded but he could tell he was getting stronger. And ripped. So he pushed through the sessions on the wave of Will's motivation and the promise of Daisy running greedy hands over his body, purring about his abs and the little cut in his deltoid.

But analyzing Will's friendship made Erik's Y chromosome ache. Men didn't pick apart and classify relationships the way girls did. At best, Erik could conclude he admired Will. Looked up to him. He wasn't a father figure, but in Erik's eyes, Will was definitely the alpha male. Which made Erik the beta. The behind-the-scenes man. Where he liked best to be. But now with James, a new buck was on the scene. Not exactly locking horns with Will for breeding rights—James was gay—but definitely shifting the status quo by sheer personality.

Erik shared this observation with David, who laughed in his face. "First of all, you're the alpha male."

"Me?"

"What, you think it's only how tall you are or how much magnetism you have? It's about pack mentality. You bring out the best in people."

"Say what?"

"Haven't you ever noticed everyone calms down around you?"

"No."

"You're human valium, dude."

"Get outta here," Erik said, giving David a shove to emphasize.

"I'm telling you, Fish. As long as you're around, things stay chill. Your girlfriend's the same way. You both got the inner flame that never flickers. People love you. But maybe it's better you don't know it. Forget I said anything. You're an asshole, Fish. Everyone hates your guts."

Erik laughed but the reflection left him more than a little stunned. Both the content and the person it was coming from. He long resigned to David being one of his more difficult friends. They were excellent collaborators and had worked on several successful projects over the past three years. But if the best was in David, Erik didn't think he'd brought it out. David had always remained moody and unpredictable, a relentless tease and notorious practical joker. The genuine moments remained few and far between, and Erik took them at face value when they came.

"Second of all," David said, "and I realize this will be hard for you to grasp, so listen closely. What James is doing with Will is called a crush."

Erik stared at him, then closed his eyes. "I'm an idiot."

"Yes, you are. And I got even more bad news for you, Fish, because Will's eating it up."

"Not this again," Erik said. "He's straight. Come on, he's been with Lucky two years now."

David grinned. "Well Lucky ain't here, is she?"

She wasn't. Lucky had been experiencing a life path shift, leaning away from physical therapy toward emergency medicine. She was taking a sabbatical and doing a modified EMT training program in Boston. Seeing if she had the stomach for it.

"Will's definitely enjoying being a swinging bachelor again," David said. "Regardless of which way the door is swinging. And he plays James like a violin. It's fascinating in a twisted way. You watch."

Erik watched and couldn't deny it. Flying solo, Will had a little more swagger in him. He seemed augmented—taller, louder, funnier. And after the conversation with David, Erik quickly grasped James wasn't competing with Will. He was adoring him. And Will was skillfully basking in it. He soaked up James's infatuation yet he was careful not to reciprocate it. He never asked for James's attention, he simply made his pleasure in it irresistible. He increased supply by decreasing demand. Erik couldn't believe James didn't get what was going on. Until he began to figure James out a little more.

If Will was an entitled cat belly-up in a puddle of sunshine, James was a stray out in the rain. Not the alpha male, but the omega. His desire to be included and accepted made him try too hard. His jokes were always slightly too loud, his joviality a little too forced. His good moods had a touch of mania to them while his downswings were wretched. If he felt the least bit rejected he plummeted into morose, passive-aggressive silence. He reminded Erik of nothing more than a lonesome dog trying a gamut of attention-seeking tricks, a ball in the lap or a muzzle on the knee, content with any scrap given and crushed when it was taken away.

James's heart was in the right place, Erik thought. But along the way, his heart had somehow been damaged, leaving James an empty, aching vessel. And Will could fill it with a single word, or crack it into pieces with a word withheld.

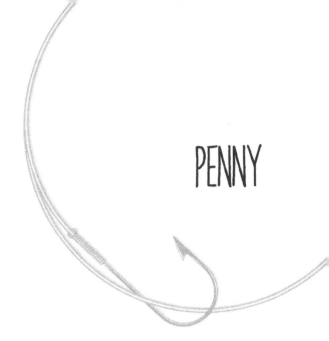

PENNY

WHEN ALONE WITH ERIK and David, James wasn't flamboyant or flirtatious. But he still seemed embarrassingly grateful to be included in their company, even if they were only sitting around playing video games at Erik and Will's place. They rented off-campus, in a quaint, slightly rundown residential neighborhood marked by narrow, two-story houses. Their place was on Colby Street, while Daisy and Lucky's little house was on the adjacent Jay Street. The two backyards bumped together, divided by a hedge.

David and another stagehand, Neil Martinez, had a place around the corner. James was in a dorm but spent as little time there as possible. "My roommate's such a douche," he said. "I should find new digs before I shoot the guy."

They were sitting around one September night. The Nintendo was broken—fingers of blame pointing in all directions but Erik suspected David had thrown it across the room in a fit of poor sportsmanship. Erik was taking it apart on the coffee table. Not to fix it. Just to tinker. It had been a long week. His schedule this semester was heavy with academic classes—statistics, especially, was a bear. Now his tired brain needed the meditative zone working with his hands always brought.

Will was at judo class. David and Neil were sketching set designs for the fall production of *Death of a Salesman*. James wasn't doing anything, just sitting and watching Erik, so intent it was unnerving. But he stayed unusually quiet, and after a while Erik forgot about him. Piece by piece he took the console apart, lining everything up in careful order on the table.

"Leave it," he murmured when James reached to fiddle with something. James withdrew his hand. The gesture was so immediate and obedient, his expression so rapt and kid brother-ish, Erik felt a surge of liking for the guy, mixed with the quiet pleasure of being admired.

"How do you know what you're doing?" James asked.

"I don't."

"You're just taking it apart for pure enjoyment."

Erik smiled a little. "I like to," he said.

James lit a cigarette and offered the pack to Erik, who shook his head. "My brothers do shit like this all the time," James said. "But with cars. They'll take an engine apart and put it together. Just for kicks."

"How many brothers you have?"

"Three. All older."

"Any of them dance?"

"Shit, no. My brothers are just like my father. They like sports, they like hunting, they like cars. Then there's me. Their personal embarrassment. They used to tease me about being adopted except I prayed for it to be true. I'd have fantasies there'd be a knock at the door and it would be my real parents come back to claim me."

Erik smiled, not knowing what to say. He bent his head back over his project, whistling through his teeth. He gave a start when James reached a finger to touch his necklace.

"This is cool. What's it about?"

Erik told him its history, explained each of the charms. When he was finished, James sat back, looking thoughtful. He drew from the neck of his shirt a silver ball chain. From it dangled a set of dog tags and a copper pendant. He drew it over his head and handed it to Erik.

Erik put down his screwdriver and took the necklace carefully, knowing a talisman when he saw one. The dog tags were stamped KORO-DOWSKI, MARGARET C.

"My sister," James said.

"Korodowski?"

"My real last name. I use Dow for the stage."

Erik nodded. He looked closer at the copper pendant. It was a flattened penny.

"We called her Penny," James said. "My mom had three boys and always wanted a daughter. My father said one would eventually turn up. Like a bad penny. And she did turn up. With me."

David and Neil had drifted over to listen and look at the tags.

"You're twins?" Neil asked.

"Yeah."

"What happened?" Erik asked quietly.

"She was in the 14th Quartermaster Detachment," James said. "They were deployed to Saudi Arabia last February. They were only there six days and a scud missile destroyed the barracks."

"I remember seeing the story on the news," David said. "I had no idea your sister was... Dude, I'm sorry."

"I'm sorry," Erik said. "That's horrible."

James took the chain back from David and put it over his head.

"Is it why you transferred here?" Neil asked.

James lit another cigarette. "My mom went off the deep end. Penny was her baby. She was everyone's baby but for Mom she was..." James sighed, exhaling the smoke through his nose. "Mom was always fragile. Meek. Put on earth to serve my father and my brothers. Penny died and something in Mom just turned off. Went out."

David flicked the lighter, held the flame a moment and then released the tab.

"Exactly," James said. "And I was fucked up over it. I came home destroyed. Came home thinking people would be sympathetic about me losing my best friend, my twin. I actually thought grief might make us all closer. Fat chance. My dad never knew what to do with me. It was like I was the price he had to pay for a daughter. Now Penny was gone and she was the only thing standing between me and him. And my brothers. It turned into a free-for-all. Whatever grief they had, they took it out on me. And my mother was checked out. She started drinking her pain away. It was a mess. I needed to get the hell out but I felt New York was too far away. So I came here."

"Shit," Neil said. David looked grim. Erik couldn't think of anything to say.

"It's funny. Abandonment takes all forms, doesn't it?" James said. "David's father died. Neil, yours too. Fish, your old man took off. Mine was present, but made a campaign of not being there. Which is worse? Having no male influence in your life, or having the wrong male influence? I mean, who was your father figure, Fish? Your go-to guy?"

Erik ran a hand through his hair. "My uncles, I guess. My mom's brothers. No, actually, not really. They were there but I can't say they were my substitute father figures. Maybe my basketball coach? He was definitely an influence but pretty much when I had a problem, I went to my mom."

"Do you still? Is she still your first phone call?"

Erik smiled. "Daisy's my first phone call."

David snorted. "Or you just roll over in bed."

"Well, who do you call, Dave?" James asked.

"These days?" David scratched the back of his neck. "Leo. Or him." He pointed at Erik.

"Shut up," Erik said, laughing.

"Yeah, you laugh," Neil said.

"No shit," James said. "I've only been here a month, but I already know if I need a body buried or a secret kept, I'm calling you, Fish."

Will arrived home then, his hair damp with sweat and his face red with exercise. "What's up, assholes," he said. He tossed down his backpack and chugged the last of his pineapple juice. Then gave a hearty belch.

"What's with you and the pineapple juice?" James said. "You suck that shit down twenty-four-seven."

"Vitamin C," Will said, walking into the kitchen. "Keeps you from breaking out."

Erik chuckled. "Among other things."

"Don't give away trade secrets, Fish," Will called.

"What?" James said, looking from the kitchen to Erik and back again, eyebrows wrinkled.

Secure in the privacy of a private joke, Erik shook his head with a smile and went back to tinkering.

DIFFICULT TIME SIGNATURES

WILL CHOSE NOT TO DANCE in the fall concert. Instead he put all his energy into his senior project. Challenged by Kees to step away from classical ballet and create a work for the contemporary dancers, Will was struggling to come up with an idea. All through September he spent long hours listening to a variety of music, either loaded into his Walkman while working out or running, or playing on the stereo at the apartment.

He sat motionless or sprawled on his back in front of the speakers. He sighed and cursed a lot. Occasionally he jotted something in a notebook, only to tear out the page and throw it in a crumpled ball at the wall. Erik sensed the clouds of creative frustration releasing the first drops of creative terror and, he had to admit, he was more than a little fascinated. This was the eternally self-assured William Maurice Kaeger on the verge of panic. What would he do?

Then one evening James burst into the house on Colby Street, breathless and panting, waving a tape. "I got it," he said. "Listen."

He popped the tape into the stereo and tossed the empty case to Will, who looked and passed it to Erik. It was Philip Glass's soundtrack for the movie *Powaqqatsi*. Out of the speakers blasted, of all things, a coach's whistle. And then an explosion of joyful sound made Erik's eyebrows first fly up, then wrinkle as he took in what sounded like an indigenous drum-and-bugle corps. First a hypnotic, repetitive foundation of acoustic percussion, followed by a cavalry charge of trumpets over fat tuba bass notes. Then a children's choir layered a simple melody on top of the rhythmic cadence.

Will unfolded his tall body and stood up.

"How do you count this?" Erik asked, losing the beat and finding it again.

Daisy got up and helped James push the coffee table aside. Will continued to stand still.

"Is this four-four?" Daisy said.

"It goes between four-four and six-four," James said. "Some phrases have ten beats."

"I like this," Will said, both hands on his head. "Holy shit, I like this a lot." He looked visionary. His chin nodded in time to the drums. His head tilted, his eyes closed. Fingers dug in his hair as his feet moved in a simple pattern. Three steps forward, one back. Three forward, one back. The back step became a hop. Then a hop with a half-turn to repeat the sequence facing the other way. Eight steps against ten beats in the music.

"It doesn't match up," Erik said.

"It's not supposed to," Will said.

Rapt, Erik watched as Will kept building on the theme, changing levels and changing dynamics. Will turned Daisy in one direction while he and James faced the other. The phrase became three dimensional. Will added arm movements, picking up the sharp percussion.

"Are you writing this down, Erik?" Daisy said. Her cheeks were growing pink.

"Write it? I can't even count it."

"Don't worry, I have it," James said. "Wait until you hear the next section. It's in five-four time. It's sick."

"Look out, you almost hit the TV," Erik said.

"I can't do this here," Will said. "I need to get into a studio. Can I get into a studio? What time is it?" He popped the tape out of the stereo. "Who's coming with me?"

Daisy sat back down on the couch, but James couldn't get out the door fast enough. He and Will were gone three hours. When they came back Will looked positively feverish. His notebook, so pathetically bare before, was three-quarters filled with scribblings, the whole ballet sketched out in its pages. Will took the idea to Kees who both blessed it and sunk his teeth into it.

Will went into rehearsals with James as his assistant. James was perfect for the job. He possessed near total recall when it came to choreography. Not only every step committed to memory, but the spacing of every dancer at any given moment in the music. Even more valuable was his ability to catch Will's improvisations on the fly and repeat them back, a human camcorder. He patiently coached the dancers who couldn't grasp the difficult time signatures. He stepped in for anyone who was absent. If Will couldn't run a rehearsal, James did, and was careful to be humble and self-effacing about it. *Powaqqatsi* was Will's baby and James was smart enough to be unobtrusive even as he became more and more indispensable. Will needed him. Publicly depended on him. James had hitched a ride on a comet and was on a trajectory to the popularity he craved.

The contemporary dancers went crazy over *Powaqqatsi*. Like a benignly infectious disease, the excitement spread through the conservatory. Ballet dancers showed up at rehearsals either to watch or to learn the choreography. Even the stagehands found time or excuses to wander by the third-floor studios.

"I still can't count this music," Erik said, watching.

"I'd kill to dance this," Daisy said. "I'm serious. I'll trip someone and not even feel bad about it."

"It's brilliant," James said. "I can't stand it, it's so brilliant. Fuck ballet, I'm going to the dark side."

Kees turned around, grinning. "Better not let Marie hear you."

"I meant it lovingly."

Daisy checked her watch and sighed. "We should go, James. Our rehearsal starts in ten minutes."

James didn't answer, he was deep in concentration. Daisy tapped his arm. Then pulled it. Finally Kees helped her peel James's fingers off the barre and she dragged him out.

The classical section of the fall concert was no throwaway. A guest choreographer from Atlantic Dance Theater had come in to stage his ballet *No Blue Thing* to the music of Ray Lynch. Daisy had a gorgeous solo piece and a pas de deux with James. The program was shaping up to be one of the conservatory's best. As they moved through October, the creative energy in Mallory Hall shifted from carefree to industrious. The strong pulled ahead and the weak began to flail.

No Lancaster conservatory student could shirk their academic studies. Those pursuing a Bachelor of Arts had to complete eighteen credits from the liberal arts program. A Bachelor of Fine Arts required twenty-four, plus another twelve in dance history and anatomy. Students had to maintain a 2.0 GPA or they couldn't perform in main stage productions.

Both Daisy and Will were getting their BFA. Not surprisingly, their dance partnership applied itself well to academic study. Working together, they sailed through the coursework with little difficulty. Except for anatomy—every dancer dreaded the notoriously grueling course. Only rote memorization, a hundred mnemonics and Lucky's tutoring got Will and Daisy to a pair of C grades last year.

This year their nemesis was dance history, with heavy reading and papers due every other week. James was in the course too, and struggling to keep up. Oddly, the photographic memory he possessed for movement didn't translate to written material. He admitted he'd never been a strong reader. Half the problem was sitting still. Will loved to read and regularly practiced meditation techniques through his martial arts training, but it was an effort for James to focus. Will didn't mind chatty people, but people with the fidgets drove him batshit.

"Hold *still*," Will said one night at Colby Street. "Good Lord, man, you're like a two-year-old."

"Put something heavy in your lap," Erik said.

James looked over. "Say what?"

"When I was a kid and couldn't sit still at the dining room table, my mom would put the phone book in my lap. Something about the weight makes you settle. Do we have a phone book?"

"No. Come over here, James." Will was lying on the couch reading. He moved his feet so James could sit down, and then he put his legs across James's lap. "There. Think heavy."

Will returned to reading, the fingertips of one hand rubbing along his hairline. From the easy chair, Erik watched James become silent and still. His focus was on his book but his hand rested on Will's shin in a manner both mindlessly casual and deliberately proprietary. Erik felt an involuntary squint of his eyes, along with a strong but confusing urge to defend his territory. He couldn't take his eyes from James's hand. Outlined white against Will's jeans. The flat ridge of shin bone against his palm, fingertips curved around calf muscle. Slowly moving back and forth. Up toward Will's knee. Down toward his ankle. Up toward his knee again, going further this time, fingers kneading.

My mind is open, Erik thought. After three years in a conservatory program at a fine arts university, he was completely accustomed to gay men being part of his daily life. He had it worked out. They were them. He was him. He knew when to make jokes and when to be cool. He had nothing but the utmost respect for Kees, and considered him a close friend.

True, there had been uncomfortable moments with a few of the more aggressive types. Boys with overt tactics, looking more to provoke and shock than to connect. It pissed him off, but he knew better than to make a scene. The conservatory thrived on gossip. One good altercation and he'd never hear the end of it. It was better to turn off and not engage. Harder. But better. He got used to it. And as long as homosexuality wasn't blatantly and personally in his face, he rarely gave it more than five seconds thought.

My mind is open, he thought again, watching James's hand stroking Will's leg.

Just fucking stay out of my face.

Erik closed and stacked his books. Without a word he put on his jacket and shoes.

"Going home?" James asked.

"I live here, remember?" Erik said.

Will looked up. "Goodnight, Fish."

"Night, ladies," Erik said. And then wished he'd kept his mouth shut. He went out, walked through the hedge into Daisy's backyard, up the steps into her kitchen, where the teakettle was whistling. Erik shut off the flame and moved the kettle to a back burner.

"Oh, here you are," Daisy said, coming in. Her hair was damp. She had on a pair of Erik's flannel pajama bottoms and a tight white T-shirt.

The cold Erik had let in made her nipples press against the material. His restless eyes narrowed at them. He slid his gaze down along the lines of her body as the night got up on its knees, hungry and intent.

"Do you want tea?" she asked.

"No," he said, walking by her and taking her hand.

"Where are we going?"

"Up."

"You're not even going to say hello?"

He turned, took her face and kissed her. "Hello." He walked through the living room, pulling her along.

"Are we in a mood?"

"We are."

"I only have one condom here. Just so you know."

"At the moment, one is all I need."

She laughed, following him up the stairs. "Since we're on the subject. I mean, I was going to wait until your birthday to tell you."

"Tell me what?"

"That I went on the pill."

Erik turned around and looked down at her.

She smiled at him. "I just started. You're supposed to keep up a second method for the first month. But then..."

He kept staring at her. She stepped up, level with him, and touched his bottom lip. "I can't wait," she said. "Nothing between us."

Erik closed his eyes. "Get up there," he said.

EPIPHANY, PART TWO

"QU'EST-CE QUI SE PASSE?" Daisy said later. Her naked body curled up against his side, head on his chest. "What are you thinking about?"

"Nothing." His body was relaxed and normally after sex his mind would be peaceful. Instead it was tangled in knots. He turned the snarl over and over, unable to find an end to draw out.

"You keep looking out the window to your place. Is his car still there?"

Erik put the pillow over his face. She peeked under it. "You think they're hooking up?"

"I don't want to know."

"But you can't stop thinking about it."

Erik took the pillow and bopped her lightly on the head. "Stop knowing me."

She laughed. "I'm sort of fascinated with it myself. Am I a voyeur?"

"Go over and voyeur away. Feel free."

"I kind of want to," she said absently.

"It doesn't bother you?"

"Two men having sex?"

"I mean, Lucky's your best friend."

Daisy pushed up on her elbow, her fingers in Erik's chest hair. "She is. And in a manner of speaking, so is Will."

"So is Will hooking up with James cheating?"

Her chin rose and fell. "In the strictest sense, I guess it is, yes."

"Are you going to tell her?"

"I'm not the morality police," she said. "And right now I have nothing to tell. You don't either." Her hand caressed his face, her thumb moving along his eyebrows and trying to smooth the wrinkle of worry between them. "But I can tell it's bothering you."

"No, it's not," Erik said. And then, because he was bothered, and because ultimately he laid all his troubles at her feet, he sighed against her hand and said, "Yeah, it is."

"It's not like there's never been speculation and jokes about Will being bisexual. This isn't news to you."

"Well, it's one thing to joke about it and another thing to see it happening." He looked up at her. "I don't know why I care. Honestly, I don't know why it bothers me so much. Easy to say it's because he's cheating on Lucky. But that's not it. Not entirely. I don't know..."

She was quiet a moment, stroking his head. "He's your friend," she said.

"David's my friend and I couldn't care less who he sleeps with."

"No, I mean Will is your closest friend. You don't have a lot of close male friends, Erik. You cultivate those relationships carefully. Even cautiously."

"Something, something. Psychology. Fathers?" he said, smiling.

"Paging Dr. Freud. Whatever the reason, it's still true. You've grown this friendship with Will over the years. You've put time into it. You're emotionally invested in it. You're close with him. It's not sexual but you're tight. And along comes James and he's able to dial into Will not only artistically but perhaps physically."

"I can't compete on that field."

"Please, Will would go to bed with you in a heartbeat."

"Stop," he said, groaning. "I have enough bad visuals going on right now."

"I know you're not threatened by it," she said, toying with his necklace.

"Just revolted." He hated admitting it, but homosexuality still repelled him at some primal level. At the same time he was keenly aware of something which tasted a lot like...

"I'm jealous," he said, with a weak laugh. "It's fucked up."

"Come on," Daisy said, "it sucks when you feel pushed out of a friendship. Sucks for anyone. But this won't last long. Will's having a fling. It's nobody's business but his and Lucky's. And when she comes back—" Daisy raised up her hand and let it hang there. "I think a lot of things will go back to normal."

Erik took her hand between his. "I don't dislike the guy. He's all right when he stops trying so hard and just chills."

"He's unpredictable," she said. "And he's making Will unpredictable. You don't like that."

"I don't like that I don't like it," he said.

"Well, you only like when people act the way you expect them to." She moved fully up and onto his body, her legs between his. With her forearms crossed on his chest and her chin on top, she was unbearably beautiful. Sometimes she looked at him a certain way and his heart reset itself, closed up coyly just for the pleasure of opening to her again.

"Stop knowing me," he said, running his hand along her cheek and into her hair.

She smiled. In the glow of the Christmas tree lights, her eyes were like a Caribbean sea. They stared into his for a long time.

He sighed. "Fine, I'll go back and get another condom."

"One?"

"Lots."

She moved off him. "What a nice boy you are."

He stepped into his jeans and pulled on sneakers. Zipping his jacket over his bare chest he leaned and kissed her. "Don't go away."

"Nowhere I'd rather be."

It was clear and cold outside. A bright full moon hung straight overhead, washing the backyards in silver. Erik let himself into his kitchen. The living room was dark except for one small table lamp. The couch was empty, but James's jacket was still slung over the back. Two textbooks were on the coffee table.

A pair of jeans was on the floor.

Erik looked at them, open-mouthed. Then he looked away and exhaled abruptly.

Well, there you have it, he thought. *No more speculation.*

Like Hansel and Gretel he followed the trail upstairs: a sneaker on one step, its mate further up. Another pair of jeans on the landing. A sweater flung against the baseboard moldings.

"Outstanding," he whispered. He imagined this would be funny some-day.

It might even be a little funny right now.

Behind him the bathroom door opened, then quickly closed again. *Fucking hilarious*, Erik thought. Shaking his head, he went into his room. He clicked on the bedside lamp and opened his side table drawer.

Empty.

"Not funny," he said.

He turned off the lamp and went to stand in his doorway, leaning on the jamb, arms crossed. The bathroom door opened again. Will came out, a towel around his waist. He smiled. As if they had run into each other on the street.

"What's up, asshole?"

"You cleaned out my rubbers, dude. That ain't cool."

"No," Will said, inclining his head. "It ain't."

"I had nine in there. I believe. Were you planning to use all of them?"

"Just a minute." Will walked down the hall, noiseless on his cushioned feet. His confidence was absolute. Not a shred of digested canary on this cool cat. After a moment he slipped back out his door and returned two of the three-packs.

"Thank you," Erik said. He looked at Will. His friend gazed back, half-naked, poised and self-aware. Apologetic about the pilfered prop-erty but nothing else. "Goodnight, Will."

"Be safe, Fish."

Erik waved the hand holding the condoms.

As he walked back to Daisy's, he waited to be upset. He should be upset. He, who didn't mind homosexuality as long as it wasn't in his face. Will and James were not only in his face but in his bedside table drawer. He should be disgusted. Appalled and confused. Betrayed.

He felt weirdly fine. And slightly curious. He looked down at the con-doms, his mind trying to grasp what the hell they could've been...

"Dude," he said, stopping to look back over his shoulder. "Did you top or bottom?"

Top, Will's voice replied.

"Jesus Christ." He shook his head free of the imagery and went inside.

"I worried you got locked out," Daisy said, moving the covers aside.

"No." He shed his clothes and got in with her. "Those two bitches stole all my Trojans. I had to shake them down."

"What?"

"I wouldn't mind so much but I buy the expensive kind. Ribbed for her pleasure. Are they ribbed for his pleasure, too, I wonder? How does that work?"

"Stop. You are joking."

"You know, I think Will is physically incapable of blushing. He didn't even break a sweat. He barely blinked, for fuck's sake."

"Are you serious?"

"Hand to God. A trail of clothes. My top drawer burgled. Will in a towel."

"Quel queutard," Daisy said, eyes wide, a half-smile around her incredulous mouth.

"Is that French for slut?"

"I don't believe it."

"I do. I had an epiphany walking back over here. Want to hear it?"

She nodded, still open-mouthed.

"James isn't changing Will or making him act differently. James is just making Will act more like himself."

Daisy looked at him a long moment. "And you're all right with it?"

"I wasn't all right when I didn't know what was going on. Now I know something is unquestionably going on and I'm strangely all right with it. Furthermore, what I am with it doesn't matter. Epiphany, part two."

"So if he has sex with another guy it doesn't count?"

"It counts. Sex is sex. It's a betrayal on some level."

"But only Will and Lucky know which level, they're the only ones who can make that call. Maybe they have an agreement for while she's away but who's to say they don't have an understanding even when she's here? She's always known what Will is…"

"True."

He ran his finger over her forehead and down the bridge of her nose. She lay on her back, arms over her head and her temple tucked by an elbow. The light pooled under her high cheekbones and in the hollows of her collarbones.

"It'll be all right," she murmured. "Will's in control."

"I know." Moving the covers, Erik ran his hand down the length of her body. He knew how her breast curved to meet his palm. He knew where she was soft, where she was tight and where her bones pressed close to her skin. He knew this body. This woman. This love. His hand moved up, over her heart, feeling the beat of her life under his touch.

"What are you thinking?"

"Nothing." He shook his head. "And everything."

She moved up on her own elbow, mirroring him. Her teeth curled gently on his bottom lip as she slid her hand between their stomachs, closing him up in her fingers. Opening them. Closing them. Sliding. Stroking. Making him hard. He licked his thumb and ran it around her breast, her nipple rising up to meet his touch. Her scent through his nose, her tongue sweet. Desire rich in the back of his throat. She reached past him for one of the condoms and tore it open. He watched her roll it on him as she'd done... How many times now? A thousand? Two thousand? Another month and they wouldn't need them.

"Qu'est-ce qui se passe?" Her eyes found his and held still.

"I don't want to sleep with anyone but you." His finger traced her jaw as a strange vulnerability gripped him. "And I don't want you to sleep with anyone but me."

She slid her hand along his, holding it against her face. "I only want you. No one could hold me in the dark the way you do."

Then her hand glided over the top of his head, curved around the back of his neck and she pulled him to her. Her kiss opened all the way for him and he toppled, rolling onto and into her body.

Fingers in his hair, she ran her mouth up his neck. The secret skin behind her knee, like silk, as she hooked her calf in the small of his back and dragged him further down into her heat.

"How many did they leave you?"

"Six," he whispered.

"Oh," she said, touching his mouth, then licking it. "It'll be an early night then..."

SLIGHTLY CRUSHY

WHEN MID-SEMESTER GRADES came out, James's GPA fell below the cutoff at 1.94. He had the opportunity to appeal but officially he was out of the fall concert. To make matters more complicated, his understudy was injured, which meant Marie now had to scramble her casting and find someone to partner Daisy in *No Blue Thing.*

Daisy was ten scrambles ahead. No stupid girls were in ballet and she was not about to get saddled with a third-string cavalier. As she soaked in the claw foot tub, her eyes were hard and far away. Shaving at the sink, Erik looked at her through the mirror. He noticed when she was in her personal war room, all the green seemed to leach out of her irises, leaving them a flat, steely blue. The eyes told the truth. In any other situation, she might have more compassion. But when it came to dance, Daisy had no use for people who didn't pull their weight. She'd thrown all useless mouths overboard and was intent on sole survival.

"Two weeks until the concert," she said. "This is going to be tight."

Erik rinsed lather off the blade. "I take it Will can't sub for James."

"No. He needs to focus on *Powaqqatsi.*"

"Did you talk to Marie yet?" he said, looking a little cross-eyed in the mirror, upper lip pulled taut over his teeth.

"Not yet, I'm too upset. I don't want to go in screaming and crying like a diva. It'll only make her more nervous and she'll pair me up with... I can't even think who she'd pick. I need to bring her a solution, not a problem." Daisy drummed her fingernails on the rim of the tub. "I think I'm going to teach John Quillis the part. On my own."

"Who's he?"

"He's a sophomore. I've had him in partnering class a few times and he's decent. And smart. He's like James—he picks up choreography fast and retains it." She looked up at Erik then. A bit of green was back in her eyes, and her smile was mischievous. "And he's just slightly crushy on me, so I think he'll take direction well. You know?"

"I know nothing about being crushy on you or taking direction," Erik said, toweling off his face. Looking up in the mirror he saw Daisy smiling at him. "What?" he said to her reflection.

"I love this," she said. "I miss Lucky but I love having you here all the time. And it's not just sleeping together every night. It's little moments in the bathroom and the kitchen. Being a couple. And being able to talk to you about anything. I love it."

This is my life, Erik thought, gazing back at her.

Will and James were still carrying on, or whatever you wanted to call it. Erik had chosen the path of least resistance and simply removed his face from the affair. Now most of his clothes were in Daisy's drawers and closet. His toothbrush was next to hers on the sink. They were together all the time. Not just making love at every opportunity but making a life. Entrenched in each other's daily business: food shopping, clothes folding, dish washing, cracking the bathroom door and handing a roll of toilet paper in.

Last night in bed, she gave him his birthday present. It was a new charm to hang on his necklace: a tiny pair of gold scissors.

"Sax," he said, remembering the Swedish word. "This is awesome."

"Yeah?" She was chewing on her bottom lip, looking uncertain. "I wasn't sure."

"Why?" He put the scissors into her hand so he could unclasp the chain behind his neck.

"Because your necklace is such an heirloom. Your history. I felt kind of funny adding to it."

"Why?" he said again, carefully threading the jump ring of the charm onto the chain.

"I'm not part of your history."

He looked at her as he fastened the necklace again. "Aren't you?"

She stared back.

He slid down to his elbow, hovering over her, holding her gaze in his. "You are," he whispered.

She was his history. And his future. Looking at her now in the bathtub, he toyed with the notion they would have a place together someday. They would be home. Together in ordinary time, writing their story.

JAMES APPEALED TO THE DEAN and somehow he wangled a reprieve. He had to pass a couple of makeup exams and clock a certain amount of hours at the academic resource center, but he was back in the concert. And behaving himself. Marie made it clear John Quillis was more than ready to understudy if James blew it again. Daisy had taught John the role and Will helped, generous with tips and tricks, skillfully coaching and guiding John to a higher plane of confidence.

"I must say I'm impressed with that kid," Will said. "Keep practicing with him and you'll have yourself a nice prince next year." He ruffled the top of Daisy's head and then his hand grew still. He looked down at her and his eyes misted.

"Oh no," Daisy said, knocking his hand away. "Absolutely not, William, don't you dare start bawling."

"Just a little bawl?"

"No. I am too tired."

She was exhausted. It came as no surprise to Erik when she said she wanted to go home for a weekend before technical rehearsals started.

"I need my mother," she said, putting clothes and a toothbrush in a bag.

"Go get spoiled. Sleep all day. Everything will be all right." He kissed her goodbye and watched her drive down Jay Street. No sooner had the car turned the corner when a cloud seemed to pass in front of the sun and the world was a slightly less pleasant place to be.

Erik walked through the yards and into his kitchen. Will was sitting at the small table, a mug between his hands and a cigarette burning in the ashtray.

"Water's hot," he said.

Erik made himself tea. He leaned back against the sink, blowing across the surface and watching Will stare out the window. This was not Will's usual meditative staring, but a morose and troubled reflection.

"Qu'est-ce qui se passe?" Erik said.

Will glanced over. "Dig you with the French."

"Two years hanging with you and Dais, I finally have some game. I can ask what's up or ask for a blow job."

"Just be careful whom you're asking for what."

Erik shrugged. "You'll suck my cock eventually. I'm just playing hard to get."

Will gave a chuckle and lowered his forehead into the heel of his hand, the smoke from the butt held in his fingers making a wreath around his head. Feeling he should stay present while still giving Will space, Erik hitched up and sat on the counter.

"Dude," Will said. "I've gotten myself into a hell of a mess."

"James not going quietly?"

Will glanced over. "All these years and you never asked me flat out about my persuasions."

"Well, when you swipe all my condoms, and boxer shorts are spilling down the stairs, it's not hard to put two and two together. But it's nothing to do with me."

"It's one of the things I love about you, Fish," Will said. "You're not oblivious to shit but you mind your business."

"Do you need my help here? Or do you want me to sit, look cute and keep minding my business?"

"I don't know what I need." Will flicked his ashes and ran a hand through his hair. "Actually I do know. I need Lucky."

"You miss her?"

"Like fucking crazy. I never set any boundaries on sex but when it came to my time and emotions and a long-term relationship, I always knew it would be a woman. And more and more, I'm realizing it's Lucky. She's the whole deal. You know?"

"What about James?" Erik asked, lifting the tea bags out of his mug and leaning to drop them in the garbage.

Will didn't answer for a long time. Emotions flickered in and out of his face as he smoked and thought. "I did it for fun," he finally said. "I was attracted to him. And curious. And acting on impulse and it was...convenient. Makes me sound like an asshole but it's the truth. Judge away."

"I'm not judging you," Erik said. "You're the closest friend I have. And in a weird way, it took Lucky going and James coming to make me see it."

Will smiled. "Your friendship is one of my havens."

"You don't seem the type to need a haven. You're the most self-actualized person I know."

"Am I? I guess I am." He took a long drag and stubbed out his cigarette. "James is a good guy. In the beginning I dug him on a whole lot of levels. As a collaborator, he's been key this semester. But damn, he's a needy fuck."

"He's damaged."

"I don't do baggage. Everyone has a backpack or a carry-on bag, but James has steamer trunks. I told him from the beginning we had an expiration date. It's temporary. And he acted fine but I can see now it's not. I should've seen it before but I was in fuck everything mode." Will sighed, putting his forehead into his hand again. "And I'm going to have a really big problem on my hands when Lucky comes back."

"Will you tell her?"

"We've always been honest with each other. Sometimes brutally, but it's how we work. We didn't make a vow of fidelity when she left this semester. I know she's been on some dates in Boston. So I probably will tell her. I think I'll have to because James seems the type to use psychological warfare."

"You mean he'll threaten to tell her."

"Absolutely. And I can put the kibosh on that kind of shit right away."

"Well," Erik said, sliding off the counter. "If there's anything I can do."

"I own this and I'll handle it. But accept my apology in advance in case it gets kind of tense next semester."

"Done."

"And for the love of God, Fish, if you're going to swing, do it outside your degree program."

Erik set his cup in the sink. "Good to know."

He walked out of the kitchen, but turned back after a few steps. "Listen, maybe this goes without saying but..." He shrugged off self-consciousness. "A lot of times the only things between Daisy and a ten-foot drop to the floor are your hands. And I trust your hands. I trust you know she's the world to me and you always got her back. Which means you got mine."

Will nodded, solemn as a soldier receiving orders. "I won't ever drop her. Or let her get in the middle of my shit."

Erik threw his arms wide. "And dude, I just listened to your boyfriend troubles. How hip was that?"

"You'll be giving me fashion advice next," Will muttered, tapping another cigarette from the pack.

"Just out of curiosity, this..." Erik gestured to himself. "Doesn't do anything for you?"

Will made to get up out of his chair and Erik sprang back two feet, laughing. "No, no. Sit. Never mind."

"One," Will said, holding up a finger, "don't start what you can't finish. Two, walk away now so I can look at your ass."

Erik ran away.

"Even better," Will yelled after him. "When you run it gets all high and tight. Like a girl's."

CATHEDRAL

WITH DAISY ON THE PILL, their lovemaking was even more frequent and intense. The spontaneity it allowed them caused a bit of a circus the first month.

"I don't know why I bother wearing pants anymore," Erik said.

"I know," Daisy said. "I pick clothes in the morning based on how good they'll look on the floor."

They were doing it all over the damn place. Seduction on the couch, sneaky trysts in the dressing rooms under the stage or the storage rooms where old sets were kept. Erik woke up hard every other morning, rolling half-asleep onto Daisy or pulling her on top of him. Or he was pulling over in the car or pressing her up against the kitchen counter or surprising her in the shower. But even better than the freedom was having nothing between his body and hers. He'd never been inside a girl bareback, never felt that gripping, vital heat without a condom. Finally he could give Daisy one of his firsts and have a kind of virgin experience with her.

She's the only woman I've touched this way, he thought. He held her in his lap, pushed up deep inside her, his hungry hands coursing along the avenues of her body. Arms and legs wound around each other, foreheads pressed together tight. Her entire body clutched him. The air roaring in his head, eardrums bulging against the dark and firework flashes of yellow and orange behind his closed eyelids. The taste of her mouth in his. And through it all he was sliding and pushing inside her and she was sliding and pulling him in. Hard against slick. Tight, hot and aching.

"God, Erik," she said, the air falling out of her voice. "I want to come."

"Dais…" He'd turned the corner. A hole opened in the night, beckoning him. He was right on the edge of coming but he'd been with her long enough he could control it and wait for her. He knew her body. Knew it by feel and sight and sound. She was closing in on him, contracting down, like a hand slowly curling into a fist.

"It feels so good."

"Let it go, Dais."

"I feel it."

"It's right there. Let it come. Come to me."

She jumped with her silent scream. He followed, gathering the air she left behind. Her kiss crashed into his as a moan passed from his throat to her mouth and back again. As what he had burst forth into her body.

Only me.

Time and space reassembled. Riding out the last of the tremors, Erik held tight to Daisy, rocking her in his lap, stroking her head on his shoulder. He could feel her heart pounding against his, the last little trembles making her body twitch.

"I love us," she said softly.

He smiled, feeling the world to his bones. "I love us, too."

"It's so good." She ran a hand back from her forehead, gathering her hair up and away from her neck.

"Happy birthday," he said, running his mouth along her throat, tasting her scent.

She took his face in her hands and kissed him. "Being twenty rocks."

Carefully he helped her down to her back, pulling a pillow into place, pulling up the covers and tucking them around their bodies.

Another December.

Another *Nutcracker* Mercenary Season.

Another anniversary.

"Two years," she said.

Fingers twined, he set his mouth against her wrist, feeling her pulse beat. "Twenty-four months."

He loved her. Sometimes it was just part of the world, like air and water. Other times, like right now, he looked at Daisy and could not get his mind around the emotion he felt for her. "Love" didn't seem an adequate word anymore. What vibrated in his heart and head and bones was bigger than the world, beyond everything he'd imagined love could be. Even the phrase "making love" had morphed out of context. Lately he was struck by the literal idea of making love. Not just a sexual expression but a creation-ary one. As if with each conversation, each shared experience and each time their bodies came together, they were assembling something larger. Adding bit by bit onto some magnificent structure. A cathedral within their private universe.

"I love you so much," he said. *You can't know. You'll never know how much. I'll never be able to say it all.*

He put his head down next to hers. Her lips brushed his face, her hand stroking the back of his neck.

"I don't know where I stop and you begin," she said. Her voice had the slurred and sultry rhythm which meant she was growing drowsy. "Everything I am is so woven in with everything you are. It's like... I can't explain. I can't explain love anymore, Erik. It doesn't mean what it used to."

I am the only one.

Erik moved closer against her as a great bell in the cathedral began to toll.

She knew.

Of course she knew.

HOW WELL YOU DEAL

ERIK RETURNED TO SCHOOL from winter break on the fourth of January. He made good time on the six-hour drive from Rochester, pulling up in front of Colby Street around four in the afternoon.

Daisy met him at the curb. "How was your drive?"

Erik kissed her. "Not bad. A little snow when I got into Pennsylvania." He pulled his backpack and duffel from the backseat and shut the car door.

"Are you hungry?"

"Starving."

"I have soup ready at my place and I can make grilled cheese."

"Perfect. Let me drop my stuff off."

He followed her to his kitchen door. They went into the living room where a clobber of bags, boxes and jackets was spilled. "When did Will get back?" Erik said, heading to the stairs.

From overhead came a long, loud moan. Erik looked up at the ceiling, then back at Daisy, eyes wide.

She smiled. "Will came five minutes after Lucky did. And pretty much every hour since."

Erik dropped his things and headed back toward the kitchen door. "Let's eat."

Later in the evening Will and Lucky wandered over to Jay Street, dreamy-eyed and sated. David, Neil and James came by as well. They sat around the living room drinking wine and smoking. Will had Lucky in his lap, caressing her as she told entertaining war stories about her EMT course. As he listened, Erik covertly watched James, looking for exchanged glances with Will or any signs of tension. So far the air was neutral and relaxed. If anything, both boys seemed to be going out of their way not to make eye contact.

"So are you definitely going down this road now, Luck?" David asked. "Do you have the stomach for it?"

"I don't," Lucky said. "There are stories I'm not going to tell you guys. Suffice it to say, I saw some horrible shit. And I discovered I'm not one of those people who can un-see things. I would not make it. If I did it for a living I'd be institutionalized within a year."

"We can't have you locked up," Daisy said. She held out her arms. "You had her all day, Will. Share."

Lucky extricated herself and went over to squeeze next to Daisy in the easy chair. "I missed you," she said, kissing her friend. "I missed you guys so much. I was bummed about missing the fall concert. What's the gossip for spring?"

Will had news. *Powaqqatsi* had been such a triumph, Kees was recommending it be expanded and reprised at the spring production. Will was already going through the entire score and picking which segments he wanted. "Definitely the second section," he said.

"'Anthem'?" James said, stubbing out his cigarette. "You add it onto the original and you have a good ten minute ballet."

Will nodded. "Dais, the part I played for you, where the tambourine comes in? I see a pas de deux there. I thought about making it for Aisha Johnson."

"She's gorgeous," Daisy said. "Aisha and who else?"

"Me."

Daisy pointed at him. "It's your graduating concert. You better be dancing something with me."

"I will. But there are no senior boys in contemporary this year. I know Kees will let me dance in my own work. Dais, you'll help me? I have a bunch of stuff I need to try on you."

"Why don't you try it on Aisha," Lucky said.

"Because if it doesn't work on Dais, it doesn't work at all."

Daisy arched her neck, smiling. "I'll help you," she said.

"Good," Will said. "I need it."

James looked up hopefully, but if there was a need for his help, Will didn't voice it.

Spirits and energy were high as the semester began. The weather was unusually mild with plenty of sunshine, which kept at bay the customary mid-winter blues. Will was on fire with "Anthem," the new section of *Powaqqatsi.* In contrast to the fiesta feeling of the opening section, "Anthem" was stately and majestic. A winding, synthesized baseline in five-four time set an almost foreboding tone, like the rumblings of a volcano. Then the brass erupted in the refrain, echoed by flutes and tambourines.

Aisha Johnson wrapped her six-foot, sinewy body like a python around the sensual choreography. She coiled her limbs about the music and squeezed every atom of oxygen out. You couldn't take your eyes off her.

"Dude, she is smokin'," Erik muttered to Will, after peeking at one of the rehearsals. "Like Tina Turner."

"More like Grace Jones," Will said. "She either gives me a total hard-on or scares the living shit out of me."

Over in the ballet division, Marie Del'Amici was staging a work called *Who Cares?* A collaboration between the famed choreographer George Balanchine and the composer George Gershwin. It was a light-hearted ballet—jazzy and schmaltzy, pure spectacle. David would be lead set and lighting designer for the production, which would serve as his senior project. He envisioned a New York City skyline across the full length of the stage. They'd go all-out on the lighting, David planned, wiring up eight full boom stands and all of the overheads. Plus the set itself would have built-in lights.

"No fish in tanks," he said, sketching out his idea in the set shop of Mallory, surrounded by his crew. "These are people dancing as people."

Daisy had a solo, and was cast with James in a pas de deux to the song "The Man I Love."

"Great, you get to babysit again," Erik said.

Daisy exhaled and shrugged.

"Why wouldn't Marie cast you with Will?"

Her smile was tired and resigned. "Because this is ballet, honey. A lot of times it's not how well you dance but how well you deal."

Will, besides dancing in *Powaqqatsi,* was featured throughout *Who Cares?* But his main pas de deux was with a girl named Taylor Revell. He and Daisy were crushed not to be cast together, but they wisely opted to be professional about it. "Man up and dance," Will said, sighing.

"James is a wild card," Daisy said. "And he's taking anatomy this year and already flailing. Anything could happen."

"I notice John Quillis is already learning James's part."

"No stupid boys are in ballet," Daisy said.

ERIK WAS OUT RUNNING one Sunday afternoon in late February when a car slowed on the other side of the street and tooted its horn. Erik squinted and saw it was James. Checking traffic, he jogged across as James rolled down the window.

"Where you off to?" Erik said, panting.

"I have to go home a couple days."

"Everything all right?"

"Yeah. Tuesday is the one-year anniversary of Dhahran."

"I'm sorry?"

"Dhahran. Where my sister was killed—"

"Oh, right, that's right. I'm sorry."

"They're dedicating a monument at the army reserve center. Some general is coming. Big to-do. I have to be there."

"Of course." Helpless, Erik touched James's shoulder lightly. "I'm sorry. I know going home is never easy for you to begin with."

James nodded, staring straight out through the windshield. He wore mirrored shades. A scruffy growth of facial hair marred the line of the goatee he usually kept so scrupulously neat. "All three brothers in the house. Waiting for me like vultures. Mom's probably already drunk. I'm already an anxious wreck and I haven't even gotten out of town. And I'll miss two days of anatomy class which will be a bitch. But," he said, slapping his hands down the steering wheel, "if Penny can go to war, I can damn well go to her memorial. Right?"

"Right."

James grinned suddenly. "And if shit gets serious, I know where her old guns are kept."

"Hey, don't get yourself arrested before the concert," Erik said, laughing.

"I'm kidding. I'll be all right. What doesn't kill us...doesn't fucking kill us."

"Drive safe, James."

"See you in a few days."

Erik thumped his fist twice on the roof of the car, then took off running. James tooted the horn again and pulled out.

It started falling apart soon after.

Early March sucker-punched them with arctic temperatures and snowstorms. Coursework and rehearsals intensified. Will was struggling with the ending of "Anthem" and struggling with James's wounded and reproachful presence. James had gone dark since his sister's memorial service. He was the omega dog now, passively pathetic as he vied for Will's attentions, resorting either to martyred brooding or biting sarcasm when he couldn't get it.

Then March spit on its hands and it started to rain. It rained for two solid weeks. The frigid dankness drove everyone into a funk. The air was a tangible, clammy and soporific substance. Skin absorbed it. Muscles sopped it up like a sponge. Half the students were irritable and antsy. The other half were lethargic, suspended in a wet, grey void. The rain beat incessantly on the windows and rooftops. Beat incessantly in heads and hearts.

"Anthem" continued to flounder. "I can't *end* this goddamn thing," Will said, cursing in two languages, nearly howling in frustration. Rehearsals were tense. In a creative slump, Will hadn't the time or energy for neediness. Daisy, being naturally grounded and pragmatic, could hold the atmosphere calm, but just barely. She instinctively knew to keep still and quiet and let Will find his own way to water in the desert. She could follow him in French or English. If she had a suggestion, she knew how to unobtrusively make it and, even better, make it seem Will's idea.

She understood his directions but more importantly, she understood his silences. If he didn't respond, she retreated with no hard feelings. His approval wasn't necessary to validate her relationship with him.

James, on the other hand, needed constant validation. He sulked if his advice were rejected. Or he became argumentative. He spoke the wrong language or spoke too much. He stepped on toes and got in the way. Meanwhile, he was weeks behind in anatomy and dancing erratically in rehearsals for *Who Cares?* This put Daisy on edge, which put Erik on edge.

"Dude," Will finally said to James. "You can't come to my rehearsals anymore." It was the first day of spring.

"I feel bad," Daisy said to Erik. "But James has become impossible. Nobody wants him around. He's so toxic. I bought him a cup of coffee and tried to talk to him afterward and he just broke down and cried. Said he was in love with Will and he didn't know what to do."

"Jesus, what a mess," Erik said.

"He looks totally strung-out, too. Do you know if he's still doing coke with David?"

"Only if he's buying it. David's not generous with his stash."

"True. And God knows James is always strapped for cash. But I swear he's on something. So does Lucky."

"Like what?"

Daisy shrugged. "A lot of dancers take uppers because they suppress your appetite. I know ecstasy is rampant in the conservatory but I thought that stuff just made you all touchy-feely and mellow. James is hardly mellow."

"You think Lucky knows about Will and James?" Erik said.

"She totally sees the infatuation. She's no dummy and James is so transparent to begin with. She probably knows Will slept with him, and my guess is she's more pissed about his choice of partner than the sex. Jesus, you couldn't find a more indiscreet guy."

"You know, I haven't heard her and Will moaning in the night lately." Erik meant it as a joke but Daisy's face was sad as she nodded.

"I haven't either," she said. "And it's weird, but the house feels empty without it."

A BLIND LEAP

JOHN QUILLIS WAS TWENTY but looked fourteen. He had copper red hair, a wholesome Boy Scout expression and to his everlasting torment, the conservatory had christened him "Opie." To compound the pre-pubescent image, his voice was still making up its mind about changing. It cracked when he got excited or upset, or just decided not to show up at all.

He appeared in the doorway of the set shop in Mallory one afternoon, waving at Erik to come over. "Daisy's hurt," he said, his voice skittering.

"What happened?" Erik said. "Where is she?"

"In the training room. It's her ankle."

"Leo, I gotta go," Erik called. Still wearing his work gloves and safety goggles, he headed out the shop door. "What happened?"

John was pale under his freckles as he trotted to keep up. "James dropped her."

"On purpose?"

"I don't know what the hell to think. She was jumping and turning into arabesque. It's a blind leap and she has to trust he'll be there to catch her. Dude, he wasn't even *looking.* Two of us yelled his name and then Dais was on the floor."

Erik stopped. "Hold up. Let me ask you something."

"What?"

"Do you think he was high?"

John opened his mouth, then shut it and looked away. "I can't go to court with anything but I know he's been hanging with a crowd that does a lot of pills. Uppers. Ecstasy. That kind of thing."

"Great," Erik muttered. He started walking again. They reached the second floor and headed down the hall where the training room was. "Is Lucky working today?"

"Yeah. She's got Dais's foot in an ice bath. But she needs to get it x-rayed. Plus she took the weight of the fall with her hand. Her little finger might be broken."

"I'll fucking kill James," Erik said. It was out of his mouth before the thought was finished in his head.

"Well, take a number," John said. "I wouldn't want to be him walking home tonight."

Daisy was sitting in a chair, her left foot in a deep basin filled with ice. Her left hand was cradled in her lap, also wrapped in ice. Will was sitting next to her but he got up when he saw Erik. "Give me your stuff," he said, holding out a hand. Erik pulled off his gloves and goggles, handed them over.

"Hey," he said, sitting down and sliding his arm around Daisy's back. She tilted her head against his kiss but didn't look at him. She didn't look at anyone or anything, just straight down at her foot. Her eyes were steel blue and her lips pressed into a tight line.

Lucky came over with Max Tremaine, who ran the athletic training department. "I want her in the ice another ten minutes," he said. "Then let's take her over to the health center and get it x-rayed. I don't think it's broken. Probably a bad sprain. Who's got a car?"

"I do. I'll take her," Erik said.

"I'll go with," Lucky said.

"Does it hurt bad?" Erik asked Daisy.

"I'll be all right," she said dully. Her jaw twitched a little. Erik could see how hard she was thinking, calculating recovery time and contingency plans. He kept his palm flat between her shoulder blades, not patting or stroking her. Such caresses would only make her crazy. Everything and everybody just needed to be still so she could think.

He watched as Lucky unwrapped the ice pack from Daisy's hand. Her little finger was red and swollen. A bit of bloodied gauze fell away and

Erik winced when he saw the nail torn to the quick. Lucky whisked the gauze away and wrapped a fresh one around the fingertip. "Put the ice back on, honey," she said.

Erik kissed Daisy's head again. "I'll get the car. Be right back." He stood up, motioning to Will, who followed him out into the hall.

"Where is he?" Erik said

"I don't know."

"I'm gonna kill him."

"I'll handle it." Will's arms were crossed, the fingers of one hand drumming nervously on his bicep.

"I thought you were handling it."

"Fish—"

"Don't 'Fish' me, all right? I've stayed out it. I've been sympathetic. I've minded my business. But now he's screwed up over you to the point of coming to rehearsal high and injuring my girlfriend. Now the sympathy ends and it starts being my business."

"I'll take care of this."

"I don't want him anywhere near her."

"I don't either but I can't control this. Thinking he was high doesn't prove he was. I don't know what's going to happen now. What he's going to dance or who with."

Erik looked at him a moment, at the crossed arms and twitching fingers, knowing Will didn't fidget unless he was upset. "You gonna rough him up?"

Will didn't look away. "I'll do what I have to."

"Do something, man, or I will." Erik exhaled, rolling his eyes. "I'm going to get my car."

THE ANKLE WASN'T BROKEN or sprained, just badly wrenched. Ice and a week's rest were prescribed. A bone in her little finger had a hairline fracture. All they could do was tape it tight to the ring finger to stabilize it. The torn-off nail was more painful.

Everyone waited to see what, if any, disciplinary action would be taken against James. It turned out to be unnecessary: four days after Daisy was injured, mid-semester grades came out. Once again, James came in under the required 2.0. No appeal this time. He was dismissed from his roles and put on academic probation. Shunned and shamed, he skulked from class to class, head down, hugging the wall. Erik didn't know if Will had roughed him up or not. He didn't care. He was too worried about Daisy.

The fall had spooked her badly. John was going to learn James's part in "The Man I Love" but rehearsals didn't go well. Daisy was tentative on her ankle, hesitating at key moments. She couldn't mesh with John and it made him nervous and balky. He zigged and she zagged. Then he was terrified she would fall and he would grab at her, throwing her off. After an agonizing and frustrating week, John knocked at the door of Jay Street.

"I've been doing a lot of thinking," he said. "And I'm going to Marie tomorrow and telling her what everyone already knows."

"Which is?" Daisy said.

"You need to dance 'The Man I Love' with Will."

Will got up from the couch. "Ope, come on. You can dance it."

"I know I can dance it, but it won't be what it should." He saw Daisy about to get up and pointed at her. "You sit. Stay off that ankle."

Daisy's lips twitched as she suppressed a laugh. John had matured considerably the past few months. He was standing taller, exuding confidence. Looking and acting a lot like Will, Erik thought.

"You worked hard," Daisy said. "I feel terrible you keep getting all these chances taken away."

"One chance got taken away last fall. But I got a matinee out of it. And now I am gifting this chance to the person who should have it. Look, Dais, I have years ahead of me. This is Will's last concert and it's your last concert with him. Let me do this." The plea was impassioned, but John's voice didn't skitter once. Like John, it had made up its mind.

"Opie, you're a prince," Will said. "But I don't know if Marie will—"

John held up a finger. "One, don't fucking call me Opie. Two, I got this. What, you think you've cornered the market on charm, Kaeger?"

"The puppy bites," Erik said under his breath.

Will crossed his arms and raised his eyebrows. "Well. I'll just sit my schooled ass down."

"And I'm getting up," Daisy said, rising from the couch. "Come here and hug me, Opie."

John blushed. "Fine, you can call me Opie," he said, going over and hugging her. "Next year, no more Richie Cunningham bullshit."

"Next year you will be the fucking Fonz," Will said.

"Damn right, bucko."

OUT OF THE SHADOWS

JOHN WENT INTO MARIE'S OFFICE with charm and a solution. He and Will switched roles: Will would dance "The Man I Love" with Daisy and John took Will's place with Taylor Revell.

"Was Taylor all right with it?" Erik asked. He was walking Daisy up to the studios for rehearsal.

"She was," Daisy said. "She was a complete sweetheart. Plus..." Daisy checked back over her shoulder and leaned in confidentially. "I think she digs Opie."

"Win-win." He slid his arm around her, brushing his mouth along her head. "Are you happy now? Happier?"

"Much." They lingered outside the studio door, kissing, until Will came out and broke up the clinch.

"Ease off, Fish," he said. "Excessive snogging makes her stupid."

"I'm just getting into character," Daisy said, smiling and letting herself be led away.

At Marie's invitation, Erik sat on the floor to watch a few minutes and John sat by him.

"The Man I Love" was an elegant, romantic piece. Sensual, but in an understated way. While first rehearsing it with James, Daisy had said the partnering was a bitch. John had agreed. Now Erik watched as Will wrapped his body around the steps. It was odd to see him struggle. Both he and Daisy were struggling. As they deconstructed one particularly difficult lift, Will's brow kept twisting in concentration and Daisy had on her war room expression. Erik looked on, fascinated, as they worked it out with Marie, flailing, dismantling physics.

Gradually they stopped talking, which meant they weren't thinking as much, which meant the magic was starting.

"Here we go," John mumbled.

Erik watched Daisy poised in the far corner of the studio. She was in her soft slippers, an elastic brace on her left ankle. She gathered her body and ran to Will and caught his hand. He lunged, weight low, as she threw her leg over his back, rolled like a cartwheel and came to a dead stop, poised on his shoulder in arabesque. In previous tries she held his hand for support. This time she let go right away. Her arms free, she relied completely on Will to turn momentum into stillness, convert the roll over his back into a pose on his shoulder. And he did it hands-free.

"How do you *do* that?" John said, holding his head. "How do you stop her right there? Jesus, I wanted to shoot myself with this lift."

Will bent his knees and put Daisy down, not letting go until she had both feet on the floor. "I feel it," he said. "She's got those sharp hip bones. I feel them roll over my back and I catch the left one with my shoulder blade. Come here, Ope."

John went into the lunge and Will picked up Daisy as if she were a pillow, put her precisely on John's back, fitting her like a puzzle piece. "Feel her hip bone?"

"I do," John said. He raised and lowered his weight a few times and Daisy moved up and down with him easily, the pose unwavering. John looked over at Erik and his expression turned sly. "Now you, Fish. C'mere."

"You're not picking me up," Erik said, laughing.

"No, dumbass. Put Daisy on your back."

"Go on," Marie said. "Try it."

Erik crossed his arms. "I already know how her hip bones feel."

Daisy's head whipped around. "Watch it, Byron."

To loud laughter, Erik got up from the floor. "And that's my cue to exit," he said with a wave to all. "I'll be down in the shop."

As he walked down to the basement, he whistled the refrain of "The Man I Love." He felt suffused with relief. Knowing Will was partnering Daisy made the pieces of the universe shift back into proper place. Still, once in the shop, helping David wire the tiny lights outlining the buildings of the Manhattan skyline set, Erik wanted to double the number of bulbs. He wanted a ton of light in pink and red and blue to flood out the past couple of weeks.

IN THE MIDDLE OF THE NIGHT, Erik and Daisy were startled off the edge of sleep by Lucky. She was calling out her lover's name but not in the throes of passion. "William," she said, from the hall right outside Daisy's door. Her voice was a blade, slicing the peace of the slumbering little house.

"The hell?" Erik muttered, picking up his head.

"William, can you get up and explain to me why James is standing out in the backyard?"

Daisy picked up her head. "What?"

"What?" Will's voice came from Lucky's room, slurred with sleep.

"Mom?" Erik said and Daisy giggled against his back.

Lucky wasn't amused. Her footsteps stomped down the hall and back again, in and out of the bathroom. "Your little friend is standing in the backyard, looking up at the windows."

They stumbled into their respective doorways, half-dressed and blinking. Lucky stood outside the bathroom, wrapped in a towel, dignified and furious.

"What is he doing?" Erik asked.

"Well he's not holding up a boom box playing 'In Your Eyes.' I would find that quite romantic. Right now it's just creepy." Lucky pushed her tongue into her cheek and looked daggers at Will. "Plus I like being able to walk naked through my kitchen without worrying about peeping Toms. I know he's gay but I'm rather particular about who sees me in the altogether."

"I'll go talk to him," Will said.

"No," Erik said, holding up a hand and making a sudden decision. "Let me."

"You?"

"You'll make it worse. I'm human valium." Before Will could protest or debate, Erik went downstairs. He unlocked the kitchen door and stepped onto the little back porch. The air was soft with the first breath of spring. A few peepers were having a late-night conversation.

He squinted into the yard. "James?"

A rustle by the hedge. Erik went down one step. "It's Fish. Come on, James, I know you're there. Come talk to me."

James stepped out of the shadows. Hands thrust deep in the pockets of his leather jacket. He looked small. Lost and forlorn. A stray dog.

"You all right?" Erik asked.

"No."

Feeling an odd sense of responsibility, Erik decided to take the time. Everyone had turned against James. Erik, too, was angry with him, but at the same time something in his heart couldn't shut down completely. He knew James felt abandoned now. And it was the worst thing for him. Erik owed him nothing, yet he felt compelled to guide James back to a safe place for the night. "You want tea or something?"

James looked up, eyebrows wrinkled in shock. Then his face softened into teary disbelief, as if the act of kindness were too much. "No, I... No. Thank you."

Erik sat down on the steps. He didn't beckon to James, but made his body language inviting. James came closer and took a seat on the bottom step, wiping his wet face. He felt in his pockets absently. "I forgot my smokes."

Erik went back inside and got the communal pack of cigarettes and lighter from the kitchen window ledge. Just in case this went long, he lit a burner on the stove and pushed the teakettle onto it.

Outside again, he gave James a cigarette and took one for himself.

"You don't smoke," James said.

"I save it for special occasions." *And it levels the playing field,* he thought. *Come sit and share a bad habit. We'll be as one in the same vice.*

James closed his eyes as he pulled in the first drag, distilling the hit of nicotine. "I don't know what to do."

"You can't come prowling around here at night. It doesn't help to scare the shit out of Lucky and piss her off."

"I know. But Will won't talk to me."

"Look, I know you care about him a lot—"

"I'm in love with him. You don't understand."

"—but you can't... I do understand."

"You don't," James said, his eyes flaring. "You're a baby, Fish. Yeah, your old man left, but so what? You grew up loved. You had a solid foundation to walk on. Now you live a fucking fairytale with Daisy and you tell me you understand? You never got beat up and abused for loving who you loved. You never got chewed up and spit out. You never had your heart broken. Wait until you lose Daisy one day then you come tell me you understand, all right?"

Erik kept his face neutral. He closed his heart and his pores, letting James's words bead up on him but not penetrate. James was angry and ranting. Erik was a convenient target.

"I'm sorry," James said, rubbing his forehead. "I'm sorry, I just..."

"It's all right. You're hurting. I know I don't understand completely but I know what you're feeling is real."

James took a few more drags, exhaling raggedly. Tears tracked down his face and he made no move to wipe them away. "Thanks for coming outside."

"No problem."

"I always liked you, Fish. You don't pretend to be something you're not."

"You think Will is pretending?"

"Don't you?"

Erik shook his head. "He loves who he loves."

James looked at him, squinting through smoke. "I think you're the only man he loves."

"Well, I don't know about that."

"I do. You're the best thing he's got. You're one of the most decent human beings I've ever met. You had no reason to come out here but you did. So forgive me for saying this, but your old man's an asshole and he doesn't deserve you for a son anyway."

Now Erik's eyebrows flew up in surprise. "Damn, James. Heavy shit."

"Well, it's true shit." James stubbed out his cigarette beneath the toe of his boot. He reached behind his head and drew out the ball chain with his sister's dog tags. Erik could see his hands trembling. It took him a minute but he slid off the flattened penny and held it out to Erik. "I want you to have this."

"No."

"Take it."

"This is yours, James. It's your... No."

"Please. You gave me the best of you tonight. This is the best of me."

Catering to the moment, Erik took the shining copper oblong and put it in the pocket of his sweatpants. He wouldn't keep it but he'd accept the gesture tonight. Hold it a few days and then return it once James realized the foolish drama of it. He'd keep the sentiment, not the token.

"I feel better knowing I'll be in your pocket," James said. "And I don't mean that in a gay way."

Erik smiled. From inside he heard the whistle of the teakettle. "You want a drink?"

"No."

"Need a lift back to campus?"

"No, no. I've already bothered you enough. I'll go away now."

James stood up and Erik did likewise, stubbing out his own cigarette.

"Thanks, Fish." James held out a formal hand and Erik shook it.

"You're safe?"

"I'm good. Sorry to trouble you. All of you."

"Well, you got to see Lucky naked. Night's not a total loss."

James chuckled. And with a wave he loped down the porch steps and out through the hedge.

Erik shut off the burner, locked the kitchen door, killed the porch light and went upstairs. He brushed his teeth and got into Daisy's bed. She rolled up against his back, curling an arm around him, pressing her palm flat to his heart.

"All right?" she whispered drowsily.

"All right," he said. "Go to sleep."

"You're so good. I love you."

"I love you."

And I am good.

He reached in his pocket and closed his fingers around the penny. He almost drew it out to put on the bedside table. But then he left it where it was and soon fell asleep.

The next morning, April 9, James was found unconscious on the bathroom floor of his dorm. In his hand was an empty bottle of prescription codeine belonging to his roommate. He was rushed to University Medical Center and survived the overdose. Then he was taken home to Greensburg.

It was ten days before Erik saw him again.

THE MAN I LOVE

THE CONSERVATORY WAS REELING in the wake of James's suicide attempt. Rumors layered on top of nervous intrigue, piling up in Mallory Hall like poor scaffolding. Erik kept his ear peeled to the whispers, but in all the talk of James, he did not hear anyone mentioning Will's name. Not romantically anyway. People guessed James had snapped after losing his spot in the concert and losing his role to Will. A few went a little deeper and pointed out it was no secret James was crushy on Will and it had made the atmosphere of *Powaqqatsi* rehearsals tense. But nowhere was there even a whiff of innuendo the attraction was mutual. Nobody hinted anything had happened.

Between Erik and Daisy, Will and Lucky, and even David, a single look was exchanged. A complicit agreement.

"Entre fucking nous," David said through his teeth.

The days passed in quiet productively. The atmosphere around Mallory was subdued, but serene. No one admitted James's absence, although shocking and tragic, was a relief. Erik kept the penny in his pocket, meaning a dozen times to track down James's address and mail it, but then forgetting. He and David put in long hours at the shop. Daisy and Will worked hard polishing "The Man I Love" and came home exhausted. Lucky fussed around making healthy dinners and icing sore joints. The air at Jay Street was comfortable and sweet. One night Erik and Daisy lifted their heads out of sleep at the sound of Lucky moaning

Will's name. They smiled at each other, biting back laughter, and lay down again.

Then it was Sunday of tech week, and the stage crew met in the shops at nine in the morning, ready to bring the *Who Cares?* set up to the stage.

"You're going to be two heads short," Leo said, his voice a rasp. "Hell of a bug is going around."

"You feel all right?" David said.

"I feel like crap, children."

"Go home," Erik said. "We can handle it."

"You're short two heads. I'll get the sets up with you and wire the booms. Then I'll go home."

It took three hours to get the New York City skyline arranged to David's satisfaction. Then they had to hustle to hang the boom stands before the dancers arrived at one o'clock.

Neil Martinez dragged himself in around one-thirty, muffling a cough and looking slightly feverish, but insisting he was good to work. Leo went home. Kees arrived, saying Michael Kantz was sick as well.

"So I'm in charge," Kees said, looking around at the company. "Are we clear?"

"Of course, darling," Marie said. "You can be in charge of coffee."

During the focus session, Erik sat with David in the house, taking notes and making cue sheets, as David discussed the lighting design with Marie. When they were ready for a first run of the ballet, Erik went into the booth to test a few of the cues.

"Hey."

Erik turned his head. Daisy was coyly peeking around the door.

"Get over here," he said, tossing his pencil aside. He swiveled in his chair as she bounded into the booth. He pulled her into his lap and drew her down on his chest, letting the seat rock back.

"You look familiar," she said, tracing his bottom lip with her thumb. "Have we met?"

"I made you come your brains out last night but we weren't properly introduced, no."

She laughed, the color rising up into her face.

He pulled her down to kiss him. "Jesus, that was out of control."

Daisy sat up and moved one of her legs, straddling him in the chair. He put his feet on the console, leaning back to look at her.

She perched high on his lap, slim and neat in pink tights and her purple leotard with the criss-cross straps. Her dark hair pulled up in a bun, all errant strands and curls secured. Last night it had spilled down her back in tangled waves. He'd wrapped its length around his fingers, drawing it aside to run his mouth up her neck, tasting salty sweat and perfume.

"You were incredible," he said.

"Me? I didn't do a damn thing, just took what you gave."

Erik smiled, his eyes far away with memory. He had her down at the corner of the bed, on her stomach while he came into her from behind. He stood over her, holding her wrists crossed in the small of her back. Watching himself slide in and out of her, listening to her come. Then come again. He was completely in control. He was young and on fire. He could go all night.

"Give it to me," she'd said, gasping, pushing back against him, her legs trembling, her back arching and desperate.

"You like that?" he whispered, his voice husky with power.

"I want it. All night long. Every night. The rest of my life, just keep doing that. God, you fuck me so good..."

The uninhibited language and the raw ache in her voice had made him want to throw back his head and roar like a lion. His grip tightened on her wrists. He held her down and gave her what he had, crazed and consumed, wanting to make her scream the house apart.

He looked at her now, shaking his head. "You were so hot," he said, running his hands along her legs, kneading the muscles of her thighs. "You have no idea."

Daisy blushed again, even her ears were red. "I can't believe some of the shit I was saying."

"I loved it." He raked his hands through his hair, looking up at the ceiling, still astonished at how they had stepped off the edge of them-selves. Just when he thought they had run the gamut of sexual possibil-ities, when he was sure the structure was finished, convinced they had come together and connected in every way conceivable...something like last night happened.

You fuck me so good. It wasn't a word they typically threw around in bed but the more he threaded it through his mind, the more natural it felt. Not crude or belittling, but truthful in a way he couldn't quite articulate. Authentic. And safe. Because the night had been raw, but it had still been loving.

Savage tenderness.

Another spire on the cathedral.

"I really was just fucking you," he said, leaning on it, seeing if it would still hold weight.

Daisy's eyes widened and she put her fingers on his lips, laughing and looking over her shoulder to the open door of the booth. "Yes, you were," she said.

"The way you were coming." He took her hand off his mouth, entwined her fingers with his. "I've never seen you like that."

"When you had my hands behind my back? And you were just holding me down?"

"It was insane."

"It was amazing," she said. "Giving everything up to you. I loved it." Her voice was a low purr. Her fingers tight with his, her eyes deep in his, her warm weight in his lap. She leaned down, barely a sound as her lips moved. "When will you do it again?"

"Soon as we get out of here." Happiness flooded his chest as he stared up into her eyes. Long rolling waves of emotion and desire. He wanted her badly, was hard with it. And yet he wanted for nothing. Everything was perfect. Right here. Right now.

"Promise?" she said.

He nodded. "I'm gonna make you forget your name."

Her pupils dilated, black eclipsing blue. "I swear. I totally want to ditch this rehearsal and go back to bed." Daisy, who had never missed a rehearsal in her life. Daisy, who went to class whether she had her period or a fever or a nail torn off. Daisy, saying she would walk away from the theater right now. For him.

"Me too," he whispered.

Then Marie's voice trilled from the front of the auditorium, breaking the spell. "Where is the man I love? Will? Daisy?"

"The man I love all right," Daisy said, swinging her leg off and getting up.

"I love you," Erik said, laughing. He caught her hand, holding onto the connection a few more precious seconds.

She ran her other hand through his hair. "I love us," she said, and kissed him.

"Us."

He held her fingers as long as possible as she went out the door and down the aisle. She walked a few steps, then stopped. She turned around and pointed at him. He stared back at her through the glass of the booth. Her smile was sweet. Her eyes were wicked. She turned again, leaned gracefully by the seat where her bag was and pulled out her pink practice skirt. Deftly tying it around her slender waist, she walked down the aisle and up to the stage where Will was waiting. Will held out his hand and she took it.

Neil popped up from behind one of the buildings in the skyline. Cupping his hands he yelled, "Fish, can you bring up the special for the set?" His voice broke and he coughed against one fist.

Erik slid those levers forward. Half the set lit up, the buildings meticulously outlined in tiny lights. The other half stayed dark.

"Dave, I think we got cables crossed back here," Neil said. "Something's not right."

David slapped his clipboard down on the seat beside him and got up. "Leave it up, Fish," he called back. He took two quick steps, planted a hand and foot on the apron, gracefully hopping onto the stage. He passed Will and Daisy and disappeared behind the set.

A moment later, his head popped up. "Fish, take it out. I need a couple minutes to fix this. Why don't you guys do your run so you're not standing around?"

Erik slid the levers and the set went dark. Daisy and Will walked upstage. She gave him a playful shove as they slipped into the wing.

Marie Del'Amici remained in the front row. Kees brought her a cup of coffee. He took his own cup and sat in one of the rear rows. Erik could see his bald head from the lighting booth.

Lucky crossed from stage left to stage right, rolling up an ace bandage. She did a little skip, a tripping leap and a twirl, and disappeared behind the curtain to a smattering of applause. John Quillis then crossed the stage with more impressive moves, and exited into the same wing to a chorus of boos.

"Are we ready?" Marie called.

They were.

Everybody in place.

Everything was perfect.

I love us, Erik thought. *All of us.*

The music started.

Will and Daisy made their entrance.

Three-quarters of the way through the pas de deux, James Dow walked in.

IN MY POCKET

WHEN JAMES DOW CAME into Mallory Hall on the afternoon of April 19, 1992, he was carrying a second generation Glock 17 pistol with a high-capacity magazine. The weapon had belonged to James's late sister, Margaret.

James entered the backstage area, coming into the wings at the left of the stage where fourteen students—a mix of dancers and tech crew—were watching Will and Daisy in their rehearsal. James opened fire, shooting five dead and wounding six others. The remaining three fled the wings.

Erik didn't hear the gunfire backstage. Between the volume of the music and the glass of the lighting booth, the sound never reached him at the back of the house.

Will said he was aware of some kind of commotion in the stage left wing. But he'd been dancing down on the apron with Daisy, where the music levels were most intense. The commotion was behind him. And it had been right at the moment of the difficult lift on his shoulder, so his concentration was especially focused.

Daisy was facing the wings as she ran to Will, the light from the boom stands in her eyes. James was backlit, in silhouette, but perhaps Daisy did see him, although her memory blacked out long before the shots were fired. The rest of her life, she would remember little from the day.

It would be years before Erik could reconstruct the shooting as a linear event. Until then, his mind only island-hopped from one terrifying image to the next, out of order and overlapping. Within the fragments, only his physical memories were clear and intact. If a true mental narrative had existed, it was gone. Later, in the remembering, and the telling, he felt he was making half of it up.

He didn't know it was James. Not right away. Someone came out of the wings as Daisy ran to Will. Stage left from the vantage point of the performers but stage right from Erik's perspective. The lift was a lighting cue, number thirty-four: bring up the mid-shinbusters, intensifying the pink wash onstage. Erik was watching Daisy throw her leg and roll over Will's back. He slid the levers, timing the cue to the both the choreography and the modulation in the music. In his right peripheral, he saw a third person onstage but he thought it was Trevor King, the assistant stage manager. He guessed Trevor had seen an errant screw or nail on the floor and was getting it out of the way.

Except Trevor King was black.

The guy on the stage was white.

Perhaps Erik would have paid more attention to the discrepancy if Daisy didn't overshoot the roll and teeter a little precariously on Will's shoulder.

"Uh-oh," Erik said softly. He remembered his mouth holding the shape of the O as he sat forward a little, then he exhaled a chuckle when Will's hand came up to steady Daisy, holding her left leg. The laugh was half relief, half admiration. Will had her. He always had her. She was good and balanced now. Will let go and extended his arm again. Just as the white man who wasn't Trevor extended his arm.

Erik had never heard live gunfire in his life. When a lick of flame erupted from the man's sleeve and three punching bangs split the Gershwin melody, Erik continued to sit with his hands on the console. An incalculable length of time passed before he could associate sound and action. Even then his mind refused to grasp it, refused further to put a name with the face.

He heard those three shots clearly and he never forgot their rhythm. Two quick bangs. A pause. A third.

Two shots and Will jerked up, back arched, his left arm flying up into the air with a spray of red. All the weight leaning forward on his leg went straight up into the air as well, the force of his writhing body knocking Daisy off his back. Then James fired a third time and Daisy's scream cut the theater in two.

Erik stood up, his chair rolling back and away. On the other side of the glass, Kees stood up too, coffee in hand. Marie must have jumped up. David said he and Neil both looked over the top of the set before hitting the floor. In the stage right wing, John pushed Lucky to the ground and threw himself on top of her, pinning her tight as she screamed for Will.

Will's body imploded, crumpling down on the floor. Daisy crashed down next to him, the pastel tones of her dance clothes now stained red.

Erik only just registered she'd been shot when the man with the gun jumped off the stage, firing into the orchestra seats. Three shots to the left, four to the right. Then he started coming up the aisle. Erik watched for incredulous seconds before recognizing the close-cropped hair and the gold earrings. Only then did he dive to the floor of the lighting booth with the full realization.

James.

A cacophony of screams, running footsteps, slamming doors. And more hard, sizzling pops rattling the air. Erik rolled further under the console, kicking cables and equipment aside, pulling himself in. Another series of shots, closer now. Then the windows of the lighting booth exploded. Erik cried out as shards of glass rained down on the console and spilled onto the concrete floor. He wrapped his arms around his head, a bristling ball of fright through which pierced a single thought:

My mother doesn't know where I am.

A lull then. Near absolute quiet except for the tinkle of falling glass. And a steady whooshing noise Erik gradually recognized as his own breathing. A faint lucidity crept around his brain. He clutched it, fought to put things back in order.

What happened? What just happened? What is happening?

He was on the floor of the lighting booth with broken glass all around him. Glass James shot out. James had a gun. James was in the theater with a gun. He came onstage and fired. He shot Will.

He shot Daisy.

What Erik did next would be held up by some as heroic. He would never understand why. He felt his actions were more suicidal than anything. Daisy was shot. She could be dead. And that pulled Erik out from under the console because if Daisy were dead, his life was over as well. He didn't go out of the booth to stop James. He went out to see if he was going to die today.

He wasn't a hero.

He was in love.

He crawled through the broken glass and went out of the booth.

Like a crab, Erik emerged into the aisle, crouched down low to the carpeted floor, up against the side of the booth. The silence roared in his ears. He wasn't afraid. He breathed a little shakily through his mouth, but he felt oddly calm. A little floaty, even. He looked at the stage. Will was curled up on his side. Daisy was on her back, her arms splayed out.

James was down around the tenth row. The silence shattered as he squeezed off another round. A strange squeal of impact and a chunk of plaster fell from the decorative frieze around the stage. It hit the floor with a thud and a puff of dust and Daisy turned her head toward the sound.

She was alive.

Erik felt a pure, relieved joy. Then he was terrified. The raw fear flooded his young body, seizing his limbs and guts, twisting around him like a thick steel cable. Death's presence loomed over him, tall and terrible. His heart was thudding so hard against the wall of his chest, it had to be audible. And his chest barely had a wall to thud against, it felt wide open, with a cold, electric wind blowing straight through. He was a core of stunned terror.

Daisy was stirring now, pushing up on one elbow, turning her head to one side, then the other.

Don't move, Erik thought. A fleeting image of her crossed wrists in the small of her back. In his mind he seized them, held them tight, held her down. His body hard on top of hers in the dark, shielding her. *Don't move. Lie down. Stay still.*

She could still die. He had to get to her before she died. He had to be there if she died. He had to get past James.

In the aisle, facing the stage, James stood still, the gun at his side. Out of the corner of his eye, Erik saw something move. To his right, in one of the rows, a brown dome of a head, stealthily creeping along, a long-fingered hand on the tops of the seats.

Kees's face rose. He looked to James, then looked back and saw Erik. He widened his eyes.

"Get down," Erik mouthed. Kees's head immediately sank. The teacher obeying the student.

Obeying the alpha male.

Erik's hand went into his pocket. His fingers closed around a flattened copper penny.

"You bring out the best in people," David had told him. "Haven't you ever noticed everyone calms down around you?"

I am the alpha male.

"You're one of the most decent human beings I've ever met," James had said. "Your father doesn't deserve you as a son."

My father doesn't know where I am, Erik thought. Silently, he moved down a few rows. He glanced at the brass letters on the sides of the aisle seats. O. N. M. He leaned against the side of the seat. Swallowing hard, he took his fist out of his pocket and gazed down at the medallion in his palm. "James," he said. The air was thick and resistant at the back of his head as he looked up.

James's head flicked around.

"James," Erik said again, making his gaze level, willing his voice to be steady. "Come talk to me."

James didn't move. He'd shaved off his goatee. It ought to have softened his face, made him young and approachable. But looking back over his shoulder, he appeared hard and remote. Drained of all empathy and human emotion. Not a flicker of recognition as his eyes slid up and down Erik's body.

Erik couldn't speak. His throat was clenched.

"You don't have to do this," Kees said then.

Erik didn't dare look back. He imagined Kees rising from behind the row of seats. Not quite standing. Just showing himself. A slightly irritated dread swirled through Erik's stomach. It made him feel stern. *Get down,* he thought. *You can't lead here.*

But Kees went on speaking. "You can stop, James." His voice was deep and gentle. And dangerously useless.

Stand down, Erik thought.

James's upper lip twitched. Then his whole mouth twisted in contempt. He whipped around fast. A shot rang out. Kees howled. Erik squeezed his eyelids and tightened his jaw as he heard Kees fall between the rows. Still Erik didn't turn away from James. He stayed still, leaning against side of the seats.

When he opened his eyes again, James stood over him, breathing hard, pointing the gun at Erik's face. The muzzle was squared at the top, rounded at the bottom. Two circles on its blunt end. One open. One closed. One for death. One for decoration.

Erik shifted his gaze to look James in the eye. He was trembling all over, and he fought not to show he knew it. He set his teeth. Slowly he raised his fist and opened it, showing James what he had. What he'd carried with him all this time. He swallowed hard and said, "You're still in my pocket."

James blinked then. A bit of clarity seemed to come into his face. Erik kept his eyes steady, acted as if he were standing, towering over James instead of crouched on the floor at his feet. His heart was exploding but he stayed still. He looked at James and tried to think through to him, tried to get James to take him.

I am human valium. Take me. I am the alpha. I lead this pack. I have you in my pocket. I am decent and good. You always liked me. Let me lead. Let me calm you again. You don't have to do this.

James blinked again, rapidly. Keeping the gun fixed on Erik, he turned his head and looked back at the stage. His eyes swept the rows of seats and then came back to rest on Erik, who still held up his palm with a bit of flattened copper in it.

"This is yours," Erik said. "This is the best of you and you gave it to me. I had it in my pocket. I didn't forget."

James licked his lips, staring down into Erik's hand.

"The best of me is on the stage," Erik said, tilting his head. "And I'm going there. She needs my best and I need to be in her pocket. Do you understand?"

James's eyes swiveled to the side. Then closed. He opened them and a stream of tears fell down his haggard face. He nodded, staring off to his right.

"Thank you, James." Erik said.

James looked at him, his expression startled by this courtesy, just as it had been when Erik offered him tea nearly two weeks ago. His surprise dissolved into a terrible anguish. The nodding head began to shake. He backed away two steps, his free hand to his brow. Frantic, he whirled to the stage, whipped back around and aimed one last time at Erik.

His teeth set together, Erik stared down the omega male.

I lead this pack. Not you.

He didn't move. Didn't blink. Not at the double-holed muzzle of the gun. And not when James, his face contorted and tear-streaked, bent his arm to set the muzzle under his own chin.

When the gun fired, only then did Erik close his eyes.

I am the—

SCREAM IF YOU GOTTA

THE SOUND OF THE LAST GUNSHOT seemed to echo forever. An awesome noise sending Erik's mind reeling backward down a long tunnel. Warp speed through successively faster rectangles of light. Like the Emerald City hall in *The Wizard of Oz* as it framed the epic retreat of the Cowardly Lion.

I am. I lead. I have you. I am. I have you. I am. I am...

Gradually the sound faded. Instead of crashing through a window, Erik came with a thump to a gentle halt. A solid weight nestled against his shoulder blades and he remembered he was sitting up against the side of row M.

He opened his eyes.

I am.

He looked at space. At the wall of the theater, at the plaster frieze around the stage and the curtain within it.

"I am," he said.

The auditorium was wrapped in screaming silence. Within this noiseless shroud, time slid out of proportion. A load of adrenaline tipped from the center of Erik's chest and cannonballed into his stomach, splashed along his limbs until his fingernails were electric and quivering. Still he sat, pulling in breath after trembling breath and staring at the space where James had been standing. Negative space now. His stomach roiled and burned. A high-pitched whine took over one ear. A cold sweat began to creep down from the crown of his head, tingling and prickling along his hairline, dripping down his back.

His eyes skittered around and finally lowered to the floor. To James's sprawled body. The gun by his hand. The halo of red in the carpet around his head.Clutching the arm of the aisle seat, Erik got up. He stepped over James and started down the aisle on wobbling legs. He stumbled, grabbing more seats until he steadied and began to run.

"Get down, Fish," someone cried from behind him.

"It's over," he said, not looking back. "He's dead. It's over. Get help."

Hand and foot on the apron, springing up onto the stage just as Lucky and John came creeping out of one of the wings. Neil's head rose over the Manhattan skyline, David came crawling around the side. The theater was twitching, unfurling tentative feelers and tasting the air.

Blood pooled around Daisy and Will. *Too much blood,* Erik thought, just as his foot slid in it and he fell down by Daisy, his hands in a viscous puddle. Her head flopped over to him. She was white as death, her eyes dimmed to slate and frozen wide open. She looked at Erik, yet she looked through him.

Lucky was down by Will, raising up his left arm. A bloody mess where Will's hand should have been.

"Towels," Lucky yelled. "Look in dance bags, look backstage. Dressing rooms, wardrobe. Anything that looks clean, grab it. We need help here."

Daisy's left inner thigh looked torn open, as if she'd been mauled by a bear. Erik swallowed hard and pulled off his outer T-shirt, wadded it up thickly and pressed it against the heinous gash of flesh and tissue. She cried out, her hands flying up, trying to bat his away. Her spine twisting, she tried to move away from him, get away from the pain.

Erik gritted his teeth, knowing to help her he had to hurt her. "Lie down, Dais," he said—using the harshest tone he'd ever used with her—and he pushed the improvised bandage firmly against the wound. "Lie still."

"Where's the shot, Fish," Lucky said. "Knee?"

"Inside of her thigh."

"All right. Medial. Femoral artery. Find the pressure point. Top of her leg, right in her groin." She pointed on her own body to the place. "Heel of your hand there and bear down."

David, Neil and John came flying from backstage with towels.

"John, come here," Lucky said. "Take his arm. Keep the towel in place on his hand. Your other hand here, this is the pressure point. Feel it? Keep holding it tight. Neil, get in here. See his side? The bullet went straight through. Pressure front and back. Good, keep it there."

Lucky came to Daisy then. She snatched the towel David was trying to fold into a bandage. "Move," she said. "Out of the way. Go get Will's feet up, get them elevated. Fish, you keep pressure going. Let me in here." Swiftly she replaced Erik's shirt with the folded towel. "Oh, Jesus," she said, a frantic edge in her voice. "Fuck, this is not good. We need help."

Not letting up on the pressure, Erik jammed his elbow into Lucky's side, just hard enough to startle her, shock her back on track. "Don't you fall apart on me, Luck," he said through clenched teeth. "You know what to do. You're the only one who knows what to do. *Do it.*"

Lucky pressed her lips, drawing air in through her nose. "She breathing, Dave?"

David now lay on his stomach on the floor, holding Daisy's head. "She's awake."

"Neil, Johnny—is Will conscious?"

"He's with us," John said.

"Pressure, then," Lucky muttered. "Pressure, pressure..." Her lips moved vaguely, as if reciting.

Daisy moaned, her upper body writhing. "Squeeze my hands, Marge," David said, giving them to her. "Hard as you want. Go ahead and break my fingers. I know you always wanted to." Daisy moaned again and David began to speak soothingly in French. His voice was pitched low in his chest. It didn't falter even as her face kept coiling up into spasms of pain and her knuckles were clenched white around his fingers.

Time dripped by.

"Will breathing?" Lucky kept saying.

Sometimes John answered, sometimes Neil. "He's breathing," they said.

"I'm breathin', babe," Will said once. His voice was soft and shaky, but it was there.

"Don't talk," Lucky said.

David kept whispering in French.

Daisy said nothing.

Little by little, Erik became aware of the presence of campus security. Then police began to fill the theater, sleek and menacing in vests and helmets. Like an invasion of black bugs they swarmed the aisles and wings, multiplied to fill the stage with authority. Loud voices. The crackle of walkie-talkies. And everywhere Erik glanced he saw guns.

Paramedics then. Hustling in pairs with bags of equipment. They were vested as well but more benevolent in shades of blue. One of them, a large black man, knelt down by Daisy's shoulder. His partner—slight and trim with a baseball cap—settled by her legs. Brisk and calm, he introduced himself as Greg, asked Erik and Lucky's names, then quickly unzipped a bag and pulled on gloves. "You two keep those hands where they are."

"Hey there," the black medic said, up by Daisy's head. "My name's Lewis. I'm a county paramedic. Can you tell me your name?"

Erik exhaled in relief when she did.

"All right, Daisy. Do you know where you are?"

"I... I'm at school."

"Good. Do you know what's happened?"

Her head lolled side to side.

"Do you remember anything?"

"The glass..."

"What's that?"

"I heard it."

"You heard gunshots, Daisy. You were hit in the leg. We're going to take a look at you and get you to a hospital as fast as we can."

"Did I fall down?"

"You could say so. We'll get you out of here. Besides the leg, can you tell me if you have pain anywhere else? In your back or your neck?" His large, competent hands began to move along her collarbones and arms. "I see you're squeezing your friend's hands there, excellent. No broken bones in your arms. Do you have pain in your head? Chest or abdomen? No? Just the leg."

Deftly he withdrew a penlight and shone it in each eye, held up a finger and had her follow it.

"How long ago was she hit?" Greg said, moving in by Lucky.

"She lay here bleeding about five minutes before anyone could get to her," Lucky said. "We've had pressure on it about twenty minutes now."

"Did she lose consciousness at all?"

"I don't think so."

"All right. Erik, you keep the pressure. Exactly what you're doing. Lucky, you scoot back and ease up on the wound, let me in here. Let's see."

Greg moved the towel dressing and Erik looked away. He had an awful ache between his shoulder blades from holding his position, holding the pressure, but he didn't move. Daisy had her arm over her eyes, blocking the light from the lanterns over the apron. Her other hand was still clamped around David's fingers.

"Bleeding's relatively minimal at the wound, Lew," Greg said, replacing the towel. "Your hand there again, Lucky, please. Good."

With a pair of shears Greg cut through the ribbons of Daisy's left pointe shoe, straight up her pink, bloodied tights. A quick slide of the blades and he tossed the material aside. With his gloved hand he felt around the thigh and Daisy cried out, her head lifting out of David's hand, teeth bared.

"It's all right," David said, his voice cracking.

Greg's fingers ducked into the hollow under Daisy's knee. "Popliteal fossa has no pulse. Bullet got the femoral artery or else the hematoma is compressing it."

"Scoop and scoot, man," Lewis said. "Get an IV in, let's fly."

They flew. Let rip with jargon and acronyms. Another EMT came over and relieved Erik of his pressure duties, and finally he could get up to Daisy's head. David scooted away to make room for him.

"I'm here, Dais," Erik whispered, sliding his hands where David's had been.

She turned her head toward the sound of his voice. "Did I fall down?" she asked again.

He ran his hand carefully along her face. "You fell down," he said. "You're going to be all right."

"Give me a vein, give me a vein," Lewis said under his breath, his fingers palpating along Daisy's arm. "You're a little thing with little veins aren't you..."

She did look little. Small and defeated. Down by her leg, Greg was packing fresh gauze and Erik made the mistake of looking. At the sight of the gunshot wound, he clamped his teeth on his lip, fighting not to break apart.

"IV going in, Daisy," Lewis said. "Big pinch here and some sting. Scream if you gotta."

She didn't scream, just closed her eyes and moved her hand with Erik's against her mouth. She set her teeth against Erik's knuckles. Tears began to slide from her eyes, running diagonally toward her ears.

"It's all right," Erik said, lying down on his stomach to put his head by hers.

She was breathing harder now, her eyes flitting all around. "Where are you?"

"I'm right here. I won't leave you." He glanced up, catching Lewis's eye.

"She your girl?" Lewis said lowly.

Erik nodded.

"Where are her parents? How far from home is she?"

"Two hours."

Lewis gave a grunt, his hands busy. "I can't let you ride in the back of the bus," he said. "You can ride up front if you keep cool, stay out of the way and don't puke."

"Thank you," Erik said, forcing his voice into calmness, digging down and pulling it together from some unknown reservoir of strength. He was grateful for the simple directions, which he repeated like a mantra: *keep cool, stay out of the way, don't puke.*

He stayed by her as Greg and Lewis immobilized her leg. When they needed to get a backboard under her, he helped by keeping her head and shoulders in line as she was rolled toward the uninjured leg and back again. His fingers were beginning to throb from her clamping grip, but he kept a hand in hers as the team counted off and lifted her onto a gurney. He helped the medics hand the gurney down from the apron of the stage. The theater hummed with purpose. Huddles of police and EMTs in the aisles, working on the injured. Working around James's body, which still lay in the aisle, covered now with a sheet.

Will's gurney was handed down from the stage. He was swaddled up in white sheets. Lucky walked by his head, lovingly holding his long, thick ponytail.

A man in a grey suit fell into step by Erik. Reaching into his breast pocket he withdrew a badge. "Detective Nikos Khoury, Philadelphia PD. I need to ask you some questions about what happened today."

Erik's heart twisted in his chest. "I can't," he said, walking. "I have to go with her." He felt annoyed and affronted. He was busy keeping cool, staying out of the way and not puking.

"I need to speak with you now, son," Khoury said, and the entourage stopped.

Erik looked at Lewis, who shook his head. "We need to go, man."

Erik felt he would either blow up or burst into tears. Nobody understood. Nothing needed to be asked. Nothing required investigation. No need to search the building or question the witnesses. It was all James's doing. James and only James and he was a clump of white sheet in the aisle and it was *over*. Everyone could just move along and let Erik do what he needed to do. Which was stay with Daisy.

"I can't," Erik said again, his voice rising. "I go with her."

"Hey now," a third voice broke in. It was a campus security guard. He put a hand on Erik's shoulder. "Listen to me. Listen. She has to go. You stay and talk to the police, while it's fresh in your mind. You take the time and tell them everything that happened. Believe me, this will be the better way. You'll get it done. You go to the hospital now and they'll only make you leave there to go down to the precinct. Am I right, Boss?"

Detective Khoury nodded. "We need to clear this building. We have a command central setup in the health center. You come there, give me the time, and then you can go be with her."

"Let go, Erik," Lewis said. "We don't have time for this. She doesn't have time."

Erik willed his fingers to loosen but they wouldn't. It was Lucky who had the bravery to let go of Will and come to Erik's side. Swiftly she took his hand out of Daisy's and into hers. She kissed Daisy's fingers and tucked them into the sheet. "I got him," she said to Lewis. "Go."

"Trust me," the security guard said, patting Erik's back. "Cooperate now and then you're done. We'll get you over to the hospital as soon as we can. I'll drive you myself."

Erik stared as the two gurneys carrying Will and Daisy were wheeled away, up the aisle and out the lobby doors.

At least they were going together. Will always had Daisy's back.

Lucky squeezed his fingers hard.

"We'll stay together, Fish," she said, as if she'd read his mind. "We'll go do this together. We won't leave each other."

Detective Khoury motioned toward the back of the theater. Holding Lucky's hand, Erik started up the aisle, David following behind.

SPLENDID ANGUISH

HE RODE ACROSS CAMPUS in a patrol car, in the back seat with Lucky and David. The streets were lined with emergency vehicles, a sea of flashing red and white lights.

Lucky's composure cracked as soon as they pulled away from the curb. She sank her face into her hands. A cry broke between her fingers. Erik put his arm around her and let her settle, sobbing, on his chest. There she slumped, dead and exhausted weight, making the keys in his front pocket dig painfully into his hip. He reached in to retrieve them. When he pulled his hand out, the flattened copper penny was wedged between two fingers.

Numb and stupid, he stared at it. Last he remembered, it had been in his hand. When had he put it in his pocket? More importantly—why had he put it in his pocket? Mouth open, eyebrows drawn down he looked out the window, as if the answer were out there. His mind was dumb grey space. An erased blackboard. Blinking and disturbed, he stuffed the penny and the keys in his other pocket.

"Front row seat to the end of the world," David said, face pressed to his window, looking up and out.

Erik looked out his side. Cops were everywhere, weapons drawn. K-9 units, too—officers going in and out of buildings with their German shepherds. Hearing the distinctive hum of helicopter rotors, Erik tilted his head up the glass to see the aerial surveillance.

More patrol cars were parked in front of the health center, cops patrolling the sidewalk and perimeter. Inside they stood at doors and windows, vigilant eyes constantly sweeping while the regular clinic staff buzzed around. But other people were there, too. Erik didn't know if they were counselors or social workers or just volunteers, but they were competent and kind and efficient. They ushered the victims in and circled the wagons, pulling close a protective force-field and saying reassuring things. *Come sit down. Let me get you a drink. Are you cold? Lie down. How do you feel? You poor thing. It's all right. Take some deep breaths. Let's call your parents. I'll help you.*

Detective Khoury sat Erik down by a window. A woman brought him some tea.

"Start from the beginning," Khoury said.

Erik tried, but it was hard to tell a coherent story. His mind kept dissolving and melding back together, losing the thread. He did better answering when Khoury asked him things.

"When was the last time you saw James?"

"About ten days ago. He left school after a suicide attempt. I saw him the day before."

"Where?"

"He came over to my house. I live with Will Kaeger. The guy they just took to the hospital with my girlfriend."

"He came to your house. Was he your friend?"

"He was in my circle of friends, yes. But not like my best pal or anything."

"How did he seem to you that night?"

"Strung out. Stressed out. Sad. A lot of people were mad at him."

"Why?"

"Few reasons. Couple weeks before he was high in a rehearsal and he dropped my girlfriend. She twisted up an ankle and broke a finger."

"Was disciplinary action taken against him?"

"No. Nobody could prove he was on something. I heard he hung with a crowd doing a lot of shit but I have no proof there either."

"Why else were people mad at him?"

"Well right after the incident he failed. Not failed. I mean, he didn't make his minimum GPA so he couldn't dance in the concert. Will took over his role."

"Will is your roommate?"

"Yes."

"Were he and James friends?"

"Yeah. And they worked together on some choreography last semester."

"Any idea why James would want to shoot him?"

Erik licked his lips. "I think James may have had a thing for Will. A lot of people thought that."

"A thing?" the detective said.

"James is gay. Was gay. He had a thing for Will."

"Is Will gay?"

"No, he's straight. That's his girlfriend over there."

"So James had a crush on your straight roommate. They were friends to a degree and artistic collaborators as well. That was the extent of the relationship?"

"To my knowledge, yes."

"Could there have been more?"

"Nothing that I saw." Which was not a complete lie. He hadn't ever *seen* James in Will's bedroom. He once saw a pair of jeans on the floor and Will in a towel.

"Did you know James owned a gun?"

"No. I know his father and his brothers hunt."

"You don't hunt with a Glock."

"His sister was in the army. Maybe it was hers."

"Do you know his sister?"

"No, she died. Last February. In Saudi Arabia."

"I see."

"But how could it have been her gun, wouldn't the Army have taken it back?"

"A Glock isn't Army issue, no. Do you have any idea why he would have wanted to shoot your girlfriend?"

Erik shook his head, his throat tight. "She didn't do anything to him."

"Why would he have wanted to shoot you?"

"I don't think he did."

The detective tilted his head. "He shot the windows of the lighting booth out. He must have known you were in there."

Numb and stunned, Erik went on shaking his head. "He liked me."

"In what way?"

"As a friend."

"When he came over to your house the night before he attempted suicide, what did he want?"

"To talk."

"To Will?"

"He was out in the backyard, staring up at the window. Will's girl-friend saw him first then we all got up. I said I'd go down."

"Why you?"

"He liked me." He showed Khoury the penny, told him what it meant. Told what happened, as much as he could remember. "He trusted me. I know he did."

The detective again took him through what happened in the theater. "You came out of the booth?"

"Yes."

"That was an insane thing to do, Erik. You could've been killed."

Erik's face burned and he looked at the cop through narrowed eyes. "She's my life," he said. "She was shot down and bleeding to death on the stage. What was I supposed to do?"

Khoury put a gentling hand on Erik's arm. "I said it was an insane thing. It was also a courageously beautiful thing. If it were my wife or daughter, I would have gone out too."

"You're a cop. It's your job to go out," Erik muttered, staring between his knees to the floor.

"True. Which makes your insane act all the more beautiful. Still, I won't want to be around when your mother gets her hands on you."

She doesn't know where I am, Erik thought. "Jesus, she's gonna kill me," he whispered absently.

The interview went on a while longer. The detective repeated a lot of the questions, twisting them into different angles. Erik's answers, though not articulate, stayed consistent. Finally Khoury thanked him and gave him his card in case he remembered anything else.

"You might see me at the hospital later," Khoury said. "But give me a ring even if you don't. I know your girlfriend will be all right. But will you call and let me know?"

Erik nodded, and shook the proffered hand.

His tea had gone cold. The same woman brought him another cup. Apologetically she said she had tried his mother's number three times but no one was answering. Erik tried twice himself.

"My brother should be home," he said. His jaw felt like it weighed ten pounds. "But he's deaf, he wouldn't pick up. I'd need to call on a TDD."

"Do we have a TDD?" the woman said to one of her colleagues.

"What's a TDD?"

"The thing for hearing impaired people. You type over the phone line—"

"Wait," Erik said, holding his head. "She's in Florida."

He was an idiot. Christine was down in Key West with her boyfriend, Fred. Erik fretted another five minutes over how to reach her, before thinking to check his wallet where, sure enough, he'd written Fred's number. Of course. He always wrote down everything.

He was exhausted then. After being questioned, the additional mental effort to produce this phone number was nearly too much.

The women dialed and spoke to Fred first, paving the way. Then Erik took the phone and Christine got on. It was surreal. Through the receiver she was crying and saying things, and his mouth was moving and he was saying things. Moments went by but they didn't pile up into memory. They fell like wheat before the plow of a recurring image—James firing and Will rearing up, throwing Daisy off his back. It cut a swathe through his mind and he looped through a dull confusion to arrive at the present again, wondering what had happened.

"I love you," his mother said. "I love you, Erik. I'm coming there. I'll get a flight and I'll be there as soon as I can."

"I'm all right," he said, as more images swept through his mind like an express train, bearing down closer and closer until the train hit him with an explosion of glass fragments.

He wandered, waiting for David and Lucky to be finished with their interviews. He got hugged a lot. By dancers and stagehands. His classmates and friends. He held crying girls, thumped the backs and shoulders of shivering, red-eyed boys. From them he learned the carnage James had left in the wings before he stepped onstage. Five students dead.

"Trevor King," they said. "He was first."

Allison Pierce was gone. Fat okey-dokey Allison, getting on Erik's last nerve since freshman year. Now she was dead.

"And Aisha Johnson."

"And Manuel Sabena."

"Taylor Revell."

The faces raced before Erik's eyes. Aisha, the gorgeous Grace Jones double whose dancing ruled *Powaqqatsi*. Gone. And Taylor, who had switched partners so Daisy could dance with Will. It might have been her on the stage and Daisy in the wings. Erik's mind swam into an alternate scenario, automatically thought *Thank God* before clamping down in shame. He shook his head hard. "Who else is hurt?"

Like a jigsaw puzzle, pieces of experience were fit together. Who had been where. Who had seen what.

"Where's Kees?" Erik asked.

"I saw him leave in an ambulance but he was sitting up. It looked like his shoulder was shot. Or his arm."

"Marie Del'Amici is in bad shape," someone else said. "She was shot but somehow she crawled between rows to hide. They didn't find her right away."

"I saw them working on her. They had a defibrillator."

"Where's Daisy?" they asked Erik. "What happened to Will?"

"Does anyone know?"

"What is happening?"

"Opie, what happened to your face," Erik said to John, whose cheekbone was scraped red and bruised.

"I must've fallen on something," John said. "When I pushed Lucky down." He crossed his arms tight over his chest, his young shoulders trembling. "You think he would've come for her next, Fish? After you?"

Erik felt a little sick. "I'll be right back," he mumbled.

In the men's room he ran the faucet cold and splashed his face, breathing through the nausea. The water fell crimson back in the sink.

He stared at it, then looked up at the mirror. He stepped back to see more of his reflection.

He was covered with blood.

He looked down. Streaked and dried in the hair on his forearms, caked in his fingernail beds, smeared across his shirt like some abstract painting. It capped the toes of his work boots and had turned the knees of his jeans to maroon leather.

Dizzy and shaking, Erik sat on the tile floor, back up against the wall beneath the paper towel dispenser. He stared at his hands. At Daisy's blood on them.

He felt branded. Eerily and irrevocably owned. She'd marked him. He'd marked her in blood once—the night of her eighteenth birthday, the night she gifted herself to him. She'd bled and he'd used it as ink, writing his name on her leg. Now he was claimed. He'd gone through gunfire and terror to pass the last test, the final ordeal, and his reward was now in his hands. On his hands.

It's all there is, he thought, turning his palms up and then down, taking it in. *No one but her. After today I can love no one but her.*

"You live a fucking fairytale with Daisy," James had said angrily. Erik would never know if James had come into the theater targeting Will, and if everyone else was collateral damage. Maybe Daisy had been a target. Perhaps Erik too. Or their fairytale. The vendetta could have been generalized or specific. But if James had come into the theater with any intent of destroying Erik and Daisy, he had failed. The fairytale was over, yes, but a truer, grittier human tale had begun in its place. A book with the strength of blood in its bound pages.

Erik began to cry. He didn't know if it was from fear or joy, but unable to stop it, he wrapped his arms around his legs, put his mouth on his knees and caved into it. He listened to the sound of his chest-wrenching sobs echoing off tile. He was both frightened and fearless. His own splendid anguish ricocheting around him. This was the real story. This was how it started. Not with locked eyes during romance and sex, but with blood. With locked eyes in a crisis. With *I am here.* Helping even though it hurt. Making your fingers let go even as your heart was breaking. To do what you had to do to survive so the story could go on being told.

The bathroom door creaked open. Another pair of blood-stained work boots and maroon-spattered jeans. David, crouching down. Back in the theater, he'd looked pale and grim. Almost stoic. Now he looked terrified. Though the florescent light was harsh, his pupils were enormous, eclipsing the deep brown irises. His eyes were black pearls, slick with tears, fringed in fear. "Erik," he whispered.

Erik could not remember the last time David had called him by name. "I'm all right," he said between sobs. "I'm all right."

David put his hands on Erik's shoulders. Put his forehead against Erik's brow. Erik clenched handfuls of David's shirt. Head to head, like twins in the womb, they hung onto each other, floating in the madness.

David, Erik thought, filled with a desperate affection. *Her blood is on you, too. You are in the story now. You are part of my pack.*

"Come on," David said after a minute, wiping his face on a sleeve. "Let's get out of here." He stood up, put a hand down. Erik slapped his opposite palm against it and let David pull him to his feet. He went to the sink and splashed his face again, scraping the blood out of his hairline and eyebrows. He soaped his forearms, got as much as he could out of his fingernails. Watched the red fade to pink and swirl down the drain.

David handed him a couple paper towels. "You good?"

"I'm good." He balled them up and fired at the garbage can in the corner. Perfect shot.

"Come on," David said. He thumped Erik's back, ruffled his hair. "Fishy, fishy in the brook, come along on David's hook..."

THIS IS MY SON

FOR AN HOUR AND A HALF, Erik, Lucky and David sat in the main waiting room of Philadelphia Trauma Center. The admitting nurses would not tell them anything, other than Will and Daisy were both in surgery. Not even to Lucky, who covertly switched her grandmother's sapphire ring to her left ring finger, laid the jeweled hand casually on the counter and said she was Will's fiancée.

Frustrated and depleted, they dropped onto couches and chairs. After a few minutes, Erik summoned the energy to get up again and call his mother. Christine could not get an evening flight out of Key West. The earliest flight she could book was eleven o'clock the next morning. Erik wrote down the information and said he would pick her up at the airport. Or someone would.

"Call me when you leave the hospital," she said. "If you go somewhere—anywhere different—you call me."

"I will," he said, and then yawned.

"Don't you dare not call me. I need to know where you are, Byron Erik."

"Yes, ma'am," Erik said, leaning his head against the payphone. It was one of their ongoing riffs: she called him by full name—which he'd always detested—and he retorted with *ma'am,* which Christine loathed.

Back in the waiting room, Erik sank into the couch cushions and put his feet up on the coffee table. He stared at nothing. Felt nothing. Soon,

Lucky toppled over and pillowed her cheek on his leg. He rested his hand on her shoulder, yawning again, his face splitting. He was a little hungry but too tired to do anything about it.

Lucky slept. The boys sat and withdrew further into their exhausted selves. David's eyes blinked and finally closed. Erik absently played with Lucky's spiral curls, wrapping them around a finger and picking at the dried blood in the ends. His mind dipped and rose on waves of disjointed thought until he too, fell asleep.

At the touch of a cold hand on his brow, he opened his eyes. Looked up at Daisy's face.

I've slept a hundred years. I'm an old man now. And she's grown old with me.

Then he realized it was Francine Bianco's hand. Daisy's mother, perched on the arm of the couch, her palm now cupping his jaw.

"Erik," she whispered, except in her accent it was *Erique.* "Oh darling, what's happened to you?"

Erik felt bruised and scraped. He put his feet on the floor, disoriented. Lucky's head was no longer pillowed on his legs. David was gone, too. Joe Bianco walked over and Erik recognized his expression immediately: he was in the war room. Jaw tight, his blue eyes turned to hard slate, shoulders cloaked in disciplined control. He crouched down and clasped a hand on Erik's upper arm. "How do you feel?"

Erik breathed in, let it out, testing his lungs. "I'm all right."

Joe indicated the blood-smeared T-shirt. "Any of that yours?"

Erik nearly replied it was all his daughter's blood, but quickly nipped the words and shook his head. "Where's Daisy?"

"Still in surgery. Will is in recovery. The doctor is talking to Lucky."

On the other side of the waiting room, Erik saw Lucky sitting with a doctor in green surgical scrubs. A few seats away sat a familiar, suited figure. Detective Khoury raised a hand in acknowledgment. Erik raised his back.

"Who's he?" Joe asked.

"A cop. A detective, I mean."

"Have you talked to police yet?"

"Yeah," Erik said, a hand to his now throbbing head. He was insanely thirsty. And the thought of a cigarette leaped unexpectedly into his mind. He was a careless, clumsy social smoker but right now, a slow, deliberate drag into his throat and lungs and the bracing rush of nicotine would be perfect. He wanted it.

"Do you need a lawyer?"

"Joseph," Francine said.

Erik blinked, confused. "No. I'm a witness."

Francine spoke sharply to her husband in French. Joe didn't look at her but his face softened and now both hands touched Erik's arms and shoulders. A warm palm on his face and a tug on his ear. A father's touch.

"Are you sure you're all right, Erique?"

"I'm fine."

"You poor thing," Francine said, her voice cracking. Her arms wound around Erik again. She was holding him like a mother, but she was crying like a child. Erik struggled to think straight. He needed context. He needed a drink.

"Where's David?" he asked.

"I sent him down the street to the Sheraton," Joe said. "I told him to get two rooms and whoever else needs to stay can stay. Franci, chère, come here. You can't keep crying on the boy and he's about to collapse. Cry on me."

"I'm sorry," Francine said, wiping her eyes. "Where is your mother, Erique?"

"Florida. She's coming tomorrow morning. I need to get some water. Do you want anything?"

"No, no. You go."

Erik hesitated, nearly asked Joe for a cigarette, knowing he'd have them. But he didn't want to smell like smoke later when he saw Daisy.

If they let him see her.

They better let him see her.

He found a bank of vending machines and got himself a Coke. Downing half of it in a few greedy swallows, he was mildly amazed his wallet was in one pocket, and his keys in another. Bits and pieces of an ordinary life. Clearly he'd gotten up this morning and put things in his pockets, but the morning was forgotten. Yesterday eluded his grasp as well, along with the previous week. Time rewound to James stepping onto the stage and no further.

James.

Erik reached back in his pocket. The flattened penny slid coolly against his fingers, the edges both sharp and soft. He took it out. In the glow of the vending machine light the flattened metal looked dull and morose. It seemed to give off a shamed vibe. As if it didn't want to be looked at. Erik put it away again.

In the waiting room, Lucky was sitting with the Biancos.

"How's Will?" Erik asked.

"The shot in the side was clean. In and out. Cracked a rib but no internal organs hit."

"What about his hand?"

"He's lost two fingers, pinkie and ring. Middle finger is fifty-fifty, they have to watch it. Index should be all right. Massive soft tissue damage to his palm. The tendons are a mess. I don't know about the carpal ligament but all the bones in his wrist are intact, thank God. Surgeon says he did great." Lucky's voice fell apart. She let out a tremendous breath and seemed to deflate under the drape of Erik's arm. She sniffed hard and Francine passed her a tissue.

"Will they let you see him?" Erik asked.

"Detective Khoury is in there now," she said, pressing the tissue to her eyes.

"Mr. and Mrs. Bianco?"

The party turned as one to the surgeon who had appeared in the waiting room. His scrubs were navy blue and he wore a patterned skull cap. Joe stood up.

The doctor came closer. "You are Margaret's father?"

Margaret? Erik thought, startled. *Margaret is James's sister.*

"I am Joseph Bianco, Marguerite is my daughter. This is my wife. This—" he touched Erik's shoulder. "—is my son and the young lady is my daughter's roommate. But she is family."

"I'm Dr. Akhil Jinani. I'm a vascular surgeon and I operated on your daughter this evening." He and Joe shook hands. "Please, sit down."

Erik stared at the Indian doctor. Dark-skinned and a bit of black hair threaded with silver peeking beneath his cap. Yet his features were young, almost pretty. A boy's face in an older man's body.

"Marguerite is resting and doing fine," Dr. Jinani said, the words brisk and tight within the lilting accent. "And they are moving her from recovery into the ICU. She is not going to die, Mrs. Bianco. And right now there's nothing to indicate we will lose the leg."

He paused to let them all digest and for Francine to get another tissue. Erik was still stupidly struggling to grasp Daisy sharing a name with James's sister.

"I will try to make this as simple as possible," the doctor said. "In surgery tonight we explored the gunshot wound and found the damaged femoral artery. We were able to stop the bleeding and I placed a graft to bypass the injured section and establish flow distally. In other words, the pulses behind her knee and the top of her foot were restored, and the leg began to warm up."

"Which is good," Francine said.

"All good signs, yes. I am optimistic she will recover fully and retain the use of her leg."

Another pause then, as the question passed unasked around the circle of people. To ask if she would dance again seemed trivial when set against the relief of her being alive and all right. But this was Daisy.

Dr. Jinani looked around his audience carefully. "I briefly heard what happened at the university," he said. "On the news. And naturally we had to cut her out of tights and toe shoes. I assume she is an accomplished dancer?"

They nodded as one. Francine's eyes closed and she held the ball of tissues tight to her lips. Erik thought about the purple leotard with the criss-cross straps. It was Daisy's favorite. Gone. Dropped in a ripped and bloodied heap on the emergency room floor. Most likely thrown away by now.

"Mrs. Bianco," the surgeon said. "It would be foolish of me to make promises about her future in dance right now. But let me say being a dancer was on Marguerite's side today. She's in phenomenal physical shape. I was somewhat amazed. Despite the shock and blood loss, her heart rate was steady all through surgery. She required no transfusions. And her blood pressure is quite satisfactory right now. As is the blood flow to the lower leg. Circulation is our priority and what we must monitor tonight. We can only go as far as we can see."

"Of course," Francine said, sniffing and blinking rapidly. "Of course. She's alive. Nothing else matters."

"Does she have any other injuries?" Joe asked.

"Only minor ones, sir. An incomplete fracture of the left fibula bone. That's nothing—the tibia is what bears the weight, the fib just gives backup. I doubt it would need to be pinned. Swelling of the left ankle may indicate some ligament damage. She will have a full orthopedic assessment tomorrow. As I said, the vascular issues must take priority. It does no good to set a broken leg if we cannot get blood to it."

"Of course."

"But if you need an orthopedic surgeon, I recommend Dr. Bonanto at the Kendall Center. For this kind of case, he's the one you want."

"I'll get him," Joe said.

Dr. Jinani looked at Erik then, taking in his weary and bloodied appearance. "Were you there when it happened? Are you all right?"

Erik nodded.

The doctor nodded as well and his expression was both sympathetic and ironic—a corner of his mouth twitched as if he were trying not to smile too broadly. "Would you like to see your sister now?"

Erik exhaled soft laughter. Busted. Yet grateful. "I would," he said. "Let my mother go first though."

Francine made to stand up but Joe set his hand on her knees, stilling her. He looked at Erik. "You go on in."

"No," Erik said. "No, you go."

Joe smiled then, raising a finger. "You go now, son."

Erik went. The nurse got him a gown and she walked him to Daisy's room. "Is she awake?"

"She was awake in recovery but then we started her on morphine for pain and she's dropped off again. The best thing she can do is sleep right now." The nurse stopped at the last door on the corridor and paused, her hand on the knob.

"All right?" she said.

Erik drew in a breath. "All right."

He went in.

"Isn't she cold?" It was the first thing he thought. "She's always cold."

"She's fine," the nurse said, with a reassuring smile. "She doesn't feel cold."

They had her in an over-sized hospital johnnie, white with little blue flowers. Emerging from the short sleeves, her arms looked fragile, bony, like a starving child's. A flimsy blue sheet was tucked around her waist and her right leg. Her left leg was exposed, the thigh swathed in gauze, the calf and foot stabilized between two long foam planks. IV lines in one arm, a blood pressure cuff on the other, along with a pulse monitor clipped to her index finger. A tube ran under her nose, delivering oxygen.

The nurse moved aside a rolling tray with some kind of monitor. "Go ahead, you can get close."

Gingerly, Erik moved in. He felt the slightest misstep—a tube jiggled, a machine jostled, an inadvertent knock against the bed—might kill her. He curled his fingers around her hand, drew it into his palm, squeezed it. His other hand hovered above her forehead. He glanced at the nurse, who nodded. "You can touch her, it's all right. Talk to her." She stepped out of the room.

Erik laid his hand flat on Daisy's forehead. Her skin was cool and dry. Miraculously her hair was still up in its ballet bun, although falling loose, toppled slightly sideways now. He bent lower, brushed his lips along her hairline, inhaling for just a hint of her perfume. A trace of sugar-soap scent would have been enough to soothe him. But her skin smelled sharply of alcohol, and dully of sweat, and another underlying odor, plastic and manufactured, like adhesive tape or latex.

Erik carefully set his cheek on her head, not allowing any weight to press on her, but letting her feel his skin. He closed his eyes. He waited to weep, but no tears came. Nothing but this numb shock, and an all-encompassing, pervasive sadness with no outlet.

Talk to her, the nurse had said, but he couldn't think of anything to say. Not when she was like this, shot down, ripped open, broken. Not even smelling like herself.

"I'm here," he said, moving his cheek over her brow, letting her feel him, breathe in his presence. "I'm here, Dais. I love you."

She made a small sound—a single, feathery hum in her throat. The fingers in his fluttered, then squeezed weakly. She moved her head in the direction of his voice, her shoulders twisting, turning into him. She put her nose against his neck. Inhaled. Again the little sound in her throat. And she was still.

Erik put his hand on her face, fingertips sliding into her hair.

He didn't pat or caress her. It would make her crazy right now. She wouldn't be able to think.

He rested his head on hers and held her still.

WHISPER TOGETHER

DETECTIVE KHOURY EMERGED from Will's room chuckling, saying Will was too zonked out on morphine for any kind of conversation. Khoury would be back in the morning. Lucky was allowed in then, and Erik could go too, if he kept it brief.

Much as Daisy had, Will turned his head and leaned into Lucky's neck, inhaling with a palpable relief. Erik found himself smiling at the primitive impulse. As if a sedated person were robbed of all senses except smell. They hadn't the strength to open eyes or reach out. They were merely looking for the soothing scent of a loved one.

Erik leaned and rested his face close to Will's, letting him sense his presence. Will's head turned. The eyes fluttered and managed to open. They rolled a little drunkenly, focused a couple seconds on Erik, then the lids dropped again.

"Whazup, asshole," Will whispered thickly. His mouth curved up a little. He looked quite pleased with himself. Then his features melted into neutrality and he was asleep again.

It was eight o'clock then, and the ICU's visiting hours ended, although family would be allowed a single hour later, from ten to eleven. Erik, Lucky and the Biancos left the hospital and went to the nearby Sheraton where David had been quite busy.

Erik never knew if David charmed someone's pants off or if it was simply an act of benevolence on the part of the hotel. But management upgraded them to the presidential suite, with its three bedrooms and three baths and every amenity they could possibly need. David himself had driven back to Lancaster and gathered clean clothes for Erik and Lucky.

"You go digging through my underwear drawer, Alto?" Lucky asked.

"Hell yeah," he said. "I know you—you'll be locking Will's door before they get the IV out of him. I figured you'd want your nice panties."

Lucky went to swat his arm, but the swat became a caress and she kissed his face tenderly. "You're a prince, Dave."

He was a prince. Erik barely recognized his gentle kindness. David, always so moody and difficult, was here for him, a beacon in the fog, beaming a purposeful, dependable light.

Erik got into the shower, turning it as hot as he could stand. More blood swirled in the water around his feet. He used the entire little bottle of shampoo and wore the soap down to a sliver.

A brisk knock on the door and David's voice floated over the curtain. "You want tea?"

"Yeah. Two b—"

"Two bags and milk. Jesus, Fish, I know how you take your fucking tea." The door slammed. Erik shook his head and had to smile. When he finally emerged, pink and dripping, the tea was on the vanity and the bloody clothes taken away. Erik didn't know where—he never saw them again. He dressed in the clothes David had brought. He retrieved his wallet and keys from the side table, then he picked up the penny. Stared at it a long time.

He did not put it in his pocket. He left it.

They sat at the table in the suite's living room and ate room service. Nobody made much conversation. Erik had reached a strange mental tipping point where he went utterly numb, nearly on the verge of indifference. He found himself thinking about basketball. Big game tonight. With Magic Johnson retired and Doc Rivers flopping, could the Lakers beat the Clippers and will themselves into the playoffs? Erik glanced over at the television. It was turned on to the news, with the sound muted. Would it be heartless of him to switch to the game? Probably.

He felt oddly and inappropriately bored.

The phone rang.

"I can't get up," Francine said, sighing. "I'm so tired."

As if her words were a signal, Erik felt leaden then. Bed beckoned enticingly. His head longed for a pile of pillows with smooth, freshly-laundered cases. His mouth actually watered at the thought of lying down.

Stooped and stiff, Joe trudged to the phone and answered.

"Eat, darling," Francine said to Lucky. "Just a little more."

Lucky picked up her grilled cheese and took a grudging bite.

Joe turned around, speaking in French, his voice raised in alarm. The lethargy of the room split apart with a crackle. Francine stood up.

"What?" Erik said.

David had gone pale. "I think they're taking her back into surgery."

Erik jumped up, bumping the table with his knee, making plates rattle and glasses slosh. "Joe, what happened?"

Joe hung up the phone and looked at Lucky. "Reperfusion," he said, as if accusing her of a crime.

Lucky shook her head, eyes wide. "I don't know what that is," she said. "I'm sorry, I don't know."

Erik ran into the bedroom to grab his sneakers and jacket. About to dash out again, he stopped and looked at the penny. It lay on the bedside table where he had left it, orange and sinister under the lamplight. It glared at him.

It didn't like to be left.

He put it in his pocket and followed the Biancos back to the hospital. There they learned reperfusion is when blood supply returns to tissue after a period of oxygen deprivation. Instead of restoring normal function, it brings on inflammation and cell damage. Dangerous pressure begins to build up.

"Marguerite began to shows signs of distress and complain of severe pain in her lower leg," said Dr. Jinani. "Despite the morphine drip."

They were in the family waiting area of the ICU, a smaller room within the unit.

"We soon lost the distal pulses and took her immediately back into surgery. I feared she was developing acute compartment syndrome."

"Which means?" Francine said. "What is it? Could she die?"

"No, Mrs. Bianco. She is out of danger but it was a serious emergency situation. In essence, her body was not rejecting the graft itself, but the oxygen the graft was bringing. We had to immediately relieve the pressure building up in the compartment of the leg—hence the name of the condition—or else blood would stop reaching her lower leg. And the tissue would begin to die. Then she could lose the limb."

"How did you stop it?" Joe said. "What did you do to her?"

"Sir, it was necessary to perform a dual fasciotomy. We made incisions on the medial and lateral aspects of the lower leg and removed a small amount of fascia to relieve the pressure."

"How deep?" Erik said, feeling a little sick as he tried to picture this. "Are you cutting into her muscle? Will she be able to walk?"

"No, the incision is just deep enough to relieve the pressure without damaging muscle tissue."

"And it was successful? It's working?" Joe asked.

"Yes, sir, the distal pulses have been restored and the limb is warm. She must be closely monitored through this first night."

"And then what," Joe said. "You'll close the wounds tomorrow?"

"Sir, you must understand," Dr. Jinani said. "The incisions must be left open until the pressure is fully relieved. I am thinking for a week."

"Oh my God," Francine whispered, putting her face in her hands.

"And it can take up to a month for the fasciotomies to heal completely."

"A month," Erik said. "She'll be in bed a month?"

"Not necessarily. My thought is she will remain in the ICU for a week while the wounds remain open. I will close them one at a time, roughly speaking, over a period of ten to twelve days. Then she will be able to walk, either with crutches or a walker, and we can send her to rehab."

Nobody spoke then. The hospital hummed with quiet purpose around them. A voice over an intercom. A nurse walking by, her sneakers squeaking on the linoleum. A phone ringing sedately.

"Can I see her?" Francine said. Her eyes were closed but her spine was straight.

"She's heavily sedated right now, Mrs. Bianco, and—"

Her eyes opened. "I don't need to have a conversation with her," Francine said, her voice velvet around steel. "I just need to see her."

"This is our only child, doctor," Joe said.

"I understand. Just for a few minutes," the surgeon said. He looked at Erik. "And you?"

Every particle of Erik's being resisted. *I can't,* he thought. *I can't do it. Not with her leg sliced open. I can't look at her like that. Don't make me.*

Joe put his hand on Erik's face. The firm, warm palm. A soft tug on his earlobe. "Come," he said. "I need you to come, Erique. We'll make each other strong." The pat of his hand again. "I am afraid, too. Come with me. I ask you."

Erik shut his eyes tight. Teeth set together, he nodded and got up.

BACK AT THE HOTEL, Erik collapsed on one of the queen beds, heeling off his shoes.

"Bad?" David asked.

Erik ran his hands through his hair and held them there. "They were long cuts, man," he said. "I thought they'd be little."

"Show me."

Erik freed a hand and drew a line a couple inches beneath his knee bone to the top of his sock. David drew in his breath with a hiss. "Just on one side, right?"

"Both."

"God." His face twisting a little, David crossed his arms tight on his chest. "And you could like...see her muscles and shit?"

"Everything. All the flesh underneath exposed. She kind of moved in her sleep, moved her toes, and you could see the tendons flexing."

"Jesus Christ."

Erik swallowed hard and shook his head, trying to flick away the image. "I don't want to talk about it."

"Don't. You're done. Hit the sack. You want tea or something?"

"No."

"Don't forget to call your mom. She called before, I talked to her a little while."

Erik's hands were numb and stupid as he brushed his teeth, pulled on sweats and a T-shirt. He called Christine. Again the auto-pilot sensation of his mouth making coherent conversation without his brain's participation.

"You went out of the booth," she said. "David told me how you... Oh, Erik..."

"I'm sorry, Mom."

"No. No, honey, I... I just need to get to you."

"I'm so tired."

"Put your head down. Stay with David. I'll be there tomorrow." More comforting, murmured words flowing over the line, saying goodnight, saying she loved him. She was coming.

After hanging up, Erik toppled into bed like a felled tree. David brought him a glass of water and a blue, triangular pill.

"What's this?"

"That, my friend, is a valium."

"I'm human valium," Erik said.

"Not tonight. Take it or I'll find one in suppository form and get Daisy's mother to help hold you down."

Even with the dire threat, Erik hesitated. And David smiled at him. His true, genuine smile. "Nothing will keep you from waking up if she needs you," he said.

"I know."

"She's asleep, Fish. You should be, too. I'll wake you up, I promise."

Erik swallowed the little helper and lay down. He pushed the pillows around, piling them behind him. Dave could laugh, he didn't care. The way Erik went to sleep best was with Daisy spooned up against his back. If she couldn't be here, he'd fake it.

David dropped into the easy chair in the corner of the room, clicking the reading lamp over his head. "That light bother you?"

"No." Then Erik sat up on an elbow. "Dave, are you reading the bible?"

"Yes," David said, licking his finger and turning pages. "Shocked?"

"Only because you're the least religious person I know."

"True. But there's this one prayer, my Aunt Helen likes it. Here, Psalm 41." He looked up with his irreverent grin. "That would be one of the Psalms of King David, naturally."

"Naturally."

David read out loud:

*Blessed are those who have regard for the weak; the
Lord delivers them in times of trouble. The Lord pro-
tects and preserves them—they are counted among
the blessed in the land—he does not give them over
to the desire of their foes. The Lord sustains them
on their sickbed and restores them from their bed of
illness.*

A long moment of silence. "Read it again," Erik said.

David did, lingering over the last line, "Sustains them on their sickbed and restores them from their bed of illness."

"Thanks for being here, man," Erik said.

David looked back at him. "Go to sleep, Fish."

Erik put his head down, wiggled back into the pile of pillows on his
shoulder blades, willing them into Daisy's pliant body.

"Fishy, fishy in the brook," David said, "go to sleep while I read the
Good Book."

Smiling, curled on his side with the charms of his necklace tucked
in a hand, Erik closed his eyes. He took roll call of his talismans: Saint
Birgitta, the fish, the boat. And Daisy's charm, the tiny gold scissors.

Scissors which cut.

The long, hideous cuts on Daisy's leg. Bright red diamonds of flesh in
her smooth skin.

He opened his eyes again.

"It's all right, Fish. Go to sleep."

Erik shut his eyes. He waited. For either sleep or panic. Neither came.

"Dave?"

"Yeah."

"Read the rest of it."

"All my enemies whisper together against me; they imagine the worst
for me, saying, 'A vile disease has afflicted him; he will never get up from
the place where he lies.'" David's voice cracked.

"Keep going," Erik said drowsily. Now the edges of his mind were
beginning to unravel. The pillows were warm and soft on his back, like
Daisy. One of his hands became her hand. Daisy's long fingers woven

with his. He ran his fingertips over the edges of his nails, but they were her nails. She was here now. Holding his hand.

"But may you have mercy on me, Lord; raise me up, that I may repay them. I know that you are pleased with me, for my enemy does not triumph over me. Because of my integrity you uphold me and set me in your presence forever."

"In your presence forever," Erik said, yawning.

Forever, Daisy whispered on his neck.

And Erik was asleep.

SHAPED BY OUR SCARS

"I AM SUCH a practical person," Daisy once told Erik. "To a fault. I don't like drama. I don't coo over babies or cry at movies..."

She didn't cry at movies. Erik had to think hard to remember if he'd ever seen Daisy cry. Really break down and weep from her guts. Sometimes she choked up in the throes of an emotional moment with him, but he was always choking right along, which made it a sweet, shared cry. Once or twice he saw her reduced to teary-eyed frustration after a grueling class or rehearsal. But if dance were a cause for sobbing, it was with an air of "I'm letting it out. I'll be over it in a minute." Productive crying. Cathartic and purposeful.

But when they dialed back the sedation the next morning and let her come up through the fog. When she opened her eyes and took in where she was. When her parents explained, and Daisy gradually began to comprehend what had happened. And when she finally went grabbing at her leg, struggling to sit up but only getting as far as an elbow, just enough to push aside the draped cage over her calf and see what had been done to her...

No, Erik had never seen her cry like this. It tore him apart, how helpless she was against it. She couldn't roll on her side or roll against him or curl in a ball or fall on her knees with her face in the floor. She had to lie there on her back and take it. Take in how her leg was deliberately and gruesomely sliced open.

It didn't matter it was done to save her life. It didn't matter Daisy Bianco was a pragmatic girl who veered away from unnecessary drama and found comfort in practical action.

Nobody was tough when their leg was cut open from knee to ankle.

She cried into her hands at first, but then her fingers hooked into claws, her nails were in her forehead. She was scratching her face and then she howled like a widow, like a madwoman.

Erik peeled her hands away from her face, where already red welts were rising at her temples. He took her wrists, put them up around his neck, and he bent over the bed to hold her. Into his chest she screamed, her breath hot and wet in his sternum. No words, just a keening moan—a thick, drunken blur of despair.

He held her, knowing these tears would do her no good—they served no purpose, they would do nothing to fix her. But he didn't say a word. Nothing he could say would console her. He wouldn't insult her by even trying. He just made himself a strong and immovable wall for her to fling herself against. He held her tight and held still.

It was a long and ugly jag, with streaming eyes and running nose and dripping mouth all soaking into Erik's shirt. Her hair a wild, sweaty tangle in his fingers and her skin hot like fire beneath her gown. She cried so hard she spiked a fever. She wept until she made herself sick, another moment Erik had never seen. Not once in twenty-eight months.

Daisy was particular about puking in private. She practically made Erik leave the state whenever she was hungover or laid low with a stomach bug. But now she was retching helplessly on her misery. A nurse was supporting her back. Erik was holding the basin with one hand, Daisy's hair with the other, and he was helping her heave it up. As calm and unconcerned as the nurse.

"I'm sorry," Daisy said, gasping between bouts.

"Don't be," he said, gently wiping her face with a damp cloth. "Just get it out of you."

At Dr. Jinani's order, the nurse put some kind of magic in Daisy's IV line and within minutes she was out. Erik sat bedside, one hand holding hers, his other laid flat on her cooling forehead. Within his grip, her fingers twitching intermittently. Beneath his palm, her eyelids trembled and fluttered. She was asleep, but hardly peaceful.

Erik knew the fasciotomies were necessary and they saved her leg. Yet he sat with his insides twisting in misery. He could not bear to see her sliced open while he was whole and unscathed. The scales needed to be balanced. While he had no intention of putting his eye out or recklessly slashing himself, he still felt a desire to be scarred. He needed some kind of ritual injury, too. A permanent reminder.

Daisy, he thought. And he finally connected his love to an image of the flower, a little white-petaled ringlet. The spirit of Daisy, crushed and broken on the ground, trod upon and left to die.

I won't leave. I will never leave you.

He set his lips on her temple. "I won't let you die," he whispered.

He had an idea.

HE WENT TO SEE WILL. He still hadn't had a minute alone with his friend. Either Will was asleep or in pain, or his parents were there, or Lucky. But right now he was alone, staring out the window, his heavily bandaged hand on his chest.

"What's up, asshole," Erik said, putting a bottle of pineapple juice on the bedside table. Will glanced at it and his mouth briefly formed a smile.

"Don't steal my line," he said.

"How do you feel?" Erik asked.

"Like I got shot. How do you feel?"

Erik breathed in and out. "Changed," he said.

Will nodded.

Erik sat in the chair next to the bed. "How bad does your side hurt?"

"Percoset's a beautiful thing."

"How about the hand?"

Will held it up, letting Erik see it from both sides. "This is going to make jerking off difficult."

"You're a lefty?"

"Isn't everyone?"

Erik laughed, but Will didn't join in. He watched Erik with troubled eyes.

"Is Daisy awake? I mean... Does she know?"

Erik nodded.

"Bad?"

Erik shook his head. "Not good."

Will closed his eyes, let his head fall back on the pillow. "I'm sorry," he said.

"Sorry for what?"

Will turned his head toward the window. "I know why I was shot. But why he had to put a bullet in her—"

"Hey," Erik said, putting a hand on Will's arm. "Hey. Look at me."

Will breathed in and looked back. "I'm sorry."

"You talk to the police?" Erik asked.

"Yeah. A little last night but I was kind of loopy."

"Kind of? You were stoned."

"You saw me?"

"I came in. You don't remember?"

"No."

"You kissed me."

Will's eyes widened. "Did I really?"

"No."

His face twisted. "Asshole. Anyway, the detective. Kary?"

"Khoury."

"Right. He came back today and I told him everything."

"Everything?"

"Everything. I know you tried to cover my sleeping with James and I appreciate it. God, I love you for it. You're my fucking best friend. But I wanted it all out there. If we try to hide shit it'll only come back and bite us in the ass. And hide it for what? Because it will somehow justify what he did? He had no right..."

Erik nodded.

Will looked away. "But I'm sorry," he whispered. "I'm so sorry, Fish. I told you I'd take care of it. And you trusted me not to let Dais get in the middle. You told me you trusted my hands. Between her and the floor..."

"Stop," Erik said. He'd never seen Will like this. Inside-out. Frantic and fretful. Sure of nothing.

"It's killing me," Will said. He rolled his lips in and his eyes squeezed shut. "What they had to do to her leg. And when I think about how I dropped her—"

"Dude, you were shot."

"You trusted my hands."

"He took your fucking fingers off. This isn't your fault."

"It is, Fish. He was coming after me."

"If he was coming solely after you he would've shot you and only you. He was on a tear. He shot his way through the wings and killed five people. He shot Daisy. He shot Marie and Kees. He almost shot me. And he would've gone for Lucky next."

Will looked at him, his mouth working hard to hold back the emotion. "You stopped him." The tears rising up in his dark eyes began to spill over. "I watched you talk to him. He had the gun in your face. And I couldn't get to you. He could've killed you. You... You don't know, Fish. You don't know what I did, you don't know how I..."

"I do know." Erik got out of the chair, moved to sit on the edge of the bed. Will tried to sit up but grimaced in pain. Erik helped him the rest of the way, gathered Will's forehead against his collarbone and let him cry. "I know," he said.

"I'm sorry." The words kept squeezing through Will's sobs. "I told you I wouldn't let her get in the middle. But she ended up right there. Right smack between us..."

"It's all right," Erik said. "It wasn't your fault. Cry all you want but you'll never make me believe this was your fault."

Will was shaking. He cried hard, his good hand in a clutching fist around Erik's shirt. Much as he had with Daisy, Erik held still against the storm. The arms cradling Will were fearless and secure. No rubbing or patting to make light of the vulnerable moment, no robust back-thumping to couch it in masculinity. The time for such bullshit had passed. Will needed him. Will loved him. And like Daisy's love, it was part of everything. Abundant as air, free-flowing as water. And precious.

"I still trust you," Erik said. "If I had to, I'd carry you out of that theater on my fucking back."

Will shook in his arms. "I'm sorry."

"It's all right, man."

After a minute Will pushed him away, roughly wiping his face. "Jesus, you're such a crybaby."

"Yeah, I love you too," Erik said.

Will pointed at him. "Don't. Just don't. If I tell you how much I love you, it's going to get embarrassing. You'll really cry. Then I'll cry. Someone's cock will get sucked. It will rapidly get out of hand and we'll wind up on Jerry Springer." He ran a hand through his hair and nudged his chin toward the bottle of juice on the table. "You wanna open that for me?"

Erik twisted the cap off and handed it over.

"Thanks," Will said, taking a sip. "Apparently hospitals make Lucky horny. Who the fuck saw that coming?"

Erik laughed, and even Will managed a smile, shaking his head against the bottle.

"Listen, I need your help." Erik told Will what he wanted to do, and Will made a short phone call on the spot. After hanging up, he wrote down an address for Erik.

"Ask for Omar. He does all my ink. He'll be waiting."

Omar had been following the coverage of the shootings on TV. In the inner sanctum of his tattoo parlor in South Philly, he listened to Erik's story, then took pencil and paper and began sketching. He grasped what Erik wanted right away. Not cute or cartoonish. Simple. Realistic. He even consulted a botanical book he had on one of his many shelves. He suggested the petals not all be perfect, maybe one or two could be tattered. Erik liked the idea, as long as the flower didn't look like it was dying.

"Oh no," Omar said, in his sing-song Jamaican patois. "We'll keep her alive, my friend, but we won't ignore her scars. We're all shaped by our scars."

Erik watched as Omar went over the pencil with a black pen, watched the design come to life.

"It's a daisy," Omar said, "but it's just a little...dark."

"It's perfect."

"Do you want any lettering—her initials, or the date?"

Erik wanted just the flower head. On the inside of his left wrist. It took Omar less than twenty minutes to ink him. It hurt, but not as much as Erik wanted it to.

He went back to the hospital and sat at Daisy's bedside, tenderly running his hand over her face and hair. She stirred under his touch and began to wake up. He smiled as her eyes grew lucid and settled against his.

"Feel better?" he whispered.

She hummed in her throat. The corners of her mouth flicked upward and she turned her forehead into his palm. The tattoo was inches from her chin. Erik waited. A moment's silence passed with her head bowed against his hand, and then she seized his wrist. Her mouth slowly opened as she moved his forearm back from her face. She blinked hard. Her fingers slid to carefully touch the puffy swollen skin.

"Erik..."

He sat still. She looked a long time, her lips trembling as she ran fingertips over her representation sunk into his skin.

I have set you in my presence forever, Erik thought, remembering Psalm 41. *I uphold you. You're in my skin. And I am not leaving.*

Still holding his wrist, she looked at him. "Does it hurt?"

"Yes," he said. And he encased the word in bronze and set it aside, marking the one and only time he would ever lie to her.

Her face dissolved beneath a stream of tears. She took his hand and drew it along her neck, tucked it beneath her jawline, curled against it as much as she could.

"Nobody loves me like you," she whispered.

PART THREE: DAVID

EXECUTIVE DECISIONS

DAVID DROVE ERIK to the airport to pick up Christine. At the gate he accepted a hug and took her carry-on bag, retreating tactfully so she and Erik could have a moment alone.

Christine, warm and loving on the phone yesterday, now stared unblinking at her eldest. She'd been a competitive swimmer in high school and still retained a long, broad-shouldered physique. It gave her an uncompromising presence and made her appear taller than she was. Her golden-brown eyes matched Erik's—right down to the red rims and circles beneath. Two deep lines angled from the sides of her nose, framing her full, proud mouth. Lines Erik had not seen before. The grey at her temples was new to him as well.

"You scared the shit out of me," she said.

"I know."

"I need a minute to be angry about it."

He nodded. "I know."

She took Erik by the shoulders and shook him. Hard. Like he was seven and had run into the street without looking. "You could have been killed," she said, her voice a razor-edge hiss through her teeth. "My *God*, Erik, what were you thinking?"

He let her do it. He'd surpassed her in height years ago, he could have easily disengaged. But she was angry and frightened and he let her.

"Never again," she said. "Don't you *ever*..." She held him away, put a finger up by his face. "If I lose you, I will die. Do you understand?"

He nodded, closing his palm around her pointed finger and pulling her hand toward his face.

"Never again," Christine said as he pressed his mouth into the heel of her hand. "You see someone with a gun, you hide or get the hell out of there. Don't you ever..." She closed her eyes. She shivered and drew a long breath in through her nose. Erik watched the moment of fury pass through her. Then her eyes opened and both her hands touched his face.

"Oh my God," she said, her voice worn down to a thread. "Honey." Her arms gathered Erik up and he crumpled into their grip. Together they sank on a pair of leather chairs and she held him tight. Her hand strong on his head. Her mouth on his hair.

"I'm sorry," he said.

"It's all right," she said, rocking him. "You're all right." Her voice was unwavering. "I'm here now." She took his head in her strong hands. Her brown eyes swept his face. She seemed to be looking for something. Erik stared back, defenseless, without guile. Christine smiled, her eyes bright with tears. She kissed his face. "I'm proud of you," she whispered and pulled him to her again.

She took up a firm position behind Erik's back, keeping a gentle hand on his shoulder through the hours and days. She took David under her wing as well, shocked nobody had come for him.

The truth was, David didn't have many to come. At the time of the shooting, his Aunt Helen was clear across the country, visiting friends in California. David spoke to her on the phone, but Erik didn't know if an offer to come to Philadelphia was made and declined, or if the offer hadn't been there. Either way, David did not seem to need her presence.

"You don't want her to come?" Erik asked. As he was practically sitting in Christine's lap at any opportunity, he couldn't understand it.

"No."

"Why not? I mean, she's all you have."

David shrugged, squinting through the smoke from the cigarette he never seemed without these days. "What could she do?"

Erik was bewildered but he didn't press it. All his own resources were reserved for getting through the days and being strong for Daisy. He had none to spare. David shadowed him nearly everywhere, somehow drawing whatever sustenance he needed by appointing himself Erik's bodyguard. Erik was glad to have him. But he could not take care of him.

Erik and Christine stayed in the suite at the Sheraton for two days and then moved back to Colby Street. Erik took Will's bed and gave his mother his own. They stayed because funerals lay ahead.

Four funerals in three days.

Not including James, the death toll rested at six. Marie Del'Amici, shot in the chest and head, lingered three days in a coma and died Wednesday. Her husband had her body cremated and took the ashes back to Italy. Likewise, Allison Pierce's body had been flown home to Indiana for burial.

The remaining victims were Pennsylvanians and Erik and David went together to pay their respects. Neither of them owned a decent suit, so Christine took them shopping. Groomed down to the shoelaces, they went on Thursday to Trevor King's wake in Allentown. The next day—on what should have been opening night of the dance concert—they went to South Philly and attended Manuel Sabena's funeral in the morning, Aisha Johnson's in the afternoon. Will, finally discharged from the hospital, came to Aisha's as well, his arm in a sling, his hair brushed back into its ponytail by Lucky.

Taylor Revell's funeral, on Saturday in Narberth, was the hardest. Daisy desperately wanted to go but her incisions were still open and she was confined to the hospital. Erik said he would go for both of them. He didn't want to. He was sick to his stomach over it, thinking of how Taylor had switched roles with Daisy. A simple act of goodwill and she signed her own death warrant. What did you say to acknowledge such cruel, karmic events?

"Thank you"?

"I'm sorry"?

Words were useless.

He sat in the pew of the church, bolstered by Christine on one side and Will on the other, needing their bodies pressed right up against his arms. David and the Biancos sat in front of him. Behind were Leo Graham and his wife, and Kees with his lover, Anton. Safe at the center of this battle formation, Erik got through the funeral service. They drove back to Colby Street but he could not get out of the car. Hunched over in the passenger seat, his body refused to move. He didn't cry. He felt quite calm. But the reserves were depleted. He was an old, weary man. It took the combined effort of David and Leo to get him back inside where he fell on his bed, still in suit and tie, and slept.

Christine made one of her rare executive decisions and declared she was taking him home. Erik was grateful to regress into a childish state, let her take charge and pull him out of school.

It wasn't as dire as it sounded. Only five weeks remained in the semester but the vice-chancellor of student affairs made a blanket ruling: anyone affected by the shooting could take an incomplete on their spring semester coursework and pick it up in the fall, with no loss of tuition dollars.

Even though Will was taking the incomplete and going home, Lucky decided to stay and finish her finals. David chose to stay as well, although he was crushed by the loss of his senior project. With a heavy heart he watched his treasured sets for *Who Cares?* dismantled and put into the storage room. Leo declared the project complete and David could graduate. But David was unfinished and unsatisfied with a sympathy degree. He deferred graduation and planned to come back in the fall and do at least another semester. Leo pledged to support him.

A community network came together to send Erik and Will home. The landlord guaranteed the apartment to them in the fall. U-Hauls were provided free of charge. A squadron of stagehands, led by Leo, showed up at Colby Street to help Erik, Christine and the Kaegers pack up the boys' belongings. Briskly they sorted out what was necessary to take and what could be left behind in storage at Mallory Hall. The crew made the apartment spotless, then went across the backyard to help the Biancos extricate Daisy from Jay Street.

The first of her fasciotomy incisions had been closed—"Beautifully," Dr. Jinani said—and the second was scheduled for five days later. She had already started in-house physical therapy and, as soon as she was discharged, she would start a more intensive program at a rehabilitation hospital.

When Erik came to the hospital to say goodbye to Daisy, he ran into Dr. Jinani, who was just leaving Daisy's room. Learning Erik was going home, the doctor shook his hand and wished him well. "I am sorry to meet under such circumstances," he said in his precise cadence, every syllable clipped and groomed into place. "But I am so glad to know you. And Daisy. You make a lovely couple. Truly I believe your support has been key to her recovery."

Daisy had kicked the hospital johnnies to the curb and devised creative loungewear out of her own t-shirts and sweatpants with the left leg cut off. Sitting up in bed reading, she looked pretty, but frail. She'd lost weight. Her face was drawn and pinched. Marie's death had devastated her. Taylor's lay heavy on her heart and mind. Holding her, Erik was torn. He hated to leave her—was on the threshold of being afraid of the separation—but his bones cried out to go home. Christine wanted him to come home. And he hadn't yet seen his brother, who wanted him too.

"You go," Daisy said, hugging him. "I want you to be with your family. I'm all right. I promise."

I can't breathe without you, Erik thought. He kept it silent. He didn't want to heap any more troubles on her already occupied mind.

"I'll come back," he said. "It won't be long. I'll figure something out for the summer."

"We'll figure it out," she said, caressing the back of his head.

He took her face and kissed her—between her eyebrows, each closed eye, her nose, her chin and then her mouth. On a sudden but sure impulse, he reached behind his head, unclasped his gold chain and put it around her neck.

"No," she said, but her eyes closed and her hand came up to hold the charms against her throat.

"Please. I want to. Just until I see you again."

"All right."

He thumbed the tears from beneath her eyes. "I love us."

"I love us," she said. "Call me when you get home."

CHRISTINE AND ERIK SAT IN A BOOTH at a diner, just over the New York border. Erik downed two Cokes but only picked at his cheeseburger. Christine put down her coffee cup and threaded her hand through plates and glasses to find his.

"I don't want you to think I'm taking you away from her," she said.

"You're not dragging me home, Mom."

"You know what I mean."

"I want to see Pete," Erik murmured.

Her thumb ran across his knuckles, caressed the tiny, red scabs where broken glass had nicked him. "I'm going to be clingy a little while. I need to know where you are. I'll be checking on you while you sleep."

Erik managed a small smile. "I know."

"Come be at home and rest. Collapse. Let me fuss over you and charge up your batteries. Because she's going to need you."

He nodded.

"Do you want to call her?"

He checked his watch. "She's probably at physical therapy now. I'll call her when we get home."

"Try to eat, honey." She let go his hand and picked up a knife. "Cut it in half. There. Eat half."

He took a bite, concentrated on chewing but it was tasteless cardboard. Having the goal to build up his strength for Daisy helped him force it down. And keep it down.

He offered to drive the next leg but Christine waved him off. "Sleep," she said. And he did. The entire rest of the trip. He woke when they were pulling into the driveway. His brother was waiting on the front step, in the company of his two dogs.

Peter Fiskare was eighteen, soon to graduate from Rochester School for the Deaf, which he'd attended since kindergarten. He was blond, like Erik, but with his father's dark blue eyes and a much harder expression. He projected a steely reserve bordering on indifference. He seemed aloof but nothing could have been further from reality. Living in a world of silence, Pete's eyes were honed to capture and process visual cues. His whole body was attuned to the deeper vibrations of human experience. He kept most of his thoughts and emotions veiled, yet he missed nothing. Erik was one of the few who knew the depth of Pete's heart and the complex feelings living there.

Coming down the walk, Pete's face was wide open, stripped down to raw relief and residual fear. He ran the last few steps and jumped, flinging arms and legs around his brother and toppling them both onto the grass where they rolled, pummeled, punched and hugged.

"You trying to be Rambo or something, you fuckwit?" Pete said. Speaking aloud was yet another indication of his emotional state. He'd stopped voluntarily talking after his father left, preferring to communicate solely in sign language. Only the most dire of situations—positive or negative—made him use his voice.

Erik flopped on his back in the grass, then looked up at the golden retriever sitting close by. She gazed down, a little disdainfully. The tip of her tail lifted in greeting as she accepted a pat on the head. Such was the demeanor of Drew, Pete's guide dog. Or as Pete put it, his business associate.

Drew was a hardnosed professional. She was trained to one job: alert Pete to noise. Everything and everyone else were mere distractions to be tolerated. She accepted praise and dignified affection but any attempt to get her to romp or play was coolly ignored. Being a companion and buddy was the exclusive domain of Lena, a lovable but dopey border collie who had twice washed out of service dog training.

"Phenomenal instincts," Pete always insisted. "Zero attention span."

But it was Lena now who put her muzzle against Erik's knee and stared up at him. Her liquid brown eyes, usually rolling and hyper, were serene. Filled with a bald, penetrating compassion.

Erik squinted at her, confused. "This is Lena, right?" he asked Pete, who nodded, looking just as perplexed.

Erik got up on his knees to study the dog. Her gaze was proud, as if she'd finally found her purpose.

I am here, little one, it said. *And I understand.*

Feeling terribly little, Erik stared back. Lena put her paws on his knees then, standing up to lick his face. He put his arms around the silken coat, burrowed his head into Lena's warm flank and exhaled.

"What's going on here?" Christine said, coming up the walk.

"I think I've been dumped," Pete said.

Lena shadowed Erik's every move. Pete hadn't been exaggerating about those instincts. The merest frisson of anxiety and her ears went up. Erik's chest tightened and she was there. If a lump came to his throat, she came to his side.

She did her best work at night. Erik's body was gripped by a surreal fatigue. But disturbing dreams were keeping sleep from being restorative. Horrific night terrors where he was back in the theater, crouched in the aisle trying to pull James back from the edge. Only this time James laughed in his face and shot him. Erik felt the impact of the bullet like a fist to the chest. No pain. Just a spectacular flow of blood through his hands and sickening sense of helplessness as James went back down the aisle and hopped up on the stage to finish what he'd started.

Erik's own blood rose up around him. A river of red down the aisle. He could not stop James. He could only watch. One point-blank shot to kill Will. Then another to kill Daisy. Then more blood surging over the lip of the apron and water-falling into the orchestra seats. A shattering of glass and the thud of falling plaster chunks. And everywhere blood.

Nothing predicted the onslaught of the dreams. They plagued him night after night, then mysteriously retreated, only to return again. Lena could not stop the nightmares from manifesting, but she rescued him from their clutching grip, bringing him back to the waking world where she could guard him. She slept on the floor by his bed, at the precise spot where his hand could reach down and find her. As soon as he began to stir restlessly or thrash, her paws were on the mattress and her nose in his neck.

Pete began bedding down on Erik's floor, too. And with his brother and both dogs close by, Erik began to string together consecutive nights of good sleep. The shadows in his face smoothed out. His appetite returned and he put some weight back on. But his heart was with Daisy. He was exposed and fragile without her. It hurt to breathe. His arms ached to hold her, his eyes longed to connect with hers. The sleep he craved was with Daisy pressed against his back and Lena on the floor by his head. Snugly bookended between the greatest love and understanding he'd ever known.

SVENSK FISK

THE FASCIOTOMIES WERE CLOSED now. The vertical scars running down Daisy's calf were livid and ugly, crosshatched with staple marks. But neither closing had required a skin graft, which was further indication her repaired artery was pumping plenty of blood and oxygen to the lower extremities. Dr. Jinani was pleased enough to tease her.

"My dear," he said, "when it comes to being shot in the leg, you are a champ."

He originally wanted her to do her rehab at the Magee Center in Philadelphia. But sensing the strength she drew from her family, he agreed she could go to a facility closer to home as an outpatient. On the fourth of May, three weeks after she was shot, Daisy returned to Bird-in-Hand.

"I'm fucking home," she said to Erik on the phone, her voice a purr of relief. They talked every night, Erik following both her progress and her setbacks.

"'Rehabilitation protocol,'" Daisy said, reading to him from a lengthy document. "'Following compartment syndrome release with open fasciotomy.' Nice to know this is common enough to warrant protocol."

"You know, *release* used to be a much sexier word," Erik said, curled in bed with the phone tucked under his ear. "Now all it evokes is your leg muscles bulging out."

"I told you not to look when they were changing the dressings."

"Well you looked. I couldn't not look if you did. Think you're going to one-up me in the looking department?"

"I'm sorry, did you just say compartment?"

"Cute. But really, it was the most disgusting thing I've ever seen in my life."

"Thank you, honey," Daisy said. "I try to corner the market on all your extreme experiences."

"You have the freakin' monopoly," Erik muttered.

The first two weeks at rehab, her trainers left her leg at rest and concentrated on getting her endurance back. Daisy worked side-by-side with one man who was a double amputee, and another who was a paraplegic. They did grueling cardio workouts solely with upper body strength, propelling their chairs in laps around the outdoor track, or in specialized treadmill racks indoors. For strength training, the men used heavy free weights while Daisy worked with resistance bands. Her exercises focused on her core, back and shoulders, and keeping the good leg conditioned. She needed strength without bulk, and had the additional goal of maintaining her flexibility. She worked with a stretching coach daily, and saw a massage therapist three days a week.

"This does not suck," she said to Erik.

"Is there a release in those massage sessions?"

"Cute."

She phased into active strength training for her injured leg. She started in the pool, using the resistance of water to gain the suppleness back in her left knee and ankle and build up the strength in her quadriceps. Long hours just learning to put weight on the leg again. And then walk on it.

She often sounded tired and frustrated on the phone. Her heart wanted pliés and relevés while her body could only handle supported baby steps. Sometimes she cried and Erik, unable to hold and comfort her, wanted to tear the walls apart. Just as her little triumphs brought him joy, her stumbles filled him with aggravation. Those were the days he wanted to take the penny out of his pocket and chuck it in the street. Only a gripping superstition kept him from doing so.

So the rest of May passed. Cardiovascular training. Treadmill. Elliptical. Weight training. Strengthening and conditioning. Stretch. Massage.

Ice. Elevation. Little by little, the left leg began to come back. All the while, the therapists were keeping her right side strong. Her right leg was her ticket out: Daisy was a southpaw in the sport of dance, a natural left turner, balancing on her right leg and spinning counter-clockwise. All her dancing was right leg dominant. It inspired an Abbot and Costello routine Joe Bianco ate up with a spoon:

"At least he shot you in the right leg," he would say.

"You mean the correct leg." Daisy always went along.

"Right, he shot your left leg."

"Right."

"No, the left."

"Right."

JUNE ARRIVED. And Erik began to rebuild.

The carpet in Mallory's auditorium had to be replaced, stained as it was with blood and human gore. The upholstery on two rows of seats was unacceptable for public posteriors. With minimal debate, the university decided not only would the carpet and seats be replaced, but the theater was getting a full overhaul, including a new electrical system. And in an astonishing cut through normally-clogged bureaucratic channels, the plans and the budget were approved and the project went out to bid. When construction crews rolled on site the first week of June, Leo Graham had created four summer internships within their ranks, securing two of those spots for Erik and David.

Erik drove down to Pennsylvania the weekend before his job started. His car ate up the rolling, scenic miles of Amish country, passing farms and vineyards and produce stands. Just at sunset he turned up the dirt road at the sign marked *Bianco's: Farm to Market*. Outside the driver's side window were hills of apple and pear trees. On the other side, grape vines were rigorously bound to posts and wires, following the ridgeline in near-military formation.

Just where the private driveway branched from the road was a funny little statue, a squat, ugly creature somewhere between a dragon and a turtle. It crouched at the base of a signpost which read *La Tarasque.* It was both the name of the house and the name of the odd, lizardy beast—a beloved legend from the region of France where Joe Bianco was born (Joe told Erik Tarasque was also the name of a beloved anti-aircraft gun towed by the French military).

Erik rounded a bend and the farmhouse came into view, pale grey with black shutters and a yellow door. Francine's treasured flower beds sprawled on either side of the stone walk, a riot of colors competing for attention. The porch ran the full front of the house and wrapped around both sides. Daisy was waiting, her red sundress bright against the grey shingles. As Erik switched off the engine, she took up her crutches and came carefully down the steps, swinging the last few feet as fast as she could. His necklace bounced at the base of her throat, catching the sun. With a cry she let her crutches drop to the ground and flung her arms up around his neck. He locked his arms around her slender waist, buried his face in the curve of her sweet-smelling shoulder and exhaled.

"Dais," he whispered.

"Never again," she said against his face. "I never want to be away from you again."

"Never," he said. "God, I missed you so much." The words didn't do it justice. He could feel the cells in his body perk up, as if he was severely dehydrated and Daisy was a long cool drink of water. They stood a long time in the driveway, holding each other without speaking. And then a longer time passed in kissing.

"Let's go in," Daisy said, smoothing her hair. "My parents went out to dinner. It's just us."

His lips tingling, Erik opened the car door to get his backpack from the front seat. Walking across the lawn, he slowed his step to Daisy's swinging gait, a hand lightly on her neck. He knew she used the crutches in the evenings, whether she needed to or not. Mandatory rest. Sun went down, she went off the leg.

"Guess what I did this week?" she said.

He could barely answer, he was too consumed with stuffing his eyes full of her.

"I don't know. Pressed twenty pounds with your left leg?"

"Twenty-five," she said, smiling. "But guess again."

He wound a length of her hair around his fingers, dying to undress and wrap himself in its soft length. "I don't do guessing games," he said. "Just tell."

"I had a follow-up appointment with Dr. Jinani. And while I was in Philly, I went to see Omar."

"Why?" It took a moment to sink in. "Wait. You didn't."

"I did."

"You got a tattoo?"

She nodded, biting her lower lip, nose wrinkled.

"What did you get? Show me."

"Come inside."

He set his backpack down in the front hall and followed her into her bedroom. The door clicked shut. "Now go find it," she said.

He brought her over to the bed, into the light of the table lamp, where she put down her crutches and stood still for him. He searched her arms, her shoulders, lifted up her hair and peered at her neck. Finding nothing, he crouched down and inspected each leg. His fingers reverently touched the starburst pucker on the inside of her thigh and the long, raised zippers of flesh on either side of her shin. Still nothing.

He stood up and slid her little sundress over her head. It wasn't on her back, nor her stomach, nor under her bra. He got distracted there a few minutes, running his tongue in circles around her breasts, breathing in the sugary scent of her skin.

"Keep looking," she murmured.

He knelt down once more, his fingers poised around the waistband of her underwear.

"You're getting warmer."

He eased them down and saw a splash of color by the jut of her hip bone.

"Oh, Dais," he whispered.

"Do you like it?" she asked, her hand in his hair.

Inked into her a skin were stylized red letters spelling out Svensk Fisk, but in such a way they cleverly formed the shape of a fish. The little loop of the E made the eye, and the top of the first K was the dorsal fin. The legs of the final K were elongated and curved, creating the tail.

"It's amazing," he said. "Did it hurt?"

She gave a dismissive snort. "Ruptured femoral artery. Compartment syndrome release with open fasciotomy. A tattoo is nothing. Omar cried the whole time, though."

On his knees before her, Erik put his fingertips to the little red fish, then his lips to it.

"I thought hard about where to put it," she said. "Somewhere only you could see."

He gazed at it up close, far away. He laid his head against her stomach and viewed it sideways. He traced the letters with his fingernail as his heart swelled and grew in his chest, a seed blossoming and blooming until he was a wide-open flower in the sunshine of her love. He laid the inside of his wrist against her hip, his daisy pressed to her fish.

"Nobody loves me like you," he said.

WE OWN THIS PLACE

THEIR FIRST DAY of work, the boys arrived at Mallory Hall and Erik froze. He hadn't been in the building since the day of the shooting—six weeks ago—let alone in the theater. Nauseous and anxious, he dug in his heels at the auditorium doors and David did an inspired job of getting him inside.

"We're going in," he said, like a platoon leader. He had Erik by the shoulders, half-hugging, half-shaking him. "We're going in. This is our theater, we own this place. Say it with me."

"We own this place," Erik said, his voice sticking in his throat.

"All my enemies whisper together against me. They imagine the worst for me, saying... What do they say, Fish?"

"He will never get up from the place where he lies."

"My enemy does not triumph over me. Fuck the fucking fuckers. Come on, Fish, we're going in there. You're lying down right in the aisle where it happened, and then you're getting up again."

"Raise me up," Erik said, a little stronger now, caught up in the call to arms. "Raise me up, that I may repay them..."

"We're going in." David yanked the theater doors with both hands, threw them open wide, and they went in.

Erik sat in the aisle by row M, his back against the seat sides.

"Here?" David asked.

"Here."

"And he was where? Like this?" David stood a little in front of Erik but Erik waved him off.

"Don't. Don't be him. Just...let me do this."

David moved out of sight. Erik closed his eyes. Opened them again.

His hand went into his pocket.

He was still carrying the penny around. And every time he tried to analyze why, it was as if a garage door came down in his mind. It was easier not to think about it.

"You all right?" David crouched by him.

"I have dreams," Erik said. "I'm sitting right here and he shoots me. Then he goes back onstage and shoots Will and Daisy. Shoots to kill. And there's nothing I can do about it."

"You tried, Fish," David said, a comforting hand on Erik's shoulder. "It was a crazy thing to do but if anyone could have done it..."

Erik put his head down. Tears wet the knees of his jeans. David pulled him close. "It's all right. You got him to stop. You did."

"I didn't mean for him to..."

"Nobody did. Nobody knew this would happen. Nobody imagined it."

Wiping his face on the back of his hand, Erik looked around. He looked good and hard at the bloodstains. It was them or him now. He'd either get up and face it, or sit here forever.

He got up and went down the aisle, hopped on the apron of the stage. David followed and stood center, hands on hips, looking stage left.

Erik walked past him, through the black curtains of the wings. He looked down at the floor. Bloodstains here, too, but something else. A block of graffiti, roughly forming the outline of a human body. He crouched down, peering at the multi-colored words. Signatures. Messages.

RIP Trevor.

Love you, my brother. Be with God.

Trevor, angel, I miss you so much.

Trevor King, forever in our hearts.

"Trev died here," Erik said.

The scuff of David's work boots as he came over. "Right there, yeah. The police outlined him in tape, just like you see in the movies. People came back and filled it in."

Erik stood up and walked further backstage. He found four more graffiti-filled outlines. Aisha. Manuel. Taylor. And Allison Pierce.

He patted his pockets. "I need a pen," he said. "A Sharpie or something."

"I'll get one."

Erik sat cross-legged by Allison's outline, his fingers resting lightly on what would have been her shoulder. David brought him a marker. Erik lay on his stomach and found a few inches of space. "Okey-dokey, girl," he wrote. And couldn't think of anything else. He felt lame and useless. He signed beneath the words, then went around signing the four others.

David was back in the middle of the stage. Erik joined him. They got down low, practically put their faces on the floor, mapping the blood-stains. Here, from Will's wounds. And over here, from Daisy's.

"So much of it," Erik said. "Jesus, it's even more than I remembered."

"Fuck the fucking fuckers."

"My enemy does not triumph over me."

"We own this place."

Together they stared down the blood on the stage floor.

The blood blinked first.

They shrugged, young and dismissive, full of resilient bravado. They spit their contempt for fate, rubbed it into the stage floor with their steel-toed boots, and got to work rebuilding their theater.

THE MIRROR TELLS THE TRUTH

THEIR LANDLORD WAS TAKING the summer to give Colby Street a much-needed paint job and tend to some other maintenance issues. So Erik and David took a dorm room on campus, sharing digs with the students attending the conservatory's summer programs. On weekends, they headed out to Bird-in-Hand. There they bunked in the Biancos' carriage house, which had been converted into a little guest apartment. It was a sweet, homey space overlooking Francine's rose gardens, with two bedrooms, a shared bath, galley kitchen and living room. David took one bedroom. Erik took the other and Daisy came in with him.

Since his first visit as a freshman, Erik found the Biancos astonishingly hip to their daughter's relationship. No coy pretenses about sleeping arrangements, no raised eyebrows when Daisy took her things over to the carriage house. When it was time to say goodnight, Joe and Francine simply said, "Goodnight, sleep well." In the morning, they said, "Good morning, sleep well?"

Having their own space in the carriage house was lovely. It would have been lovelier had Daisy and Erik actually been having sex.

Her hands were warm and encouraging in the night and his body responded. Yet his mind was elsewhere. Detached and idly watching from a corner of the room. "It's hard to explain," he said, although he knew he didn't have to. Under his touch, Daisy's body was open, but ambivalent. She could take it or leave it.

"I'm not numb," Daisy said, her eyebrows wrinkling. "I like touching you and holding you. But I just feel so tired."

"Tired's one thing but I feel unwired," Erik said. "I don't feel like me."

She put her face against his chest. "It'll be all right. Our bodies are probably freaked out still. We'll just keep throwing time at it."

Time was kind and plentiful for them. All the weekends through July and August, when Daisy's pain levels became more manageable and she gradually gained some mobility back, they lay naked in bed together, as comfortably twined as they could get. They kissed. They never tired of kissing. They talked the hours away. They laughed. They stared—they could still lock eyes and go into their private universe, and they went there frequently.

But they weren't making love.

Not much, anyway.

Some nights she woke up screaming, and he soothed her. Unlike his Technicolor night terrors, her dreams were without imagery. "It's pitch black," she said. "And huge. There's nothing to see but I can sense it goes out for hundreds of feet and up for hundreds of feet."

"Is it a room? Or a cave?"

"I don't know. It's just the biggest darkest space I've ever known and it's terrifying. I'm trapped there. No one else is in the dream. No story. No circumstance or context. It's just vast black space and I can't get out. It's right behind my own eyelids and I can't open them." She moved further into the circle of his arms, shivering with unspeakable revulsion. "It doesn't sound like anything but God, I just feel sick when I wake up..."

"It's real," he said. "It's real and it's something. I know, Dais. Believe me, I know."

Erik's dreams were on him again, too. He'd wake up yelling into the dark and Daisy would bring him back into the light. She curled up against his back, her hand flat against his pounding chest, her head on his head, murmuring him back into rest.

But rarely back into her body.

DAISY'S TEAM OF TRAINERS and therapists was more than pleased with the rate of her leg's progress. Both calf and thigh were getting stronger by the day. Oddly, the most challenging injury to overcome and the most chronically troublesome all her life was the ligament damage in her ankle.

"Come on, Marge, that's like being shot in the ass and going blind," David said in mock disgust. "Can't you do anything right?"

Once, not long ago, Daisy would have rolled her eyes, clucked her tongue or outright ignored David's teasing. Now she laid her temple against his upper arm and laughed. David was allowed to call her Marge now. Daisy allowed him anything. He'd proved himself Erik's true and trusted friend, and Daisy herself was too singularly and fanatically focused on her goals to be bothered by his ribbing. Nothing bothered her.

Or so it seemed. The brave face she put on in the daylight was nothing indicative of what transpired in the dark.

Only Erik knew what came in the night.

He watched Daisy work. Nobody worked harder, fought tougher. He could see, almost taste the frustration, and he knew the unending aggravation from her leg's unwillingness to cooperate was nearly unbearable. It was offensive to her. For Daisy was so used to her body doing what she told it to do. Every dancer was.

"Dancers are narcissistic as hell about their bodies," she said. "We love the mirror."

They were lying in bed, up in the carriage house. The last full moon of August hung in a corner of the window.

"You have a fierce vain streak if you're a ballet dancer," Daisy said, "and you feel no shame about it. You're entitled to it because you've been working your body to death for years. You hate the mirror. The mirror tells the truth. Ballet is so cruel because it allows one right way to do a step or pose, and fifty wrong ways. And on those good days, when you look in the mirror and you see it, you see your reflection looking just the way you want it to? Then God, you love the mirror. It's our drug. It's every dancer's little, twisted addiction."

He could take it as a cue to launch into a pep talk, assure her she would find the fix again. But Erik understood her at a much more elemental level. She didn't need him telling her what she already knew. He let her be, and let her work it out.

"It's so hard," Daisy said. She was sitting up now, looking out the window, out over her mother's rose gardens bathed in silver moonlight. "I don't know what I'll do. I've had one vision all these years, being a principal dancer in a ballet company." She looked back at him. "I don't know if it's going to happen now. I'm fighting like hell, but at the same time... I feel like I need to start thinking like you, and having some other irons in the fire. What's my Plan B?"

"Any ideas?"

"None. I don't know what else I am," she said, her voice splintering apart. "I can't think of anything else I..." She trailed off, sighing, her chin on her hand. "You have so many books on your shelves, Erik. I just have one."

He lay on his elbow with his body curved close to her. His hand ran down the length of her hair and along her spine, then back up again. "Think you would ever teach?" he asked.

Her mouth twisted. "I guess. Keesja says nobody plans to be a dance teacher. It just naturally evolves for some. Maybe it will with me."

Erik watched her, helpless. Helpless with love for her. And admiration. All these weeks he'd been watching her gather her will during physical therapy, amass every shred of cunning and ingenuity, and settle the bit of recovery between her teeth. It broke her down. She fought and lost. She cried bitterly, but they were her productive tears, her means to go back and try again.

Now she was turning her laser focus inward, taking an unflinching look at what she might or might not be able to do, facing up to the practical decisions which might need to be made in the near future. And making a plan. Or at least, making the plan to make a plan.

He laid his palm on her leg, across the scars on her inner thigh.

"We're all shaped by our scars," Omar had said, as he inked a daisy into Erik's wrist.

"I love you so much," Erik whispered. He loved her calm, pragmatic poise. She took on her problems without drama or tantrums. Beneath her stillness lay rich and complicated passion. Erik knew how scared she was. But afraid or not, Daisy would look her life in the face and do what she had to do.

"I'll be there," he said. "Whatever you want to do. Or not do. I'll be there."

She looked at him, the moonlight in her eyes. "I know how to dance," she said. "And I know how to love you."

"There's a book on your shelf," he said.

They stared, breathing each other, pulling into their little haven.

"I don't know what I'd do without you," she said.

"You'll never have to know." He smiled, reached and tucked her hair behind her ear. She lay down again. In what had become a ritualistic gesture lately, he set his daisy tattoo against the little red fish inked by her hip.

PETAL BY PETAL

THEY CAME BACK to Lancaster in late August.

The girls moved into Jay Street. The boys moved into Colby. They unloaded and unpacked, then clipped back the stray branches in the gap of the hedge separating their backyards. Open for business.

After a week of classes, they threw a little dinner party. Daisy and Lucky cooked. David and Neil came over. So did John Quillis, now firmly established as part of their clan. John's height was up an inch and his voice down an octave. His face was shedding its babyish curves, sporting a careless growth of beard. He looked adult. And a little haunted. In the light of the kitchen table, they all looked older and battle-worn. Yet as they ate and laughed and passed around a bottle of red wine, they talked optimistically about what lay ahead.

Lucky was designing a dance therapy minor to go with her physical therapy major, and using Daisy as her case study thesis. Daisy hadn't yet been green-lighted to go back to class. She was doing her therapy and her training sessions and had christened the fall semester, "Operation Irons in the Fire." She was taking psychology, creative writing and art history, and auditing a course in French literature.

She was also teaching.

Kees took over as director for both the contemporary and ballet divisions, holding down the fort until a new ballet head could be hired. Short-staffed, he wanted Daisy to cover some of the lower-level technique classes. She balked at first. "I don't teach," she said, partly indignant, partly terrified.

Preoccupied and stressed, Kees would have none of it. "Consider this your senior project. Teach the damn class or I'll flunk you."

To her surprise she was good at it. More than good. "She's a natural," John said. "Like who didn't see that coming?"

"Duh," Will muttered.

Will's appearance had shocked everyone: he'd cut his hair. Not a mere trim, but cropped close down to the scalp. Even after a week, Erik barely recognized him. He gaped all during dinner, still getting used to the startling presence of Will's facial features. He was all eyes and jaw. Exposed and raw. Dangerously handsome.

"Dude," Will said, "you keep staring at me like that and we're gonna have to take it upstairs."

Erik rose out of his seat. "Let's go."

John got up as well. "I'll witness." And the table broke up laughing.

"What possessed you to do it?" Daisy asked, touching Will's head.

Will shrugged. "I just felt the need to do something dramatic. You and Fish got tattoos. You know what I mean." He massaged his left wrist as he talked. The surgeons had saved the middle finger—no end of jokes there—and Will had spent the summer in intense rehab, gaining back control of his maimed hand. It pained him—both the lingering discomfort in his palm and the phantom pain from the two lost fingers.

"Was Lucky mad?" Neil asked.

"Furious," Lucky said, smiling.

"Only because I did it without telling you." Will sunk a little in his seat. "I didn't think that part through too good. None of us is really into surprises anymore."

"No shit." John said.

"But once the shock wore off... What the hell, it's just hair. It grows back."

Lucky ran her hand over Will's crown. "It's like velvet," she said, a little dreamily. "Especially when you rub against the nap."

"Yeah, with your inner thighs," David muttered and again the table broke up.

Erik laughed along, but he kept an ear peeled the next few weeks, listening for Will and Lucky's customary noises in the middle of the night. Either they were having quieter sex or, like Erik and Daisy, they weren't having much at all. Erik desperately wanted to ask. Hit the gym or go for a run and bring up the topic. Ask Will if he and Lucky were having trouble in bed.

But he didn't. It was awkward. And such a fucking drag. He thought his physical relationship with Daisy would get better back at school. Back in the cradle of their romance.

It didn't.

Their desire was back—whether it was from the campus vibe, or from the memory of past sexual encounters splashed all over the apartment on Jay Street, the love call was loud and undeniable. Yet the love itself was unremarkable.

Daisy had to struggle to come. Moves and tricks Erik had once brought her around in minutes, but now brought only an indifferent, dulled pleasure. "It feels good, it's just not taking me anywhere," she said, her voice filled with a confused frustration. "It's like I'm stuck. I don't know."

"I know," Erik said, confused by his own experience. He felt like a klutz in bed. Getting aroused was no problem, the urge struck often, but once in the act, he couldn't get completely into it. He wasn't exactly stuck, but he couldn't seem to find the hook during sex, the ability to step off the edge of himself and fall headlong into a climax. It was like sleeping with one eye open, or one foot planted on the floor: he couldn't give over to pure pleasure anymore, he felt constantly braced for something.

Cruelest of all, sometimes the sex was sweet and connected, but followed by an anxiety so intense, it left them reeling and shaking, if not outright physically sick. It was a sucker punch tactic filling Erik with an angry dread. They'd be cuddling together in the afterglow, minding their own damn business, and little by little he would start to feel sick, feel the unexplainable fear coming out of the dark.

"When the wolves come," Daisy said. To her the angst was like a pack of hunting beasts loping over the horizon, coming to tear them apart.

Erik fought it. Tried to make a stand, using all the mantras and talismans at his possession, still the undefinable terror ensnared him like a trap, a fish in a net, dragged down by a churning undercurrent of *something is wrong, something is wrong,* and no means to fix it other than throwing more and more time at it.

Beside him Daisy shivered, caught in the same net. "Why is this happening?"

"I don't know." He had no answers. He could not help her, could not save her from the wolves plucking her apart, petal by petal.

"I don't know what to do," she said. They clung to each other, shaking it out, trying to beat it back with jokes.

"We have the most amazing pillow talk."

"Right? Most people have a cigarette. We have a panic attack."

They were both free-falling, gripped with a terrible foreboding they could not explain. Shivering, freezing cold, pulling their clothes on and seizing extra blankets.

"Let me spoon you," she said through chattering teeth.

"Please."

She pressed up against his back, knees behind his, her hand flat against his knocking heart. Lying this way, with Erik sandwiched between her hand and her body, pressure from both sides, seemed to be the only calming remedy.

"At least we're both feeling it," he said.

"We're in it together."

"I can't think of anyone I'd rather have a nervous breakdown with than you."

"Oh, honey. You say the sweetest things to me."

"I'm trying to be funny about it. I don't know else what to do."

"I love you. We just have to get each other through it and...fuck sex."

He laughed. "Fuck sex."

"Fuck this."

"Fuck this fucking fucked-up world. Jesus Christ, what the fuck."

"I love you. You're fucked-up and I love you."

"I love your fucked-upness."

They were trying so hard but they were young. Unskilled and powerless at three o'clock in the morning when they ought to be consumed with each other. Instead they were being eaten alive.

PEPPARKAKOR

ERIK WONDERED HOW MANY important conversations had taken place while he was either up a ladder or holding one.

He was holding one now for Joe Bianco, who was replacing a section of Christmas lights on the porch of La Tarasque.

"You having nightmares?" Joe asked.

"Sometimes."

"How often?"

"Few times a week," Erik said.

Joe grunted, yanking at the strand of lights which was caught on a nail. "Every night for me when I came home from Vietnam."

Erik pictured a younger version of Joe, maybe longer hair and a moustache. Bolting out of bed, gasping and sweating, waking up from the war.

"For how long?"

"How long every night? Years. The bad dreams. Jumping at loud noises. Always looking for danger. Years, it took."

Still holding the ladder, a foot on the first rung, Erik looked out over the property, at the last light of day turning the horizon pink and orange. The leaves were dead on the Japanese maples. Francine's gardens were neatly wrapped up for the coming winter. Shrubs encased in burlap, the mulch piled high. Wood smoke hovered on the air.

"Was it different dreams?" he asked. "Or just the same one over and over?"

"A handful of different ones."

"And you still have them?"

"Sometimes. Some things still have an effect. The sound of a helicopter. Not something I hear often but if I do, it makes me nervous. And thunder. I still hate thunder. Catch."

Erik caught the string of dead lights and handed up the new one, then the hammer, which Joe hooked through a belt loop.

"For me it's always the same dream," Erik said. "Just the one where I watch James and can't do anything about it this time."

"What about Daisy?" Joe's accent always seemed stronger when he was speaking names. Daisy's name, especially, which softened and slurred into Dézi.

"What about her?"

"Is she having nightmares?" He glanced down at Erik and raised an eyebrow. "I never pretended you weren't sleeping with her. You want me to start now?"

Erik smiled at his shoes then looked back up at him. "She has them, too," he said. "She wakes me up or I wake her up. I'd say at least three nights out of a week, someone is waking somebody up."

Joe held down his palm and Erik put a few nails into it. "I went to war, Erique, and saw death rain from the skies." He kept speaking, punctuating each quiet sentence with a blow of his hammer. "I took apart land mines so my men could get through, then I put mines back together to kill other men. I blew up bridges and set fire to trees. I saw children gunned down in the fields where they played. I saw women with their bellies sliced open and men with their limbs blown off. I heard screaming in the night I cannot ever un-hear. But I did my tours and came home to build a life where my own child could be safe. I deal with the nightmares because I think of them as extra insurance. I take them on. I can carry the burden, just as long as my family is safe."

He stopped, a forearm on the top of the ladder, the hammer poised in the air. "Then a boy with a gun goes after my daughter. Now it is my own child with her leg sliced open. My Dézi screaming in the night. And it turns out nothing I did made any difference."

Erik looked at him, seeing Daisy's mannerisms and expressions flit in and out of his face.

"What can you do with a world like this? No insurance exists. You can't control who lives or who dies. All I know, Erique, is if my only daughter is having nightmares, then I want you sleeping next to her. Not just because you love her. But because you understand her."

Joe indicated the switch with the handle of the hammer, and Erik threw it. The porch lit up, gold and twinkling.

"Ça y est," Joe said, and carefully came down the ladder. He was struggling with an arthritic hip, resigned it would eventually need to be replaced. He was touchy about being coddled though. Erik helped him fold up the ladder and stow it as unobtrusively as possible.

"Come with me a minute," Joe said as they went back inside. They hung their jackets on the pegs in the mudroom, then Erik followed Joe's limping gait down the hall to the small study next to the living room. The inner sanctum. Joe's desk and bookshelves, antique map collections, and his two beloved Meyer lemon trees by the southwest windows. Both were in bloom, and the citrus smell from the blossoms was strong.

"I'd like you to have something," Joe said, opening a drawer in his desk. He drew out a small box of navy blue leather, a double, flourished rectangle embossed in gold on its top. He handed it to Erik.

Erik looked at him a moment, then opened the lid.

"I can't take this," he said, staring down at the Purple Heart.

"You can," Joe said. "I am giving it to you."

Erik shook his head, bewildered. "Why?"

"Because, Erique, this is what you do for the boy who looks a killer in the eye and calls him by name. The boy who crawls through broken glass to get to your daughter. The boy who stares down her wounds and is there when the thunder wakes her up in the night. Technically speaking, a Purple Heart is not the right medal for this situation. But it's my medal. And I would like you to have it."

Erik couldn't speak.

"And one other thing," Joe said. "If you cross paths with your old man someday, and he has nothing good to say to you? You show him your medal. And you tell him Joe Bianco is proud to call you his son."

If Joe had smacked him in the chest with a two-by-four, Erik could not have been more felled. "You're killing me," he whispered, clutching his decoration.

"You and me both, mon pote."

HE'D COME TO LA TARASQUE for Thanksgiving. They had all come. Will was free because Canadian Thanksgiving is in October. Lucky waved the Bianco's invitation at her mother and conveniently forgot to mention her boyfriend's inclusion. And David came because wherever they went, he followed.

Now the four of them were plonked down at the long farmhouse table in Francine's kitchen, making gnocchi. By intense principle, Francine never made turkey on Thanksgiving, a notion which struck Erik, Lucky and David as bizarre. Almost on the verge of treasonous.

"Turkey is vile," Francine said. "You wait. I'm going to convert each and every one of you tonight."

She and Daisy had prepped one batch of plain gnocchi dough, another with butternut squash, and a third with spinach. Watching Daisy in the kitchen, working side-by-side with Francine, ricing potatoes, kneading dough, laughing, joking, Erik was so happy and so in love, he was practically choking up.

He couldn't take his eyes off her. He didn't know how he'd missed it before, but the shape of Daisy's physique had completely changed. The training of the summer and fall was evident in her lean muscles and athletic curves. Nothing near Lucky Dare's hourglass figure, but still, quite a respectable pair of boobs was up high in her tight sweater. And what she did to a pair of jeans, in Erik's opinion, should have been illegal. She was gorgeous. Moving confidently and competently around the kitchen. Chattering French. And smiling.

A few weeks ago she was given the all-clear to go back to class. And just before they broke for the holiday, she put her left foot into a pointe shoe and went up on her toes. The pain was there—a sharp bite in her inner thigh, an ache in her calf and shin, and a morbid complaint from her ankle. One way or another, those pains would always be there. But now Daisy was back up on pointe, her leg straight and true. Erik always marked it as the day Daisy's smile came back.

She sat down at the table, kissed him carelessly, then joined the others in rolling out snakes of gnocchi dough, yellow, orange and green. They cut the snakes crosswise and rolled the knuckles off the tines of forks, dropping them onto floured wax paper. Daisy could make two dozen in a minute. Will soon got the knack. Lucky, David and Erik just made a mosh of their gnocchi, but Francine walked among them like a nursery school teacher, praising, coaching, ruffling heads. Joe poured wine with a lavish hand. Then he sat quietly, rolling perfect, ridged gnocchi off the tines of his fork. Three yellow, three orange, three green. Each one precisely the same size.

"Erique, darling, tell me," Francine said. "At boarding school I had a friend who was Swedish, and at Christmastime her mother would always send her these wonderful cookies. They had orange zest in them, and black pepper. I loved them, but I forgot what they are called. Do you know these cookies?"

Erik was about to shrug apologetically when his memory nudged him in the side and he heard himself say, "Pepparkakor."

"Yes," Francine said, her face lighting up.

Erik laughed as if he'd sunk a half-court shot at the buzzer. "I totally pulled that out of my ass," he said. "Pepparkakor. They were the Christmas cookies."

Daisy was smiling at him. "Who made them?"

"My grandmother. She made one batch without pepper for me and my brother, and another with just a little pepper for my mom. Then my dad would get his own little box and they'd have both pepper in them and pepper sprinkled on top. He liked them really hot."

"Is she alive?" Francine asked, with wide, hopeful eyes. Mentally she was already tying on an apron and zesting oranges.

"No, she passed away and I'm not in touch with my father's family. But maybe my mother knows someone..."

Francine touched his wrist. "No, no, darling, don't go to any trouble. I'm just happy you remembered the name. Pepparkakor," she said, as if it were a private joke. Then she clapped her hands and surveyed the efforts of her many slaves. "Are we done here? Yes? Let's eat, then."

The gnocchi were thrown into boiling water then divided up into two giant bowls, one tossed with butter and sage, the other with a light tomato sauce. A wooden bowl had an arugula salad, and a platter held a mountain of roasted asparagus. They took plates and served buffet style, then sat at the kitchen table. No candles, no china or silver, no formal place settings. Bread, parmesan cheese and wine bottles went hand to hand, up and down the table. Francine pressed seconds on them. Then thirds. Joe went up an impressive fourth time, sat back down with a tiny portion and ate it in the admiration of his stuffed company.

"Where do you put it all?" David asked, regarding Joe's trim physique. "Do you have a third leg or something?"

Joe smiled conspiratorially at him. "Beaucoup de place dans la bitte."

Francine threw her napkin down the length of the table at him, as the boys let out a yell of laughter. Even Erik, who needed no translation.

"He said there's room in his cock," Daisy mumbled to Lucky.

Lucky threw up her hands. "Cock? How can you even say 'cock' at the same table with your parents? How do you even acknowledge your father *has* a cock?"

Will choked on his wine and turned away. Francine shrieked with laughter and even Joe, normally so deadpan, had his face in a hand, shoulders quaking.

Lucky patted Daisy, who was sprawled on her, laughing. "Francine, can I come live here?" she asked. "Please? Just let me come live here and eat, curse, make lewd jokes and screw in peace. Honestly..."

"I love you," Daisy said, gasping, running her knuckle along her streaming eyes. "Oh my God, I love you." She toppled onto Erik now, giggling. "I love everybody so much..."

YULETIDE CAROL

WITHOUT FAIL, THE BIANCOS always cut down their Christmas tree the day after Thanksgiving.

Snow was in the forecast. Already a cold snap had moved in with a nasty wind chill. Daisy decided to bail. Being outdoors on such a day would make her leg miserable. If she weren't going, Erik didn't want to either. Francine, with a mysterious expression, said she had errands to run. Everyone else bundled up, piled into Joe's truck and headed out. The tree farm was by Sadsbury, which meant they'd be driving through the infamous village of Intercourse. David was beside himself and Joe promised to pull over by the signpost so a picture could be taken.

Daisy went into the kitchen to wash up the lunch dishes. Erik sidled up behind her, slid his arms around her waist, hugging her.

"You're such a mush," she said, rubbing her cheek on his head.

"I am," he said. He moved her hair, kissed her neck, hugged her against him again. He was only having a moment, wanting to hold her, but then Daisy started unbuttoning her shirt. She tilted her head, giving him more of her neck, her fingers finishing the last button and parting the lapels. He slid his palms over her soft skin, unhooking her bra. She turned in his arms and they kissed, groaning open-mouthed with their hands everywhere, seizing it.

She unbuckled and unzipped him, put a hand down his pants. Those strangely disconnected wires came together with a sizzle and he was hard, closed up tight in her fist and wanting. His fingers yanked her jeans open, slid deep and found she was wet, spreading for him, ready.

They kissed and clutched, writhing in a fevered celebration. It hadn't been this way in a long time. This was good. Possibly this could be great.

Holding their clothes together, they ran through the cold to the carriage house. The little rooms were frigid, so they went into the shower and steamed the hell out of the place. Erik's hands ran in soapy strokes all over Daisy's body, with its new weight and the hard curves under wet, silken skin. Within the grappling passion they were relaxed, completely turned on, turned further and further into each other. They were themselves again. Finally.

Erik picked her up, pressed her up against the tiles, her butt resting on the soap ledge and her toes braced on the other wall. He pinned her high so he could lick her breasts while he moved in her. Moved out of her. Held still a teasing moment and then gave it back to her slow. Water and desire crashing on his skin. Perfect.

"God, that's good," Daisy said. A little hitch in her voice as he thrust deeper. She held his wet head, turned his face this way and that as she kissed him. She touched his mouth and he sucked on her fingertips.

"You're so tight," he said.

"It's so good." The air was falling out of her voice. She was going somewhere. He could feel it. Her eyes were filled with green.

"Look at me," he said against her mouth. "I want to see you come."

He was pure grace. A master of her body again. It was like throwing a line out, feeling the hook catch the edge of her climax and reeling it in. Poised on the lip of his own desire, he pushed further into her as he slowly wound the line tighter. Listening for it, feeling for it, waiting for her edge to touch his. It was almost there. Just right there.

"Erik..."

"Come, Dais. Come to me."

Through her mouth like a distant wind blew the sweet sound of no sound. Usually Erik jumped, following it. Now he just let their joined edges crumble away from his feet, let himself dissolve and come with an exquisite slowness. Moaning into her neck as she clung to his shoulders, riding out the tremors.

"Jesus," he said between the aftershocks.

Her fingers dug deep in his wet hair and she kissed him, laughing deep in her throat. "Now that was us."

"Totally us." His arms were spent and he set her down. She took the bar of soap and started working a lather over his body, her hands warm and slippery along his chest and stomach and limbs. He soaped her, then, and they wound arms around each other, sliding and kissing, sending tiny iridescent bubbles through the damp air.

"Now I don't feel bad missing the trip to Intercourse," Erik said as they dried off. Daisy laughed and popped him with the towel.

Sleepy and sated, they peeled open the covers of their bed and slid in. They lay on their sides, Daisy up against Erik's back, her hand on his chest.

"Oh, look," she said. Outside the window, it had started to snow, little icy flakes like glitter, not yet sticking.

Perfect peace. No anxiety. Not a wolf in sight. Pressed tight between Daisy's body and the palm of her hand, Erik felt his bones melt away. A sweet sleep, sweeter than he'd known in months, began to creep over the crown of his head. It laid soothing fingers on his eyes, wove a gorgeous warmth through his muscles.

This, was his last wakeful thought. *This moment. Right here.*

Right now.

This is my life.

THEY NAPPED A LONG TIME. Everyone zonked out in the snowy afternoon, and eventually wandered back into the kitchen for another laughing, boozy dinner.

"Can't we just stay here," Lucky said yet again. She sighed happily, tucked in Will's arms and peeling one of the little clementine oranges from a bowl on the table. His chin rested on her shoulder as he ate the sections she fed him.

"I'm in," David said. "Screw the theater, I'll raise chickens."

They joked around, elaborating the fantasy, but Erik felt serious about it. Still high from sex and refreshed by good sleep, he was firmly under the spell of this wonderful house. He was shaping a dream, a sweet vista unfolding before him. A house like this, a kitchen like this, dinners like this with friends like these. A lifetime of fuck-the-turkey Thanksgivings.

With Daisy.

After dinner they set up the tree. Will built a fire and Joe put on Christmas music—he had an ironclad rule forbidding any holiday songs produced after 1959. The living room filled up with the scent of pine and all the vintage, old school standards. Daisy sang as she passed ornaments up to Erik on the ladder. When Nat King Cole came on, David serenaded them with his version of the Christmas Song:

> *Roast nuts chesting on an open fire.*
> *Nipfrost jacking off your nose.*
> *Yuletide Carol getting laid by the choir...*

The smell of baking began to waft as well. "You remember the errand I ran today?" Francine said. With a flourish, she brought a book out from behind her back and showed the title to Erik—*Lights of the North: Swedish Christmas Traditions.*

"Does it have pepparkakor?" he asked, flipping the pages.

It did, and they were in the oven. Before anyone else was allowed, Francine and Erik tasted them carefully.

"Yes," Francine said.

"I remember these," Erik said. "Wait. Something else. You're supposed to break them. Everybody take one, don't eat it yet."

He remembered. You held the cookie in the palm of your hand, made a wish and pressed down on the center. "If it breaks in three pieces," he said, "your wish will come true."

"What if it doesn't break in three?" David asked.

"You still have cookies." Erik looked around the room at his circle of loved ones, then down at the treat in his palm. Happiness pulled his chest apart. He threw it onto his growing vision of the future. How every Christmas, Francine Bianco would make pepparkakor for him, a tin of rounds flecked with citrus and heat, golden and crisp with memory.

This, he wished, and pressed his finger onto the cookie, which broke cleanly into three pieces. Daisy moved by his side, eyes shining as she held up her hand and showed him her own triumphant thirds.

Later he lay in bed, Daisy's head pillowed on his heart, his hand resting on her cheek. They had made love again and it was gorgeous. Sweet and spicy like the cookie flavors lingering in their mouths. The night was gentle around their spent bodies. Will and Lucky were laughing softly in the other bedroom.

In the dark, Erik whispered, "Do you ever think about marrying me?"

The curve of Daisy's smile filled his palm. "If I marry anyone, it'll be you," she said.

He scooped up a handful of her hair and held it to his face. He smiled into its damp softness, his tongue tingling with orange zest and pepper and Daisy.

NO HEROICS

"I WANT TO DANCE 'The Man I Love' again," Daisy said.

Erik was startled, thinking it was the last thing she'd want. "Why?"

A ripple of defiance along Daisy's jaw and her eyes flared. "Because fuck him. That's why."

It was early January, the beginning of another semester. The two couples were at Jay Street, having pizza and discussing the advent of the spring dance concert.

Will stopped chewing, looking at Daisy. Then he slowly swallowed his food, nodding his head. "Three months," he said. "We have three months."

"You're physically ready?" Erik asked.

Daisy nodded. "I can do it."

Lucky was only picking at her dinner. She didn't seem to be feeling well. "Are you mentally ready?" she asked.

"I am." Daisy looked at Will. "I need to dance it. Otherwise, it's..."

Will put his hand on her head. "I'm in," he said. "I want this. And you're right. Fuck him."

"What does Kees say?" Erik asked.

"He's on board with the idea," Daisy said. "But he has to get permission from the trust."

Who Cares? was copyrighted and could not be performed anywhere without express permission of the Balanchine Trust. Marie Del'Amici had gone to great lengths to secure permission last year. All Kees could do was ask again.

"We got it," Daisy told Erik a few days later. "The trust will let us do it. Kees had a meeting with Michael Kantz and it's final, we'll dance it."

"Nothing else?"

"For me? No. It's enough. No heroics, just the one pas de deux with Will."

"Well, I call it pretty heroic," Erik said.

He was busy with his own project: an art student wanted to present his senior portfolio in the Black Box Theater, making an interactive, multi-medium experience of art, poetry, music and light. Erik was commissioned as lead designer. It felt good to be immersed in the creative process, getting his hands dirty, getting his mind dirty, helping someone build a dream.

Class. Rehearsals. He worked, and Daisy worked. They came home at night to Jay Street where the two couples were living all the time. David and Neil came over almost every evening. John Quillis was a regular visitor. They ate together, studied together, gathered close and took care of each other.

"Lucky's pregnant," Daisy whispered in bed, one night toward the end of January.

"I know, Will told me. Said the condom broke over Thanksgiving."

"Lucky doesn't want to have it."

"And Will does."

"It's the exact opposite of what I expected. I thought she'd be the one to..."

"So did I."

She sighed, moved closer up against Erik's back. Her fingers played with the charms on his necklace. "I guess it's one of those things where you think you'll feel one way, and then it happens, and it's all different."

"I think it's the shooting," he said. "Life is so tenuous. Lucky's afraid of it and Will wants to fight it."

"You're right. God, I feel terrible."

"I feel helpless."

"Nothing we can do. Except just be here. Be ready to do what they need when they need it."

A week went by, a week of tense, whispered conversations and the sound of tears through thin walls. Will was spending nights alone at Colby Street. Jay Street felt lopsided, like a table missing its fourth leg. At the same time, the little house felt immobilized for war. Poised and braced, balanced on a single eggshell. Wolves paced on the horizon, primed for the hunt.

Erik woke up one night, not to tears or wolves, but a warm thickness in his blood, a pleasantly familiar feeling in his lap. Daisy had a hand down his sweatpants, stroking a very cheerful erection.

"Good evening," she whispered against his temple.

"What's up," he said, his eyes closed.

"You."

"How 'bout that."

"This is impressive."

"Thank you," he said, his voice still slurred with sleep. "I worked a long time on it."

She was pushing his pants down his hips, and pulling him toward her. "You should put that in me."

"I should, right?"

"Yes."

They rolled. She was pulling her own clothes away and aside. Half asleep, he took her by the waist and languidly worked himself into her heat. Her breath left her chest with a dry little puff as her butt settled into his lap. Sweetness radiated off the nape of her neck.

"I love when you wake me up," he murmured. He slid his hand under her shirt, filled it with one warm breast. She sighed and pushed further back into his lap.

And then a startling noise from outside their door, a knocking into the wall. A human sound. They flinched a little, then froze in the embrace. Daisy looked back over her shoulder. Erik put a finger to his lips.

Footsteps. Another thump. Silence.

More silence.

Erik touched his fingertip to Daisy's lips. She drew it into her mouth and pushed back hard on him. He started to move in her again. Throwing out the hook, looking for her edge. Hot, wet, squeezing pressure all around him. Sugar. Skin.

Noise again, just beyond their door, and now a cry.

"Daisy."

Daisy pushed up on her elbow, looked over at the door. "Luck?"

"Daisy." Louder. Urgent. An edge of panic.

"Stay here," Daisy whispered, pulling her shirt down and her pants up and hurrying out. Erik sat up, strained to hear something even as the sound of his own quickening heartbeat filled his ears.

"Oh my God. Erik, help me..."

He exploded out of bed, tying his own pants, tripped over something as he burst into the hallway. Daisy came flying out of the bathroom. "She's having a miscarriage. I need to get Will, stay here with her."

"Wait." But she was down the stairs and seconds later, the back door slammed. Erik stared at the floor. The drops of blood on the scuffed wooden planks. A trail leading to the bathroom. His heartbeat grew louder, heavier, a sledgehammer against the inner wall of his chest. He had to go in there. He had to.

Do it. Now.

Blood like a constellation of stars across the white-tiled bathroom floor. Lucky sat on the toilet, wearing nothing but a T-shirt, hunched over, her face in her hands. Erik reeled back, hesitating. This was a bathroom. A private, insanely intimate place of bodily function and his entire instinct screamed at him to get out of here and leave the lady alone. Don't embarrass her.

But this lady with the blood-streaked legs was Lucky. The same Lucky who got down in the blood on the stage floor and saved Daisy's life.

Erik knelt down on the lilac shag rug and gathered her into his arms. She was crying. "I changed my mind."

"I got you, Lucky. I got you, hold onto me."

"No, please, I changed my mind. Don't let it—don't let it happen, please, I changed my mind."

But then a slow and steady dripping in the water beneath her, and she screamed against Erik's shoulder, not in pain but in despair. Her whole body contracted desperately, trying to hold it back, hold onto the baby.

Erik yanked a bath towel from the rack, wrapped it around Lucky, hiding the bowl and her legs, trying to shroud this in some kind of dignity. He held her tight as she hung on his neck.

"Let it go, honey," he whispered against her hair. "Let it go. Hold onto me, I got you. Let it go."

Her body relaxed in his arms, he felt her surrender. Another cascade of drips, muffled beneath the towel, and Lucky buried her face in his neck, moaning like a wounded animal.

A commotion of footsteps up the stairs and Will was there then. He slid in on his knees, and Erik carefully handed Lucky off to him, scooting back and out of the way.

Will buried his hands in her hair and rocked her, holding her head on his chest. Lucky was sobbing. "I'm sorry, I'm sorry."

Will picked up her face, kissed it all over. He was crying too. "It's not your fault," he said. "It's not your fault, honey. It's all right."

"I changed my mind, I wanted it."

"I know. It's all right. I just need you to be all right. I just need you, nothing else. It's all right, Luck. I just need you..."

Erik helped Will put Lucky in his car to take her to the campus health center. He stood on the porch, watching the red tail lights disappear down the street and turn a corner.

They always leave in the middle of the night, he thought.

He went back inside.

Daisy was in the little front hall, wrapped in a throw blanket and shivering. Erik shut the door, then lurched into her. She opened her arms and caught him. They slid down to the floor, clutching one another.

"Thank you," she whispered. "Thank you for helping her. You were so good. You were so good to her."

He was shaking so hard his bones hurt. The thought of the blood in the bathroom was making him feel sick. "I can't go back up there," he whispered, filled with shame about it, feeling cowardly and weak but he couldn't, he could not go back in there.

"What's the matter? Tell me."

"The blood. I can't, Dais, I can't do it again."

"I'll take care of it. No, no, it's all right, I understand." Her kisses on his face, her hands soothing on his head. "I'll clean it up. It won't upset me."

The wolves were on him. They had him by all four limbs, one tearing open his chest, another devouring his belly, a third at his throat. They had him. "God, Dais, what's happening to me?"

She wrapped him in the blanket, in her arms and legs, and her hair. "It's all right. It's all right..."

They leave in the middle of the night.

He couldn't shake the foreboding thought, couldn't discern who he meant by "they." They left. It left. Everything left. Nothing would stay in place. It was a constant clutch and grab and fight like hell to hold onto anything good anymore.

BEGINNING OF THE END

THE WINTER WAS COLD, bleak and relentless. The sun never seemed to break through the veil of sickly grey clouds pressed down over Lancaster. All ice and slush and mud, a dirty film on the sidewalks and windows. A dull malaise permeated the student body. The whole campus seemed to be shivering, sunken in on itself, looking for warmth within instead of reaching out to build a fire.

Will found Erik in the bathroom late one night, sitting on the floor with his head in his hands.

"Dude, you all right?"

"Yeah."

"What happened?"

"I don't know," Erik said. "Dais and I were fooling around, her period came in the middle of it and I...got all light-headed." He blew out a huge breath. "Can't shake this one off."

Will ran cold water on a washcloth and handed it to him. "Not surprising."

"Her period never freaked me out before."

"You weren't having nightmares about her bleeding to death before. Girls weren't miscarrying in your arms before."

Erik grunted, holding the cloth to the back of his neck, his eyes sweeping the tile floor and remembering blood. Lately, he saw blood everywhere.

He wasn't doing well.

In the apartment on Jay Street, nobody was doing well. Lucky was withdrawn, a shadow of herself. Even her curls lost their spring—they gave up, and unwound into sad, mournful tendrils.

Will looked haunted. Nobody had ever seen him so subdued and distracted, even as he wrapped himself in work and preparation for the spring concert.

Daisy chain-smoked and lost weight, her body diminishing back to ballerina fragility. She was jittery and frenetic, prone to weeping for no reason. She lost her stillness.

Erik was smoking regularly, too. He buried himself in work, buried the struggle against constant anxiety and the never-ending visions of blood. The nightmares came regularly. He woke up Daisy. She woke him. Sex was infrequent and unremarkable.

David's mean streak was back. He regressed into old tactics, like a child acting out, looking for love by asking for it in the most unloving ways. But everyone was too consumed with their own wars to pay much attention.

They gathered together in the evenings, yet each struggled alone. The winter was hard and long. One night, as they sat around watching TV, David brazenly cut cocaine out in the open, razoring the snowy powder into neat snakes on a little mirror on the coffee table.

Had the color of cocaine been the irresistible temptation? The pristine whiteness? Its seductive purity?

Erik flinched at the harsh, sucking sound of David doing two lines.

"Anyone?" David said.

They stared. Not a glance was exchanged. Everyone was making up their own mind.

"I'm good," Will said. A beat of silence. Then he stood up. "On second thought, fuck everything." He went over.

"Fuck this fucking world," Lucky said, and crossed.

Daisy got off Erik's lap. "I don't care anymore."

Erik followed. "I could get shot tomorrow. Screw it."

They knelt around the altar of the coffee table. Will patted David's head, and David smiled like a well-praised puppy. He was the high priest now: King David, singer of songs, bearer of gifts and bringer of comfort.

In later years, Erik viewed that night as the beginning of the end of the world. The descent into hell.

And he never forgot David had opened the gate.

EMOTIONAL HAMBURGER

THE NIGHT OF THE spring concert, Daisy and Will's comeback, Kees asked Erik if he would mind having company in the lighting booth.

"I need to be somewhere soundproof so I can cry in peace."

"You just want to be with me, Keesja."

"Yeah. And if anyone tries anything the least bit cute, you and I will take their asses *out*."

Erik who was a bit of a controlled wreck, could think of no one he'd rather have in the booth with him than Kees, who was a blatant wreck.

Fate was kind, putting the anniversary of the shootings, the nineteenth of April, on a Monday. The ceremonial recognition wouldn't overlap with the concert, which was scheduled for the following weekend.

The contemporary division had the first act. Daisy and Will's pas de deux would be the first number in the second act. During intermission, Erik sought out Joe and Francine Bianco, standing with them at the back of the theater, pressed on all sides by the crowd. The space buzzed with conversation and anticipation.

They chattered nervously at each other, laughing too hard and too loud. Adrenaline kept flooding Erik's chest as the minutes ticked by. It seemed it would never be time. And then it was nearly time. His heart was pounding. He caught Kees's eye and tapped his watch. Joe tugged his earlobe. Francine kissed him.

Erik went back into the booth and Kees followed. They drew on their headsets. Erik rubbed his cold hands together, chafing his fingers, blowing on them.

"Wat denk je, mijn vriend?"

Erik smiled. "I'm dying. How about you?"

"I am an emotional hamburger."

A crackle in Erik's ear. "Five minutes," David said. "Flash the house-lights, Fish. Neil, intermission music ready to fade out."

Erik reached and slid the master switch, dimming the house down, then up again. Once more. The murmur of the milling audience intensified, then people began filing back into seats. Erik and Kees fidgeted relentlessly, tapping pencils and fingers, jiggling knees, spinning in their chairs, inhaling and exhaling loudly, over and over, trying to whittle away these last, agonizing minutes.

"Me amas, Neil?" Erik said into his headset.

"Te amo, Pescado," Neil said from backstage left.

"Dave, how we doing back there?"

"Nobody's thrown up yet," David said.

"Great, I get to puke alone," Kees muttered.

"Where's Dais?" Erik asked.

"Warming up."

"Tell her I love her."

"Tell me first," David said.

Erik smiled into the headset. "All my enemies whisper together against me," he said.

"They imagine the worst for me, saying, 'He will never get up from the place where he lies.'"

"Raise me up, that I may repay them."

"For my enemy does not triumph over me."

"Amen," Kees said.

"Amén," Neil said.

"Now tell her I love her," Erik said.

"And grab both their asses for me," Kees said.

"With pleasure." Another crackle and David was gone. Erik stared at his own reflection in the booth glass, fingertips rubbing his chin.

"Tums?" Kees offered him a couple from the bottle kept in the booth.

"Thanks, I've already had eleven tonight."

"You guys keep booze back here?"

Erik smiled, but his eyes slid away guiltily. David had cut a couple lines before coming to the theater. Erik had passed. Barely. The idea of being high at Daisy's return to the stage was unthinkable to him but damn, it was hard to pass up.

She was a sick mistress, Lady Cocaine. The rush to the brain, the dizzying clarity, the euphoria of everything being all right. But she got bored of you so quickly, and then left without saying goodbye. In her cold, slushy wake, you crawled, a strung-along, anxious mess. Erik was starting to hate her.

And he was starting to need her.

"Bring down the house," David said over the headset.

Erik's chest tightened, released fiery hot waves into his stomach and arms.

Kees held out a formal hand. "Merde."

Erik shook it. "Merde." He brought down the master switch with his left hand while his right hand hovered, fingers poised over a section of levers as if he were about to play a chord on the piano.

The curtain rose with a velvety hum.

"Lights up," David said. Erik pushed the levers forward and the cyclorama began to glow a rich, twilight blue.

"Cue sound."

Out floated the lush, measured tones of the introduction to "The Man I Love." From the upstage left wing came Daisy and Will. She in her pink dress, bourréeing in fifth, her hand tucked in Will's elbow, her head tilted toward but not quite on his shoulder. Tall and tender in black, Will walked beside her, his maimed hand covering her fingers.

And then the auditorium erupted.

Both Kees and Erik jumped in their seats, reared backward, open-mouthed in shock as the applause came roaring down from the balcony and met with the ovation coming from the orchestra seats, whirling together in a thunderstorm of clapping, stamping triumph drowning out the music.

"Jesus," Kees said, stumbling to stand up, his hands on top of his head.

Erik stood up as well, leaning over the console to peer out at the audience. "What is *happening...?*"

He scanned the crowd: on their feet, applauding and whistling.

Will and Daisy reached center stage. She turned on her toes, bour-réeing backward, still with the choreography, but the music was lost.

"Oh boy." He could hear David exclaiming low in his ear. "Holy shit. Holy shit. I don't believe this."

Daisy kept moving, her feet lightly gathering up the inches of the stage floor, her arms liquid patterns. She turned under Will's arm, his other twining around her waist and she fell back, languid, melting, her eyes never leaving his. Will caught her, but clumsily, he was breaking down, breaking out of the dance, his face crumpling. Instead of bringing Daisy up into the next phrase, he brought her up and crushed her to his chest. She came off pointe, stood in her flat, pedestrian feet. Her shoulders were heaving, shaking and she buried her face into Will's shirt. The intensity of the applause rose up another level. People were yelling now, as if at a rock concert.

Erik's hands closed up his mouth and nose as the enormity of it dropped onto his shoulders.

Kees put an arm around him. "Good Lord, I haven't seen an ovation like this since I watched Cynthia Gregory in *Swan Lake.* And that was after the show, not before." His other arm joined the first, hugging tight as Erik cried into the steeple of his fingers.

Neil called over his headset, "Dave, what do we do?"

"Kill the music. Just run it back to the start. Stand by, everyone, stand by, let's just let this pan out."

Erik didn't think it could possibly last any longer, yet on and on it went. Will was whispering to Daisy, coaxing her head up off his shoulder, and finally he got her to turn around. They stood there then, clasped in each other's arms, stood and faced it, accepted the moment as rightfully theirs. Will was shaking his head over and over, laughing, wiping his eyes. Daisy's face had bloomed with her full, bright beautiful smile.

Erik leaned and put one hand flat on the glass of the booth, palm to the stage. He usually did this at curtain call, but tonight everything was out of order, upside-down and unbelievable.

Daisy wormed one of her arms free from Will's embrace. She touched her fingers to her mouth and turned her palm out back to Erik.

He thought his heart was going to explode. He needed no other high. This was enough.

This is my life.

A whole minute went by before David spoke again. "Erik, can you hear me?"

Erik ignored the tissue Kees held out and roughly wiped his wet face on his upper arm as he sat down. "Yeah, I can hear you."

"Start taking the stage lights down. Leave the cyc lit."

"Lights going down."

As the stage dimmed, Will and Daisy retreated into silhouette, disappearing through the upstage wing. The applause petered out as the audience sat.

"One day you'll tell your grandchildren about this moment," Kees said.

David waited another fifteen seconds of murmured shuffling and blown noses, and then gave the cue. "Sound up."

And they began again.

TORQUED AND SHADOWY

DAISY COULD BARELY get out of bed after the concert.

No more driving force toward a goal, nothing to work for or look forward to. She had relentlessly pursued recovery, then rehearsal and finally performance. The curtain was down and the theater of her heart sat empty. She went around empty-eyed and depressed, wandering lost in the vast, dark cavern of her dreams. The light came back into her face when she was on cocaine, but only for interludes growing more and more fleeting and requiring more and more juice.

David brought new offerings for the coffee table altar at Jay Street. They all smoked up one night and then, as if bestowing communion, David laid ecstasy pills in each of their palms.

"We call this a high roll," he said. "You can thank me later."

They all locked eyes and swallowed. In a few minutes, Erik felt as though he were swimming in caramel. Everything—*everything* was wonderful. He stared open-mouthed as the world turned inside-out and revealed all its beautiful mystery.

Ecstasy, he thought, and with a profound flash of insight, he got it. He understood *everything* and he wanted to touch and love all of it.

In this psychedelic, sugar-glazed euphoria, he and Daisy practically floated upstairs. Her eyes filled with green swirls, her smile wide open, giggling and carefree. They kissed with laughing tongues and lips, deep in one another's mouths. Erik couldn't get out of his clothes fast enough.

He was in love with the world. So horny, Daisy's eyes on him could make him come. He could rub up against the air and come.

Daisy gave him a small push and he fell back on the bed. Hard as iron and melting soft into the blankets. She crawled along him, naked and lucious, her kiss pulling him up, drawing him into her. He crossed the boundary behind her eyes and he was in her head, kissing him, who was her, which was us.

I begin where you end, I end and you begin and we are forever. I just want to fuck you forever.

A stab of anxiety, like a bloodstain on a white tablecloth. The euphoria tilted under his feet. He was going to fall off. He dug his fingers into her hair, clenching his fingers through it, holding on.

"Do that again," she murmured.

He pulled and released on her hair, sucking gently on her tongue. She moaned in her chest. "Again. Harder."

He kept kissing her, clasping the lengths of her hair in his fists and pulling tight. She straddled his thigh, grinding down, sliding along him. Her hand gripped his cock tight. He was so hard. He wanted in but he wanted to see it through, watch her rub one out. She was getting off on him. He could tell where her sweet spot was hitting his knee. So soft and wet.

"Come," he whispered, pulling her head back hard. "Make that sweet little pussy come for me."

He dragged her until the pain revealed itself in her liquid eyes and she came against his leg. It was gorgeous. She came with her whole body, even her voice. Wild and terrible it careened off the walls, like a goddess giving birth to the world. His own voice rose up to meet it and he exploded hot in her fist, overflowing like caramel between their bodies, it was so beautiful...

He let go her hair and was mesmerized by the strands wafting free from his fingers. Later he was slightly disturbed by what he'd done. Yet his veins were filled with a sick need to do it again.

And do it harder.

From there it spiraled out of control. They got addicted to those high rolls, and with no more sweetness to be found in their sex, they delved instead into a vein of bitter gratification. They unplugged the

Christmas lights and drew the curtains, pinning the edges so not a chink of light penetrated. A rolled up towel along the bottom of the door and the room went pitch black. The infinite cavern of Daisy's nightmares. A thick, tangible darkness where they went at each other, scratching and clawing, balanced on the edge between enjoyable discomfort and outright violence. Distilling the pleasure out of pain. It felt good to hurt. It was normal to hurt. Joy was fleeting and treacherous but pain was dependable. It sucked, but you could trust it to suck.

In the dark Daisy yanked Erik's head back and kissed him hard enough to draw blood. It should have repelled him. Instead, as soon as he tasted it, he was like a shark tracking wounded prey. He took her down to the floor and he was on her, high and crazed, torqued and shadowy. He pinned her fast and took her hard. His teeth on her bones, blood in his mouth, his weight holding her down in the endless dark. Lost in the gleeful, twisted part of his soul that wanted to fuck her into pieces so no one could ever hurt her again.

Me. Only me. Only I love you and only I hurt you.

But hurt required feeding. Like a drug habit. It slid around corners of the bedroom and demanded more. Hurt was the lord God and they would have no other verbs before it. Hurt stood over their beds, exacting devotion and sacrifice.

"Tie my hands," she said one night. And he did.

"Pretend you're raping me," she said another night. And he did.

"Look at me," he said, a hand at her throat as he thrust hard and deep. His index finger pushed her chin up and her mouth closed. "Look only at me."

Night after night he pushed her to where he thought she'd surely say no. Too much. Enough. No more.

"More," she said, not taking her eyes from his. "Harder. Erik, *please...*"

Only he had what she needed and she begged him for it. She gave him purpose. She was the antidote to all the useless helplessness of his dreams.

Then came a night when Erik, higher than he'd ever been in his life, pulled out of Daisy and turned her roughly onto her stomach. His whisper coiled in the sludgy dark like a viper. "I want to fuck your ass."

She didn't say a word. He heard the scrape of a drawer, some rifling around and then a condom was in his hand. His drugged brain could barely keep up with his body, registering what was happening five beats after it had happened. In this surreal fugue state, he was stretched out on her back, worming her legs apart and pushing into her unyielding body.

"Let me in." He didn't recognize his own voice.

Her fingers twined with his beneath the pillow, clenched to the breaking point. Her neck arched in pain. He took a small, reverent taste of the tight, hot agony and had to fight not to come. He moved further into her and she moaned. With his mouth he moved her hair away from her neck, set his teeth at her nape. "Does it hurt?"

"So bad," she said, her voice thick with arousal.

He dug in with his teeth, admiring his own controlled skill. He slid one hand beneath her body. She spread her legs for him, opened up slick and swollen. Her lips caressed the tattoo on his wrist. "I feel alive when it hurts."

"So do I. Only when it hurts"

"I want to come."

"Come, Dais. Come for me. Come until it hurts."

He came just as she did. Brain joined body and he came so hard he saw the rear side of his skull, saw back to yesterday and out into next week. He lay on her, breathing hard, wondering if he'd pushed himself too far and he was cut loose in space, his sanity roaming lost around the universe, never to return.

It wasn't such a bad notion.

Gradually a tingling returned to his limbs and a dull ache between his eyebrows convinced him he was indeed present.

"Get out of me," Daisy said drowsily, as if asking for an extra blanket. Erik carefully got out, chucked the condom, then lay down again and didn't move. They sprawled there, passed out, sated and spent.

They woke up and turned to each other, fingers seeking each other's faces in the dark. They couldn't see, but by touch they knew no joy was in their eyes.

"We make love and it's horrible afterward," Erik whispered. "We're sweet to each other and it makes us physically sick. But if you bite me or scratch me or draw blood, it's fine. If I pin you down or pretend to rape you or fuck you in... We go right to sleep. It's peaceful then. And I don't understand."

"What's happening to us?" In the dark, her voice was small and lost.

"We're better than this."

"We used to be."

"I can't do this anymore," Erik said. He got up and flung open the curtains, flooding the room with weak light from the street. "No more. I'm not hurting you in bed again. I won't."

He plugged in the Christmas lights and Daisy began to cry. Erik drew her out of bed and into the shower. She cried as he washed her hair and her body. He cried over the welts he'd raised on her back and the fingerprinted bruises on her upper arms and thighs. Back in her room they stripped the linens off her bed and remade it. Lay down in the clean sheets, weeping tired, defeated tears.

He held her all night. She slept all the next day. Erik could not get her out of bed. He came downstairs after his third attempt, sat on the bottom step in the living room with his head in his hands.

Will and Lucky came in the front door. Lucky took one look and squeezed past Erik to go upstairs. Will sat on the step next to Erik. Put arms around him.

"It's all right, Fish." Will's cheek moved against the top of Erik's head. His hand rubbed circles between Erik's shoulder blades. "It's all right."

"I feel like it's all falling apart," Erik whispered.

"It's this place," Will said. "I can't stand being here anymore. We all need to leave. And we will. Soon. It's almost over, Fish. You'll get out of here with Daisy and go somewhere new."

Whatever Lucky said or did, Daisy got up. She pulled strength out of some hidden, bottomless reservoir and rose to do what she had to do. Her mouth was set and her eyes flat blue. She was in the war room. She went to class and studied for finals. The curtains of her room remained open. She and Erik lay in bed at night, clasped in each other's arms and staring. It was all they had left. They stopped feeding the hurt and found they weren't hungry for anything else. So they stopped having sex.

Just stopped.

FISHY, FISHY IN THE BROOK

IT WAS HOT the May afternoon when Erik went to David's place, looking for coke. He found David in bed.

With Daisy.

No words. No altercation. Not then. Erik stood in the doorway as David flipped a handful of covers over his and Daisy's bodies. Then the three of them simply stared at each other, frozen, as the world exploded in slow-motion.

Erik didn't know what made him turn around and leave. Shock, he supposed. Or maybe a human body could only take so much stress before it went numb. He felt numb walking down the stairs, walking through the living room of David's apartment, going out the way he came in. He closed the front door without a sound. Politely. So as not to disturb. What a fucked-up thing to do.

He had trouble reconstructing what happened next. More shock, he guessed. His mind shutting down what was impossible to comprehend. Up in his hot, airless room, he sat on the bed staring at the wall. Trying to determine if he indeed saw what he'd just seen. He couldn't feel his limbs. His face burned, his lips tingled, but the rest of his body didn't seem to be present. He was nothing but a head. A head trying to process an impossible math problem where one plus one equaled three.

I just saw David fucking my girlfriend.

He would have laughed. It was absurd.

Then the problem turned grammatical. A matter of tenses to solve here.

He fucked my girlfriend.

He is fucking my girlfriend.

Will he fuck my girlfriend again?

He could not wrap his mind around it. The problem was unsolvable. He rearranged the factors.

Daisy fucked David.

He stood up. Now the rest of his body was back and filled with a shaking nausea.

She slept with him. She's sleeping with him. She will keep sleeping with him.

It was not only unsolvable, but intolerable. He stood up, hands on the crown of his head, pressed down to keep his mind contained.

What would he do?

"It's this place," Will had said. "We all need to get out of here."

He needed to get away. Yes. He picked up his backpack. He could not stay here. Not in this room. Not in this house.

Not in this town. Not anymore.

A panic began to creep over his head. He had to get out of here. Recklessly he stuffed in some clothes. Random things. He didn't even think. He was getting out. He couldn't stay.

He stopped. Blinking. What was happening? What had just happened?

How could she do it? Like a wet bar of soap, the idea she would cheat on him flopped and slipped through his hands. He couldn't catch it. It made no sense. They were together all the time. They were *together.* They were in love, they were bonded. Their love defied description. They were each other's sole means to survive.

They were inked into each other's skin.

What in hell had just happened?

From the window. Voices and action outside. He leaned on the sill and looked out at the backyard. Daisy was hurrying up her back steps. Little blue skirt, a white shirt. Her arms crossed over her middle, her head down. Hurrying. Scurrying.

And a few steps behind, David.

David, following Daisy. Into her kitchen. She was trying to get away. He was following.

Erik's eyes narrowed.

Betrayal had refused to stay in his hands, but the notion of theft slammed into Erik's chest and he crossed his arms over it, holding on tight. Now he had his answer. It was David. David wanted Daisy. He'd always wanted her. He wanted her but she went to Erik. And David had bided his time, waiting for a chance. A chance to take her away, chew her up and spit her at Erik's feet.

He should have known.

He never should have trusted David.

"You only want what you can't have," Erik whispered.

Erik closed his eyes. Opened them again. Looked down at his feet and the image of Daisy there, used, thrown out, thrown back at him because David was done playing with her.

"You son of a bitch," he whispered.

Outside, the sky was pale grey, veiled in sickly clouds. The heat was intensifying. Erik walked through a cloud of tiny buzzing insects as he came through the hedge and into Daisy's yard.

Through the screen he saw David, sitting with his back to the door—at Daisy's kitchen table.

Sitting in Erik's place, smoking.

I get a panic attack after sex with Daisy, Erik thought. *David gets the cigarette.*

He yanked the door open. David whirled in his chair, white-faced and trembling. He stood up, crushing the half-smoked butt into a saucer.

"I can explain."

Erik stared at him.

"This is all my fault," David said hoarsely. "It's my fault, Fish, not hers."

Erik advanced on him, fingers opening and closing in fists. "Fishy, fishy in the brook," he said. "What to do with David the crook?"

David started to speak but Erik hadn't come here to listen. He seized David by the shirt collar and threw him against the wall.

Though the fight was vicious, his brain was oddly detached. Off sitting in a corner, making up little rhymes to finish *fishy, fishy...*

Not his to take, but still he took.

Blood spraying from under his hands. David's blood spattering onto the walls of Daisy's kitchen.

I found you in bed, and the walls shook.

"You like fucking her?" he said. The dark, dangerous voice coming out of his throat was alien to him. "Did it feel good? I bet it did, you son of a bitch..."

Pots and pans clattering from the counter, a shining arc of silverware across the floor, chairs skittering sideways.

For King David, I was forsook.

"Hope it felt good," he muttered. "Because it's the last good thing you're gonna feel in your life, Alto."

Hands on his shoulders then, pulling at him. Daisy's hands. She was screaming at him to stop. He shook her off violently, hoping she stayed to watch.

As I kill you, let her look.

A crunching clatter and a cry of pain behind him as Daisy fell onto the floor. And David, who had been passive up until then, punched him. Hard in the jaw, as if defending the woman he loved. Erik's eyes burned. His aloof brain smashed together like two cymbals and he turned back on David in a rage of fists and kicks.

Then different hands were on him, stronger ones. "Let go, Fish."

A forearm across his collarbones and an index finger set into the hollow of his throat, pressing down against the nest of nerve endings there.

"Enough," Will said, his voice a low growl. His finger pressed down harder—a defense move he'd learned in Taekwondo. Fiery pins and needles shot down Erik's arms, leaving him no choice but to let go.

"I'll kill you," he cried, kicking David's side.

"Come on," Will said, pulling him back. "You're only giving him what he wants."

Erik got another kick into David's ribs with the hard toe of his work boot. He felt the soft give of flesh and the resistance of bone. "I'll fucking *kill* you."

"Come on, Fish, let's get you out of here."

Erik fought, struggled, writhed, but Will's strength was absolute and his arms were a straitjacket about Erik's torso.

As he was being dragged away, Erik looked back just once. His eyes passed through David, lying in a bloody heap on the floor, and found Daisy.

Daisy, on her knees in the wreck of her kitchen. Daisy, her hands in her hair, pulling it from her temples. Daisy, her mouth open, and those eyes, dear Lord, those beautiful blue eyes he'd stared into so many times, making time itself stop, making the world go away.

The eyes he had let look into his soul.

He'd trusted her. He'd put himself into her hands, been vulnerable with her in the dark of night, let her see him at his weakest. And she'd gone to David.

Through the doorway he stared into her eyes. Time did not stop. The world stayed as it was. The connection was gone. The bond was lost. She'd killed it.

"Erik," she said, her hands coming out of her hair, falling into her lap.

Then the screen door slammed shut.

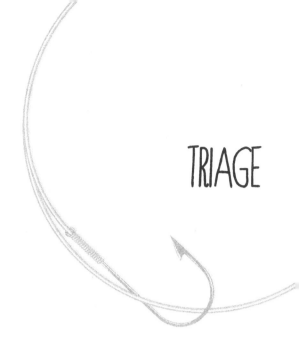

TRIAGE

"I DON'T WANT TO see her," he said to Will.

"You shouldn't," Will said. "Cool off. Nobody will fault you if you get out of Dodge a little while."

Erik sat on his bed, staring straight ahead.

"Fish," Will said. He crouched down by Erik's feet. "There's an explanation."

Erik flicked his eyes to Will. Stared at him.

"I mean," Will said. He floundered for words, reaching to run his maimed hand through hair no longer there. "This was just something reckless and stupid. You can work it out..."

Erik looked away. "Leave me alone."

Will shut the door. Erik remained in his room the rest of the day, with the door shut, although the house was empty. Will did not come back. Erik lay on his bed, staring at the ceiling, watching it get dark. The silence inside the house screamed. The ambient noises from outside puzzled him. How could the world just be going by? Didn't anyone realize what had happened?

The slam of a screen door made him sit up. He looked out the window, through the hedge to the girls' backyard. Daisy was sitting on the back stairs. He could see her white shirt in the dusk, and the glowing red tip of her cigarette. The minutes slipped by as she smoked, her arms around her shins, chin on her knees. She lit a second cigarette off the end of the first and smoked it. Then a third. Her gaze never moved from the windows of Colby Street.

I know you're there. Come talk to me...

He could go over.

They could smoke and talk. She could explain.

They could work it out.

He fell back down on the bed again, unable to stop the tears. Great, shuddering sobs in his chest and throat, a lament smothered into the pillow. She was sitting there smoking, wearing the same skirt and shirt that now smelled of David. David was all over her body. Cells in her mouth, fingerprints on her skin, semen dripping out of her. She'd taken her clothes off for David. She'd opened her mouth for David, opened her legs for David. She'd let David inside her, moved under him like a lover. Her arms up around his neck, her knees hugging his hips.

Was he supposed to sit there and smoke and listen to her explain all that? And then say it was all right?

How could you do it? Erik went to the window. Stared through his tears to the tiny, balled-up figure on the back steps. *How could you? What were you thinking, what made you go? What did you need?*

Then he knew what the explanation was.

She needed the pain Erik wouldn't give her anymore.

He was useless to her.

She went to get it from David. Worse than letting David love her, she'd let David *hurt* her. She'd betrayed both Erik's love and Erik's pain.

It wasn't to be borne.

"It's over," he said. "We're finished. You're useless to me now."

He drew in a deep breath, balling his hands into fists, setting his jaw. *Feel nothing.*

He picked up the backpack he'd started filling and set it on the bed.

It's over. You will feel nothing. Neither love nor pain. Ever again.

He began to gather more things together.

Through the night he sorted and packed. A swift and brutal triage of what had to be taken and what could be left forever. He pulled together his belongings and pushed aside Daisy's, letting some fall to the floor and chucking others into the garbage. He loaded trash bags and duffles into his car, and before the sun came up, he left.

"I will explain," he said to his mother, six hours later. "But not now. I'm home but pretend I'm not here. I just need some space. Then I'll explain."

He shut himself up in his room and slept for two days. The house was quiet around him. Christine was working. Pete wasn't home from college yet. Lena was there, though. She lay on the floor by Erik's bed, occasionally putting her paws on the mattress and licking his face. He pushed her away.

The morning of the third day, he summoned his will and got up. He was brushing his teeth, staring in the mirror at his haggard face and scruffy growth of beard, when his hand flew up to his neck.

His necklace was gone.

He dropped the brush, minty foam dripping from his mouth. His hands felt his neck and chest in wild desperation.

Gone.

How could it be gone?

He looked in his bed, yanked sheets and blankets and shook them out, waiting to hear the clink of gold links on the floor.

Nothing.

He went through his backpack, his pockets. He combed the floor. He went all over the house. Through all the boxes and bags of possessions he'd brought from Lancaster.

It was gone.

Was it on him when he left school? Of course it was.

I think it was.

Of course it was. It was always on him. He must have lost it on the way home. At a gas station. Or a rest stop.

Devastated and crushed with guilt, he sank onto his bed, weeping for all that had been lost. Lena put her nose in his neck and whined high in her throat. Erik hooked an arm around her, pulled her close, felt her solid weight and warm panting. She rested her muzzle on his shoulder, licked his ear, whined again and laid her silken face against Erik's wet one.

I am here now. And I understand.

She was here now. But she'd die someday and be gone. Like every-thing else. Everything was temporary. It all left in the end. Sooner or later it pulled down the driveway in the middle of the night. Or it was shot down or sliced open. It dissolved into bloody drips in the toilet or it ended up in bed with another man. Nothing good would stick around.

Pain, however, was in it for the long haul.

Pain stayed.

Erik let go of Lena, turned from her comfort and buried his head beneath the covers.

This was his life.

PART FOUR: DIANE

A JILTED WOMAN

TIME WAS A formidable enemy.

Time was an infinite road into a barren wasteland. A rocky, potholed path comprised of increments Erik could not fathom: weeks, months, years—they only meant pain and loss to him. Together they made up a more ominous concept called a lifetime. His life was unfolding before him without Daisy.

Those first few weeks of late spring after he arrived home were lost to him. Nothing imprinted. His short-term memory was short-circuited. Later, he would look back on those months as if through the wrong end of a telescope, wondering how he'd done it, just how he'd survived. He had no active recollection of doing so.

Time frightened him. It made him physically ill. If he thought in any length of time longer than a day, he could not get out of bed in the morning. When he was in a good place, he could manage a twenty-four hour cycle. During the slumps, he had to hold his own hand through minutes.

And yet, time could be an insanely elastic and devious thing. First it stretched before him like a snake, hissing words like *forever, never, always* and *infinite.* Then one day Erik woke up and nine months had passed. He should have felt triumphant, instead he felt bewildered. Where had it all gone?

If he wasn't grappling with time, he was dodging never-ending attacks of memory. The world was a war zone: recollections booby-trapped every corner. Free associations waited on rooftops to take pot shots at him. Everything reminded him of Daisy. Everything. For those first nine months, he didn't go to movies, rarely read a book and avoided music as much as possible—music was the worst. He kept the radio in his car tuned to sports networks or NPR, and if ever he were subjected to songs, he imagined a filter in his head rendering the lyrics meaningless.

Given his way, he would destroy every known copy of Elton John's "Tiny Dancer."

Where once he'd been surprised to discover the depths of his passion, he was now equally astonished at how well he could shut down. *You will feel nothing* was his mantra whenever memory staged a sneak attack. *It was another time, another life, and it's over now. They are gone, you are here, and you will feel nothing.*

His most secret weapon was staging a re-enactment of the shooting in the theater. Only this time, everyone was gunned down and killed.

She died. Everything that happened after was a dream. She's gone. She was gone a year ago. Will's gone. Lucky, David, Neil and Opie—everyone who was in the theater is gone. They're just outlines of graffiti backstage. You've been asleep. It was a dream.

It's time to wake up now.

DAISY PHONED REGULARLY those nine months. Christine soon wearied of fielding the awkward calls, and Erik had his own phone line installed. He rarely answered it, screening every call by letting it go to the machine and picking up when it was warranted. He never picked up for Daisy and didn't return any of her calls. He wouldn't speak to her. Could not speak to her. A few times she managed to catch him live on the phone, and each time he froze into silence.

"Talk to me," she would whisper. It was a stranger's voice, a pathetic keen of agonized chagrin. "Erik, please talk to me. I'm so sorry."

In his mind she was still on her knees in the kitchen at Jay Street. Kneeling in the bombed-out crater of their love, beseeching him. He gazed over the top of her bowed head and said nothing. Like an Easter Island statue he stared out to sea, stony and resolute, refusing to engage or acknowledge, until she hung up in tears. Then he would crumple on the floor, undone, and he'd have to start all over again, scrabbling to collect the bits and pieces of his life and glue them together.

She continued to call. Saying she was sorry, saying she'd do anything.

But what am I supposed to do? he thought.

He kept throwing fire at the bridge, and she kept putting the flames out and shoring up the timbers. He laid land mines, and she picked her way through them.

Figures, Erik thought. *Her father's a fucking sapper.*

The last time she got through to him, she was pulling heavier artillery.

"I can't believe you're just going to give up," she said. "One stupid mistake and you're going to walk away from me. Walk away from us. Without a fight. Without even a word."

It would be any man's cue to whip around and bombard her with a million heated words. Unleash hell, give her a ripshit battle to decide the war.

Erik couldn't do it. He had no fight left in him. His throat was sodered tight and the shaking anger in her voice merely made his heart shrink further and further into a corner.

"Say something," she cried. "Yell at me, curse at me. Say you hate me. *Say* something, Erik..."

I can't hate you, he thought, almost startled she would demand it of him. *I could never hate you.*

But now I can never love you.

The two nevers cancelled each other out. Leaving nothing.

I can never love her. And I can never love anyone else. This is my life now. Everything is ruined.

"There's nothing to say," he whispered. "It's over."

"It's not. Erik, please, you can't—"

He hung up.

Will's calls were harder. Will had done nothing wrong. Will was an innocent bystander. But Will was also a conduit to Daisy. If Erik wanted nothing more to do with her, then he couldn't have anything to do with any of her.

Will phoned relentlessly, leaving messages. At first they were warm with sympathy.

"Fish, call me. Let's talk about it. I feel terrible."

Then they turned cool with jokes.

"Dude, when I said you should get out of Dodge a little while, I meant for like a *day?* We're going on weeks here, this is crazy."

Finally they were hot with hurt and anger.

"Fish, what the hell are you doing? This isn't funny anymore. This isn't about Daisy. This is you and me, all right? Fucking call me already."

Erik made a stone of his heart and ignored the pleas which grew more emotional and angrier. Finally Will got through by calling at three in the morning.

"Hang up this phone and I will kill you."

"Jesus," Erik muttered, half-asleep, his heart pounding from the shock of the phone ringing. "What do you want?"

"What do I w— I want your fucking meatloaf recipe, that's why I'm calling every day. Jesus Christ, Fish, it's *me.*"

Erik breathed in through a clenched jaw.

"Fish, what are you doing?" Will whispered. "Talk to me."

"Did you know?"

"Did I know what?"

"Did you know she was fucking him?"

"Jesus, no. I'm as shocked as you are. Nobody saw it coming."

"Including me." Vulnerable from fatigue, tears stung his eyes. He bit down on his lip until he felt the plate armor of his stubborn resolve slide into place. *You will feel nothing.*

"Look," Will said. "I don't know all the details, but my gut tells me this wasn't an ongoing thing. I think it was just something stupid and random."

"It was David wanting what he couldn't have."

"And you beat the shit out of him. I would've done the same. But now what about Daisy?"

"What about her?"

A bubble of frustrated silence on the other end of the line. Will inhaled then exhaled roughly. Erik imagined him slumped in a chair, his face in a palm. The lines of his body etched with pain. Good. Life was shit and everyone should hurt.

"Let me get this straight," Will said. "You're leaving her. You've left her. This is it. You're gone."

"Yes."

"Just like that. What you have with her means nothing."

"Clearly it meant nothing to her," Erik said.

"No discussion, no goodbye, no... You're not even going to hear her side of it?"

"I have no desire to hear her side of it. She wants David, fine, she can have him. God bless. And when he chews her up and spits her out, I won't even say I told you so. Because I'm such a good guy."

"Dude," Will said, his voice softening. "She did a shitty thing to you. Nobody will say otherwise. You gotta be dying a thousand deaths and I'm so fucking sorry..."

Erik's eyes narrowed, his body tensing. He could handle an argument with Will. He welcomed a screaming match, but compassion would destroy him. Empathy would dissolve the pathetic, flimsy barrier he'd worked so hard to jerry-rig out of nothing. "Well," he said. "I'm glad we agree there."

"Come on, man," Will said. "She fucked up but she loves you."

Will's love was bright, firm and clear, slipping through the holes of the phone receiver and shining into Erik's eyes. He flinched from it, a mole squinting into the sun.

"She didn't fuck up," he whispered, turning from the light. "She fucked David."

"It was a mistake, she'll be the first to stand up and say it. Won't you even let her—"

"Let her what? Explain? Apologize? And then what? I just get back with her and pretend nothing happened? What am I supposed to do?"

He could hear the click of Will swallowing. "I don't know, but you can—"

"No. Will. What am I supposed to do?" His voice cracked open. "Tell me. What?"

"Dude…"

"What am I supposed to do?" The words were nearly soundless now. He wanted to scream it. Wanted to crawl through the phone and dump it in Will's lap and get answers. Will needed to tell him the next move. Right now. Or else…

"Fish, I… I just know you guys love each other."

Love isn't enough.

Neither love nor pain. Ever again.

"Forget it, man," Erik said. "I'll never be able to look at her again without seeing her in David's bed. That's my last memory of her. That's my souvenir. That's what I got. I don't ever want to see her again. You can tell her to just leave me the hell alone."

"All right. Fine. Your fight with Daisy is your fight with Daisy. What about me?"

"What about you? What the hell do we have left to talk about?"

"You're done with me? Pardon me sounding like a jilted woman but I thought I meant something to you."

He did. Will's friendship had no price. But Will was the open door back to Daisy. Now he was a dangerous liability.

Both of them had to go.

Erik hardened every soft and compassionate thing in his heart. He erased the previous version of events. He rewound, took it back. Back to the beginning, where Will was no innocent bystander. And he rewrote the past into a story he could live with.

"I'm done," he said. "I was done when you fucked James and brought all this shit down. It all goes back to you and him. None of this—"

"No," Will said. "No, you are not doing this."

"—would have happened if you picked a goddamn persuasion and stuck to it. If you hadn't strung him along like a toy and then threw him aside. You're no better than David."

"Don't you put this on me, Fish."

"You brought it down," Erik said. "You fucked him over and he came into the theater looking for you. I wish he'd just shot your sorry ass and been done with it."

"You are fucking unbelievable," Will said.

"And I'm done being one of your goddamn casualties. No wonder you're on Daisy's side—you cheated on Lucky and got away with it. I'm telling you, I'm done. I'm through with her. I'm through with both of you."

A long exhale in his ear. "Well. I won't take up any more of your time."

"Don't. And don't fucking call me anymore."

"Believe me, you miserable bitch, I won't," Will said. "But let me say one last thing, Fish. Actually it's something you said once, allow me to paraphrase."

"What?"

"You can't *breathe* without her."

He hung up.

Watch me, Erik thought. And he threw the phone across the room.

HE TOLD HIS MOTHER, in the most general of terms, what had happened at school—Daisy had left him for David. Christine was shocked and sympathetic. She took his side. Daisy's endless phoning confused her. Undoubtedly she sensed she didn't know the whole story, but she stayed supportive and tactful and gave her son his space. She worried. She was his mother: she couldn't not be concerned about Erik's shadowed eyes and the handsome face becoming more and more gaunt. He worked long, arduous hours at a handful of jobs, doing anything and everything to stay distracted and tired. And still she heard him pacing in the night, the jingle of Lena's collar following wherever he went.

Christine worried, but she'd never coddled him before. He was a man now. He didn't need her to sort it out. He would take it apart and put it back together again. He'd let down and cried to her only a few times. Most nights she merely stayed up with him and his inconsolable melancholy. He didn't want to talk. He just wanted her presence. So she brewed a lot of tea and sat close by.

Yet Christine herself was heading into a new phase of her life. She had a man—Fred had been a constant companion for five years by then. Fred was getting ready to retire. Christine wanted to sell the house, downsize into a condo with Fred until Pete was out of school, then possibly move down to Key West.

"What's your plan, honey," she asked one December evening. "What do you want to do?"

Erik, whose plans went to D, minimum, had started to think about it himself. "I think I want to get into a community theater," he said. "Working tech in a place like the Walnut Street down in Philly—it appeals to me."

"Will you go back to Pennsylvania?"

"No. It's... No, I'm done there. I know I have to get my degree. I should be able to transfer my credits to one of the SUNY schools and finish it in a semester, a year at the most."

"You did get into Fredonia. And Geneseo," she said.

"I'm thinking Geneseo. It's a great town, and there's the Geneseo Playhouse. It's got a great reputation. Maybe I could do an internship there or something." He looked over at his mother and smiled. "Don't stay here for me, Mom. I'll be all right. I can coach basketball, I can tend bar, I can do construction. I'll put something together."

"You always do." Christine put her hand on his cheek, caressed his rough face. "My heart's broken for you, honey. I'm so sorry it ended up like this."

He closed his eyes and leaned into her hand. "I'm sorry about the necklace, Mom," he whispered. "I looked everywhere. I don't know what happened to it."

"I know," she said, her hand sliding down his arm and squeezing his wrist. "You didn't lose it on purpose."

He put his head in his palm, pulling at his hair. He didn't understand how precious legacies were carelessly lost while the token of a killer stayed safe in your pocket. Nothing made sense. Nothing held still. Nothing behaved the way he expected it to.

"These things happen, Erik."

He didn't know if she meant the necklace or Daisy. Maybe she meant his father.

He didn't ask.

OUR BODIES REMEMBER

SUNY GENESEO ACCEPTED HIM. He guessed his application essay had clinched it—the one and only time he would play the Lancaster shooting card. He wrote of being a survivor, of second chances, the memory of those killed being the motivation for what he wanted to achieve in life. It was humble, moving and brilliant. And he meant none of it.

He shied from dorm life, and took a small apartment off campus. Alone. He wasn't there to make friends. The less people knew about him, the better. He erased Lancaster from his resume and if asked, told people he'd transferred from Buffalo State.

The tuition was less here than at Lancaster. By living frugally and working hard, he could spread the last of his grandfather's money across this semester, and into the fall if necessary. The courses he needed to graduate were mostly general education credits. His schedule was a mongrel of math and science, plus the advanced stagecraft required for a BA in theater arts. And for his aching soul, he enrolled in both piano and classical guitar.

Which was how he met Miles and Janey Kelly.

Miles was a professor of piano and voice at Geneseo. Janey was a clinical psychologist at the college's counseling center. She also played piano and sang, and both she and Miles were active at the Geneseo Playhouse.

The relationship worked perfectly—this childless musical theater couple in their fifties and this withdrawn young man with no interest in the party life of college. The Kellys took him in and Miles became Erik's new mentor. Not a Leo Graham by any means, nor did he possess any of Kees's flamboyant style. Yet his edges lined up against Erik's with a satisfying click. They collaborated seamlessly at the playhouse. They ran together almost every night, shot baskets on the weekend, went for beers and talked themselves dry. Despite the thirty-year age difference, they got along like brothers, and Erik felt at home in Miles's undemanding company.

The Kellys also gave music back to Erik. Janey was avidly social and a superb cook. The doors of the spacious brick house on Ivy Street were always open on weekends, the living room and kitchen filled with their theater friends. Drinks and dinner gave way to long jam sessions: guitars, upright basses, ukuleles, harmonicas, someone showed up with a banjo once. Erik was usually the youngest guest present, but he stayed all night, playing, absorbing, learning, losing himself in the keys and the strings.

Sometimes the parties had a slightly younger demographic, which gave him the opportunity to get laid. As a twenty-three-year-old emerging from a stretch of self-inflicted celibacy, he was dying for it. But he was wary of encounters with girls his age. They were looking for love. He wanted none of that—the idea of opening himself to another relationship and leaning into its joy alternately terrified and exhausted him. He felt no pride in his blunt quests to blow a load and hit the road, but such were the hard facts of life.

And who could I love now anyway?

Women of a certain age suited his needs better. His most regular and reliable booty call was a married friend of Janey's. Not his finest moment, either, but it allowed him physical connection while avoiding the peril of becoming emotionally invested. He didn't have to look for an excuse to leave after sex. He *was* the excuse.

They liked him though, those older women. They shivered and moaned under him. They were lavish with their praise, letting him know in no uncertain terms what he was doing to them. He was wild. They swore they never had it so good in their lives.

He didn't care.

Sex remained an unpredictable pleasure. Sometimes it soothed him, other times, too many for his liking, the horrible anxiety flooded him when it was over. He wanted sex, outright jonesed for it, but he hated when the wolves came afterward. He hated even more being in the throes of the act and struck with a wicked compulsion to scratch his partner's skin or pull hard on her hair. To have "hurt me" on the tip of his tongue. To want the bit of pain nestled gently in his teeth, clamping down just hard enough.

He kissed differently, he noticed. No slow, gentle buildup with fingertips caressing the woman's mouth. He got straight to it and, frankly, past it as soon as possible. Just a checkpoint. First base. He didn't want to kiss. It was too intimate, his mouth a vulnerable gateway to the depths of his wounded, trembling soul.

The mindless, heartless coupling was his sole vice. He still had no head for booze. He didn't smoke anymore—cigarettes only reminded him of Daisy. He couldn't afford coke and even if he could, he wanted nothing more to do with her cruel high. He would forever equate cocaine as a wintry bitch, cloaked in wanton destruction, full of empty promises she could make everything all right.

HIS MOTHER SOLD THE HOUSE and moved in with Fred, so Erik stayed in Geneseo the summer of 1994, working at the playhouse and coaching basketball at the Y's summer camps.

Daisy's calls had tapered off while he was still living at home, and she began writing instead. Simple postcard bulletins. The missives then followed him to Geneseo—Christine must have given her his address. Sometimes he read them, sometimes he didn't, depending on what kind of mental state he was in. The Philadelphia postmark let him know she was still with the Pennsylvania Ballet—just enough information to process. Opened or not, he threw out the letters afterward. To spare himself the pain of lingering over and dissecting her words, he saved nothing.

Then one night she left a message on his machine. His mind nowhere near a good state, he stopped the playback after hearing, "Erik, it's Daisy," and deleted it. Then he called his mother and chewed her out for giving Daisy his phone number.

"I don't want to talk to her," he said. "If anyone from Lancaster calls for me you can tell them—"

"I'm not your goddamn secretary," Christine said. "And I don't lie for you. Answer the phone and tell them yourself."

They each slammed down their ends of the line. They rarely argued and it made Erik feel sick. Later he called back and apologized but the malaise didn't go away. He wasn't feeling well. He seemed to be spiraling down into a funk. He wasn't hungry, he couldn't sleep. The piano wouldn't talk to him, his guitar was sulking. Work felt empty, he couldn't find his three-point shot. Sex was as appealing as a stomach flu. Time turned back into the enemy. Some days it was a chore to get out of bed. Some days it was an ordeal just to breathe through his mantras.

You will feel nothing. There is nothing more to feel. Neither pain nor love. They died. What happened after was a dream. They are gone. You are left. It's time to go.

One evening the playhouse was rehearsing *You Can't Take It With You* and a thunderstorm rolled through Geneseo. It was biblical outside, with multi-branched lightning illuminating the skies and thunder rattling the windows. A tree came down in the park across the street, falling slowly and majestically onto the power lines where it teetered for a moment.

Inside the playhouse, the entire circuit panel shorted out. A Fresnel over the stage exploded. The sound system let out a horrid shriek of feedback, followed by two short bursts of static. A beat of silence. Then a third angry buzz.

The tree finished its descent, taking the power lines with it. And then the transformer blew.

At the epic boom, everyone jumped in their shoes or out of their seats. More than a few people screamed. The company stumbled around the dark theater, clutching their chests, groping for hands, finding each other, gasping with both fright and the laughter of a near-miss.

In the chaos, nobody noticed Erik Fiskare had run away.

He'd been in the lighting booth, of course. The explosion and the piercing feedback had him immediately on his feet. Those rapid bursts of crackling static—two quick, a pause, then a third—and then that final apocalyptic detonation. It all came back to him. He ran. Not toward the stage this time, but away, far away in the farthest direction he could find.

He hid in a corner of the dark, empty green room, shaking, trying to pull himself together, to come back to the here and now.

Miles Kelly finally found him. "Well, here you are."

The beam of a flashlight played around Erik's body, hunched over in a chair. His hands were tucked tight under his legs because it was the only way to keep them from shaking.

Here I am, he thought.

"Are you all right?"

"Yeah," Erik said. His voice was an adolescent squeak. He cleared his throat. "Just... I wasn't feeling well. Just need a minute."

Miles took a step closer, peered at him in the milky beam of light. Erik gave him a flimsy smile, then immediately looked away for the smile was too weak a dam for the flood of hysterical weeping behind it.

"Are you sure?"

"I'm fine, I just need a minute."

"Do you want me to get you some water?"

"Yeah. Thanks."

"I'll be back. I'd leave you the flashlight but it's pitch black in the halls."

"I'm fine, you take it."

Once Miles was gone, Erik pulled his hands free and let the shaking overcome him. In the dark, his teeth chattered. He was going to be sick. He couldn't be sick here. He couldn't move, either. He put his head down on his knees, counted his breaths, said his magic words.

Feel nothing. Neither pain nor love. Nothing. Feel. Nothing.

The door to the green room opened and shut. Footsteps approached. With a great effort, Erik arranged his face and picked up his head, squinted toward the beam of the flashlight. "That you?"

"It's Janey."

She held out the bottle of water to him, watched as he fumbled the cap off and spilled most of it down his shirt trying to drink.

"What's the matter, Erik?" she said. She sat down next to him, put a light hand on his back. She was kind, one of the kindest women Erik knew. He liked her. Maybe he could trust her.

"What frightened you?" she asked.

"The sounds," he whispered.

"In the theater just now?"

"Yes." He took another, more controlled sip of water.

"Drink slow," she said.

He exhaled roughly. Pulled more air in. Beside him, Janey sat patiently, neither pressing him to explain, nor dismissing him.

"I lied to you about something," he finally said. "I didn't transfer from Buffalo. I was at Lancaster University."

Janey inhaled sharply through her nose, then made a small noise in her throat. "You were there during the shootings?"

Teeth clenched tight, he nodded.

Her hand pressed against his back, and her other hand crept around his fingers. "Were you in the theater when it happened?"

"Yeah." He held tight to her.

"I see," she said. "The static and feedback and the explosion. All of it must have reminded you."

"I think so. I think that's what happened. What's happening."

"You're having a flashback." Her arm was fully around him then, pulling him close. "It's perfectly understandable."

A fresh round of shaking gripped his limbs. He tried to laugh. "This is just really weird."

"Sometimes our brains forget but our bodies remember."

"Yeah."

"Did you lose friends?"

"My girlfriend was shot," he said.

"Oh, Erik. I'm so sorry."

He should have clarified what he meant, should have explained Daisy was shot but she'd survived, she was still alive.

They all died. You are left.

Then he was weeping, crumpled over in Janey's lap and she was holding him. An arm around his shoulders, her hand stroking his head as she rocked him, as if consoling for the death of a loved one. Clasped in her calm, firm embrace, Erik was horrified by the idea of it being easier to do this, infinitely easier to grieve for the loss of Daisy if she really were dead.

I wish she had died, he thought with a passion.

Then right on the heels of that came, *I wish I had, too.*

Which was terrifying in its cold, clinical certainty. He thought it again, tried it on for size, like jacket off the rack: *I wish I were dead.*

He raised his arms, felt the fit of the sleeves, smoothed down the lapels, buttoned a button. *I wish I were dead.*

It fit well.

JANEY CAME BY HIS PLACE, bringing some pasta salad. And a business card.

"I don't feel comfortable counseling you, Erik, we've been socially involved for too long."

"Of course."

"So what I say now, I say as your friend: you need to talk to someone."

She asked if he'd ever seen a therapist, if he was on any antidepressants or had ever taken any meds for the stress. He lied and said he'd been in a support group at school for a little while. He fabricated a prescription, he forgot the name now, but he hated the way the pills made him feel, and stopped after a few months. With the taste of fraud in his mouth, he took the proffered business card and thanked her.

"It's a colleague of mine. She's excellent with PTSD cases."

"All right."

"In both my personal and professional opinion, you'd benefit from counseling. Traumatic events can stick around in the folds of your brain for years afterward, and the most innocuous of things can trigger them."

"I know."

"You have quite the arsenal of two-word responses, don't you?"

Janey was no fool. Her eyes swept him head to toe, front to back, and he nearly cowered, feeling exposed.

But she was kind. "You're an adult, Erik. I'm giving you this card, and I won't check on you. But..." She stepped to him, and cupped his chin in her hand. "Promise me."

"What?"

"If you ever feel you are going to hurt yourself, you call me. You wake me up at two in the morning. You bang on my door. If it ever comes to that. Do you understand?"

"I will," he said, then smiled sheepishly. "I will call you if it gets to that."

"Promise me."

He promised, and with the best of intentions he tacked the card on his bulletin board.

But of course the next day he felt better, and when you feel better, it no longer seems as urgent to take steps to maintain feeling better. He began to string better days together. A week of feeling good. It was so much easier to be reactive than proactive. Two weeks. The episode was long ago and far away now, no longer meant for him.

He left it behind.

He pumped up his basketball and hit the court. He sat down at the piano, picked up his guitar. He whistled. It was getting lighter in his head. He'd dodged another bullet. He was fine.

Soon enough the business card was tacked over with layers of this and that, buried on the bulletin board, and Erik was back to letting the months go by.

I'M DONE NOW

ERIK GRADUATED IN DECEMBER of 1994, the same time the Kellys left Geneseo—Miles had landed a new job at SUNY Brockport.

Erik braced himself for a bereft depression after they were gone. Truly Miles had been his closest friend. Perhaps, he had to admit, his only friend. But instead, time went into one of its surreal elastic phases.

He kept himself hyper-busy. He was now working full-time at the playhouse. Besides doing set and lighting design for the seasonal productions, he was the mastermind behind a partnership with the public school districts, devising a student theater program. Classes and workshops ranged from elementary through middle grades, with internships for high school students.

Erik taught lighting, set design, basic stagecraft. He coached basketball at the Y, gave guitar lessons, played piano at a few watering holes. He had a few girlfriends. Nothing serious, just females to keep company with. He kept his thoughts and feelings at bay. Most of the time. Occasionally he went through cycles of depression and anxiety but he did his best to ignore or tough out the dark spells. On a couple of bad nights he toyed with the idea of going for counseling. Inevitably the light came back around and the need for help was dismissed.

Time left him alone. It passed quietly if he didn't pay too much attention.

Two years passed. And one April night, Daisy called.

She hadn't reached out by phone in a long time. Long enough to make him relax the vigilance on the caller ID, plus he was distracted tonight, too much on his plate. Getting home late from a rehearsal, combined with burning dinner, no clean gym clothes, and a broken shoelace making him late for a basketball game. The phone rang and he didn't check the little box, he just picked up.

"It's Daisy."

While the calls had tapered, the written communications stayed steady—little notes, a scribble on his birthday. A Christmas card. When her return address changed abruptly from Philly to New York City, he opened the envelope to read about her new gig with the Metropolitan Opera Ballet. Then he chucked it.

"Are you there?"

He was caught off guard by her voice. Usually it was tentative and submissive. Laced with apology. Tonight it was soft, but confident. Conversational.

"I'm here," he said.

"Hi," she said.

Say hello, he thought. *It won't kill you.*

"Hi," he whispered.

"It's the nineteenth," she said. "I was thinking about you."

The nineteenth of April, the fourth anniversary. "That's right," he said. He slid his fingertips along the side of his nose, his face melting into his palm. Eyes closed, he tested his memory. Was it still there?

Yes, it was still there.

She was still there—rolling on top of David with her hair a tangle.

"How are you?" she asked.

Shattered, he thought, one helium balloon rising above the bunch crowding his mind. "I'm fine and I have to go," he said. "I'm late for a game."

"Erik, please," she said. "It's been almost three years. Are we ever going to talk about this?"

Three years and she was still linked to David in his mind. He couldn't even have a conversation without seeing them in bed. It was ruined. He couldn't do this. Without another word, Erik hung the receiver back up, and went to his game.

Days later, UPS knocked on his door, needing him to sign for a large box. The return label read *D. Bianco* with a Manhattan address.

He slit the tape with a kitchen knife, and opened the flaps to find a veritable time capsule of his belongings. Things obviously left in Daisy's room at Jay Street.

My necklace, he thought. *It's in here. She had it.*

He unpacked the box, stacking everything carefully, sure the next item retrieved would be his lost treasure. He took out a pair of jeans, two button-down shirts, and his Mickey Mouse T-shirt. All the clothes were folded nicely and smelled of fabric softener. Daisy must have washed them. Next he found his Leatherman and Swiss Army knives, a plastic baggie with a capo, guitar strings and picks, another baggie with his ring of allen wrenches. His hardcover book of Swedish folk tales, his zippo lighter.

He unpacked it all and the box was empty. Taped to the inside was an envelope with a note. Not a card, nor her nice stationery, but a scrawl on half a piece of loose-leaf paper:

> *I'm sorry, Fish. I regret what happened more than you will ever know. I will always regret it. I think about you every day. I'll love you until I die. And I'm done now. I won't contact you anymore. Dais.*

He stared at the *Fish*, not recognizing his own moniker, not coming from Daisy. She'd never called him Fish.

He put down the note and inventoried the items again, went through them twice, including the pockets of all the clothing.

His necklace was not in this box.

He sat on the floor, surrounded by bits and pieces of a past life, and wasn't sure what it all meant.

DRUMMED OUT

"DIRECTORY ASSISTANCE, what listing please?"

"Last name Bianco," Erik said. "First name Daisy. On West Eighty-Sixth Street."

A brisk tapping of keys against a background hum of voices and more tapping.

"I show no listing for Daisy Bianco."

"What about Marguerite Bianco?"

"Margaret?"

"Marguerite."

"Spell that, please?"

He did, and waited through more tapping.

"I show a listing for Marguerite Bianco on West Eighty-Sixth. Hold for the number, please."

A click and a crackle, then a chopped, automated voice began intoning digits. Erik wrote them down and hung up.

He was falling apart.

It began a month after Daisy sent back his things, when it dawned on him he was waiting to hear from her. She said she was done, but so what, she couldn't have meant it.

I'll love you until I die, she wrote. She wasn't done. She'd never be done.

Month after month passed, and nothing in his mailbox.

He realized he wanted to hear from her. As painful as the communications were, he'd looked out for them. Even with no intention of responding to her, he must have subconsciously needed the regular bit of assurance the bridge wasn't totally burned.

More months passed, and he realized the depth of his reliance. The streak of cruelness at its bedrock. He'd been punishing her. She was full of guilt and remorse and he sucked on that like a piece of candy. A gobstopper of spite set like a sticky, snarling pitbull at the door kept slammed shut in her face. Knowing damn well her unrelieved chagrin meant she would hold her end of the structure up, no matter how much firepower he threw at it.

But then she had enough.

I'm done now.

Daisy let go and the world collapsed. Erik was buried in rubble and ruin. Buried alive. His chest torqued tight around his heart. He couldn't get food down his throat. Couldn't get words to come up. Tonight he was pacing his apartment, riddled by an agitated depression and filled with a shamed remorse over the loss of his necklace.

It was the loss of his necklace making him ashamed and depressed, wasn't it?

He was more than certain Daisy didn't have it. She would have sent it to him by now. He knew her. She would not keep something so precious, simply out of... He couldn't even formulate a motive for keeping it. She would not have sent back his things and kept just the necklace.

She doesn't have it.

But it's an excuse to call her.

Just call her.

Because you can't breathe without her.

Her number now in hand, with a need to stop the insanity and take drastic action, Erik dialed.

One ring.

Two rings.

"Hello?"

It was a man. A crossbolt of confusion went through Erik's mind, pierced the mental sheet of paper with his scripted lines and pinned it to the opposite wall.

"Hello?" An edge of annoyance in the voice.

"Yeah, hi," Erik said. "Is Daisy Bianco there?" *I must have dialed wrong. I was nervous, I switched some digits.*

"No, she's not, can I take a message?"

Open-mouthed and stunned, Erik couldn't think what to say. "No. I mean, yes..."

"Who is this?"

"It's... I knew her in college, I was just calling to—"

"Erik?"

His eyes widened as his stomach turned inside-out. "Yes?"

A chuckle in the voice now. "Fish, it's John."

"John?"

"Quillis."

Erik stood up, a hand to his head. "Opie?"

An exasperated sigh. "Oh for fuck's sake, will that name never die? Yes. Opie."

The face, with its red hair and earnest expression, parted the fog of confusion like a ray of sunshine. "Holy shit."

"My thoughts exactly."

"How did you know it was me?"

More low laughter. "I took a wild guess."

"How are you?"

"Not bad, how about yourself?"

"What are you doing there?" Erik said. And then a coldness swept over his limbs.

"I live here," John said.

"You live..."

"I live here, Fish."

Erik's mouth fell open. Closed. Opened again. "Oh."

A long pause.

"Well," John said. "This is awkward."

"I'm sorry," Erik said. "I didn't know."

"Of course you didn't." John's voice was friendly, but unapologetic. Authoritative. He wasn't overtly challenging Erik. Rather he was calmly staring down a potential threat. Sizing up this new buck on the scene who wanted to fight for breeding rights.

He's the alpha male.

"Ope, I'm sorry," Erik whispered. "I was just…"

"It's all right, Fish. Do you want me to give her a message?"

"Yeah." He cleared his throat, pulled himself together. "Daisy sent me back some of my things she had with her."

"I know. Was everything there?"

"I'm looking for my necklace. I don't know if you remember it but it was—"

"The gold one? With the fish and the boat? Sure, I remember it. You lost it?"

"It's been lost since school and I thought it would be in the box but it wasn't. It was valuable to me and I thought she wouldn't want to send it in the mail. If she even had it, I mean. I've looked everywhere and this was kind of my last—"

"I gotcha. I don't know, Fish. I haven't seen it but then again, it's not exactly something she'd show me." John cleared his throat. "I'll let her know you called and asked about it."

"I appreciate it. Thanks."

"You doing all right?"

"Yeah. Yeah, I'm good. How about you?"

"I'm good."

A pause. Erik licked his dry lips. "How's Dais?"

"She's fine," John said. "She's fine now. She was pretty bad for a while."

Erik closed his eyes. "Bad how?"

"She was cutting herself."

Erik sat down and said nothing.

"She was in a hospital upstate for a while. It was bad. And it's only just started to be better for her. So I'll let her know you called, but… I don't want to sound like a douche or anything, but I'd appreciate if you wouldn't make a habit of it."

The words felt like a reprimand. A beat down. Erik's face burned and stung. His fists curled in rage and then loosened in impotent helplessness. It was over. He was being dismissed. Stripped of his medals and drummed out of the ranks.

"You understand, right?" John said.

"I understand. Thanks, Ope. John. Sorry."

He laughed. "You can call me Opie. It's fine."

"Take care of yourself."

"You too, Fish. Bye now."

Erik depressed the end button with his thumb and let the phone drop onto the floor. He sat. Staring. He didn't know for how long. Then he pulled on a jacket and went out.

He walked. Hours. No destination other than a corner store to get a pack of cigarettes, his first in years. He chain smoked, one after another, leaving a trail of butts. He leaned against walls like a hoodlum. Sat on park benches like a homeless man. Tried to think.

She was cutting herself.

Erik couldn't even grasp what that meant. Had she tried to slit her wrists? Had John saved her from a suicide attempt? His gut twisted as he screwed up his eyes, dodging his head away from a vision of blood running down Daisy's arms.

It was bad. It's only just started to be better.

He walked and smoked. Waited to feel something.

She was cutting herself.

Daisy was in the hospital. It was bad for a while. Now she was living with John Quillis. And she was better.

Erik thought her motivation to send his things back was simply reaching the bottom of her well of sadness. She mailed the box, said goodbye and made to carry on, empty and alone. Above all, alone.

Not the case.

She returned him because she had found someone else. She said goodbye, shut her own door and now John stood there as a sentry. The alpha male. A line drawn in the sand. A perimeter of piss around his territory.

The man she loved.

Don't make a habit of it. You understand, right?

He could. He'd always liked John. He was crushy on Daisy but in an innocent, non-threatening way. Part of the conservatory lore.

"Keep an eye out for her, Ope," Erik had said after James had dropped Daisy in rehearsal. "I don't trust that guy and I don't want him anywhere near her. You see trouble, you stop it. Rough him up if you need to."

John looked skeptical at first, and then embarrassed: he was a dancer, he didn't know anything about roughing people up. But Erik had showed him a few things, showed him how to punch, and with marching orders in hand, John had taken his place in the ranks. He'd been down in the blood with Will the day of the shooting, making his bones. Initiated into the circle. One of Erik's pack. If anyone was going to take Erik's place…

Jesus, he was groomed to take my place.

He stopped, turning his face into the wind, letting memory blow over him. A rehearsal for "The Man I Love." Him and John watching Will and Daisy. Will had picked Daisy up and set her on John's back, advising him on how to catch her hip bone in his shoulder and stop the roll into the arabesque lift.

"Now you, Fish," John had said, turning his head and looking at Erik with a sly, conspiratorial expression.

Not me, Erik thought. *Not me now.*

Now John slept with Daisy against his back. Her hand over his heart. Or maybe he spooned her. Holding her all night and keeping her safe from the wolves. He'd wake up and put his face into the curve of her neck. Run his tongue up the bumps of her spine. Grow hard against her legs and butt until she…

Erik started walking again, lighting another cigarette. John Quillis. It made sense. Another dancer. Someone who spoke Daisy's language. Earnest and kind and devoted. Protective. Appreciating if Erik wouldn't make a habit of calling.

John holding her in the dark.

Partnering her in the day.

Daisy's face pressed to the back of John's neck. The hip bone he'd learned to catch with his shoulder now lovingly pushed up against him. The hollow by the bone where red letters were inked. Erik's fish swimming in the shadow of another man's body.

Again.

He chucked the rest of the cigarettes and went home. He ran a low-grade fever for two days. Then he ran an emotional fever for a week, alternating between impassioned conversations with himself or crying in the shower.

A postcard showed up in his mailbox. The front was a panorama of the Metropolitan Opera House. Daisy's pretty handwriting filled the back:

> *John told me you called. I was out of town at an audition.*
> *I'm really sorry, but I don't have your necklace. You were*
> *wearing it last time I saw you. I'm sorry, Fish, I know how*
> *important it was to you. I feel terrible it's lost. I hope you*
> *find it. D.*

Bewildered, Erik sat down and stared at the card.

She didn't have it. He knew she didn't but he had hoped.

Not even *Dais,* this time. Just her initial. The bare minimum.

D for dismissed.

Twice she'd used Fish in her notes to him. She'd returned not just his things, but his name.

She was gone.

You will feel nothing.

His necklace was gone and Daisy was gone now. Really gone.

Feel neither love nor pain. They died. You are left. It is time to go.

He boxed it up tight, took it to the backyard of his heart and buried it.

DEAD CENTER

"JANEY?"

"Erik, honey, how are you? Goodness, we haven't heard from you in months."

"I know."

"Miles is out for a run."

"Actually," Erik said, "I called to talk to you."

"Did you now?"

"I promised you I would."

As he'd hoped, Janey went into her professional voice. "Are you all right?"

Erik was sitting on the floor of his apartment, curled up, mouth on his knees. "I think I'm in trouble."

"What's the matter, Erik?"

He squeezed his lips in. He'd been so afraid to call her. Now he was even more afraid to tell her the reason why.

"I'll help you, Erik," she said. "Tell me what's happening."

"I think I'm losing my mind."

"Do you feel like you're going to hurt yourself?"

"I can't stop hurting."

"Talk to me. Tell me."

"I can't do this anymore."

"Where are you?"

"Janey, I lied to you about so many things. I never got help in college. I never went to a support group and I let you think my girlfriend was killed but she wasn't, she's alive, she's with someone else now. She's alive and I feel like I'm dying and—"

"Erik, slow down, I will—"

"He told me not to call again and I won't but I don't know... I need to talk to someone and I can't find the card you—"

"*Erik.*" She'd never raised her voice to him and like a slap it startled him into open-mouthed silence.

"Where are you?" She was calm and professional again.

"Home. And I can't do this anymore."

"Erik, listen to me, I'm going to make a call. Two calls. You sit tight right there, don't move. Don't move a muscle until I call you back, do you understand?"

"All right."

"I will call you back. I promise. I'm going to get you help."

"All right."

"We'll find you, Erik. We'll get through it. I will call you back."

Disconnected, he sat on the cold floor, dead center in a ring of wolves. Their eyes glowed green and malevolent as they watched him open the blade of his Swiss Army knife. He touched the tip to the inside of his left wrist, tracing the daisy petals.

I have set you in my presence forever.

He'd done this to himself.

He had to cut her out of him or he would die.

Shaking his head hard, he took the blade off his wrist, closed the knife again. "You don't have to do this," he whispered. "You can stop."

I am the alpha male.

I lead this pack.

And John lives with Daisy.

The wolves took a step closer, tightening the circle.

I am the omega. A stray out in the rain. Like James.

The wolves nodded. Erik opened the blade again.

Janey called him back. She stayed on the phone until a friend arrived, a man Erik vaguely remembered from the Kellys' house parties. He was kind. He didn't ask questions or probe. He made gentle talk as he took the knife away, closed the blade and slipped it into his pocket. Then he drove Erik downtown, to the office of Dr. Diane Erskine, who was waiting for him.

So it started.

THE DEFINING MOMENT

AT FIRST GLANCE, when he was trembling and disoriented, Erik thought Diane Erskine was old, maybe in her sixties. More lucid at his next visit, he realized she was one of those women who went grey early, eventually becoming silver-haired while still in their prime. She wore her silver hair short, in a pixie cut. Her eyes were grey as well and she tended to dress in neutral tones. She exuded a sleek, expensive class, but she was oddly colorless.

Therapy perplexed Erik. He went into his first session assuming they'd talk about the shooting. He took up the entire hour talking about his job at the playhouse and the student theater program. He didn't even touch the subject of college, let alone the shooting. He walked out with a confused dissatisfaction, certain he'd botched it out of the gate and accomplished nothing.

He started going in with an agenda, a comprehensive list of things to talk about, in order of importance. Yet half the time, the plan was forgotten, the list went untouched, and he would be babbling on a tangent of the most pointless, inconsequential crap.

It was nervous babble, partly because Diane would never direct the session. She responded to whatever he brought up, but if he had nothing to talk about, she didn't help him by prompting a topic or line of discussion. Not a baited hook dropped. Not a bone thrown. She simply sat. And waited. The silence would stretch past awkward into agonizing, until Erik reached for anything and started rambling.

He was also slightly alarmed at the cost of therapy. While wouldn't be out on the street because of this, he wanted the assurance he was getting his money's worth.

It was unsatisfying. Touching a little on Daisy here, a bit on the shooting there, a dash of his mother, a drop of David, a shake of childhood. It all led to the first six weeks feeling like a bad technical run-through: a lot of disassociated parts but no show.

"What exactly is supposed to happen here?" He made the mistake of asking, back before he learned asking questions was pointless because Diane only parroted them back to him.

"You feel something is supposed to be happening." Often she left off the upward, inquiring inflection at the end of a question, making it a statement.

"Shouldn't this be... I don't know, deeper?"

"This feels shallow."

"Well, I mean, shouldn't I be crying or something?"

"Do you feel sad, Erik?"

It was enough to make you crazy, if you weren't already.

He tried going in cold, no preparation. Tried the approach of having nothing to prove and trusting Diane wasn't grading his sessions. He realized he did trust her. He was getting used to her, getting used to this hour of self-centered introspection. Week after week, he made and kept his appointments. He never looked forward to a session. Sometimes he outright dreaded it, constantly on the verge of canceling. He didn't like therapy, but, he admitted, he didn't dislike Diane.

He went. And they dug.

Time was gentle. The weeks softly piled up into months. And he began to find things in the dirt.

For the first time ever, he took all his scattered memories and impressions and lined them up into a wobbly narrative of not just the shooting, but the events leading up to it. He began with James, how he came to Lancaster and rearranged the elements. Margaret's dog tags and the penny. *Powaqqatsi.* The stolen condoms and the affair with Will.

The telling was strange. Erik found he could narrate the events of the fall semester, but his memory seemed to cave in after December. He hopped from one isolated recollection to another, bobbing like buoys in a choppy ocean. January and February were murky and muddled. March was filled with alarming sinkholes. April disappeared entirely. He could pick up the thread again, shakily, when James stepped onto the stage. And he could go forward from there.

"Why did you even come out of the booth?" Diane asked. Her voice didn't dip out of its professional neutrality but it seemed her eyes were pressing him hard. He wondered for a moment if she had children. A son of her own who was capable of such a reckless move. "Why didn't you stay down and covered?"

"I can't tell you what my thought process was that day, I don't remember. All I know is he shot Daisy." He held out his hands to indicate it was reason enough. "I had to get to her."

"You could have been killed." She turned her lips in as soon as the words were out. He guessed she'd just crossed a line. She was here to listen, not judge. He decided to step across as well.

"Do you have a son?" he asked.

Diane nodded, and he smiled briefly at her. "I know," he said. "It was an insanely stupid thing to do. My mother... Before she hugged me, she shook me. Like she didn't know whether to kiss me or kill me. A thousand people have asked me what I was thinking. And I feel like anything I try to describe, any way I try to tell the story, I'm making half of it up. I don't know what I was thinking in the moment, Diane. I don't."

"How about what you were feeling?"

"Feeling? I was scared shitless."

"What else?"

His shoulders inched up to his ears, silently indicating he could not remember. The "I don't know" was poised in his mouth, all made, not yet spoken. He kept it back. Closed his eyes. He let the words go unsaid, let his shoulders fall again. He relaxed into the silence, and followed his mind. Let it take him by the hand and go for a walk.

"Where are you," Diane said, after a minute.

"I had to get past him," Erik said. "I had to get to the stage. If I snuck by James, he'd shoot me. But if I talked to him. If I asked him... I don't know."

"Let it spill out," Diane murmured. "Don't be articulate. We can explore it afterward."

"I spoke to him," Erik said, trying to let go. "I called him by name and said 'you don't have to do this.' I thought I could calm him down. If anyone could, I could. I was the alpha male. Human valium."

"Tell me more."

"I calm everyone down. David said so. I started believing it was true. I could talk James down. He trusted me. He trusted me with the story about his sister. He gave me the penny. I had him in my pocket."

He looked up at Diane, who stared unblinking back at him. "Were you angry with him?" she asked.

"Angry?" he said, startled. "Right there and then?"

"Or right now."

"Sure. I mean, Jesus, he was fucked-up and depressed, maybe he was heartbroken over Will. But so what? A million people are fucked-up, depressed and heartbroken. Including yours truly. You don't see me going into Geneseo playhouse with a gun. Who thinks like that? I don't know why I bothered trying to sympathize. Fuck him. He blew the back of his head off and I got up and left him in the aisle. I didn't even look back. It's not the defining moment of the day. I got nothing for him." He slumped back in the couch unclenched the fingers he'd been holding in fists during the rant. "There you go, Doc, there's anger. I got anger for him. What a breakthrough."

Diane shifted in her chair, her fingers playing with her earring. "What was the defining moment of the day, I wonder?"

Erik hesitated, then reached in his pocket. He took the penny out and gave it to Diane. "Maybe that is," he said, watching her examine it. "I've carried it with me every day since the shooting. I had it in my pocket when I was at the funerals of the people he killed. I hate his guts but I keep it with me all the time. I wish I knew why."

Diane turned the flattened coin over and over in her fingers. "Often the victims of violence make their assailant into a monster. Something less than human. They refuse to call them by name. Acknowledge their pasts or their families." She handed the pendant back to him. "You chose to keep this. And to keep his humanity."

"He trusted me," Erik said.

Diane nodded.

A long aching silence passed. Erik put the penny back in his pocket. "I just need to keep it."

"It doesn't mean you're a horrible person," Diane said. "It just means you're a person."

"I wish he'd never given it to me. I don't want to define that day, Diane, and I don't want that damn day defining me. It was an incident, not my life. If I could, I'd go back to the theater and throw the stupid penny on the floor. Leave it in the aisle. Leave it dead there with the rest of—"

They died, only you are left.

"Where were you going just then?" she asked.

Haltingly, he told her.

"You pictured them dead?"

"It made it so much easier. But then Will would call, or Daisy would write, or my heart would just laugh at me and the whole illusion would crumble. So I stopped killing them off but I still kept telling myself to feel nothing."

He felt terrible after the session. Physically awful. Weak and anxious. His chest wide open and wailing. He felt perpetually on the verge of tears, his throat seized up.

"Therapy doesn't seem to be good for my health."

"How so?"

"I mean I don't feel better. I just feel like shit. Shittier."

"Because you're feeling."

He closed his eyes. "Meaning what?"

"Erik, you cannot selectively shut down. You can't cherry-pick the feelings you want to suppress. The limbic system is not a sophisticated switchboard. It's just one primitive switch. On or off. You mute one feeling, and you mute them all. And now, if you start digging into one feeling..."

"I wake up all of them and now I'm fucked," he said, exhaling wearily.

Diane interlaced her fingers around a knee. "We've discussed before going on antidepressants."

He dropped his head back, squirming against the notion. "I don't really want to."

"Why not?"

"It just makes me feel weak."

"You're in a weak place right now."

He put his head in his hands, trying to dig for the words to articulate this fierce aversion. "I don't want to be that kind of person. I don't want to need a pharmaceutical crutch the rest of my life. It makes me feel... I don't know. Weak."

"Let me tell you what meds won't do," Diane said. "They won't make it all go away. They won't numb you, they won't fix you. If you keep coming to see me, you are going to keep feeling, Erik, and feeling bad and feeling hard. But with the proper medication, we can slice off the extreme end of the spectrum, those horrible episodes of depression and anxiety keeping you from making progress with me. Meds can hold the floor under your feet while we rebuild some of your walls."

He chewed on her metaphor, allowing himself to entertain the idea. "I guess so."

"And the goal here, Erik, my goal, is to get you off the meds. I certainly don't want you on them for the rest of your life if it's not necessary. And honestly, I don't think you will be."

With her declaring she had a goal for him, his trust in her deepened. He ran his fingers through his hair and sighed. "All right," he whispered. "All right, I'll try."

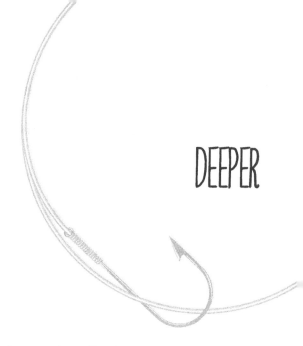

DEEPER

HE SAW A DOCTOR, who tried several medications before finding one that got the floor under his feet without giving him nauseating headaches or killing his appetite. He also got a prescription for Klonopin, to use as needed for anxiety. It was the closest thing to a wolf-killer he could imagine. Half a tablet took the edge off a panic attack but still let him go about daily business. If the pack came at night to get him, he took a full tablet and so long, suckers.

He was starting to sleep again. And as Diane had foreseen, the drugs did dull the razor-sharp edge to the depression. Which he appreciated. But they also sliced off the other end of the spectrum, and he noticed nothing particularly excited him, either.

Which he could handle.

He and Diane kept digging.

"God, the blood," he said. "I hate blood. I couldn't get it off me. Everything was just soaked with it."

"Whose blood?"

"Everyone's."

Daisy's blood caked in the hair of his forearms. Outlining his fingernails and crusted in his eyebrows.

Lucky's blood on the bathroom floor.

David's blood on the kitchen wall.

"My dreams were filled with blood," he said. "It's all over some of my memories. I'm not exaggerating when I say I think back to some of those times and it's—" He made a throwing motion with both hands, an imaginary bucket of blood. "It's splashed there."

"Your loved ones were shot," Diane said, and began to raise her fingers, one at a time. "A boy committed suicide in front of your eyes. Your girlfriend's leg had to be sliced open. You held a girl having a miscarriage. You beat up a friend who betrayed you." She was out of fingers. Her hand curled into a fist and dropped on the arm of the chair. "These are horrible, bloody experiences, Erik. Spaced over the course of a lifetime you wouldn't just blithely get over them. They all happened to you in a single year."

Erik stared past her, open-mouthed. "It was bad," he said. He admitted it. Declared it. His mind flipped up an unexpected image of himself as a small boy, in his parents' bedroom door.

I had a bad dream.

Standing at the foot of their bed with an affronted attitude. A sense of entitlement and a need to be validated.

I had a bad dream. Something terrible happened. Look at me. Agree.

"It was horrible," he said.

Diane looked at him and nodded, agreeing.

DEEPER.

"Can you tell me about David?"

He spoke of coming into the hall at the top of the stairs, seeing David's bedroom door open. Peering into the dimness to discover David had a girl in bed.

"I was about to leave. Turn around and tactfully get the hell out of there."

"Why were you there in the first place?"

He blew his breath out. "That," he said, "is not one of my finer moments."

Diane sat still.

"I went over there to see if David had any coke."

"I take it you don't mean the beverage."

"No."

"Were you doing cocaine often in college?"

"I'd never touched it before senior year. But after the shooting I started doing it. We all did. Coke and ecstasy."

"Daisy too?"

"Yes. Her and I. Will and Lucky. We got it from David. We were getting high all the time."

Diane's chin rose and fell. "I see. Let's table that for another day. Right now I'm just confused about the situation. You went to his apartment looking to score."

"Fine, put it that way. Yes."

"Why did you go upstairs? To his bedroom?"

"Because," Erik said. "I got to his apartment and the door was open. And he did have coke that day. It was left on the coffee table. It was just out, in the middle of the living room. And I immediately thought something was wrong. David would never... He was reckless but he wasn't stupid. I put some magazines over the mirror to hide it. I tied up the baggie and went upstairs with it. I thought something had happened to him."

"I see. And you went upstairs and you saw he was in bed."

He saw the bared upper half of David's body emerging from the sheets, his arms and back tensed and ropy with muscle. The unmistakable rhythm and groove of his hips. A girl's hand at the back of his head, pale against his dark hair

"Funny," Erik said absently. "When I was about six, I got up in the middle of one night and walked in on my parents having sex." He trailed off, staring at the wall. "I don't know why that just popped into my head."

"Push it a little," Diane murmured.

"I guess," he said, both pushing and pulling at the two unrelated images. "There's watching porn, and seeing sex in the movies, but when you actually see it in front of your face, you walk in on the human, unstaged act of..." He laughed a little. "When you're a kid it's sort of horrifying. When you're an adult, there's something ridiculous about it. When I saw David banging this chick, I almost laughed. But in a friendly, almost affectionate way. I could tease him about it later. *Nicely done, Dave, perfect ten for technique.*"

"But it wasn't some chick."

"He was on top of her. I didn't see who it was. But then..."

David had rolled, tumbling to his back, pulling the girl on top of him. He'd been smiling. Erik saw the flash of his teeth in the dimness. An open-mouthed grin of gasping delight. David was happy, which was such a rare thing to witness. The girl's body glided on top of his and her eyes slid past the door, then doubled back. She pushed the tangle of hair out of her face.

And then the slow-motion nuclear explosion, a mushroom cloud of disbelief, and the skies opening up to rain down death. Because it was Daisy in David's bed. Daisy sliding on top of David, making him smile like that. Naked, tousled Daisy staring at Erik, who stared back. The staring. Their way of drawing together into a private universe. Now they stared as their universe blew itself to smithereens.

"Do you think it had been going on for some time?" Diane asked.

Erik shook his head, mouth open. "I never saw it coming. I had no suspicions. None. She and I were barely having any sex but we were still so close... I never imagined she would go sleep with someone else."

"The shock must have been indescribable."

"David," he said, spitting the name on the rug. "I knew I couldn't trust him, I knew he would fuck me over in the end. Son of a bitch only wanted what he couldn't have and if he couldn't have it, he'd steal it."

"You assume he stole her?"

Erik looked at her. "What?"

"You seem convinced he seduced Daisy. Not the other way around."

He closed his eyes. "It doesn't matter who seduced whom," he whispered. "She had my heart. I gave her my soul. I helped her after she was shot. I held her head when she was throwing up. I helped her to the bathroom, in and out of the shower. I was there when she woke up screaming. I gave her every single thing in me and then she fucked David and *don't* ask me how it felt, Diane. I know you're going to. Just don't."

Diane was silent.

Erik opened his eyes. "She ruined everything."

Diane glanced at her watch. "We have to stop now."

"Yes," Erik said. "We do."

ONE NIGHT HE DREAMED of his father, and called him by name.

Byron.

Erik was out in a golden boat on a lake, reeling in fish after golden fish. Calling out *Byron* with every catch, calling to his father, who stood on the shore, waving. Erik let go his rod and reel, cupped hands and yelled over the water, *Who do I look like?*

And his father called back, *You look like me.*

Erik woke up. Calmly came out of sleep. The dream had been gentle. Uncomplicated. He lay in bed, his fingers tracing his collarbone where the chain had once hung. Staring into the dark corner of his little room, his mind was far away, walking the galleries of his life's museum, where he touched memories long abandoned.

They were there.

They were delicate, light things, like feathers, wafting away if he grabbed too hard at them. But they were there. Sensory and tactile. Blocks of scrap wood to play with. The rhythm and ring of hammers. The smoky whine of the power saw. The smell of sawdust and paint as a forest playground emerged in Erik and Peter's bedroom.

"He was a set designer," Daisy had said after Erik described the loft beds, the trees, swing and hammock.

"Maybe it's why I was drawn to technical theater," Erik said to Diane at his next session. "The smell and sound of the workshop reminded me of him."

"Could be," Diane said. "Or it could just be what you love. Not everything has to be a thing, you know."

He glanced at her. "You learn that line in school?"

"No, from my mother," she said, one of her rare, personalized engagements.

More feathers, piling up in his hands, drifting around his ankles. If he sat still, if he put aside the customary armor of anger and pride, they came to him. He made his breath hover above the snowy heaps, leaned into their silence.

"Where are you now," she said.

"With him," he whispered. A lap, and a gold necklace to play with. Strong arms lifting him up to sink a basketball. A broad back beneath his stomach, on top of a sled in winter. Gentle hands steadying the seat of his bicycle. *Prosit* when he sneezed. *Skål* for a toast.

He remembered his mother's silhouette, on top of his father like they were wrestling. They were laughing in the dark of their bedroom and Erik had thought it was a game. A game his father wasn't trying too hard to win.

"They didn't fight," he said. "I don't remember them fighting. I only remember them laughing. In their bed. In the dark."

He'd had no context for it at the time. Now its significance ripped him open.

Because he remembered when they were a family.

And he remembered when they weren't anymore.

After their father was gone, he and Pete wouldn't sleep among the trees of their bedroom. They didn't want the swings and the hammock. They recoiled from the lingering smell of wet paint. Defiantly they dragged sleeping bags to Christine's bedroom and slept on her floor until she sold their house and they moved away from the past. Tried to start again.

He sat still, the tears making steady tracks down his face. The pain pressed on him from all sides.

"You must have missed him horribly," Diane said.

What an obvious thing to say.

But what a truthful thing to say.

I had a bad dream.

"I missed him." He closed his eyes, took it out of the past and cradled it in his hands. "But I don't know if he missed me."

The forbidden thought, now spoken aloud, was a knife in his heart, slashing straight down to his guts. He thought he would die. This boyhood pain was insurmountable. He was unmanned.

"I wonder where he is," he said, surrendering to the question coiled up in his bones. A daily inquiry actively thought or subconsciously pondered, but constantly with him, a gene on his Y chromosome: *Where are you, Dad?*

"I wonder if he even thinks about me." He shook his head, opening his eyes. "I wonder if he saw the news stories about Lancaster. If he saw it on TV or read it in the paper. I wonder if he saw my name and thought *that's my son.* If he did, and even a shooting couldn't move him to find me, then either he has no heart or..."

"Or what?" Diane said.

"Or he's dead."

He looked down at his empty palms and saw white feathers. Exhaling wearily, he watched them blow away.

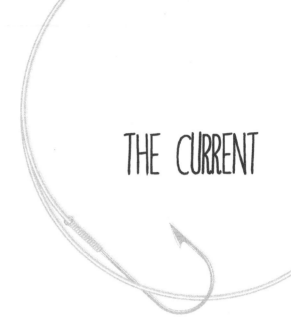

THE CURRENT

THEY DUG.

Deeper.

Erik came in one afternoon in a bad mood. He chucked his jacket off, plopped down on the couch and put an ankle on the other knee. He exhaled loudly and Diane raised her eyebrows at him, but said nothing. She always waited for him to make the opening serve.

"I had a date last night," he said. He was attempting to do this more often—get out there and open himself up to the possibility of connecting with someone.

She volleyed easily. "What was that like?"

"A disaster."

"How so?"

"She was lovely, it wasn't her. It was just my usual bullshit."

"Which is?"

"It's the second, no, third time we've gone out. We ended up back at her place and..." He trailed off awkwardly.

"Did you sleep together?" Diane said.

"Yeah. It was fine during it. Great, actually. But then afterward, I was a wreck."

"What happened?"

"I don't know. I was lying there having a panic attack. I had to get the hell out. I felt really bad but... This is like the story of my life. This always happens and I don't know why."

"You find this always happens when you go to bed with someone?"

"I'm fine before, fine during, and then afterward, I go into a death spiral. Is it cold in here?"

"I don't think so. Are you cold?"

"A little. What were you asking me?"

"How long has this been happening?"

He took a deep breath, shuffling his cards. Pointless posturing, but naturally with any kind of sexual issue, the kneejerk reaction was to sugarcoat. But if he was here to dig into it, if he was paying to dig into it, then he may as well dig into it. "Since the shooting," he said miserably. "Five years."

Diane barely blinked. "That long."

"Yes."

"So even with Daisy this happened."

"Both of us."

She shifted to lean on the other arm of the chair. "Both of you would have anxiety after sex."

"You're going to do that annoying thing of parroting everything I say back to me, aren't you?"

She smiled, her tongue pushing into her cheek for a moment. "Yes, I am."

He crossed his arms over his chest, trying to organize his thoughts without thinking too much. "Daisy and I had some issues with sex after the shooting," he said. "Two problems. Three. Two right away and the third later. First, immediately afterward it was just impossible, physically impossible. She could barely get out of a chair, much less into bed. Honestly, it was the furthest thing from either of our minds. Forget I said it was a problem. The issue was when we started again. It was weird, we both felt really disconnected. Ambivalent. Like we could take it or leave it. And I guess that's pretty normal for post-traumatic stressed people."

Diane nodded. "It's the first thing to go."

"And then we started feeling like it again, but every time it was good between us, we'd end up a wreck."

"From anxiety?"

"Sheer panic. Shaking and nauseous and terrified. Of nothing."

"And this was before? During?"

"Just after. Occasionally it was good, I mean really good during it and actually peaceful afterward. Occasionally. But then it was like we'd be sucker-punched—it would be twice as bad the next time, like we were being punished. We were flailing. We didn't know what to do. At all."

"Did you seek any help?"

He laughed. "Shit no."

"Why not?"

"Because we were twenty-one and twenty-two years old for crying out loud. Who thinks to go into sex therapy then, no matter what the circumstances? Come on." He tucked his fingers under his arms. He was nearly shivering and he pressed his feet hard on the floor to stay his knees.

She nodded, twisting the corners of her mouth. "All right, fair point. So you just muddled through it."

"We did, but we muddled together. Both of us had the same problem. If it were her lying there anxious and I was fine, or the other way around, it would have sucked. But we'd both be nauseous and shaking. We were in it together."

Diane drew a foot up under her leg. "I was just going to ask you if the loss of sex made the relationship feel diminished in any way. But it sounds as though you remained emotionally bonded. If anything, your bond grew stronger?"

"We were tighter. Definitely. We were rarely apart. We needed each other. We didn't understand what was happening but we talked about it. We tried to laugh at it."

"Yet something in your consciousness was linking sex to anxiety."

Erik raked his hands through his hair, frustrated. "I don't get it. If walking into the theater made me anxious, or rehearsing, or running a show, it would make sense to me."

"But instead sex was the trigger. Why do you think?"

"You're the shrink, you tell me."

"Do you have any ideas?"

He resisted the urge to throw the pillow at her. "No, I got nothing. I have no idea why my greatest source of joy and comfort made me feel like I was going to die. By all means, enlighten me. The shooting had nothing to do with sex."

"It didn't?"

He threw the pillow, but at the side wall, not at Diane. "Oh good lord, don't do this. What are you getting at?"

Diane's eyes hadn't even flicked toward the trajectory of the cushion—apparently worse things had been thrown in this office. Languidly she reached for her coffee cup and took a reflective sip. "Let's back up a little. How soon prior to the shooting did you have sex with Daisy? Or been in any kind of sexual environment with her."

"I told you I can't remember anything before the shooting."

Diane put her coffee cup down. "Try," she said.

Erik exhaled. "Let me think."

"Any kind of physical, loving, intimate way. What was the last time you remember before the shooting?"

The cold in his limbs intensified, grew prickling and sinister as he tried to think. "It was...." Every thought he began bumped into an invisible wall and splintered. "It was—" he began a half-dozen times, only to trail off as his mind faded out, and every time it faded out, his chest got tighter. "Diane, I'm sorry. I can't think when," he finally said. "It's gone."

"You're getting agitated."

"I know." He wasn't feeling good. Something was wrong.

"Do you feel frightened?"

"A little bit... Yeah."

Her voice dropped, not in volume, but in pitch, lower, resonant, calm. "I think this is important," she said.

He tried to get air in past the obstruction in his chest. He wanted to say *I can't breathe,* but it came out, "I can't remember."

"Try to relax, Erik. Listen to my voice. We're going to work through this together."

He was shaking now. A cold, dark wind through him, trying to blow him back from going down this road. "What's happening to me?"

Diane got up slowly, being careful not to startle him. "Your body is trying to keep you from remembering."

She took a blanket from one of the other easy chairs and held it out to him.

"It's going to be frightening but it is not going to kill you. I promise. Let it come back to you. I'm right here. I'm not going to let you face it alone."

It seemed a supreme act of bravery to put himself into her hands, but he did, wrapping the blanket around him like armor. "All right."

"Try to remember when, before the shooting, you were last sexual with Daisy."

He closed his eyes. "I don't even know where to start rewinding."

"Start in the aisle. When you came out of the booth into the aisle. What was before?"

"I was under the console with the broken glass. And before... I was watching the shit go down. And before that I was running lights"

"Now back up from there. Before James came in. Before the dancing even started. What were you doing?"

"Diane, I can't breathe."

"You can. The air is going in. You're breathing. I promise."

"All right."

"Back up. Where are you?"

He visualized the action running in reverse. "It was a rehearsal. A tech run-through. And it was Daisy's turn. They would have called her and she would have come...from the audience. No. Wait."

Like a small bright flower, the memory rebloomed: Daisy, walking down the aisle. Tying her skirt as she headed toward the stage. His mind pulled back, widening the recollection. Daisy turned back and waved at him, then walked down the aisle. Which meant she'd been...

"Where are you, Erik?"

Another flower unfolded its petals. In the booth. Of course. She'd been in the booth with him. "It was," he began, but his throat was bone-dry. He cleared it. "It was..."

"Stay here. I know it's hard."

"I feel like I'm dying."

"Tell me."

"The lighting booth."

"When?"

"Before she went onstage to rehearse, Daisy was with me in the lighting booth."

"Tell me."

It was so strange, picking these flowers. He looked at them, sure they belonged to someone else. Then he held them closer to his face, caught their scent and he knew they were real. They were real and they were his. He remembered.

"She was sitting on my lap and..." It was flooding him now, fast and furious. Not flowers but a white-water river of memory churning up in his brain, each recollection clamoring for attention and refusing to be corralled into order. His hands came up to the sides of his head, trying to hold it all in place.

"Were you having sex in the booth?"

"Yes. I mean no, not then. It was the night before. God, I'm all over the place."

"It's all right. Keep backing up. Tell me about the night before."

He opened his eyes and looked at her helplessly. "My head is spinning, I can't even..."

"Erik look at the wall. Right there, the place where it's blank. Take everything in your head and fling it on the wall. Like a movie. Put it there."

He tried, stared hard at the white expanse of space and attempted to project his thoughts onto it. He even imagined a whirring clicking noise, like a projector. It worked. The tornado in his head died down to a gentle gale. "We were in her room, and we were just... God, I remember now."

"Describe it to me, what are you feeling?"

He knew Diane wanted him to speak in present tense but it was too terrifying. Until he could figure out what was scaring him so much, he had to keep it in the past.

"We were making love but it was..." He trailed off as the images on the wall grew brighter, more vivid, dripping sweat and giving off a faint scent of sex and perfume. Desire, thick like syrup, caramel sweet and rich. The bumps of Daisy's spine and the muscles along them rippling as he thrust into her from behind, slow and sure and strong. Something almost narcissistic about it—admiring himself in his prime. All cut arms and abs, bursting with health and stamina. He was young, rock hard and raring, carefree and reckless. He could fuck her all night, she only had to ask. And she did. She begged for it.

"I had her down on the bed. I was behind her and I was just holding her down and fucking her. Sorry," he said.

"There's no shame there. When you've established that kind of trust and intimacy, sex wears all kinds of faces."

The movie on the wall, which had been silent, now offered up a soundtrack of memory as well. "She was saying...things. Like *you fuck me so good* and... I can't believe I'm telling you this."

"It's not about me," she murmured. "Go on."

"It made me feel incredible, like I really dialed into what it felt like to be a man. I was down at some elemental level of being..."

"Male."

He nodded, lost and transfixed in the remembering. "I was making her come. Getting her off, one after the other. She kept begging and I kept going and we just fed on each other. And at one point she put her hands behind her back and I held onto them. She just gave herself over to me."

"It sounds intense."

"I can't believe I forgot this."

"You didn't forget."

"God, I had her in my hands. Had her right where I wanted her and I wanted to make her scream the house down."

"You were very much in love with her."

"Yes."

"You trusted each other. You were utterly free to say whatever you wanted and be whatever you wanted. You could be loving and sweet, or you could be primal and savage. You could make love or you could fuck, it was all the same thing."

A stream of tears on his cheek then. He hadn't even realized his eyes had welled up. "I never knew anything like it in my life."

"And there seemed to be no end to it."

"Nothing to stop it."

"And when you were in the lighting booth the next day," Diane said.

He turned his head from the wall. "She was in there with me," he said. "She was sitting in my lap and we were talking about it. Talking about the night before. And we were laughing and rehashing it and sort of blushing. This coy bit of *I can't believe the shit I was saying,* but we were laughing. Teasing each other. And God, I couldn't wait to get her alone again. Get my hands on her again. Usually she was the practical one. Nothing ever swayed her from class or rehearsal. But she was sitting in my lap and she was all in my eyes. She said, *I just want to ditch this place and go back to bed with you.* But Marie called her and she had to go. And she..." He squeezed himself tight, his ice-cold, shaking hands in fists, all of him shaking, looking for a place to flee.

"Let it out, Erik."

"She kissed me one more time and she walked down the aisle. But she turned back and looked at me. And waved. And that moment right there—everything was amazing. She pointed at me and she was smiling at me. Everything was perfect. I was so happy. I swear it's the last time in my life I remember being completely and totally happy."

"You were connected to her," Diane said. "With every cell of your body."

"It was like I was still inside her."

"And you were still connected to the night before, yes. The current of sexuality was still live. It was still crackling."

"Yes."

"It was a powerful moment, Erik. A moment layered with joy. All kinds of deeply intense feelings of love and connection and arousal and youth."

"I was so happy," he whispered. "I was..." He was starting to cry as the fabric of the universe began to tear down the center, thread by thread, warp and weft separating.

"Lean into it," she said. "Don't pull back, Erik. Tell me."

"I was looking at her. But I was looking at Will, too. And David behind the set. All my friends onstage and backstage. My teachers. Everyone I loved, all of us in the theater. My life was right there. It was perfect. I was so happy..."

"And then?"

"James came in."

"And what did he do?"

The tears dripped into his mouth as he answered, "He shot it."

"Yes."

"He told me it was a fairytale. He told me the day would come when I would lose her and then I would know what it was like. He made that day come. He *brought* it to me."

"You were one of his targets, Erik."

"It wasn't just Will. He came after me, too."

"Even though you had him in your pocket all that time."

"Oh my God."

"He came and he shot down your happiness."

"He killed it." He curled over his knees, sobbing into his hands. "He took it away from me, he shot all of it down. It was gone. It was dead, all of it. And Daisy..."

The river of memory closed over his head, picked him up and tossed him along. The current battered him against the rocks, dragged him on the gravel, filled his lungs with frigid, brackish water that choked and burned. Out of the depths of his young heart poured his grief, the raging, bitter injustice of what had been done to him. He cried hard, for the undeserved ripping of pages from the stories of his life. For the senseless destruction of everything he'd held so dear.

Diane made no move to rescue him or throw a lifeline. She sat quietly as he wept. It was strange, disconcerting, crying so unreservedly in front of someone, a woman no less, who made no move to comfort him. Without a word or gesture or touch, she sat there, giving him her unconditional presence.

She was his witness.

She put no spin on his pain, just acknowledged it, a tiny piece of public within this intensely private moment of grief. His trust she would rescue him if it were warranted, was absolute.

"How do you feel?" she asked when finally he brought his face out of his hands.

"Like I have the flu." He ached all over and he thanked God he'd made this appointment late in the afternoon. He guessed he had just enough in the tank to get himself home and collapse.

"Do you see now, Erik? How when you would try to make love, terror and anxiety would immediately follow?"

"I do see it now. I can't believe... Never in a million years would I have linked those things together."

"They were already linked. You just weren't aware."

"How do you not be aware of something like that?"

Diane leaned forward in her chair. For a moment Erik thought she was actually going to touch him, take his hands in hers. But she only clasped her own hands together and looked at him intently. "What happened, Erik," she said, "was *traumatizing.*"

"I had a bad dream," he whispered.

"The way the brain deals with trauma is to suppress. It doesn't forget. It just pushes the trauma somewhere deep, where it continues to exert its power without you being aware of it." She sat back, but her gaze stayed fixed on him, holding him rapt. "It is absolutely no shock the repercussions to your relationship with Daisy were sexual. It makes perfect sense being sexual and loving and connected brought on feelings of extreme anxiety. It makes sense you are reluctant or even outright averse to leaning into the joyful moments of your life because part of you is now braced and waiting for something to come along and blow your joy to bits."

"What do I do?" he said. "How do I stop this?"

Her smile was indulgent. "You've begun today. This was a huge step. You did an amazing thing here."

"And we're out of time, I take it?"

"For today. But we have plenty of time to work this out."

COUP DE GRÂCE

HE WENT HOME. He was still chilled and feeling the residue of the session on his skin, so he took a long hot shower before falling into bed and careening into sleep.

And he dreamed.

Dreams with cruel vividness and clarity, with not a shred of the absurd to remind him these were only dreams. He was back up in Daisy's room, in her bed, wrapped in her arms and legs and hair. Her mouth swollen and hungry in his, her breath in his lungs as she whispered amazing things.

Up on his elbows, cradled in her thighs, he held her head in his hands, her hair woven around and between his fingers. As he worked his hips in her, his necklace swung back and forth by her chin. She kept catching the fish in her teeth and smiling up at him. Those gorgeous, wicked, blue-green eyes. She had him. She'd caught him. He was where he belonged and it would never end, ever.

He rolled down and pulled her up onto him, a cartwheel of limbs and a seamless, unbroken kiss. And then she was over him, leaning on his wrists, holding him down, onto him and all over him and so damn good at him. He could writhe here forever, gripped from within and without by her body on top of his. Firm flesh and soft skin, shifting muscle and bone. So small but so strong and coaxing from him emotions he didn't even know he had. They burst from him unbidden as he gasped out of their kiss, holding her head, holding her mouth still against his, fighting for breath. *I love you, Dais. I love you, I love you...*

Then the dream turned dark.

Pitch black. Thick, tangible black. His back burning under the rake of her fingernails. The taste of blood in his mouth. Her hair damp and sweaty in his tight fist. His weight pinning her to the floor, to the wall, to the bed. Her wrists crossed in her back. Holding her down. Hurting her. His teeth on the back of her neck as he tore her up because she needed it.

Down into the black.

Down...

Erik woke up coming, sweating and trembling, a lap full of sweet, strong wetness and the taste of blood on his tongue as his mouth cried Daisy's name out to the dark. The thin dark of his room. He was awake. Alone and cold. She wasn't there anymore, she'd sent him back.

I'm useless to her.

He crawled back into the shower, literally crawled and sat under the spray, curled up against the wall of the tub. He had the hot water full blast, steam billowing in clouds around him, but he was freezing again, drowning in the icy rapids. He could not get warm, could not get out of his own head. He put on his warmest clothes, even a hat, made tea and warmed up some soup but he could barely tolerate a sip or spoonful. He was sick.

He was crazy.

He pushed the bowl away and picked up the phone. He got Diane's voicemail, left what he hoped was a coherent message, and then resumed pacing around and sipping plain, hot water. She called him back in five minutes.

"Help," he said.

"Help is here. Tell me what happened when you went home."

He sketched it out for her, too anxious to be embarrassed.

"I'm sorry, Erik," she said. "We didn't leave off in a safe place."

"What do you mean?"

"It's difficult to end a session in a place where you feel safe, in a place where you can put down whatever we were discussing and leave it there. We were in the middle of something rather intense, and you took it with you."

"I need to talk to you," he said. "I can't tough it out another week."

"Of course not. I'm glad you called. I can meet you at my office in ten minutes, can you come?"

"You'd see me?" he asked. "Tonight?"

"Erik," she said, "it's my job. You've hired me. I'm on your team now."

"Thank you," he whispered.

"See you in ten minutes. Drive safely, please."

HE TOLD HER. Unloaded all of it—the cocaine and ecstasy, and all those nights in the pitch dark when he and Daisy tried, it seemed, to kill each other. To fuck each other to death.

"The last time," he said, "when I had her in the shower afterward. Her body... She was like this broken thing. The scars on her thigh and the scars on her calf. And then the scratches down her back and the bruises on her arms. Her hair was collecting in the drain because I had pulled on it. It was horrible."

"It must have been frightening."

"But it felt so good. Violence made the sex amazing and I didn't understand. I still don't. Well, maybe I do a little. I see how they were tied together in our minds. Maybe... Maybe we were trying to connect back with the night before the shooting. Because the night had such a raw edge to it."

"But remember it was deeply loving as well. And since feelings of love only brought anxiety, possibly you had to jettison it and focus solely on the raw savagery."

"I have no memory of thinking that way."

"Of course not, it was purely subconscious. You were simply trying to take control any way you could. And losing control simultaneously."

"I remember I couldn't do it anymore," he said. "Be violent in bed. But I think she still needed it. And then I was useless to her."

Diane inclined her head. "You feel that?"

"I do. I really believe Daisy needed the violence. She was hooked on it. Just like coke. I wouldn't give it to her and she went to David to get it. To ask him for it, knowing he would do anything for her."

"You must have been devastated."

"She killed me," he whispered.

"It seems you're still angry with her," Diane said after a moment.

He opened his mouth to reply of course, but then stopped to think about it. Was he angry with her? Of course he was. At least he had been. Was he still?

"Am I?" he said.

"Are you?"

He put his head in his hands, pulling the hair back from his temples. "I don't understand," he said, sighing. "I still don't understand how she could do it."

"She was traumatized as well, Erik. I'll play devil's advocate for a moment and say she may not have been entirely in her right mind when she slept with your friend."

"It's possible," Erik said, thinking of the cocaine left carelessly on David's coffee table, "she was high when she slept with him."

"Would you treat it as a reason or an excuse?"

Erik looked at her. "I don't like to treat it at all."

Diane gazed back, fingertips steepled beneath her chin. "I can't speak to her experience, Erik. She's not here. We're talking about you and your experience. About what it was like, no matter the reason or excuse, to find her in bed with David. After everything you had been through together."

"Everything I did," he whispered. "Crawled through broken glass. Stared down the barrel of a gun. And it wasn't enough. She made me feel useless."

"Yes," she murmured.

"And used." His face twisted with the pain, eyes hot and throat tight. "It was almost like another shooting. Except she had the gun this time." A swift rage filled him and he grabbed the tissue box and fired it against the far wall. "*Fuck*," he said, sinking his face into his hand again. "Sorry. I'm not aiming at you."

"I know," she said calmly.

"She was... She had my life, Diane. She had my soul. She was like this." Erik put his hands out, cupped together, open and receiving. "Like this. And I put myself there. Everything. Anything. No secrets. Stories about my father, memories of my father. I would put them in her hands and she would hold them. She understood me. And then it was ruined."

"Was it?"

"You know how when they execute someone by firing squad, the captain takes the last shot. It has a name. It's French, Daisy would know it."

"The coup de grâce," Diane said.

"Yeah. The death blow. It killed me."

"And you left."

"I left. And I know why I haven't gotten seriously involved with another woman since. Part of me never wants to hurt like that again. But God, this hurts even when I'm alone." He glanced around but there was nothing to throw.

"It's your heart," Diane said, getting up herself and retrieving the tissue box. "Your heart is breaking."

"It's breaking now? I can't do this again."

"That would be a fair statement except you never did it the first time." She set the box in his lap. "You can throw it again, just aim over my head."

"I didn't do it the first time?"

"Did you? Did you feel it at the time? You lost the love of your life. Did you take the time to feel all that grief and pain? Loss is trauma, same as a shooting incident or any act of violence. It's emotional violence. You don't forget. You simply suppress. And while you suppress, the grief gathers strength to come back at a later time. With more power to kill you. You may want to trust me on this one, Erik, because I see it a lot."

He sighed, spinning the tissue box in his hands. "You think I have trust issues?"

"I think a Tibetan monk would have trust issues after your experiences. Who do you trust now, Erik?"

He gave up his most charming smile. "I trust you."

"And I'm glad to hear it. Outside this office, who are the people closest to you? How many people do you let into your heart?"

"Not. Many."

"I'm not surprised. You were eight and trusting in the world, and your father left. You were twenty-one and trusting in the world, and James came into the theater with a gun. Then you were trusting in your relationship with Daisy, and she slept with your friend. We have a lot going on here," she said

Erik glared, thinking she sounding a little too pleased, as if he were a project. "I just want to stop hurting. I want to stop waking up in the morning and feeling like the day is already out to get me. Stop fucking *crying* all the time. Jesus, it's like I don't even recognize myself anymore."

"I don't know if it will ever cease to be a painful subject, Erik. Possibly this is always going to matter to you. The goal now is to learn to open your heart and trust. Not so much trust in love or trust in people, but trust in yourself. So if you do get hurt—and that's probably a when not an if—you will be able to survive. Because you have survived."

"But I'm a wreck. I'm on meds, I'm in therapy. This fucking woman ruined my life."

"You're alive. You're here in this office taking it on. This is it, Erik, this is surviving. It's not one event, it's a process. And it's not a linear process. You don't start at point A and just get to point B and you're fine again. It's a matrix. It's a three-dimensional scaffold you build around your life. You'll find it's cyclical. And seasonal. April might always be a tough month for you, it might be your haunted time of year. Or it might not. The point is you can lean into your weak moments the same way you can lean into joy. Pain makes joy sweeter. And joy helps you survive pain. You can't have one without the other. If you open yourself to both, you are, by default, surviving."

Erik nodded, his eyes far away, but his entire being listening to her.

"Do you feel all right about leaving it here, are you safe?"

"I think so."

"If you get home and you're not, you call me."

"All right."

"Call me. We'll come back as many times as it takes."

He paused for a moment, feeling out the professional line between them.

"I like *we*," he said.

"You won't do this alone," she said. "I'm on your team."

He smiled, glad—for perhaps the first time—he was doing this work. "Thanks, doc."

"I'll see you next week, if not before."

PART FIVE: MELANIE

ADJUNCT ASSHOLE

MILES CALLED ERIK one night in late summer of 1998, full of gossip and intrigue. The technical theater director at Brockport State had just resigned in disgrace, in a scandal involving not one, but two freshmen girls, and a boatload of video tapes.

"Video," Erik said, eyebrows raised. "Impressive. Did you see any of it?"

"No, goddammit."

The college was desperate to distance itself, sweep out the closet before any skeletons could take residence. They needed to regroup and replace as soon as humanly possible.

"And, let me guess," Erik said. "Distract everyone's attention away from the video tape to a big main stage production."

"Big," Miles said. "Big-ass, I believe was the expression used."

Big-ass productions required big-ass stagecraft, but big-ass applicants were proving hard to find. "So I said I knew this guy down in Brockport," Miles said. "No formal teaching experience—"

"Try no experience," Erik said.

"But he's good. A natural with kids—"

"Kids. Not college students. Kids."

"And a born leader."

"Miles, are you saying my ass is big?"

"I'm saying, is your resume up to date?"

"I'm incredibly flattered. Thank you for thinking of me, Miles. You're a prince. And they will never give me the job."

"Come up," Miles said. "Come up and visit us. Janey misses you. And go interview for the hell of it. Chance of a lifetime, Fish. What's the worst that could happen? They say 'Thanks but no thanks,' and you go back to Geneseo."

He went for the hell of it. And he got the job.

"I got the part," he said. This was the theater, after all.

"Someone must have liked your ass," Miles said.

Packing his possessions into a jumble of boxes, duffel bags and laundry baskets, Erik felt a new man. After a year of intensive therapy he was seeing Diane just once a month. His regular doctor had been dialing down the dosage of the antidepressants. He was nearly off them and any episodes of anxiety were few and far between. He was feeling good. Head shrunk, almost med-free and shit together. Things were interesting again. Food tasted good, sleep was a friend. He was back in shape and ready for a change.

He still felt woefully underqualified for the position, but as he toured the performing arts complex and got to know his colleagues, he couldn't help but feel a rejuvenated excitement. People were happy he was there. Grateful he was there. Miles and Janey fussed around, helping him get settled. He had an office. And a business card, for crying out loud: *Erik Fiskare, Adjunct Professor of Technical Theater.*

"So now it's Professor Asshole," Miles said, as they went for a run in Corbett Park.

"Adjunct asshole. Sounds kind of sexy."

"Sounds like a medical condition I wouldn't want."

Brockport is a village in the town of Sweden. Erik got an ancestral kick out of that. He liked the feel of the place. Beautiful Victorian houses nestled on tree-lined streets and the stately Erie Canal gave Brockport its old world charm and quaint village air. State College brought a buzzing modern energy to downtown, where Erik had his apartment on Apple Street.

He moved from Geneseo in a hurry, dove straight into the new job and never completely unpacked. He didn't hang any pictures or buy himself mugs or a bathmat. A skeleton kitchen was good enough. He made sure the windows facing the street were decently covered and hooked up the stereo and TV. The rest was just floors and walls and a drafting table.

The fall semester was a blur of activity. The theater director pitched *Noises Off* as the main stage production. Erik wasn't familiar with it. He picked up a copy of the script at the library, took it home to read and blanched. It was a British play-within-a play comedy, dependent on a thousand technical cues and effects. This was no open the curtain, close the curtain affair. He'd have to build a set on a turntable, a set to be viewed from both sides.

"I'm screwed," he said to Miles on their daily run. "This is way too big an ass."

"Then you'll have to build big pants."

In his small, Spartan apartment, Erik paced and panicked. *What would Leo Graham do?*

"He'd get to work," he said. He talked to himself a lot lately.

He made tea, sat down and read the play again. A thought tapped his shoulder and he reached for a pad of paper. An idea sat in his lap. He filled page after page with notes and sketches. The high of creative flow began to creep through his veins. He touched the groove. Took a careful taste. Put one foot on the bedrock of his own capability and tested it. Then the other foot. His talent felt solid beneath him. He trusted it. He could pull this off.

The shop had been a disaster area when Erik arrived, a disorganized mess with safety violations warranting public floggings under Leo's regime. Erik cleaned house and began to bring order from chaos. He identified his superstars, his weak links and his filler, and from them he crafted a team. Within a month, he had if not a well-oiled machine, then a respectable jerry-rigged motor humming along with an energetic purpose. The shop came alive. Erik came alive, more alive than he'd been in years.

They pulled it off. *Noises Off* was a smash and kudos rained down on Erik for the set design.

He had arrived.

He collapsed and slept through most of the winter break, reviving for Christmas with his brother. Pete had married at the tender age of twenty-four and had an infant daughter who decided her uncle was a custom-made mattress. Every afternoon Erik napped on the couch with his niece on his chest, her possessive pink fist curled around his finger. It was better than half a Klonopin.

"You're so her bitch," Pete said aloud, tossing a blanket over them. He kissed Valerie's head, then Erik's head, and tiptoed out of the living room, leaving them to drift off in the light of the Christmas tree.

Refreshed and restored, Erik drove over to Brockport State one January morning, a few days before the student body was due back. He wanted time alone to plan classes and putter around.

He was surprised to find the theater doors open. The work lights were on, throwing a harsh florescent wash on the stage. Someone was in here. A prickling wariness made the hair on his arms stand up and his eyes search for the nearest exit. Caution turned to curiosity when he heard a piano being played: the Bach Prelude in C.

C major, the friendliest key.

His heart still thumping, he walked down the aisle and up the side steps to the stage. Now a voice rose over the rolling arpeggios of the piano. The Gounod "Ave Maria" in a rich, clear soprano.

A girl is in here.

The hair on the back of Erik's neck was up now, but not with fear. Intrigued, he made his way to the stage right wings, where the concert baby grand was kept.

A slim, black woman sat at the keys. Long, cornrowed hair gathered back into a thick ponytail. Her shoulders rolled like waves as she leaned arms and hands into the music. Her head tilted and dipped as she sang, riding the phrases out. Erik stared. And listened. For underneath this woman's full, sweet voice, he heard another voice speaking to him. A little nudge in the side. A hand pulling at the tail of his shirt.

Who's she?

The woman sang the last "Amen" over the last fluid arpeggio. She lifted her hands, sustained the final note with the pedal and lifted her toe.

Erik let out the breath he'd been holding, and a long, slow whistle with it. The woman's head flicked back over her shoulder. A second of guarded surprise in her face, then a softening. A little bit more of her turned on the bench. Her eyes looked him up and down. Her mouth curved into a smile.

"Hello."

BY HER OWN ADMISSION, Melanie Winter came from nothing. She grew up in the Langfield Homes in one of the poorest parts of Buffalo—"Buffa-low, baby, about as low as you can go." Her father worked double shifts at the Trico plant, making windshield wipers until he dropped dead of a heart attack when Melanie was ten.

Her mother went out to work driving a bus, leaving Melanie and her sister in the care of their seamstress grandmother. Money was scarce. Discipline was strict. ("Fly swatter, baby, right on the back of the calf— you don't want to feel it twice.") The Winter girls were raised on tough love and pride. And music.

"Music saved me," Melanie said, her hand stroking the keys of the baby grand. Erik leaned on the piano's lid, chin in hands, listening. They had been talking for half an hour now. "Church choir first. Then Gramma bartered sewing for piano lessons. Recitals, school plays and shows, they saved me."

Her mother didn't live to see Melanie graduate from high school and go to the Eastman School of Music on a full scholarship. Her grandmother died shortly after, leaving her life savings to her granddaughters. Melanie's sister took her money and ran, heading west to Chicago. Melanie, on her own in Rochester, hoarded her nest egg and took nearly eight years to earn her degree while working, keeping both soul and body alive. She gave piano lessons, voice lessons, and supplemented with any other kind of work she could find. She wasn't too proud to sling hash. Wherever a community theater struggled, or whenever a school play was in need of help, she was there.

Now thirty-two, this position in Brockport's theater department was her crowning achievement. But like Erik, she was feeling a bit of a fraud.

"You know what I mean? How in the hell did I pull this off, and how soon are they going to find out I don't have a clue how to teach at a university level?"

Erik, just past twenty-eight, knew exactly what she meant. He told her first about his own dubious means of getting the job, his own fears of being exposed as an interloper, and then went on to describe the fall semester and its accomplishments. "You definitely feel like a freshman again," he said. "You keep looking around for the guy in charge and realizing it's you. But you know more than you think you do. And if you don't know it, you make it up."

"Make it up. Sounds like a plan. I'll just act like I know what the hell I'm doing. And it's theater," Melanie said, shrugging. "We're in the business of making it up."

Erik smiled, his eyes sweeping over her smooth, high forehead and her slanting cheekbones. She reminded him of Aisha Johnson, the *Powaqqatsi* queen, gunned down at age twenty. Something was stirring in him, an interest he hadn't felt in months. Or years? A yearning to touch the energy of someone's mind. A desire to step out of the dark and into the light of another human.

"Word on the street is they want to do *Oklahoma!* for the spring main stage production," Melanie said. "To do *Oklahoma!* as my maiden voyage? You know how much vocal work that's going to take? I think I'm going to be sick."

"If I can build a set for *Noises Off* out of the gate, you can do *Oklahoma!* And you won't do it alone."

She smiled. "Well, I know I'll like having Miles Kelly in the orchestra pit. And I think I'll like knowing you're around to talk me off a ledge."

Him of all people, talking someone off a ledge. Erik had to smile back. With some reluctance, he took his elbows off the piano lid and straightened up. "I have to go get some stuff done. But it was really nice talking to you."

"I enjoyed it too. I'm going to just sit and play a while. Will it bother you while you're working?"

"Not at all."

She gave a little wave of her hand, and then turned back to the piano. As he puttered around backstage, he listened as she went through an eclectic mix of songs from Broadway shows, old standards, a pop tune or two, and then shifted back to classical music. He was up on the catwalk, pulling lanterns off the upstage bar when she started playing the Bach Prelude in F Minor.

Daisy's prelude.

His hands froze. His head lifted, tilted toward the music. Out of the past it came, those solemn bass notes underneath the rising chords. Floating up to him on his perch over the stage, not in a painful onslaught but a gentle wisp of smoky memory, wreathing around his head.

Do a triple.

Watch this, Dave.

O mio dio, Margarita, you naughty thing...

He waited for sadness, for anger, for any of the emotions typically attached to those years. They didn't come. He was being pulled in another direction now. Erik crossed his arms on the railing of the catwalk, leaning out a little to look at Melanie at the piano. The curve of her back, the roll and caress of her hands on the keys.

Her head lifted then, and she saw him. She stopped playing and smiled. "There you are," she said.

Gazing back, Erik raised the fingers of one hand, showing his palm to her, then slowly let them drop again.

Here I am...

DREAM BALLET

MELANIE INDISCRIMINATELY CALLED everyone "baby."

Within a week of meeting, Erik was caught up tight in a crush. Crushed to a giddy rubble. The high of being smitten hit his long-sober, intolerant brain like a line of cocaine. He woke with Melanie all over his mind. He drove to work thinking about her vitality and enthusiasm, her terrific, full-throated laugh. Finding ridiculous excuses to pass by her classes in the auditorium or the Black Box, he lurked in the shadows, watching. He admired her teaching and how she kept order—shrouding strict discipline in warm, often self-deprecating humor. From the stories Melanie told him of her childhood, Erik thought he could detect her grandmother's influence.

"Minus the fly swatter," he said.

Melanie held up a finger. "I have one in the office. They better not test me, baby, I will use it."

In their free time, she coaxed him to the piano with her, waving a book of four-hand duets which they picked through. She even got him to sing with her. It was something he'd never feel he was good at, but if it meant his leg and hip could be cozied up to Melanie's on the piano bench, he'd sing his face off.

When he wasn't teaching, Erik was driving his team of stagehands in building a myriad of sets for *Oklahoma!* Besides the landscape backdrops, they needed house fronts with working doors, picket fences with workable gates. They built cabin walls, barn walls, a surrey with the fringe on top. They devised trick knife blades and host of other props.

"Be aware," Miles said privately to Erik. "You're going to have to rig a gunshot blast in the second act. Aunt Eller fires off a rifle."

"I saw that," Erik said, touched by Miles's forethought. "I'll be all right."

He also had to rig up a bit of business for the dream ballet which ended the first act. In the midst of the dancing, to a specific cue in the music, a veil had to fall from the sky. He came up with a mechanism to attach to one of the lighting bars and he picked his most musical stage-hand to man it. But the first time they tried it out, the bit of white voile drifted about, floating everywhere except where it needed to be. Hilarity ensued as the dancers tried to catch it.

Melanie suggested fishing weights sewn into the hem of the veil. Those weren't readily available but Erik got some small washers and Melanie sewed them in place with the swift competence of a well-trained needlewoman. They tried the scene again and this time the veil slammed straight down to the floor.

"Well that ain't romantic, baby," Melanie said.

Finally, after much trial and error, the veil was released and floated perfectly into the action below. Wild applause in the theater. Melanie gave a whoop and jumped onto Erik's back, wrapping him in arms and legs, her full-throated laugh against his ear.

Oklahoma! was a triumph. Full house after full house, standing ovation after standing ovation.

A few days later, after the stage was struck, the sets broken down, the props stored and the costumes dry-cleaned, Erik and Melanie went out for a drink.

"You mean like a date," Melanie said to his invitation. "Or just a do?"

"A date," Erik said.

She looked at him a moment, arms crossed. "I've never dated a white man."

"Neither have I."

She clucked her tongue, planted her palm square in his chest and pushed him away. "You are adorable. Pick me up at seven."

Erik whistled as he showered and shaved. It wasn't until he was tucking in his shirt tails that he realized today was the nineteenth of April.

Seven years since the shootings. Where would he have been at this time of the night? Probably in the waiting room of the hospital. Asleep.

He pondered that as he buckled his belt and filled his pockets: cash, wallet, keys. He paused, the flattened penny in the palm of his hand. Troubled, he sighed and jiggled it in his loose fist.

"You know, James," he said. "I think I'll fly solo tonight."

He went to his bedside table drawer and took out the blue leather case that held Joe Bianco's purple heart. He flipped open the cover and lifted out the inset.

"This is the most symbolically wrong place I can think to put you," he said, laughing as he placed the penny in the bottom of the case. "So do me a favor and keep it entre nous. All right?"

He replaced the inset, covering the penny with the medal. Then he shut the case and left.

TEN AFTER ONE

HE SLEPT WELL and woke up smiling and stretching the next morning. Lazy and smug, he combed through last night's images. It had been, in his opinion, a spectacular first date. A crazy good, touchy-feely time, culminating in ice cream and a walk along the canal.

Kissing Melanie on the Main Street Bridge, their mouths sweet with chocolate and butterscotch, Erik felt flammable. It had been a long time since he'd kissed like that: slow and soft, letting it unfold of its own accord, following where her embrace led him. Feeling her kiss go from sweet cold to even sweeter warmth. The way his mouth felt in hers. He was dialed into her, and it had been an eternity time since his sexuality had extended feelers beyond his own selfish needs and into a woman's experience. An immeasurable age since he'd been caught up in a woman like that, caught up tight with her, engaged mind and body to the point of wanting to be inside of it all. Feeling young. Feeling great. Great to be alive with nowhere else to rather be.

Nowhere else to rather be?

Erik bolted up from the pillows, noticing his bedroom was suspiciously bright with sunlight. He seized the clock: it was ten after one.

Ten after one?

He checked his watch. It was right.

"Shit," he muttered, falling back.

He considered screwing it. He'd already come this far. He could call in, claim a debilitating stomach bug and go back to sleep. But his conscience wouldn't let him do it. He got up, dressed and drove to campus.

It was April 20, 1999.

The theater was quiet and eerie. Hurrying down to his office, Erik passed the student lounge where a crowd had gathered, students and faculty huddled together on couches, standing in close groups. People were holding each other. Some were crying. Everyone was focused on the television.

Erik moved into the lounge, cautious. Like a hunter approaching a kill he wasn't sure was quite dead. Something was going on. Something big. He gazed at the anchorman on the screen, began assembling a picture from the fragments.

Some of the students released from the high school have been reunited with their parents. Now let's take a look at the live coverage from Littleton where an arrest has been made.

Officials are preparing a briefing there for parents.

I wish I could give you more information but we don't know. It's extremely chaotic out there.

A graphic flashed up, the state of Colorado. A dot for Denver. Across the top of the screen: *School Shooting.*

No confirmed fatalities as of yet as police have not completely secured the building.

Continuing to find victims throughout the school.

We have to point out the gunmen have not yet been found.

These gunmen, wearing black trench coats.

Columbine.

A hand in his, cold fingers and rough, dry skin. He turned his head. It was Melanie, her eyes enormous, her lips pressed into a tight line.

On the screen, groups of students being shepherded by police across a parking lot, their hands on their heads.

Helicopters. SWAT teams. Dogs. Ambulances.

Columbine, Erik thought.

Wasn't a columbine a flower?

"Daisy," he whispered.

You may have noticed the word on your screen "Lockdown."

SWAT teams in position.

Students still trapped inside.

"Unbelievable," Melanie said.

She moved closer into him, seeking comfort. He stayed motionless. A small trickle of sweat dripped down his back.

Conflicting stories.

Calls from within the building.

The gunmen have not yet been found.

His legs were prickling now. Maybe he should sit down.

Students inside.

Sound of gunfire.

The edges of his vision began to fade out. He was looking at the TV through a pinhole.

911 call from the library.

Still trapped inside.

The gunmen.

"Daisy..."

Erik opened his eyes. He was lying on the floor in a forest of legs, Melanie kneeling beside him. "Get back," she said. "Get back, give him some air."

Her fingers unzipped his jacket and undid some of the buttons on his flannel shirt. She laid her hand flat on his chest. His heart pounded against it. He was on fire. His blood had turned to electric, molten lava, crackling along his limbs.

I'm dying, he thought.

"Erik." Melanie's hands on his face now, smoothing his forehead. "Talk to me. Are you having chest pains?"

"No." It wasn't pain, exactly. More a slow, ripping sensation. Something had a hold of his heart and was pulling it through his ribcage. But he wasn't in pain. He was just quite exquisitely terrified.

Someone knelt by his other side and put a hand on his shoulder. "Erik."

It was Miles. He was pale behind his horn-rimmed glasses, but his melodious voice was calm and unwavering. He shifted to sit down, cross-legged, and took Erik's hand in his. "Fish, look at me."

Erik struggled to focus.

"It's Miles. Look at me. Come back to me."

"It's happening again..."

"But not to you," Miles said. "You're not there. You're here with me. Look at me."

"What's the matter with him?" Melanie said, her voice cracking with fright.

"He was at Lancaster," Miles said.

A murmuring gasp of recognition rippled through the lounge.

"Oh, Jesus," Melanie whispered.

"Daisy," Erik said. The panic intensified. It had happened again. *No known fatalities,* the news said. But in his constricted, writhing heart, Erik knew it wasn't true. Someone's son died today. Someone's daughter would die tonight. Kids would lie in hospital beds. Blood would be all over their lives. Dreams and fairytales in bloody pieces on the floor.

"Squeeze my hand," Miles said. "Stay with me."

Erik nodded, breathing hard through his mouth, squeezing Miles' fingers. He started to shake.

Squeeze my hands, Marge. Go ahead and break my fingers...

"I'm cold," he whispered. How could he be cold with this fire in his veins?

"Let's get him off the floor," Melanie said.

"No," Erik said. "No, don't." Though cold, the floor was good, pressed all along the backs of his legs and shoulders and head, grounding him.

But blood was all over the floor.

"Daisy."

"People, please back up, give him some room," Miles said. "He was at Lancaster, this is upsetting. Let him have some air. Can someone get some water, please?"

"Think we need an ambulance?"

"No, I think we're riding a hell of an adrenaline wave here, it just has to run its course. Hang onto me, Erik, just hang on. This is now. You're with me."

"Erik, think you can sit up, baby?"

He sat up. Comforting hands on his shoulders and back. His head was pounding behind his eyeballs and he felt a little sick. His limbs burned.

Someone handed him a bottle of water, icy cold and dripping condensation.

"Just a sip," Melanie said. "Hold it in your mouth and swallow slowly."

"Nice and easy," Miles said. "You're all right."

Erik sipped, water dripping down his chin. "It's not all right." He slumped and put his forehead on Melanie's shoulder. "It'll never be all right for them again."

"Is there someone I can call for you?" Her arms were strong but he could not trust them. Nothing could be trusted. Sweat dripped down his neck. Desperation swirled in him like an evil vortex. The only ones he could trust were lost to him. He'd driven them away, set the world on fire and now he was alone. And forgotten. They wouldn't look for him anymore.

"Nobody," he said. "There's nobody left."

"It's all right, baby. I'm here. I'm with you." Her hand pressed against the back of his head, her lips brushed his face.

He was about to lean further into her comfort, then recoiled again.

I already leaned into her, he thought. *I left the penny behind and leaned into the joy, and now he's making me pay. This will always happen when I lean in and trust the moment.*

"I can't," he whispered. *Blood is all over everything, blood will always follow joy. James will never let me be.*

Melanie brought her body to his, pulled him into her. "Feel me," she said. "I'm here. This is now. I'm right here."

His hands clutched the back of her sweater. The trembling intensified.

"Mel," he whispered.

"It's all right."

"Mel, I can't do this again."

Because I never did it the first time.

THE IRREVOCABLE PART

SHE TOOK HIM to her place. Once inside, hunched in one of her kitchen chairs, he couldn't stop shaking. He was cold to his bones. Melanie pressed maternal hands to his forehead and claimed he wasn't running a fever. She put her teakettle on and while waiting for it to come to a boil, gave him a pill. "Take it. You're going bye-bye now."

He swallowed it without question. If she'd handed him a cyanide capsule, he would have taken it quietly as well. Anything to make it stop.

He followed her, willing and docile as a duckling, to her bedroom, where she took his shoes and eased him into her bed, piled the covers high on top of him. She sat, holding his hand, until the sides of his mind folded in and the roof came gently down.

And then, nothing.

When he awoke, the windows were dark. Melanie was sitting beside him, propped up against a mountain of pillows, reading. He was curled up tight against the length and warmth of her legs, his face pressed to her hip. Her hand was quiet on his back.

"Hey," she said.

It was an effort to pry his tongue off the roof of his mouth. Without a word she passed him a mug from the bedside table. It was tea, hot and sweet with a lot of milk. He drank a few gulps, then she took it away and he lay back down.

"Feel better?"

He nodded. His hands and feet were warm and dry, his chest open, his stomach calm. The relief of the terror having passed was indescribable. He breathed in the peace.

"Thank you," he said against her leg.

"Don't give it a thought. You just rest. Go back to sleep."

But he wasn't sleepy. Melanie had laid aside her sheaf of papers and now he picked one up. As he suspected, they were printouts of archived news stories from Lancaster.

"I didn't want to ask you too many questions so I did my own dirty work," she said. "Miles said you were there but he didn't say you were in the fucking thick of it."

Erik was skimming the blurbs. Chunks of the past on paper.

> Lancaster University remains in lockdown tonight after a shooting incident at the Mallory Theater. Five students and one professor were killed and more than a dozen injured after a student opened fire on the conservatory's spring dance concert rehearsal.

His hands turned pages. Melanie's hand stroked his head.

> The injured were taken to University Medical Center, except for three who were rushed to Philadelphia Trauma Center. Senior William Kager and junior Margarete Bianco are listed in serious but stable condition.

"Did you know them?" Melanie asked, touching the paragraph.

He nodded, eyebrows wrinkled at the misspelled names. "Will Kaeger was my roommate. And Daisy Bianco was my girlfriend." The words were ordinary in his mouth. As if he were merely saying the sky was blue.

Melanie picked up his hand then, turned it over. "I see," she said, tracing his tattoo. "You said daisy in the lounge this afternoon. I didn't realize it was someone's name."

Instinctively he made a fist, as if to hide, then he relaxed his fingers. Relaxed into his history. It was all right. Lancaster was his past. Daisy was his past. This tattoo was part of that past. It could all be ordinary: the sky was blue, he was a Lancaster survivor and Daisy was his ex.

He turned another page.

> *Officials said at that moment Dow, still in the aisle, low-ered his weapon and was approached by Erik Fiskare, a junior.*

Melanie's fingernail, painted a deep raisin brown, made circles on the paper. "What an insane thing to do," she said. "You fool cowboy."

"I know."

> *Fiskare attempted to speak with Dow and sometime during the exchange, Dow turned the gun on himself. Fiskare was unhurt.*

"Unhurt, my ass." Melanie's hand caressed his head. "You weren't just there," she said. "You were a hero."

Erik closed his eyes, loving her touch.

"'Fiskare attempted to speak with Dow,'" Melanie read. "My God, baby, you could've been killed."

"Yeah."

"What in hell could it have been like? I can't imagine."

Nestled against her lush body, he told her. Thanks to all the work he'd done in therapy, it was easy now to tell it as a concise story. And thanks to the Valium, it was easy to detach.

As he spoke, Melanie lay down, her knees touching his, holding his hands. "Go on."

When he was done, they both lay still and quiet. Tears from Mela-nie's eyes ran down into the smooth, soft pillowcases. She brought the clump of their woven fingers up to her mouth, her breath warm on his knuckles.

"You're a hero. Why don't any of these news stories say so?"

"I don't know. I didn't think much about..."

Her fingertips shushed him. "You stopped him from killing more peo-ple. You saved lives."

He started to automatically dismiss her words. Downplay his role and brush it aside. Then he stopped and remembered the work he'd done with Diane, learning to look at certain things and call them what they were.

You watched your loved ones be shot.

It was a horrible experience.

He moved closer into the circle of Melanie's arms. Let her look at him and call him what he was.

"You're a hero," she whispered.

AGAIN HE WAS SITTING at her kitchen table, now suffused with hunger instead of fear. She'd opened a bottle of wine but wouldn't let him drink any, keeping him on the tea. It was chamomile, which he didn't care for, but it was good to sit still and let someone fuss over him, deciding what was best. He lounged, chin propped on the heel of his hand, quietly keeping her company.

She was busy with cutting board and knife. She dipped below his field of vision then reappeared with a skillet. The rapid click of the gas burner being ignited, the swish of flame, the skillet went down. She reached over here for a decanter of olive oil, over there for a pat of butter, what she wanted never far from reach. He watched her pull apart a head of garlic and competently smash the cloves one by one, under the flat blade of her knife. The papery skins were tossed in the sink. She brushed her fingers off on the dishtowel tucked through one of her belt loops. Gathering the pale yellow spheres into a pile she began to run her knife through them, quick and crisp, the tip of the blade steady on the board, her wrist rocking the handle in a precise rhythm. Once sliced, she gathered again and began to chop crosswise. Rock and run the blade through, gather the pieces, rock and run again. In the pan, olive oil and butter began to sing.

"Was your girlfriend all right? Did she ever dance again?" she asked. "If you don't mind me asking."

He didn't. "She did. Months of rehab. A lot of hard work, but she did."

"Where is she now?"

"She danced with the Pennsylvania Ballet for a while." Erik rolled his lips in, considering his next move. *Keep it ordinary*, he thought.

"Last I heard she was in New York. We're not in touch anymore. We broke up rather badly."

"I see," Melanie said. "I imagine the shooting messed you guys up nine ways to Sunday. That sucks, baby. I know it's an understatement but I just have no words."

She scooped up a pile of minced garlic with the knife and dropped it into the skillet, which gave up a satisfying, oily crackle. She shook the pan a little, reached for a wooden spoon. The smell of butter and olive oil and garlic was making Erik woozy.

"It's nice here," he said.

Melanie took a drink from her glass as she stirred, put it down and ran the back of her wrist across one eyebrow. "Do you think you'd like to stay tonight?" she asked.

He watched her swift, experienced hands without answering. He wanted to stay. He wondered if they would make love, and he wanted it as well. But what about the aftermath? What if it happened again, that awful death spiral of anxiety?

"What do I do about that?" he'd asked Diane.

"What do you usually do?"

"Get the hell out of there."

"Why?"

"Because it's... I don't know."

"No, push it a little. Finish the thought. Because it's what?"

Erik flailed around for words, dropping his hands into his lap. "It's embarrassing."

"Nobody would understand is what I hear you saying."

"Right. It's insane."

"Have you ever tried explaining it?"

"No."

"What if you did?"

He blinked at her. "How?"

"Tell the story. You don't have to get into the nitty-gritty intimate details. You could simply condense it down to its most elemental parts."

"What, so I say one night I had an intense sexual encounter with my girlfriend, and the next day I watched her get shot? And it irrevocably linked sex and anxiety in my mind?"

Diane nodded slowly, a corner of her mouth twisting. "That works," she said. "But I'd leave out the irrevocable part."

"I can't say that."

"Why not, it's the truth. And if she can't handle it, there's no emotional future with her anyway. You can fuck, leave and save yourself the anxiety."

So infrequently did Diane curse that the exchange had stayed firmly planted in Erik's mind. And if ever there were a time give the advice a field trial...

What the hell, keep it ordinary, he thought, swallowing hard.

"I'd like to stay," he said. "But there's something about... Something might happen to me. I just need to let you know something." He put his face into a hand, laughing. "I'm sorry, Mel, I'm not good at talking about this."

Melanie handed him a head of broccoli. "Rinse this off, please. And cut it in florets. You can talk and be busy. Sometimes it helps if you're a little distracted."

It did help. Occupied with this bit of business, he did his best to sketch out a coherent, generalized story of what transpired in therapy. Then he braced himself to be politely shown the door.

"So," Melanie said, "what I hear you saying is one minute she had the proverbial hand down your pants in the lighting booth. And the next minute it was Armageddon."

He nodded, rinsing broccoli bits off the blade of the knife and setting it in the sink. "Something like that."

Melanie wiped her hands off and poured herself another glass of wine. "You know, I'm no shrink, but if one minute you're making out with your girlfriend and sporting wood and feeling good and dying to get her back in bed. And the next minute the place erupts in gunfire, a man blows his head off in front of you and your girlfriend is all but bleeding to death... I don't know, I think my mind would keep all those things tied together for a real long time. Wouldn't surprise me if you two were messed up afterward to the point where you couldn't make much love."

A humbling gratitude took him by the throat. He thought he would cry from the sheer sweetness of being understood.

"We couldn't," he said. "I mean we could, but it was just...so messed up."

"And you were so young. God." Melanie scraped the garlic, golden-brown and fragrant, into a small bowl, then took the skillet and spatula over to the sink. "So what made you guys break up eventually?" She flicked the faucet on. Clouds of steam wafted up and fogged the window.

"I found her in bed with one of my closest friends."

Melanie shut off the water and looked over her shoulder at him. She reached down the counter to her block of knives, selected one and solemnly offered it to him.

Erik burst out laughing. Her expression was so dry, so perfectly ironic and beautifully timed, and he began to love her.

She put the knife back into the block. "I'll tell you what, I'm gonna feed your ass," she said. "And then I'll either take you back to your car tonight, or I'll take you back to it in the morning. You decide."

"All right."

"And if you stay and those wolves of yours end up coming, well you know what? I got a baseball bat and a whole lot of Valium. So bring it."

He reached for her then, pulled her into him. Her neck was damp with steam, her hands redolent of garlic, her body's lush, soft curves warm against him. "Thanks for taking care of me," he said.

She leaned back in the circle of his arms. "I had a good time last night," she said. "It was one of the best dates I've ever been on. And frankly, you should give a seminar on kissing."

Erik smiled at the floor, a pleased heat rising up into his face.

"I'm glad I could be here for you tonight. I'm touched you shared all this with me. And I hope you'll stay."

"I'm thinking I might."

She rested her hand on his jaw. "So much blood. So much pain, baby, and you were so young. I'm sorry."

Her thumb ran along his cheekbone. Then it glided across his lips. He closed his teeth on it, gently, but held it there. The moment swelled in electric silence as he felt something in him unwind, uncoil. A gate opened and desire coursed through his body, bright, hot, purposeful.

He took her head in his hands, brought his mouth to hers. She reached around his waist and with a definitive twist, turned off the burners of the stove.

She took his hand, led him back into the bedroom. They kissed, hungry, peeling each other's clothes off with shaking hands. The night sat up and begged, ravenous. He was alive. He hadn't died. Sons and daughters had died today but he was alive, down on his knees, naked, running his mouth over Melanie's stomach, curling his fingertips into the waistband of her underwear.

She stilled his hands.

"I'm at the tail end of my period," she said. "There might be some blood."

He gazed up at her, grateful, so grateful. Her hand played in his hair.

"Don't be afraid of it," she whispered. "You don't have to be afraid anymore."

She was beautiful. Passionate and compassionate. He didn't shy away from her blood. He let himself move into it, seeing it as a life force, full of vitality and strength. It was baptismal.

Under him, Melanie was beautiful.

"Come here," she said. Her voice a song in the dark. "Show me everything."

His body was strong. He was young and alive and he leaned far into the moment, giving his weight to it.

"God, you're good," she said, gasping in his arms.

"You're so good," he whispered, his fingers seeking her out again, finding where she was still wide open and wet for him. Wet with desire. Wet with blood. He wasn't afraid.

"Your body is amazing," he whispered, a good lover again, thinking of her first and himself second.

Later, he lay drowsily against the velvet skin of her back. Her perfume wafted rich and golden into his nose and throat. Not a sugar scent but spice. Old world and exotic. He breathed her in and murmured, "I never thought it would be this way again."

She kissed his fingers, twined with hers. "Baby, I often find as soon as you say 'never,' life throws 'always' at you."

He ran his smiling mouth along her head. "I never want to make love with you again," he whispered.

"Smartass." She turned in his arms, giggling and wicked. "I'll need an extra fly swatter under the bed to keep you in line..."

WHILE YOU'RE DOWN THERE

THEY DATED TWO YEARS. Then they found a beautiful apartment in the historic district—the sunny half of an old Victorian home with a back porch and a small yard—and moved in together.

It wasn't quite seamless. After the best-behavior novelty of moving in together wore off, they settled back into their ways and found they were an imperfect couple. Melanie was dramatic when it wasn't necessary—making mere inconveniences into dire issues. Her energy levels were unwavering, especially on Sunday mornings when Erik wanted to sleep. And her inquisitive curiosity, so charming in the beginning of the relationship, could quickly turn to pestering.

Not that he was such a prize: he had his anxious episodes, his dark, seasonal moods—especially in November and April. The intensely painful and private moments from his past were only discussed in general terms. He gave her what he could but she wanted all of him in detail. He knew it frustrated her that he'd dehydrated parts of his heart so thoroughly, no amount of drenching love and affection could revive them. It made for misunderstandings and a lot of bruised feelings.

Domestically they did all right—they squabbled about money and bickered over chores. Yet despite the clashes over stupid little things, they lived well together. He grounded her. She gave him a much-needed jolt. She marveled at how he could fix anything. He loved the clever, creative ways she made their home beautiful. They got an upright piano.

And a dog—a mixed mutt they named Harry. Naturally, Melanie called him Baby.

Most nights, Erik slept well, curled on Melanie's back, their hands twined between her breasts. Harry snored in the corner and all was right with the world. But some nights Erik lay awake, not anxious, but feeling he was acting a part in some existential play.

What am I doing?

Who am I?

And he'd look at Melanie sleeping in his arms. *Who are you?*

Those nights he worried at the relationship, even as his mind chided him to stop tinkering with a non-existent problem. Their relationship was solid. They talked, they laughed, they made a lot of love and, thank God, after sex Erik was peaceful. The lovemaking alone filled him with a gratitude for Melanie he would never be able to fully articulate.

The students loved them, and in turn Erik and Melanie were mentors, involved in the kids' lives and helping them build dreams. Most of all, they had fun. Pure, careless amusement. They had a wide social circle, went out all the time with the Kellys. They gave parties. They went away on romantic weekends. They did everything a couple was supposed to do, laughing their asses off.

"You're so good," Melanie said to him. Not just in bed but in passing. She whispered it while running her hand over his head or along his face. Growled it playfully while grabbing his ass.

"Your heart is huge. Your love is amazing."

She loved him. Why wasn't it enough?

What more do you want? Erik asked the ceiling, his fingers reaching up to toy with invisible charms on his long-lost necklace. He was happy, yet he felt strangely stagnant. Everything was right, yet something in his soul moped. Not every wire was connected. Some essential part of him still felt missing. Something felt unfinished.

You're looking for what you had with Daisy.

It was an old thought. In the dark in his new home with Melanie, a new thought gradually emerged:

Maybe Daisy was the dream.

He'd loved her in the enclosed and insulated universe of college. Sure, they moved off campus and had to start paying rent, the electric bill, buying groceries. It felt like being an adult, but were they just kids playing house?

He tried to picture living with Daisy but couldn't seem to get out of her mother's kitchen at La Tarasque. He was stuck there with her in a perpetual tableau of holiday joy, making gnocchi and decorating the Christmas tree, surrounded by their circle of friends and Nat King Cole songs. He didn't envision taking her car in to get the oil changed, cleaning the oven, defrosting the refrigerator and plunging the toilet—things he'd done while cohabitating with Melanie.

Would she and I have survived in the real world?

Maybe she was the dream the whole time.

Maybe it would've ended anyway. On its own. We would've grown different ways or pursued dreams in different places and it would've ended. We still wouldn't be in touch. There just wouldn't be all this bad feeling about it.

This was the real world: standing in the lounge of the performing arts complex, clustered with students and faculty. They clung to each other, horrified as they watched the events of 9/11 unfold on TV.

This was real: Erik holding Melanie tight in his arms, turning her face to his chest and not letting her look when the towers fell. He watched in disbelief, but he did not fall. He stood strong, his arms crossed over Melanie's back, protecting her. She'd saved him once. Now he would be her hero. He was good. His heart was huge and his love was amazing.

Melanie deserved both.

"I'D LIKE TO GET MARRIED," Melanie said.

Erik looked at her a long moment.

"To you, smartass," she said.

"You're not even kneeling," he said, with his most affronted expression.

She laughed.

"No ring? Seriously?" He gestured around them to the bedroom. "This is how you propose?"

She seized a pillow and smashed it on his head. "You know I can't stand contrived, sugary, romantic crap. We're naked in bed, this is as genuine as it gets."

His fingers trailed over her collarbones, down her chest, cupped her breasts in his palms and put his face to them.

"You want to get married," he whispered.

"I do. Let's just do it. I don't want a big wedding. I don't want any wedding. Let's just drive to city hall. I'll call my sister and you call your mother and brother. We'll go somewhere nice for lunch then we'll fly to Jamaica..."

Her voice trailed off as they both silently rejected the idea. It was two weeks after the terrorist attacks. With the smoke still billowing over lower Manhattan, who could fly anywhere, or would even want to?

"We'll go to Vermont," Melanie said. "Or Lake George. We'll take a nice trip somewhere. I haven't had a vacation in years."

He pushed up on his elbow, his other hand still running over her body. "I'd like to get you a ring," he said. "Would a ring just be unbearably contrived? Sickeningly romantic?"

She kissed him. "You're adorable. You know that?"

"So you tell me."

She turned into him, burrowed her head against his chest. "I would love to have a ring."

They got licenses, made an appointment at city hall and reservations for lunch afterward. They bought matching platinum bands. Erik owned one suit, and it was an embarrassment, so they went to get him a new one. Melanie bought a lovely sheath dress in ivory wool.

Erik asked Miles to be best man. Melanie's sister, Julia, flew in to be maid of honor. Christine would come, but Pete Fiskare was participating in clinical trials for a new kind of cochlear implant and would be under the knife in Chicago. He and his wife sent their best wishes and a beautiful set of cast-iron skillets which Melanie all but took to bed with her.

"If you ever *touch* these with soap, I will beat you senseless."

The night before, Erik approached Melanie as she strode from closet to dresser to suitcase, packing for the trip they had booked to the Berkshires.

"You proposed in bed, so I can give you this in the closet." He took her left hand, slid on the ring he'd secretly bought under Miles's guidance. A small square diamond in a simple platinum setting. Straightforward. Just like Melanie.

She gazed at it a moment, her lips quivering. She looked sideways at him with bright, brimming eyes. "You're not even kneeling."

Smiling, he put a knee down. Then he put the other knee down and the smile faded. He sat back on his heels, palms open and empty in his lap, gripped by the moment. He looked up at her. Couldn't think of anything not contrived or sugary, so he tried to let his eyes say it all.

This is me. This is all I am. It's damaged and flawed and parts of it are buried and secret and frustrating to you. I'm not a dream or a prize.

Will you have me?

"I love you," she said.

"I love you."

Her hand caressed his hair. "While you're down there..."

HE'S NOT HERE TODAY

"The Man I Love"

Transcript from the National Public Radio series, *Moments in Time*

April 27, 2002

Karen Stark: You're listening to *Moments in Time*. I'm Karen Stark, thanks for joining us.

April brings a tragic pair of anniversaries to the country. Last Saturday, the twentieth, marked the three-year anniversary of the shootings at Columbine High School in Colorado, an ordeal still fresh in our minds. And the day before, April 19th, was the anniversary of the shootings at Lancaster University in Pennsylvania. It has now been ten years since the massacre left seven dead and fifteen wounded, stunning the nation with its chilling randomness.

NPR correspondent Camberley Jones covered the Lancaster shootings in 1992 for our sister station WHPA. She went back to the university last weekend, where a memorial ceremony took place, attended by students, survivors, and victims' loved ones. The event culminated with the re-dedication of the theater, in the name of a beloved professor who was killed that fateful day.

[Sound: interior of theater, construction, voices]

Camberley Jones: It seems a cool, serene April evening at Lancaster University outside Philadelphia, but the auditorium of the Mallory Performing Arts Complex is emotionally charged. It's Friday, April 19th, the anniversary of deadly shootings in this theater ten years ago. All day flowers have been left in the building's courtyard. A candlelight vigil is scheduled for tonight. And tomorrow, the auditorium will be re-dedicated to Professor Marie Del'Amici, who was the director of the conservatory's ballet division. She was shot dead by James Dow, one of her students. He came into theater during a rehearsal, opening fire on the dancers, faculty and other students present.

Dow killed six people before taking his own life. Over a dozen were wounded in his attack. Many of the survivors have come to Lancaster for tomorrow's ceremony, along with family and friends of the victims. Memorial plaques will be hung backstage, along with a larger plaque in the building's lobby, naming the new Marie Del'Amici Auditorium.

Unidentified male voice: We should be set in ten minutes. Start clearing the stage, please. Will and Daisy, ten minutes.

Jones: William Kaeger and Daisy Bianco were two of Professor Del'Amici's students, exclusive partners during their years at Lancaster's conservatory. Both were injured in the shootings. Will was shot once in the side and another bullet took off two of his fingers. He was able to come back to dance the following semester. Daisy Bianco, however, was shot through the leg. It took her nearly a year to recover. Both she and Will graduated Lancaster and went on to build successful careers. The piece they are rehearsing for tomorrow's ceremony—in tribute to their teacher—is the same piece they were working on when James Dow came into the theater.

Unidentified male voice: Off the stage, everyone. We need those ladders off.

Second male voice: Hold on, hold on, we got people on the catwalk. Off the catwalk.

Jones: Although Dow's motive is still not entirely clear, he was dropped from the spring concert for failing to meet his minimum GPA. He attempted suicide ten days before the shooting and was taken out of school by his parents, back to his hometown of Greensburg. None of the conservatory members saw Dow again until he appeared in the theater on the afternoon of April 19th.

Dow entered the theater through a side hallway which led to the backstage area. Armed with a semi-automatic Glock pistol, he shot and killed five students and wounded six others. He then stepped onto the stage where Will and Daisy were dancing.

William Kaeger: My memory is full of holes. Some parts are clear, others are blank. He came onstage at the part of the pas de deux where Daisy does this really difficult lift on my back. It takes a lot of concentration and maybe it's why I didn't hear the commotion backstage or even see James come out. He was behind me. Vaguely—I don't know if I'm making up this memory or if it's real—I think I heard screaming when Daisy was running to me. But the music was loud and I was in the zone. I had to catch her. Then she was up on my back and...then it gets surreal in my head. I don't remember pain exactly. First my side felt like it was on fire. Then my left arm kind of jerked up. I reared back and I threw Daisy right off my shoulders.

Jones: Daisy Bianco comes to sit by Will. She remembers little of the day.

Daisy Bianco: I remember nothing of the shooting. My last clear memory is walking down the aisle. Right over there. I had been in the lighting booth with my boyfriend, then I walked down the aisle to go to the stage and... It just splinters apart after that. I don't even remember starting the dance.

Kaeger: He didn't come in until three-quarters of the way through.

Bianco: I know but I have no memory of it. Everything literally stops there. Right over there in the aisle, when I turned around to wave at my boyfriend. And then it's just a black hole, until I woke up in the hospital and I still didn't know what happened.

Jones: After shooting Daisy and Will, Dow jumped from the stage and began firing at people, wounding Marie Del'Amici and another five students. Cornelis Justi, the director of the conservatory's contemporary dance division, was sitting near the rear of the theater.

Cornelis Justi: It was like watching a movie. Cliché, I know. But there's truth in it. I just stood there and watched. With my cup of coffee in my hand, can you imagine? For five seconds I thought it was a joke. I thought the theater department was pulling a prank. Someone with a gun, seriously? Come on, this is my theater. People don't get shot in the middle of rehearsal.

Jones: Panicked, screaming students flooded the aisles, fleeing for the lobby doors and emergency exits. Justi herded as many as he could out, but when he saw James Dow jump off the stage and fire into the orchestra, Justi dove to the floor between two rows of seats.

Justi: Sheer adrenaline. I never felt anything like it in my life. Shots were coming closer up the aisle and then this awful shattering of glass. James shot out the windows of the lighting booth. A boy named Erik Fiskare was in there, he was running lights for the concert. I thought he was killed. It was madness. Then everything went quiet. I peeked up and James was standing still in the aisle. Then I saw Erik. He'd come out of the booth and was crouched down in the aisle. I was so relieved to see him, but then he started moving down the aisle. Toward James. And I remember thinking, *Dear Lord, what is this kid doing?* Then I realized he was probably trying to get to Daisy.

Jones: Erik Fiskare was Daisy Bianco's boyfriend and Will Kaeger's roommate. From where he sat in the lighting booth, he'd seen the both of them shot. He managed to hit the floor before James blew out the glass of the booth.

Justi: Erik spoke to him then. He called his name. He said, "James." And James turned his head. I'll never forget this. Not his whole body, just his head. And he looked at Erik. And Erik said, "James. Come talk to me." I remember thinking, and I still think it today... Excuse me... Thinking it was the most courageous thing I had seen in my life.

Jones: Here's David Alto, who was the set and lighting designer for the concert.

David Alto: I was behind the set the whole time. I should've been in the orchestra with Marie but I had to fix something. So I was behind the set and I stuck my head up when James fired at Will and Daisy. I hit the floor with one of the other stagehands. It felt like I didn't breathe for an hour, but how long could it have been? Five minutes? Not even. Things got really quiet so I slowly put my head around the set. And I saw Erik, sitting in the aisle, up against the sides of the seats. And James...had the gun pointed straight at Erik's face. I was frozen. Thinking *I can't watch this. But I have to...* Erik, he...was one of my best friends and he was alone in the aisle staring down the muzzle of a gun. If I made a move, he'd be dead. If I didn't make a move...

Jones: He's not here today?

Alto: ... No, he couldn't be here. Anyway, the gun went off. I didn't even have time to shut my eyes. James went down in the aisle. He was dead. And it was over. That part of it, anyway. A lot of other things were just getting started.

Jones: Five students were dead in the theater. Professor Marie Del'Amici had been mortally wounded and would die three days later at Philadelphia Trauma Center. Onstage, the situation was grave. Daisy and Will were both bleeding heavily.

Lucia Dare, Will Kaeger's wife, was also in the theater the day of the shootings. She majored in sports medicine at Lancaster and is now a physical therapist.

Lucia Dare: It's interesting. The semester before, I had been in Boston, taking an EMT training course. I thought it was something I wanted to pursue. But turns out I didn't have the psyche for it. And yet the day of the shooting, I was in the thick of it, applying what I learned in the course to my best friend who'd been shot. With my boyfriend over there who'd also been shot. This was happening in my school, to people I love. I should have been a basket case. But I was numb. I was just...

Alto: You were incredible, Luck. Come on. People would have died if you hadn't been there.

Jones: David Alto, now 32, is in remission from kidney cancer. He's watching today's rehearsal from the auditorium, wearing a black wool cap over his bald head. Lucky Dare sits next to him, holding his hand as they relive those difficult memories

Alto: I was trying to help Daisy but Lucky pushed me aside. "Get out of the way." And she was just yelling things at Fish. I mean, Erik Fiskare. We called him Fish.

Dare: I was calm with Will but I nearly broke down when I saw Daisy's wound. And Erik [laughter]—oh my God—he was leaning on her femoral pressure point and with his other elbow he just whacks me in the side. You know, like you'd slap a hysterical person. "Get it together." Or something. It worked. My hands just took over and then I was a robot. Like I could feel my brain severing the emotional connections I had to these people. Crazy what happens to you in a crisis.

Alto: The blood was everywhere. Jesus. For a long time afterward I had a really, really hard time with blood. Like if I was flossing my teeth and spit blood in the sink?

Dare: You flossed? I didn't floss for a year.

Alto: Post Traumatic Floss Disorder ... [Laughter]

Jones: Despite their joking, Post Traumatic Stress Disorder, PTSD, was no laughing matter. For many of those in the theater on April 19th, the psychological wounds of the ordeal took longer to heal than the physical ones.

Bianco: Oh, I was a mess.

Jones: Wrapped in a black shawl, Daisy Bianco sits in one of the orchestra seats. She's joined by John Quillis, who is also performing at tomorrow's ceremony. He was a sophomore in 1992, and watched the shootings from the stage right wing. He and Daisy were good friends at school, and then started dating a few years after graduation.

John Quillis: I ran into her randomly in New York. We were both going to a master class or something. I didn't recognize her at first.

Bianco: I looked like crap. I think I weighed 90 pounds.

Quillis: If that. I knew right away she was still haunted by it all. I think I knew because... Well, look, I'm the son of two psychologists. They had me immediately in therapy after the shooting. I think I was one of the few who went to counseling.

Bianco: You were.

Quillis: But even so, it was a long process. When I met up with Daisy I was coming out the other side. She looked like she was just heading into the tunnel.

Bianco: Avoiding the tunnel. I knew I was mentally unraveling after the shooting, but having the goal of physical recovery kept me slightly distracted. Not to say the physical injuries weren't devastating.

Quillis: Her scars are crazy.

Bianco: Being shot nearly destroyed me. Destroyed the essence of me. I'm a dancer. This is all I've done, all I've been since I was five. And then I wake up in a hospital bed with my leg shot up and sliced open and I had no idea what had happened. The randomness, the senselessness of it... I truly became two people afterward. There was the me who worked like hell, trained and fought and never looked back. And then there was this other me who was just...dark. Angry and depressed and constantly anxious. Things I had never been before. Feelings I had never entertained, let alone been consumed by. I didn't know how to express them. A lot of times I didn't even have words for what I was experiencing.

Jones: What got you through it?

Bianco: I don't...

Quillis: Take your time. You all right?

Bianco: John was the one who got me into therapy and got me on track to...back to myself, I guess. I got through it.

Quillis: It's all right.

Bianco: I got through it but I don't think I ever got over it. I can't... I lost things I'll never get back... Sorry, this is hard. It's... In a lot of ways I'm still two people. Part of me has moved on and evolved yet part of me is still haunted. The shooting changed me. It changed who I was and for a long time I didn't like...her.

Quillis: It's all right. Come on, let's take a break. Get some water.

Jones: Quillis comforts Bianco, leading her down by the side of the stage where they stretch together. They are in their thirties now. Quillis is a principal dancer with the Boston Ballet. Daisy Bianco danced two years with the Pennsylvania Ballet. She did a season with the Metropolitan Opera Ballet in New York City and then went on tour with *The Phantom of the Opera,* in the role of Meg Giry. In 1999 she received an invitation to join New Brunswick Ballet Theater, where her former partner, Will Kaeger, is a principal dancer.

Bianco: It's so wonderful to be dancing together again.

Kaeger: I don't dance with anyone the way I dance with Dais. Right from the start, when we were put together her freshman year, we had something special. It's hard to explain. She's calm, poised and cerebral. I'm an impulsive lunatic. But somehow those two things meshed into...us.

Bianco: We always partnered by pure instinct. So it was frustrating after the shooting. We had to relearn so much because of our injuries. All this thinking was required.

Kaeger: But we partner now in totally unique ways, and those came out of our injuries. But you're right, I remember the first time we went into supported adagio class after the shooting. I didn't think two fingers were going to make much of a difference but it was a disaster.

Bianco: We left in tears.

Kaeger: Tears. I'd lost sensation in this hand so I couldn't hold onto her, couldn't feel her weight when I was lifting her. We were falling all over the place, it was really discouraging. I was actually really freaked out by it. But little by little it became instinctive again. Dais knew how to work around my bad hand and I knew how she was going to compensate for her leg. This whole other dimension of our partnership emerged. And we had the bond of experience, too.

Bianco: War mates.

Jones: Apart from the emotional memories, was it difficult to stage this piece after not performing together for so long?

Kaeger: No. Piece of cake. I can partner her in my sleep.

Bianco: And I love this pas de deux so much.

Kaeger: It's from the George Balanchine ballet *Who Cares?* set to the song "The Man I Love." I've never danced it anywhere but this theater. And never with anyone but Dais.

Bianco: I'm grateful the music holds no memory of the shooting for me. I can hear it and not be reminded.

Kaeger: It reminds me of Marie though.

Bianco: It does. Her death was a bitter loss to the conservatory. In the aftermath of the shooting and trying to recover and come back and dance again, it was devastating not having her. Something was just missing from this building. I never stopped looking for her. I'm looking for her right now, yelling notes from the orchestra.

Kaeger: She was crazy. She had an energy like... If you couldn't keep up, then you best just get the hell out of the way. She wanted one hundred and ten percent from you all the time. But you couldn't help but want to give it to her. You wanted to give her your best.

Bianco: She made you believe in yourself. She said, 'You dance well. You must dance well.' And she was so fun, you hardly realized she was running you ragged. I try to channel her when I dance now. All her humor and motivation and energy.

Kaeger: Her Italian curses.

Unidentified female voice: Are we ready to run this? Places, please.

Jones: Bianco and Kaeger take to the stage. Twenty or thirty dancers and stagehands settle down to watch.

[Music clip: George Gershwin's "The Man I Love"]

Jones: A hush descends as the couple reaches the part in the choreography where Bianco runs to Kaeger and languidly leaps onto his back in a split arabesque. This was the moment they were shot ten years ago. There is no hesitation, no fear today. Their timing is flawless, and their colleagues burst into spontaneous appreciation.

[Sound of applause and whistles]

Jones: After an instant of stillness, Bianco slides off Kaeger's shoulders, her toe finding the floor, still in deep arabesque. Her torso melts down on her leg as he turns her, she revolves around and through and then she is off to the far corner, turning again, running, leaping onto his shoulder.

[Applause]

Jones: I sit with Cornelis Justi while the dancers take a break and ask him what this week has been like.

Justi: Surreal. Emotional. Brings everything back. Yet it's gratifying to see Will and Daisy together, to see they've remained such close friends and now are professional colleagues. And to see they still dance so brilliantly together. They still have their magic and it makes me happy. It makes me feel young. And it helps keep Marie alive for me.

Jones: For *Moments in Time,* this is Camberley Jones in Philadelphia.

SHORT, CURT AND MOODY

ERIK WAS DRIVING HOME when he heard the story on NPR. He had to pull over. He could not possibly drive and listen at the same time. Heart pounding, he pulled into the parking lot of the library and sat with the engine running, his mouth a little open.

They were alive.

Of course, he knew they were alive, out there somewhere in the world. But now they were here. In his fucking *car*.

He listened, sitting motionless, falling down a wormhole in time. Tumbling into an alternate universe and onto the astral planes of a past he'd worked hard to forget.

That music.

Those voices.

Daisy.

He gripped the steering wheel tight as he listened to her, leaning in toward the dashboard, wanting to crawl clear into the speakers and...

And what? Be there?

"He's not here today?" the reporter asked.

"No, he couldn't make it," David said.

David of all people, making excuses for him. What a magnanimous gesture. And his little pause beforehand. If you were in the know on the situation, his pause spoke volumes. The pause broadcasted.

But they had talked about him. They had made him part of the story, still included him. Kees told what happened in the aisle. "It was the most courageous thing I had ever seen," he said. And Erik almost broke down. Kees never told him.

Both David and Lucky brought up Erik's name, clarifying he was Daisy's boyfriend at the time. David watching the shit go down in the aisle. And Lucky giving her little detail about Erik whacking her in the side. He'd forgotten.

What more could they have said about him?

Daisy didn't say my name.

She said "my boyfriend." But she remembered being in the booth with him. He wondered if she'd ever discovered a link between the night before the shooting and the anxiety of their lovemaking. She'd touched a little on the subject of therapy and her recovery.

And how John had saved her.

Will and Lucky were married. No big shock, but nice to hear anyway. And they were all in Canada, apparently. Together. But not John though. He was in Boston. Were he and Daisy long-distance lovers? Or were they not together at all?

And David had cancer, his mind piped up. *Did you get that part?*

Erik turned off the radio and drove out of the parking lot. He kept his eyes on the road, steered, braked, signaled. Somehow he got home, but he had no recollection of the route. In his head, the refrain of "The Man I Love" echoed, swelling violins and woodwind arpeggios. Instead of the road, he could only see the pas de deux. Daisy in a poppy pink dress, running half the length of the stage and leaping onto Will's back, transforming momentum into crystal immobility.

He couldn't be here.

"No shit," Erik said to the windshield.

Other than, "I was in the lighting booth with my boyfriend," Daisy hadn't a thing to say about him.

Not even his name.

It hurt.

But her voice. Out of the past, through the speakers of his car, he heard her talking. It seemed incredible she was out there, real, flesh and bone, with a voice sounding exactly as he remembered. Amazing how all of them were still out there and real. Will and Lucky, Kees. John. Even David. All of them there in Lancaster, just last week, while Erik was here in New York, safe beyond the charred and smoking struts and beams of his bridge.

Daisy's voice. At one point it had fractured into little slivers of pain.

"The shooting changed me," she said. "It changed who I was and I didn't like her."

She described part of herself as haunted. Spoken of things she lost she would never get back.

Me, Erik thought when he heard it, leaning forward, his head practically touching the dash. Fingers reaching to caress the radio in a transfixed wonder. The tiniest thawing in his heart. A shift in his atoms he could not prevent.

She means me.

But she didn't say his name.

Melanie was waiting for him at the steps to the kitchen door. She had left Brockport State, landing a plum job as a music teacher at a private school. She had to commute to East Rochester every day, but the money was good and she loved the work.

"Were you listening to NPR?" she called out before he was out of the car.

"I was."

"Did you hear it? The thing about Lancaster?"

"I heard it," he said. He kissed her and went inside, crouched down to be greeted by Harry.

"They barely mentioned you," she said.

"You think so?" he said, scratching the dog's ears and neck. "No, they talked about me."

"Not much, though." Melanie had pulled two beers from the fridge. She popped one and gave it to him. "Cheers, baby."

"Skål."

"Why didn't you go?"

He sat down. "Go where?"

"To Lancaster. To the ceremony."

"I didn't know there was one." Erik took a long drink and let the day fall away from him. Harry put his head on Erik's knee.

"What do you mean you didn't know?"

"I didn't know." He drank again, running his hand along the dome of Harry's head, lost in thought and music and memory. Finally he looked up again.

"What?" he said to Melanie's incredulous expression.

"It's the ten-year anniversary and nobody called you?"

He shook his head.

She took a pull of her own beer, looking expansive. "How many more questions do I get here?"

He smiled at her. She was getting better at respecting the sore spots of his past, not probing. It had been her idea to set limits on how many questions she could ask in a given situation. "Two more," he said. "For a blow job, you get three."

She rolled her eyes. "Have you been back to Lancaster? Ever?"

"No."

"In ten years, you have never gone back and you're not in touch with anybody?"

"Mel, those are questions you already know the answers to. I told you what happened and why I had to leave. Nothing's changed."

"It's... I'm sorry, I'm not invalidating what you felt at the time, but it just seems so extreme."

"It was an extreme situation."

She tapped her nails on the table, finishing her beer. "Well. I blew my quota. I will now go and let you brood in peace."

He laughed against the mouth of the beer bottle. "I'm not brooding. I feel incredibly surreal right now. I'm in a little bit of a time warp and—"

"And possibly you will be short, curt and moody the rest of the night," she said, putting up her palm. "It's all right, as long as I know in advance."

She got up from the table and, as she passed, Erik caught her hand. "Are you sure you don't have a third question?"

"You're adorable," she said. "And no further questions. Oh, this came for you. Registered mail, I had to sign for it."

From the counter she handed him a padded envelope. She kissed his head and left the kitchen. Erik drank the last of his beer, eyebrows wrinkled at the envelope. A return address in the corner, but no name.

Slowly he set the empty beer bottle down as he realized the address, postage and postmark were Canadian.

Canada.

Daisy.

"Shit," he whispered, his heart breaking into a gallop. First the radio segment, now this knockout punch.

Breathing deeply, he broke the seal on the envelope and drew out a typed letter. He unfolded it, glanced just at the first line—*What's up, asshole?*

He knew immediately.

Not Daisy.

Will.

WAITING TO BE FOUND

25 April 2002
Saint John, New Brunswick

What's up, asshole? I know what you're thinking: how the hell did he find me? Well, I know you're isolated out there in East Bumfuck but there's this nifty new invention called the internet. It makes it really difficult for your enemies to hide from you. Especially when they work for a State University with a website. And let their pretty faces get captured in college newsletter articles. What an amateur move. Honestly, are you even trying anymore?

Well anyway, you're still a handsome little fucker. And congratulations on your recent accolade. A national award from the United States Institute for Theater Technology. Aren't we doing nicely?

So here it is, 2002. I was at Lancaster for the ten-year anniversary. Nice of you to show up. What, you think your angst doesn't smell?

Kidding.

(Sort of.)

Anyway, I was at Lancaster. Don't know if you heard but they rededicated the auditorium to Marie. They made a really nice ceremony and Daisy and I danced "The Man I Love" because DUH. Haven't danced the thing since 1993 and to tell the truth, I'm fine retiring it from my resume. It's just riddled with fucking context and I can't dance it without crying, plus Daisy gained six ounces and lifting her makes my knees creak.

(Don't tell her I said that.)

(Oh wait, you wouldn't anyway. My bad.)

So what was I talking about? Oh yeah, Lancaster. Opie was there. He's a superstar down in Boston now. He and Dais had a thing some years ago. (Don't play the dumb blond—I know you know.) They still seemed awful sweet on each other at the ceremony but probably they were just caught up in the nostalgic moment. Whatever the case, Opie did grow up nice. But who didn't see that coming?

(I don't know, why AM I telling you this?)

David was there and he's in sad shape, apparently in remission from some kind of kidney cancer. The treatment really did a number on him, lost all his hair and weighs less than Daisy. It was pretty sobering although he seems in good spirits and the prognosis looks promising. He spoke of a girlfriend, hinted they were going to tie the knot. Although if this chick is smart, she'll keep herself a dishonest woman. Dave only wants what he can't have, right?

(Jesus. My bad again.)

Meanwhile, back in Lancaster (Did I mention I was there?)... For shits and giggles, Opie, the girls and I went by the old apartments. By some weird coincidence we got there just as they were delivering, wait for it, a new stove to Jay Street. Remember the ancient fire hazard? They were JUST replacing it. So we had a good laugh and being the man I am (and the man I love, ha ha), I stepped *in to help the guys lug the old one out. And lo and behold underneath it was your necklace. It must have come off you and*

Erik dropped the letter. Heart pounding, he grabbed the envelope and went digging. With shaking hands he took out a small plastic bag.

"Holy shit," he whispered. He broke the zippered seal and tipped the contents out. A jingle as the familiar heft of the chain coiled against his palm, the solid clink of the charms on top.

"Holy shit." He closed it up in his hand, set his forehead against his fist. He breathed, laughing a little. Nearly crying. Relief settled on his shoulders like a cape, his whole being now reduced to one thought.

I got it back.

Still holding his lost treasure tight in his palm, he picked up the letter again.

> *It must have come off you and got kicked under there on (cough) the day of which we will not speak. (Yes the hole in the wall has been patched but you can see it if you know where to look.)*
>
> *Like the One Ring waiting to be found, there it was. And here it is. I should deliver it personally but then you'd have to suck my cock and it would just get out of hand. Better sent through the mail and you can suck the letter carrier's cock. Just remember to breathe through your nose.*
>
> *But seriously folks, it's a little grungy and you'll see the clasp is broken and one of the charm thingies fell off, but any jeweler can fix it up for you. I hope you're glad to see it again. Not that you'd treat its miraculous reappearance as anything SYMBOLIC or MEANINGFUL.*
>
> *Pardon me while I beat you over the head with it.*
>
> *As you can see, I'm writing not from Lancaster (I was there), but from the frozen tundra of my ancestral homeland. I won't tell you what I'm up to because the intimate, personal details of my life are not for your ears. Not until you suck my cock, anyway.*

Hope you're taking good care of your sorry ass, which I have the unfortunate honor to still love. I'm kind of stupid that way.

Under strenuous protest, Lucky says hi. She refuses to send any love until you show your face and let her smack the shit out of it. I told her not to hold her breath. She was breathing through her nose at the time.

(Don't tell her I said that.)

(Oh wait, you wouldn't anyway. My bad.)

Yours truly in Christ,

William
P.S. Don't fucking call me.

Erik opened his fist. He tipped the necklace from one palm to the other. Then cradled it in both hands, still not believing it was here. After nine years, it was back in his hands.

It must have come off you and got kicked under there on the day of which we will not speak.

It could have been lost forever. If Will and the others had not been at the apartment, the day the stove was being moved... His gut twisted at the implication. Someone would have picked it up. Looked at it. Wondered at it. And kept it.

Shuddering at the near miss, he touched each charm, saying hello: the fish, the boat and the Saint Birgitta medal. There should have been four. The little pair of scissors Daisy got him for his birthday was missing.

If anything was lost, it might as well be the scissors. They weren't part of the original. This, here in his hand, *this* was the returned treasure. His talisman. His legacy. He had it back. Closing his fingers around the warm pile of old gold, he felt complete and was humbly grateful.

"What was in it?" Melanie had come back into the kitchen.

He opened his palm and showed her. "Will found it."

Her eyes lit up. "Oh my goodness." She took the chain and stretched it out carefully. "Look, it's just the way you described it."

"I can't believe it."

"Well, well," she said. "Maybe you won't be moody tonight after all. Can I see the letter?"

He slid it across the table and got up to get another beer. She sat down and read through it, with a few chuckles more polite than genuine.

"Well," she said. "He's certainly friendly, considering you cut him off without a backward look."

Erik nodded while his insides squirmed. She was right, of course. Will had zero reason to be so amiable.

"He's got a big heart," Erik said.

"What's all this 'suck my cock' stuff?"

"It's... Never mind, I couldn't even begin to explain."

She folded the paper neatly and slid it back to him. "How many questions?"

He grinned at her. "I'm in a good mood. You may ask unlimited questions."

"Are you going to call him?"

"Will?"

She nodded. "Or at least write and let him know you got it?"

His good mood wobbled on its axis. Again, she was right. He should at least let Will know. And it made him feel cornered.

"I'll let him know I got it but...I don't know how much more I can do, Mel."

Melanie tilted her head, studying him for a long moment. The silence pulled out like strings of taffy, reminding Erik of early sessions with Diane Erskine. How the quiet would coil around him like a boa constrictor, squeezing words out of him from sheer desperation. The surprise benefit, all these years later, was awkward silence didn't bother him. He could sit easily in it. Far longer than Melanie could. She always caved first.

"Baby," she said, sighing. "Everything about Lancaster makes you go so far away from me. You get a look in your eye, like...you're somewhere you just can't come back from."

"It's hard to come back from there," he said. "Which is why I don't like going in the first place."

"I know. I just try to demystify it by throwing questions at it."

"You do? Really?"

She smiled, put a hand out on the table and Erik dropped his onto it. "I can't deal with it, Mel. I admit it. If I call him, then it's just too close a proximity to Daisy and I have no desire to get caught up in it again."

"Caught up in what? What did she do to you?" Melanie shook her head. "I mean, I know what she did. But it's like...you never got over it. You just left it."

"Honey, I spent a lot of time and a lot of money getting over it."

"Over the shooting or over her?" Her fingers stroked his wrist, close to the tattoo of the daisy. It was a gesture to soothe him. Instead he felt the bristling desperation of a trapped animal. He took a long drink, willing himself to relax. He was being ridiculous. She wasn't trying to trap him or trick him. She was his wife. They were having a conversation.

"Over all of it," he said. "It was all one thing."

"It still seems so unfinished."

"It just is what it is."

She took her hand away, rolling her eyes. "I hate that expression."

"Sometimes it makes the point beautifully."

"I just find it incredible how you could completely shut down this part of your life."

He spread out his hands. "I plead the Fifth."

"You don't have many male friends, do you?"

The swift subject change threw him. "What are you... Come on, I have plenty of friends."

"Who's your best friend?"

He smiled at her. "You."

"Thank you, but who's your closest male friend?

"Miles, I guess."

"You guess? Come on, if we had had a big wedding, who would have been your best man?"

"My brother. I wanted him at our little wedding but he was having surgery."

Elbow on the table, Melanie slid her jaw along her palm, the other hand's fingernails tapping on the tabletop.

"What?" Erik said, sighing.

"I'm just looking at my handsome husband."

"You're tapping your nails and analyzing your neurotic husband. Stop. I can pay to be analyzed if I want it."

Her nails stilled. "It's a puzzling side of you, my love."

"Oh now I'm a box. Well, there are five other sides to me, hopefully you like those."

"I like all of you, I just..."

"What?"

"Nothing." She stood up and went over to the refrigerator. "I am so glad you got your necklace back. Are you happy?"

He held it up, gazing at the charms. "I don't have a word for what I am right now."

"You'll take it in to be fixed?"

"Tomorrow. I'll take our wedding bands in to be polished, too, if you want."

Her head popped over the open fridge door. "I can defrost some chicken? Or we can get Chinese and chill out?"

"Perfect."

"Are you all right?"

"I'm fine. Are you done asking me questions?"

She stared him down. "Do you want pork or vegetable lo mein?"

THOUGH HE WASN'T OUTWARDLY CURT or moody with his wife that evening, Erik was all anxious brooding within. He kept catching himself whistling bars of "The Man I Love," which was annoying. So was the hydra in his gut, rearing a thousand emotional heads, hissing and biting at him.

He felt guilty for not attending the ceremony, then justified because he didn't know about it. Then he was insulted at not being informed, and regretted cutting himself off to the point of exclusion. On the heels of regret came relief he avoided seeing Daisy, or worse, seeing her being awful sweet on John. David was an unquestionably dodged bullet. Then again, Erik could have seen Will—another helping of guilt. But Will was in a professional collaboration with Daisy now.

In Canada.

Daisy, who was always cold, living up in Canada.

He pictured her in a long wool coat, walking along snowy streets in boots, a hat pulled low and a scarf pulled high. Dance bag over her shoulder.

Walking alone.

Was she alone?

He put his fork down, pushed away his container of lo mein.

"Not hungry?" Melanie said.

"Not really."

"Are you all right?"

"I'm fine," he said. "Stop asking me shit."

Calmly, Melanie made a gesture of reaching into her pocket and then held her empty palm out to him.

"What?" he said.

"It's a fuck," she said. "I give it."

He closed his eyes. "I'm sorry," he said. "I love you. And I'm going to take my guitar out on the back porch and be moody."

"Enjoy yourself," she said, smiling, and gestured to his uneaten food with her chopsticks. "Can I eat that?"

It was a lovely night for April. The air was velvety soft. The perpetually-strung Christmas lights made the little porch into a warm, twinkling cave, and Erik sat there a long time. Deconstructing the opening riff of Led Zeppelin's "Over the Hills and Far Away," he tried to shut his thoughts out. Tried not to let it matter Daisy hadn't spoken his name on the radio.

The back door opened.

Stark naked, Melanie lounged against the jamb, fingers combing through her plaits.

"I have a question."

Slowly Erik put the guitar down, got up, and followed her inside.

Sometime later, in the dark of the living room, Mrs. Fiskare lifted her face out of the couch cushions with a concerted effort, and weakly pushed her tangled cornrows out of her mouth. Her shoulder blades were heaving and slick with sweat.

"Oh my God," she said, gasping. "What was *that?*"

"A fuck," Erik said, falling onto the floor, panting and spent. "I gave it."

DELIVERED IN PERSON

April 28, 2002

What's up, asshole? I heard the radio show yesterday. Then arrived home to find your letter and my necklace. Mind blown. If you delivered it in person you would've been blown as well. But it's allergy season and I can barely breathe through my nose. So it's for the best.

But seriously. I'm an overwhelmed and sloppy mess from this. But I wanted to let you know I got it. And thank you. Thank you for being the kind of guy to step in and help lug a stove out. Thank you for being the kind of guy to hunt me down and send back the thing that means the world to me. I don't have words to tell you how much I appreciate it. (Other than "suck" and "cock," of course.)

I'm taking care of my ass. It's not as high and tight as it used to be, but it's in one piece. And it is sorry...

I won't fucking call you. But I fucking thank you.

    E

Part Six: Kees

TESTICULAR FAILURE

MELANIE CAME TO HIM one night, sat on the ottoman and put her hand on his outstretched legs. Erik looked up from the guitar he was stringing to see she wasn't crying, but her eyes were bright and her mouth trembled.

"Honey, what's wrong?"

"I got my period," she said.

He stared at her. He didn't want to say "And?" out loud but he was completely confused.

Melanie sighed, closing her eyes. Her mouth was set somewhere between a smile and a grimace. The last time she had this expression was when she dropped her cell phone in the toilet.

"Mel, you look like you need a body buried. What's the matter?"

She took her hand off his shin. "I stopped taking the pill a year ago."

"A year?" Erik set guitar and strings aside. "A year ago you stopped?"

She picked at her fingernails. "Nothing's happening."

He was too shocked to put a sentence together. "All right," he said, pulling his hair back from his forehead. "But..." He exhaled, hands open. "Mel, I had no idea you've been trying to get pregnant since 2002."

"I know," she whispered.

He barely recognized her. They had their moments of miscommunication, true, but this bit of clandestine business seemed deliberate and devious. It was almost manipulative.

"Oh, Mel, that ain't cool," he said, trying to let her know he was upset, but not be harsh with her. Every line of her body was already laced in misery. She was crying now.

"I'm almost thirty-seven," she said. "I'm worried something's wrong."

He took his feet off the ottoman, leaned forward and gathered her to him. "Don't cry," he said, running his hand along her hair. She had taken the cornrows out a year ago and had it straightened. "Everything's fine, nothing's wrong with you. Don't cry."

"Do you want to have a baby?" she asked.

He opened his mouth. An unequivocal *yes* should have tumbled right out but he had nothing. "I figured we would," he said. "Of course. But let me get used to this, honey. You've been kicking it around for a year. I'm just coming into the picture tonight."

"I know. I'm sorry. I just don't want to wait too long."

He held her away, thumbed away the tear tracks on her face. "We won't wait too long."

They barely waited at all.

Male plumbing is less complex than female, so Erik got tested first.

Locked in a small room at the urologist's office, a room loaded with every kind of porn in every medium imaginable, he ought to have felt like...

"A man in a room loaded with porn," he mumbled. "Candy store, my ass."

He felt ridiculous.

Trying to get comfortable in one of the recliners (he felt stupid), and staring at his cup (he felt even more stupid) he spent a few minutes laughing. Then he sighed a lot. Then he picked up one of the magazines and tried.

He tried another magazine.

"Whoa," he said, peering at a page. A naked woman with long dark hair was turned partly away from the camera, looking over her shoulder at him. She was top-heavy: giant, augmented breasts on a too-slender body. But Erik wasn't looking at her breasts. He was looking at her legs.

With keen interest his eyes trailed the length of thigh and calf, down to her feet.

Her feet were in pointe shoes.

Erik's eyes narrowed. Her feet in pointe shoes, the ribbons tied neatly around her ankles. Her legs were bare, the muscles shaped and defined. Bare feet in pointe shoes. One long curving line of leg, from her toes on the floor, up her calf and thigh to...

With one hand, he covered the woman from the waist up, so all he had were a perfect little ass, long legs and bare feet in...

Five minutes later, he put his specimen cup through the revolving door at the nurse's station and left the office. His pace was a little guilty: he'd ripped the page out of the magazine and folded it up in his back pocket.

Two days later, the urologist called. "By chance did you ever have the mumps?"

"Excuse me?" Erik said.

"Your counts are extremely low, but what concerns me more is the motility."

"The what?"

"Your sperm aren't swimming," the doctor said with patient enunciation. "For lack of a better phrase. Is there a history of male infertility in your family?"

"I'm estranged from my father, I wouldn't know," Erik said. "If it helps, he was an only child, but I don't know the reason why. My paternal grandparents are deceased. I have a brother. My brother has two children, and to my knowledge, they were conceived the old-fashioned way."

"All right, for the moment we can rule out genetic causes. Back to my original question—did you have the mumps when you were a child?"

"No," Erik said.

"Are you sure?" Melanie said from the other extension.

"Of course I'm sure," he said. And the next day at work, he closed his office door and called his mother down in Key West.

"Of course you did," she said, as if Erik were witless. "It's why Peter went deaf. You knew this."

"Pete had meningitis," Erik said, as if she were the demented one.

"That was years later. The mumps left him deaf. He got it first and you hadn't been vaccinated yet, so we whisked you out of the house to your grandfather's. But then you came down with it too. It's highly contagious."

"I see," he said, disturbed he'd gotten the story wrong all these years. "Why are you asking, what's the matter?"

"Melanie and I can't get pregnant, and it seems I'm the problem. Doctor asked if I'd had the mumps. I guess one of the side effects is sterility."

"Well, yes, they told me that. But you were three years old. They said sterility was only a risk if you were past puberty. Mumps can't be the reason."

"Maybe it isn't."

"It's not. It can't be. Tell him you were just three."

He reported back. The doctor agreed, given Erik's age at the mumps onset, it was unlikely the disease had caused such testicular failure.

"Would you mind not putting 'testicular' and 'failure' in the same sentence?" Erik said.

He would need all the jokes he could muster in the next year. Erik, this man who hated to be the center of attention, was about to be scrutinized in a way that made every atom in his body howl in protest.

"I can't tell you how many people have been touching my junk," he said to Miles as they ran along the canal. "I think if I made a list of people who haven't had their hand down my pants, it would be shorter."

"Put me on the list, please," Miles said, panting.

"It's not enough they have to handle your balls. No. They have to measure them. Did you know this? They have a little thing of rings to measure your boys. It's enchanting."

"Huh. I may register a complaint at my next physical. All I get is a finger up the ass."

Before jumping into in-vitro fertilization, the doctors were trying to boost Erik's counts through chemistry—injections of chorionic gonadotropin three times a week. Fortunately they were small-needle subcutaneous shots and he quickly got the knack of self-administration. Melanie, wanting to participate, tried once to inject him, botched it badly and left him with an ugly bruise. Ever after, she lost her nerve as soon as the needle hovered over his skin.

"I can't," she said, looking a little green around the eyes.

"Pussy," Erik said, snorting. He took the syringe away and deftly took care of business. "So much for your career as a heroin addict."

Once Melanie would have laughed. Now her smile died halfway past her lower lip and she sighed.

Banned from Needle Park, Melanie hovered over him with various homeopathic remedies, nagging about selenium, ginkgo biloba, Asian ginseng and Vitamin C. For the latter, Erik resurrected his old pineapple juice habit.

"Orange juice has more Vitamin C," Melanie said, comparing labels.

"Pineapple juice makes your jiz taste good." He nudged her side playfully, but she rolled her eyes, shouldering past to put the bottles back in the fridge.

"Only one place your jiz is going, baby."

"Yeah, in a cup," Erik muttered.

The months fell away. How quickly they passed when the sole purpose of life was trying to reproduce. You were either gearing up to get pregnant or in the business-like throes of the act. Or waiting to see if you were pregnant, or trying to console your inconsolable wife when she got her period. Then you geared up again.

Erik was growing weary of scheduled and scrutinized sex, conscious of Melanie evaluating every bump and thrust for optimal conception. He once offered to videotape their lovemaking for the doctors' critique. Melanie was not amused. Without a sense of humor to play off, Erik soon stopped making jokes, robbing himself of the only outlet for stress. He kept his mouth shut, took his shots, downed the herbal remedies and dutifully jerked off by appointment. Always taking his trusty torn-out magazine page, cropped down to just legs and pointe shoes.

TOPPING AND TAILING

"WHAT IS THIS?" Erik said.

Melanie was topping and tailing string beans at the kitchen table. She looked up at him, at the piece of paper in his hand.

"I was just looking around on the internet," she said. "Throw it out if you want."

Erik looked down at the paper, a printed list of names and addresses.

> *Byron Fiskare*
> *4732 Pinnacle Peak Hwy*
> *Phoenix, AZ*
>
> *Byron E. Fiskare*
> *49 Oak Street*
> *Santa Monica, CA*
>
> *Byron Fiskare*
> *14975 Mann Street*
> *Burbank, CA*

"What do you think you're doing?" The words were icy in his mouth. He felt violated. Worse—he felt pillaged. Sacked. She had trespassed in the most guarded room in his heart's palace. A room filled with the soft white feathers of memory. A room kept quiet and still so as not to stir them. Looking down at the list of addresses, it was as though Melanie had gone into that room with a leaf blower.

"You can't go here, Melanie."

"Don't you want to know?" she asked. "After all these years, isn't it time?"

The HcG shots made him irritable. He knew it was one of the side effects and noticed both his patience and temper were easily lost these past months. Reining himself in from snapping at his students meant he often came home and snapped at his wife.

Tonight he got in her face and yelled until his voice cracked. "You try to get pregnant without telling me and now you go looking for my father without telling me. When did I become irrelevant to this marriage, Mel? When did I get thrown out of the decision making process? And when the *fuck* did you decide you know what's best for me?"

He crumpled the paper in a shaking fist and threw it at her. "Don't you ever go looking for my father again, do you understand? He is *dead* to me. If he ever calls here, I don't want to know. If he ever shows up here, I don't want to know. If you go have *coffee* with him, I don't fucking want to know."

He stormed out, the sound of her sobs dwindling away behind him as he swiftly clipped a leash on Harry and left. He walked for hours, muttering under his breath. He cooled off, and then he felt terrible. He still felt justified, but he felt terrible.

"I'm sorry," he said later, carefully taking Melanie in his arms. "I'm sorry. The damn shots make me crazy but it's no excuse. I should have walked out or..."

"I'm sorry," she whispered. "I'm like a lunatic lately. I miss my mother." Her face crumpled and she wept in his chest. Erik slid his hand along the back of her neck, rested his cheek on her head.

"I know," he whispered.

"I miss my mother and I hate that she's missing everything."

"She sees you," he said, swaying side to side. "She sees you. She knows."

"But I don't see her seeing me," she said, her voice hitching. "And I'm thinking about my dad. I'm dreaming about him and..." Melanie picked up her head, touching her fingers under her eyes. "It just bothers me our child won't know its grandfather."

"I know," he said again, helping with his own fingertips to stay the tears. "Sometimes that's just how it is with people. My mom will be the only grandparent. It's not ideal but it's what we have, Mel."

She nodded. "They say infertility can really bring the crazy out in people," she said. "I guess I have more crazy than I knew."

"I love your crazy," he said. "And you put up with mine."

"I'm sorry, baby."

He shushed her and pulled her close. "I know how important this is to you," he whispered. "But please. Mel. My balls are under a micro-scope. Sometimes I need you to just take me to bed for..."

She picked up her head and managed a wobbly smile. "Just for your cock."

"Well," he said, looking up the ceiling. "Yeah. Kind of."

She laughed then and put her hand on his face. "Come on. Upstairs. Leave your balls. Take the cannoli."

"You're adorable," Erik said, pulling her by the hand.

"You can even pull out," she said, following. "That's how uninterested I am in your sperm tonight."

"Oh, now you're teasing."

"Try me..."

BELOW THE BELT

MEL TRIED HARD to separate making love from making babies. But the gonadotropin injections were not helping Erik's counts, and the doctors concluded he and Melanie would need high-tech assistance. Conventional insemination was ruled out. "Even with the artificial head start, your sperm will never make it to the fallopian tubes," the doctor said.

"Thanks," Erik muttered.

Overnight their life turned into acronyms. They jumped right over IVF—in vitro fertilization—to a procedure known as ICSI.

"Intracytoplasmic sperm injection," Erik said on his daily run with Miles. "You don't just flood the egg with sperm and hope for the best. You pick up one single sperm and inject it straight in."

"Sounds foolproof."

"Ah, but I like to make things difficult. They have to get my boys direct from the source."

"I'm afraid to ask."

"Percutaneous epididymal sperm aspiration."

"Showoff."

"PESA for short. I mean, who can handle a mouthful like that?"

"Your mother?"

The procedure failed.

"Testicular sperm extraction," Erik said to Miles. "That's TESA to those in the inner circle."

"I can't compete with this," Miles said.

"I feel bad you won't ever know the pleasure of getting a local anesthetic in the nuts. I mean, once you get over the nausea, a needle to the sack really makes you feel like a man."

"The only thing I feel right now is inadequate."

But the TESA failed as well. After the doctor called with the unsurprising news, Melanie went straight out with the dog. Erik stayed put.

Slumped at his desk, he pressed the heel of his hand into his forehead, feeling older than he had a right to, and relieved he was finally excused from all of this. He was done. No more would his private parts be under constant public scrutiny. No more acronyms. No more every other word being "sperm" or "semen" or "ejaculate." No more needles and specimen cups and everything below the belt. The verdict was in.

He wrote *sterile* on a post-it, taking a good look at the word. He couldn't connect with it yet. He was too occupied with liberated joy that everyone, including Melanie, would finally get out of his pants and leave him alone.

His computer beeped. He tore off the note and crumpled it as he jiggled the mouse, bringing the dimmed screen back to life. He'd been waiting for his brother. They always talked on Thursday nights, via instant messaging.

> Ptfiskare74: Hey bro... How'd it go yesterday? You hear anything?
> Efiskare: Yeah just hung up with the doc actually. Nada.
> Ptfiskare74: Nada like they found nothing or nada found nothing that was swimming?
> Efiskare: No swimmers.
> Ptfiskare75: Shit. What now?
> Efiskare: We look for a donor or adopt.
> Ptfiskare74: What are you leaning toward?
> Efiskare: I don't know yet.
> Ptfiskare74: Well...I don't know how you feel about this but if you want, I'll do it.
> Efiskare: Do what?
> Ptfiskare74: I'll donate. Don't make me spell it all out. You know how I blush...

Efiskare: Really?

Ptfiskare74: Of course. If you guys wanted. I mean I feel kind of responsible that you can't.

Efiskare: What the fuck are you talking about?

Ptfiskare74: Come on, I gave you the mumps and screwed up your boys.

Efiskare: Dude, shut up.

Ptfiskare74: I'll do it. I'll do it for you. I'll do it yesterday. You let me know.

Pete's offer kindled Erik's interest. He felt a little genuine excitement. Pete. Of course. The more he thought about it, the more it seemed like the perfect solution.

But Melanie refused. She wanted a donor. Furthermore, she was beginning to feel she wanted a black donor.

And then it was war.

Erik's ancestral hackles were up. He was not only filled with residual gonadotropin, but with insulted Italo-Swedish rage. He turned on her, wounded and angry. Was she declaring him of defective stock, his bloodline and genes of no use to her? He had no problem raising a child who was a biological niece or nephew. It would be blood. He would have a bond. A connection.

"My parents are dead," she said.

"What does that have to do with it?"

"It has everything to do with it. My parents are gone. My sister's not having any kids. I'm the only one left. I'm continuing my father's line."

"And I'm not?"

"Pete has two kids. You have both your parents and you could not care less about your father's line."

He couldn't have been more shocked if she'd spit in his face. "Fuck *you*, I have both my parents. How can you even say that?"

"You know you won't ever look for your father, Erik. You're not even in touch with any of your cousins on his side."

"You have a lot of nerve, Mel. You know nothing about what I went through when he left. Nothing."

"Maybe if you told me—"

"Oh, I see where we're going. You're hung up on knowing every little thing about my past."

"I bet you told *her* about your father."

There was no question who she meant but this was an unexpected smoke bomb. He kicked the explosive topic aside and counted ten. "Are we arguing about a donor or are we arguing about my ex-girlfriend? Please let's pick one thing."

"There is still so much you won't share with me."

"I can't share everything," he said, looking up at the ceiling.

"You can, you just won't. I'm your wife. I need to know these things."

"And I'm your husband. You've got to respect what hurts me."

"Fine. We'll argue about donors. I don't want to use Pete's sperm."

"Why, because he's my brother or because he's white? Or because he's deaf? Tell me what's going on here. Please."

"This is my father's name," she said, her throat thick with suppressed crying. "I can't help but wonder what he would think... What my mother would think if..."

Erik stared at her. "If they knew you were in an inter-racial marriage?"

Melanie looked away.

"We talked about this," he said. "We talked about this when we started dating. We talked about it before we moved in together. After we got engaged I asked if you were sure and you got mad at me. You were insulted. I apologized and said I would never ask you again. Do you remember this, Melanie?"

"It's different now."

"Different how?"

"It's different when you're trying to have a child."

"It wasn't my idea." His voice was raised. He wanted to throw something. "You went off the pill without telling me. You didn't even instigate a conversation. A whole year, you tried to get pregnant on the sly and race wasn't a problem. Only now, when I can't get you pregnant, it's a burning issue? Now we're going to have this conversation?"

"Erik, you are the *king* of un-had conversations."

"Stay on the topic," he said. "If we use your eggs, any child of ours is going to be half black."

"You're saying we shouldn't use my eggs at all?"

He opened his mouth and shut it, thinking. "Maybe it's the fairest thing," he said.

She was shaking her head, like a girl being told she couldn't have a pony. "No."

"You have your eggs," he said. "I have nothing."

"That's not my fault," she said. "What happened to you isn't my fault."

"It's my fault, then?"

"Do you even want to have a baby?" She shouted it. The words echoed off the walls. "Because I don't think you want it."

"I don't want it?"

"No."

"I did everything," he said, pushing the words through the wall of his teeth. "I did everything, Mel. I subjected myself to every test, every procedure. Every needle and every goddamn way someone wanted to crawl up my works. I never said no."

"But you never said 'I want it.'" The tears ran down her face. "Never once did you say you wanted it more than anything and wanted it with *me*."

He looked at her. Could only look.

"I'm your wife," she said. "This is a marriage, not an extended play-date."

"Mel—"

"I can't stand this, Erik. I can't stand your ambivalence anymore. I plan our social life. I plan our vacations. I plan this, I plan that and you just show up. I proposed because I knew you never would. I shocked you by going off the pill but you didn't fight me. You just tottered along without an impassioned opinion either way. That's all you do—passively go where I tell you. On auto-pilot. You can take it or leave it. You don't have a fire in your belly for anything. What if I weren't here planning and telling, what would you do?"

Erik turned away, looking out the window and counting.

"You keep secret the things you're passionate about," Melanie said. "I'm tired of trying to dig them out of you. And I can't take the way you just follow your life around instead of leading it. All the while the best of you is stuck in Lancaster with that bitch who made you feel so—"

Bitch made Erik whip his head around so fast his neck cracked. Melanie's sentence never ended.

"Feel so what?" he said. "What did she make me feel? Go on. Tell me what she made me feel."

Across the living room, Melanie stared at him.

"Useless," Erik said. His voice sounded raspy and full of sludge, like a broken old man's. "She made me feel useless. Just like you're doing right now. It's no different. I don't have what you need so you'll go get it from someone else."

"Baby..."

"It must be the type I attract," he said. "All the women I love make me feel useless. Nothing I do is enough for them. Not staring down the barrel of a gun, not taking a needle in the sack. Nothing."

Her hand soft on his shoulder then and he flinched from her touch. "Just leave me be," he said, with the last vestiges of civility he could muster.

Weeping, Melanie went upstairs. Erik stood with his forehead and fists pressed against the windowpane.

"Useless," he whispered.

A MAP, A PICK AXE AND A VENGEANCE

"CAN I ASK YOU a personal question?" Erik was running with Miles along the canal.

"Already? We just met."

Erik didn't feel like joking. "Are you and Janey childless by choice? Or did you have fertility troubles?"

"Ah. I wondered when you would ask."

"In my typically obtuse and self-centered way, it only just occurred to me."

"Unfortunately, we are childless by choice."

"Unfortunately how?"

"Consanguinity."

"Speak English."

"Janey," Miles said, "is my first cousin."

Erik slowed to a jog and then stopped, leaning over with hands on knees. "She is?"

"Technically speaking she is my double cousin. Our mothers are sisters and our fathers are brothers." Miles ran easily in place. "Shocking?"

"Surprising to learn but not shocking. I mean, it's not appalling."

"Then I'll throw in we're not married, either."

"Then why does she call herself Janey Kelly?"

"Because her name is Janey Kelly," Miles said.

Erik grimaced and looked at his watch. "My next asinine question will be in thirty seconds."

"I cannot wait." Miles began to run again and Erik fell into step beside him.

"If it's not too asinine, when did you fall in love with her?"

"The question is when was I not in love with her? I was born to love her. We were five when we realized we belonged to each other. We fought it. We denied it. We tore ourselves apart and went to live on opposite sides of the planet. I married a lovely woman everyone approved of and I made her life miserable. She had the good sense to leave me because she knew I was born for Janey and no one else."

A quarter mile passed in silence. Their sneakers slapped in rhythm. Left. Right. Left. Right.

"Born for her," Erik said. "Tell me what you mean."

"I look at Janey and my heart leaps," Miles said. "And when I am with her, I want for nothing. We wasted eight years of our youth living apart and being miserable just to make everyone else happy. We finally said to hell with everyone and decided to be together. It had its price. Three decades later and still some people refuse to acknowledge we are a couple. But we found our truth and made our choices. We chose to be together. We chose not to have children because it's too risky. And we chose not to adopt because we only want each other. Maybe it's selfish, but..."

"Or maybe it's courageous."

"I don't know, Fish. At some point, you just have to start living the truth of who you are and what you feel."

Erik stopped running. Hands on his head he turned in a circle, looking up at the skies, breathing against the fingers of steel darting around his throat.

"All right?" Miles said from up ahead.

"Yeah." He set out again, his body a heavy, sodden weight. "I'm all right."

EVERYTHING AT HOME WAS ALL WRONG. He and Melanie were dug deep in their separate trenches and fighting a quiet war of attrition. The house grew chill with words and accusations unspoken. Frosty weeks went by. Eggshells crunched underfoot. Gradually the air thawed and small overtures were attempted. The subject of adoption was raised. But by then they were emotionally exhausted and physically indifferent.

Occasionally they reached for each other in the night, but even their sex was tired. Melanie's body was present but her head was elsewhere. They rarely laughed in bed anymore. They barely talked. Their connection was full of misunderstood static. Most nights they lay back to back, Melanie hard done by and misunderstood, Erik a useless testicular failure.

Night after night, they tossed and turned their covers to mush until Melanie caved, took a pill and slept. Only when she was breathing slow and deep did Erik put the pill that was Daisy on his tongue and swallow.

The best of you is stuck in Lancaster with that bitch.

True. And now the bitch had taken up quiet residence in the folds of his brain. He let her stay, a one-woman Greek chorus observing as he went about his day at work, willingly talking back to him whenever he silently talked to her. Asking questions. Helping work out a problem. At night, he imagined her voice softer, asking different kinds of questions. Listening and nodding thoughtfully as he talked out other problems. Her hands cupped for whatever he wanted to put in them.

All the same, even as he idled away the time in imaginary conversations, he never once envisioned the crucial confrontation he ought to have had with Daisy. He never went back in time to rearrange events. To imagine himself walking into the kitchen of her apartment and saying to David, "You need to leave." Going upstairs and hearing what she had to say. Or even making his way to her as she smoked on the back steps. The next day at dawn. A week later. Even a year later.

No hypothetical do-over for the calls he didn't return and the letters he didn't answer. No yelling at her, cursing at her, telling her he hated her. He took only the best of the best and constructed an idealized castle in the air, suspended in present tense in a parallel universe. Just Daisy hanging around being Daisy.

He managed his thoughts with astounding discipline. He was almost smug about the rules. Casual mental musings were allowed. Wallowing would not be tolerated. Sexual horseplay was punishable by death.

It worked well for a couple weeks. Like a chaste Sir Galahad, he made do with the memory of their bond, their soulful friendship, their effortless support of one another and the comfort her presence always brought him. He kept alive her keen intelligence, her humor and wit, and her astonishing talents as a dancer. He consoled himself with his dumb, made-up conversations, and managed to keep the recollection of his physical relationship with Daisy locked away in a stone fortress. Every now and then he would stick an extra pillow behind him and pretend she was snugged up against his back. Her hip bone softly poking him. His heart calm under her palm.

It was all he allowed.

Until now.

At some point you just have to start living the truth of who you are and what you feel.

Miles's offhand remark was a bowling ball, sending all the stringent rules skittering and spinning. The stone walls Erik so carefully built around the ardent memories were crumbling. Through a chink in the stones Daisy appeared and crooked her finger at him.

He went. Lying in bed, in the shadow of his wife's sleeping body, Erik went looking for buried treasure with a map, a pick axe and a vengeance. He crawled back through the archives, dug in and began to catalog. And in defiance of all the laws, he wallowed in it. He scooped up the sex, poured it from his hands onto his head and bathed in it.

The memory of kissing hollowed him out, filled his chest and belly with gnawing heat. He could press his fingers sideways across his lips and in an instant, they were her mouth. But kissing was an innocent snowball tossed down the mountainside. Next thing he knew, Erik was being swept along in an avalanche of sense memory.

The thought of her lithe, muscled body made his palms ache with memory. He put out a hand and her breast curved into it. He could distill her scent out of mere air. Her perfume. Or the damp, musky smell when she was excited, writhing as he either slid her out of her clothes or pulled them enough aside to get to what he wanted.

I want. I want. His body coiled in a quenchless thirst, needing to beat fists against the walls, foam at the mouth and bay at the moon. *I want it.*

He gazed into space, remembering how she took her clothes off for him. The sight of her, wanton and hungry, breasts overflowing from an unhooked bra beneath a shirt pulled halfway up, thighs trembling inside panties pushed halfway down. The tips of his fingers prying her open. The slick, pink flesh quivering when he breathed on it. He touched his tongue to the roof of his mouth and remembered the tart, sweet taste of her. The heavy drop of her hand on his head. The noiseless rush of air through her throat when he made her come.

Lying in bed—hard, crazed, burning—he went through it all. All the lovemaking in dorm rooms and the apartment on Jay Street. Sex in the morning when their bodies were still wreathed in sleep. Sex at night when their bodies were screaming with need. Fingers and mouths, sweat and juice. Craving it. Begging and dying for it. Building a cathedral. Being in love and being wanted. So safe in a web of physical trust, he could make love to her like a sweetheart one night, throw her down and fuck her the next. It was all the same thing. Staring into her eyes without speaking was making love. Being buried in the heat of her frustration was making love. Whether her kiss crashed into his mouth, or just brushed it like a passing dream, he could taste her love. And nothing could top it. Nothing could surpass it.

Not even Melanie.

It was deplorable behavior. He knew it. It was selfish and cruel to his wife, her body curved like a parenthesis away from him. He imagined the waves of betrayed hurt radiating off her back onto his. But it was Daisy in his head in hot, candy-sweet ribbons he could not ignore.

You're cheating on Mel, he told himself. *All this maudlin, mental jerking off to the past? It's no different than if you were fucking someone else. You're a shit husband.*

He couldn't help it. Any more than he'd been able to help falling for the high of cocaine all those years ago. This high was even more addictive because it was organic. It was cooked up in the laboratory of his soul. He sucked it up from the depths of his heart, up into his nose and let it melt down from the top of his skull.

Stoned, he stared into the dark and Daisy's face materialized. She was lying on her side, staring back at him. One hit and he could put her there. One toke and he could bring it back—the serenity, the stillness. He wasn't reaching out to her merely for sex. Sex was only part of it. Sex was an extension of the love and peace and deep understanding in the depths Daisy's eyes. A connection so soulful, it was cellular.

"Consanguinity," he said, moving his mouth around the word but making no sound. A blood bond. A soul bond.

He reached out a hand, touched nothing, yet he felt her. Her jaw in his palm, her hair through his fingers. Her shoulder rising and falling with her steady breathing. Inhaling him. Exhaling herself. Staring through his eyes.

I want it, he thought, gripped by desperation, a fire in his belly. *I want this. I lost this. Why can't I find it again?*

He rolled over and looked at Melanie. His wife, this woman he'd married because he loved her. His heart ought to leap at the sight of her, or be filled with a soothed peace. He should look at her with a vision of the future, a common goal, a mission. She ought to be the love of his life.

She wasn't.

I love her. But my heart never stopped at the sight of her. My fingertips don't ache when she is not there. I don't look in her eyes and want for nothing. I don't want to fill her questioning hands with my answers.

And I never wanted to ink her into my skin.

An aching, wailing pain in his heart then, and a sickening sense of shame. He had to get out of bed, physically back away from Melanie, with an ever-growing dread. *What have I done?* His back bumped against the wall. He was trapped. He was mourning. He was grieving. He was a shitty husband, a heartless son of a bitch who had fucked up badly.

He was not where he was supposed to be.

I'm lost, he thought, stumbling down the stairs, stumbling around in the dark of his mind. *I lost everything. Why can't I find it?*

He wandered the house, trying to wear himself out. He sat at the kitchen table drinking tea, Harry's muzzle on his knee.

Where are you, Dais, he thought, projecting his yearning self out into the ether. To the far north and a dark Canadian night where Daisy might be awake, too.

Where is your home? Are you sleeping?
Who is holding you tonight?

"Who loves you now?" Erik whispered to the kitchen cabinets. "Who is the man you love?"

Harry yawned, making a high-pitched keen.

When Erik finally came back to bed and slept, the dreams, dormant for so long, came to him again.

First he was up in Daisy's room, in a caramel haze and they were fucking each other senseless, safely savage within the structure of their love. Then he was in the theater, and James sent a bullet into Erik's chest with a dull thud. He could not get up to stop James, who was shooting Daisy dead. The blood was rising up over Erik's head. A wave of it pouring over the edge of the stage. Blood like a river in the aisle, blood in his hair, blood on his hands, blood on the stage floor.

It was Daisy and blood and sex coming back to him in the night again. And when he woke up coming, coming and dying in a gasping, heaving sweat, heart pounding in his ears and a name half-formed in his mouth, Melanie slept on.

Or pretended she didn't hear.

YOUR FATHER'S TREE

THE FINAL PAPERS were signed on an unseasonably chilly autumn morning, the day before Halloween. Erik walked his now ex-wife out of the courthouse and they looked at each other.

"I'll get you a cab," Erik said.

"Why don't you get me a drink?" she said. "Let's go to a bar."

Erik stared at her, not understanding.

"Where was our first date?" she asked. "This isn't a trick question."

"At a bar."

"Right. And after we got married at city hall we went to...?"

"A bar."

"I think it'll be all right if we go to a bar to mark the occasion of our divorce. In fact, it seems fitting."

Still bewildered, Erik nodded, gesturing down the street. Melanie took his arm and they walked without talking to a small Irish pub. They sat at a sunlit table in the window, ordered drinks, looked at each other.

Melanie was wearing her hair in cornrows again, letting the grey come in at her temples. New lines creased her forehead, but when their beers came, she raised her pilsner with dry-eyed serenity.

"Cheers, baby," she said.

"Skål," Erik said, touching his glass to hers.

They drank deeply. Melanie put a finger to the bit of foam at the corner of her mouth. "You will stay in touch with me, won't you?"

"I... If you want me to."

"I do. Does it surprise you?"

Erik shook his head. "I don't know what surprises me anymore. I don't know anything anymore."

Melanie had asked for a divorce ten months ago. Erik conceded. She wondered if she might have the upright piano. He agreed. She asked if she could take the dog. It killed Erik, but he let Harry go.

Then she threw a plate at him.

It went wide and smashed in pieces against a far wall but the intent behind it was unmistakable. "You are emotionally retarded, you know that, Erik? Goddammit, you won't fight for *anything* you love," she said. "You spineless victim."

And she moved out. With the dog. It was the ugliest moment in an otherwise smooth, no-fault divorce that took less than a year.

Now Melanie leaned forward and began tapping her index finger on Erik's left hand. He looked at her, looked down at his hand as her tapping grew more deliberate.

"What?" he said. His wedding band was gone. So was hers. They had sold the diamond and used it for lawyers' fees. But she wasn't tapping his ring finger, she was tapping down by his wrist, flicking with her nail, nudging his hand to turn over. When it was palm up, her fingertip came to rest on his tattoo.

"You never got over her," she said, her voice filled with kindness he didn't deserve. "You just left."

Erik breathed slowly. "I was young," he heard himself say. His weight was down again. He hadn't had breakfast and one beer was already sinking gooey fingers into his brain.

"You started calling for her in your sleep," Melanie said. "The last few months I was at home. It was November—the dreams always come back to you in the fall. I was used to the thrashing around and the wordless crying out. But then you started calling for her."

Erik clenched his fist and turned the tattoo down to face the table. His other hand came to catch his brow.

"Hey," Melanie said, squeezing his hand. "I'm not telling you now to accuse you. I just... I worry about you, baby. You're not mine to worry over anymore, but I do. I want you to be all right. It's fall, November's in two days, the dreams will start coming again. And I don't want you to be lying next to your second wife calling Daisy's name."

It settled onto his shoulders, the great wrong he had done this fine woman. "I'm sorry," he whispered. "Mel, I'm so sorry."

"Fuck you," she said. Then she sat back, grinning. "Can you tell I'm in therapy? It's going really well, I think."

He laughed. "Hey, I'm glad I'm still worthy of one of your fucks."

"I've been back to church, too," she said.

"Growing your soul and shrinking your head," he said. "It's good stuff."

"I won't lie and say we didn't talk about you."

"You're talking about me in church?"

She kicked him under the table. "Smartass."

He smiled. "Anyway, it's only supposed to be about you in therapy."

"If I'm paying, I'll make it about whatever the fuck I want."

He let go her fingers and reached to touch her cheek. He did like her, and it made a warm little dent in the genuine sadness which had cloaked him during the divorce proceedings.

The one drink turned into a two-hour boozy lunch. The beers loosened their tongues and hearts. They cried a little, but they also laughed a lot. And afterward, when they stumbled out onto the sidewalk and Erik hailed a cab, they were still laughing.

"Your heart is huge," Melanie said, putting a foot into the well of the car.

"Your love is amazing," he said, holding the door.

She put her cheek against his. "You're good."

"You're adorable."

Erik waved as the taxi pulled away, laughing when Melanie gave him the finger out the window and catching the kiss she blew before the cab turned the corner.

"IT WAS WEIRD," Erik said to Miles as they ran through Corbett Park.

"How so?"

"It felt almost celebratory. We just got divorced and we were having a party."

"Would you rather she told you to fuck off forever?"

"No," Erik said, laughing.

"Amicable divorce is an achievement," Miles said. "And at the end of the day, you still like each other. Which is also an achievement."

"I know," Erik said. "But it just seemed weird."

"Probably because you don't have much experience with relationships ending in a healthy way."

They emerged from the park, turned left and headed along the canal's bike path. The sun's rays slanted from beneath the clouds. Leaves were collecting in crunchy piles. The air was cool and dry, the perfect temperature for running. A hint of wood smoke lingered. They reached the Main Street Bridge and headed across its span. The clouds shifted and the last of the sun threw a handful of diamonds on the green waters of the canal.

"So," Miles said. "Will you stay in touch?"

"With Melanie? I guess. I mean, sure."

Miles chuckled. "Your apple lies so close to your father's tree, Fish."

Erik stopped short. "Excuse me?"

Miles stopped too, looked calmly back with hands on hips. "I teach diction. You heard me."

"Are you actually comparing me to my father?" Erik said.

"Yes."

Erik glanced around, open-mouthed and stunned. "I don't know where you get off bracketing me with that—"

"Erik, shut up. I'll preface this by saying I love you like a son. Both Janey and I love you. But it's clear you only know two ways to relate to people: whole-hearted, complete commitment. Or estrangement. And who did you learn from?"

Erik's teeth clicked shut. He stared.

Miles answered his own question. "Your old man. From him you learned the only way to end a relationship is to walk out and never look back. You shut it off, shut it down, cease all contact and act like it never happened. It's what you did with Daisy. You did to Daisy exactly what your father did to you. Not consciously. Not maliciously. But because it was the only way you knew. And you almost did it with Melanie. If Mel hadn't orchestrated that little post-mortem after you came out of the courthouse, you would've said *vaya con dios* and never called her again."

Erik was on the defense, a sharp retort formed on his tongue. Yet at the same time Miles's words were turning a key to the gears of his mind. And the reply dissolved.

It was the only way you knew.

"Daisy hurt you," Miles said. "And you never let her explain. Or apologize."

"She cheated on me," Erik said, his voice hollow and petulant.

"Oh, stop clutching your pearls. She cheated but you never dealt with it. Instead you amputated her like a diseased limb, shut your heart down and never looked back. You may think it's closure but it isn't. You may think the Janeys and Daisys of the world come along twice in a lifetime but they don't. C'mon, move, my legs are going to cramp up."

They ran down Market Street in silence, turned left and headed for the Fayette Street Bridge, crossing the canal again. Their strides ate the asphalt in rhythmic gulps. Their open-mouthed breathing matched. The charms on Erik's necklace jingled as they bounced around his collarbones.

"Maybe you're right," he said, as they jogged down the ramp back onto the bike path.

"It was Janey's theory," Miles said. "She's the shrink."

"You're just the henchman."

Still running, Miles reached into his pocket then held out his empty hand to Erik.

"What?" Erik said.

"It's a fuck. I give it." He laughed and punched Erik's shoulder. "God, I love that line. One of Mel's greatest."

"I know," Erik muttered. "Thanks, Miles."

"It's what we father figures are supposed to do. Slap you upside the head to point out the not-so-obvious."

A babble of laughter behind them. A couple on rollerblades glided by, letting go hands to divert around Erik and Miles, then join again. Their legs planed side to side in perfect unison. Partners on the path.

Erik watched the lovers until they disappeared around a bend.

YOU STILL HAVEN'T KISSED A MAN

AT SOME POINT you just have to start living the truth.

In his heart Erik knew it was time. He didn't ask why, he didn't think it to death. He just got in his car and drove to Lancaster.

It was Monday of Thanksgiving week. The campus seemed subdued. Erik parked in the visitor lot and heeded the posted sign: *All visitors must report to the Security Office in the Wayne Administration Building.*

The office was a tiny nook in the lobby of Wayne, manned by a young man with a black watch cap and a soul patch. His nametag read *Charlie.* "Help you?"

"I was a student here," Erik said. "I was just in the area. Would it be all right if I walked around?"

"Sure," Charlie said, scooting his chair over to a computer console. "What's your name?"

Erik gave it and spelled it, handed over his driver's license. Charlie tapped a few keys, made a few mouse clicks.

"What class?"

"1993, but I didn't graduate."

Charlie grunted, typed, and then, thankfully, he smiled. "Well, you're right here, class of '93. Fill this out and I'll print you up a badge." He passed a form on a clipboard over the counter and Erik began filling it out. As he did, another security guard came in through a back door.

He was a much older guy, silver hair and mustache, an impressive beer belly. Erik glanced at his nametag, *Stan*.

"Whaddya got, Charlie," Stan mumbled, dropping his walkie-talkie into a charger.

"Just an alumni visitor pass."

Stan glanced over Charlie's shoulder at the computer screen, then stooped and looked again, putting his hands on the back of Charlie's chair.

"Erik Fiskare," he said. "I remember you."

Erik looked up, startled. "I'm sorry?" His mind raced through a gallery of his not-so-finest collegiate moments. He couldn't remember an offense so notorious, it would stay planted in a security guard's memory for over a decade.

Stan straightened up, adjusting the belt holding up his considerable girth. "Well, you might not remember," he said. "It was in Mallory Hall right after the shooting."

"Holy shit." Charlie swiveled around to look at Erik. "Class of '93. You were there?"

"I was," Erik said to him. Then to Stan, "You were?"

"Sure was. You were in a bit of a tug-o-war. Police wanted to question you but your girlfriend was being wheeled out on a gurney. I talked you into staying."

"Wow." Erik blinked. He tried hard, but could only summon the general recollection of security's presence in the theater. No faces. He recalled the agony of letting them take Daisy without him, but nobody named Stan who had acted as a voice of reason and helped him make the decision. "I don't remember a whole lot from that day," he said.

"Well I can't blame you," Stan said. "You were one scared kid. I tell you, Charlie, this poor guy was covered in blood and had a look in his eye I hadn't seen since I was in Vietnam."

"No kidding," Charlie said. His tone was amused tolerance but his eyes on Erik were awed and respectful.

"A real thousand-yard stare. His whole heart was heading out in the ambulance. He wouldn't let go of her. I told him to stay and talk to police first. Otherwise they'd only come looking for him later, wondering why he was reluctant to talk."

Erik's eyes drifted up and to his left, to the place of memory. "You know," he said. "Hearing you talk right now, it starts to... I think I remember your voice."

"You said all right but they still had to peel your hand out of your girl's. Typical, right? We think we're men and then a woman brings us to our knees." Stan's laugh started as a wheeze and then burst in a bubbling guffaw.

"She make it?" Charlie asked under the chortling.

Erik nodded at him. "She made it. She's all right." He turned back to Stan. "Talking to the police first definitely was the right choice to make. I don't remember you steering me, but thank you."

Stan dismissed it with a wave.

"No, really," Erik said. "I came back today to face some ghosts, so it means a lot to find this out. Thank you."

Stan cleared his throat. "Good to see you again, Erik," he said, and offered a hand across the counter. "Welcome back."

Erik shook his hand. Then took his license and the completed visitor's badge from Charlie and shook his hand, too. He left Wayne Hall oddly touched.

In the lobby of Mallory Hall, he stood before the bronze plaque outside the auditorium doors, tracing a finger over the raised letters:

DEL'AMICI MEMORIAL AUDITORIUM

IN MEMORY OF OUR FRIEND AND COLLEAGUE

MARIE GIULIA DEL'AMICI

PROFESSOR OF DANCE

MAY 27, 1943 - APRIL 22, 1992

He breathed in, his heart pounding. The smell in the lobby alone was an engulfing wave of nostalgia. The smell of the past. The smell of production. It was more intense than he'd imagined.

The doors to the theater were open, and music played within. Erik hesitated. He could skip the theater and head down to the shops, look for Leo. He did come to see Leo, after all.

"We're going in," David had said, one long-ago summer. "Fuck the fucking fuckers, we own this place…"

Erik glanced again at Marie's plaque, then he walked through the auditorium doors.

Here the smell of the past was stronger. He paused by the lighting booth, dark and empty. The door was ajar, beckoning. Erik put his hand on the glass pane, as if to soothe a sorrowful dog. *Not now. It's all right, I'll come back.*

A half-dozen girls were on the stage in practice clothes, flushed, panting, gulping water. One or two glanced back to where Erik stood. He kept his badge and his hands in plain sight, made his body language neutral.

Standing in the middle of the third row, talking to the girls, a familiar figure. Tall and broad-shouldered, a little thicker in the waist now, but exuding the same charisma and magnetism. And the voice—deep and full, rising up out of his chest and filling the theater.

"All right then, ladies. Go cool down. Thank you. If I don't see you, enjoy your Thanksgiving."

The girls dispersed through the wings. Erik moved further down the aisle. Kees was looking at a notebook, a pair of reading glasses on his nose, held by a chain. His bald pate shone under the lights.

Erik cleared his throat. "Keesja."

Kees looked up like a bird, then back over his shoulder. His mouth fell open. "Holy. Shit."

"We meet again, Obi-Wan Kenobi."

Kees tossed the notebook over his shoulder and fumbled at his glasses. "Will you look what the good Lord hath brought to me?"

"The return of the prodigal son," Erik said, his voice husky as it passed his tight throat.

"I don't believe what I'm seeing." Kees made his way down the row.

"Believe it."

"You still haven't kissed a man in your life but I can tell you're pretty damn close right now."

Kees came up the aisle, throwing his arms out into their full, magnificent span. Erik went straight into them and was crushed in muscle and bone. Kees's hands pummeled and patted him, he kissed Erik's head, rocked him back and forth, crooning. "Good to see you. So good to see you."

"Good to be seen," Erik said.

Kees held him away. "How are you, my man? Let me look at you. No, wait, let me finish feeling you up." He hugged Erik again.

"Keep your hands off my ass."

"You wish." Kees swatted said posterior anyway. "Now let me look at you. Sit down, come, sit down. Goddamn, I can't believe it. All these years, Fish. What the hell are you doing here?"

Erik could have made up any number of things, but this supernatural weariness he could not seem to shake left him with only enough energy for the truth. "It was time," he said.

Kees seemed satisfied, and leaned back, putting one ankle on the other knee. He was now sporting a goatee, shot through with grey. So were his eyebrows.

"So tell me, what have you been doing with yourself since you ran away?"

"Interesting choice of words."

"I call things what they are. Where did you go?"

Erik gave him the short version, a resume of Geneseo and Brockport.

"Are you married? Any little fishies of your own?"

"Just divorced. No guppies."

"No wonder you look terrible."

"Do I?"

"Well you're beautiful to me but yeah, you look a little beat up, my friend."

"I feel beat up."

Kees clapped a hand on his shoulder. "Let me buy you a beer. And a sandwich. Good Lord, you look gaunt."

"I won't say no."

"Come on. Just stop by my office, let me get my coat."

They headed up the aisle. He hadn't intended to, but as they reached row M, Erik paused and looked down, moving his feet around. The carpet was navy blue in 1992. They'd pulled all of it out and replaced it with this gold.

"Right here," he said.

"Right here," Kees said.

"I heard the radio piece. From the ten-year anniversary. I was touched by what you said."

Kees's eyebrows came together.

"You said when I came out of the booth and called James's name, it was the most courageous thing you'd ever seen."

"It was," Kees said. He cleared his throat. "Stupid and insane. But courageous. And genuine. I knew you didn't plan it. You just did it. Because of who you are. If anyone could have pulled James back from the edge, you could, Fish."

Hands in pockets, Erik moved up the aisle toward the lighting booth. He put a foot up on the step, looked back at Kees, who nodded.

He stepped in, flicking the light.

It was a mistake.

He'd come in looking for his own memories of work, of shows and tech weeks and his stagehand friends. Instead, she was here. Hanging around, sewing her shoes. Nestled beside him while he was running a show, keeping him company. Straddling his legs the day of the shooting, burning with impatient desire.

He looked out through the glass but she was there too, on the stage. Running to Will, up on his shoulder, a bloody burst and Will jerked up fast and threw her off him...

He turned the light off and the images faded away. He ran a hand along the console table. Caressed it as he'd once caressed his lover. He stepped out of the booth. "It's all I can do."

"It's enough. Come on."

They walked through the lobby and down the stairs to Kees's office. "Is Leo here?"

"Unfortunately you'll miss him. He already left for Thanksgiving."

"Michael Kantz?"

"He retired two years ago."

"So you're head of the whole dance department now?"

"I am. And having a hell of a time wearing all these hats. Marie left a cursed pair of shoes, my friend. It's just been a bitch finding a good fit and we're getting less ballet applicants."

"I really was here during the Golden Age, wasn't I?"

"You were indeed."

"You're well though? Holding up?"

"Holding up."

"How's the shoulder?"

Kees vigorously wind-milled his arm a few times. "Happy?"

"I'd be ecstatic except it's the wrong shoulder."

"Well dig your steel trap," Kees muttered, and made circles with his other arm, much more slowly and without as much range. "Hurts like a bitch on rainy days."

"Doesn't everything?"

"I tell you, Fish, much as I'm shocked to see you wander into my theater like a stray dog, I'm not shocked."

"Why's that?"

"The older I get, the more I'm convinced there are no coincidences." Kees shuffled through papers on his desk and finally extricated a copy of *Dance Magazine*. He licked a finger and went through the pages. "Here. If you can step into the lighting booth, you should be able to look at this."

As if it were a sword, he reversed the mag over his forearm. Erik took it carefully.

"There's a chair behind you," Kees said. "Or just fall onto the floor if it's too much."

Erik scanned the headline, "A Tree Grows in Saint John: New Brunswick Ballet Theater Debuts Full-Length Nutcracker."

He sat down. In the chair.

> *After two years of only being able to produce the Act II Divertissements from the beloved ballet of the Christmas season, New Brunswick Ballet Theater is debuting its first full-length Nutcracker this year, with a thriving guest list for the party scene and an army of mice and soldiers, all under the age of twelve. Co-Artistic Directors William Kaeger and Marguerite Bianco partnered with local dance schools to cast the iconic first act, and a team of industrious set designers came up trumps with the ultimate present for their iconic battle scene: a growing Christmas tree...*

The text went on for pages, but the pictures now caught Erik's eye. Children rehearsing. Stagehands constructing the tree. Then shots of Daisy and Will, dancing together in college: one from the Bach variations, another from *Who Cares?* Daisy in her poppy-pink dress.

Skimming the text, Erik turned the page. A beautiful black-and-white picture of Will and Lucky Dare. Lucky seated at a desk, poring over some papers with a little boy on her lap. Will stood by with a baby girl on his shoulder. The caption read "A Family Affair: Will and Lucky Kaeger, with their children, just another day behind the scenes at NBBT."

Erik turned the page. And there she was.

"This is now?" he asked. "This year?"

"Right now," Kees said, his voice low and kind.

Daisy. Right now.

A full-page color shot of her rehearsing, or perhaps teaching. Daisy in a practice tutu. Posed in a long, leaning arabesque, supported by Will. Behind them clustered pairs of dancers, some mirroring the pose, some simply observing. Will's head was turned back toward them. Daisy's head was turned forward and her mouth was parted—clearly she was talking through the reflection in the mirror to the couples behind her.

Without being aware he was doing it, Erik's finger traced the line of Daisy's pose.

Line, Kees had taught him, *is the picture the body makes in the air.*

Daisy's long legs, feet bare inside pointe shoes, arched and curved. Her black tights came down mid-shin, and Erik could see part of one scar along the top of her left calf. Will's hands circled her waist, his left hand nearest the camera, with its two missing digits. Erik noticed he wore his gold wedding band on his index finger.

He continued the path of his own finger, up the song of Daisy's neck and shoulders. Her hair pulled up with those same small curls falling out. Her face was more angular, her eyes a little circled. But beneath the twin arches of her brows, those impossibly blue-green irises blazed with a passion. She was in her element, vibrant and alive.

She was beautiful.

Erik traced her arms, slim and curved, reaching out and away from her, extended without break to the ends of her nails. Her left hand nearest the camera: a bracelet encircled her wrist but her fingers were bare.

"I said look at it. Don't eat it."

Erik looked up, blinked.

"You talk to her?" Kees asked.

Erik shook his head, closing the pages.

"Ever?"

"No." Lightly he tossed the magazine back onto Kees's desk. Kees stared back at him, calm, relaxed, arms crossed.

"Why not?"

Erik stood up. "I need a couple of beers for this conversation. Are you still buying?"

"What if I wasn't?"

"Then I'd buy."

Kees released an arm and gestured to the door.

FREE COUNSELING

THEY WENT INTO TOWN, got beers and burgers, sat and ate at the bar.

"Wat denk je, mijn vriend?"

"Did you know Daisy slept with David?"

"Of course I knew."

"You did?"

"I'm the gay dance teacher. I know everything. Except for the life of me, I can't figure out when you became such a stubborn, vindictive, unforgiving ass."

Erik stared. Kees calmly chewed and swallowed, took a pull of beer and stared back. "Quite the déjà vu here," he said. "I had a little chat with Daisy at the memorial ceremony. She's made a beautiful life for herself but any idiot can see she never got over you. Then I had to take Opie out to dinner and hear about the torch he's still carrying. I tell you, Fish, if I keep up this free counseling, I'm going to end up broke and fat."

Erik put his burger back down on the plate. "What's your hourly fee?"

"You're cute so I'll take you on pro bono. Talk to me, Fish. What are you really doing here?"

Erik took a long sip of his beer. He was approaching a crossroads. Daisy occupying every waking and sleeping thought. Everything in him knew it was time to stop clutching his pearls and start living the truth. And yet he was frozen. He was waiting for a comet in the sky or the tea leaves in his mug to arrange themselves into a guide. He needed something. Someone to show him.

Or bless him.

"Lately, Kees, I've been thinking a lot about the first dance concert I worked. All those nights of tech week when I sat with you, and you taught me about dance. And about partnering."

"You were like a sponge, I remember. Watching Daisy and Will, you were consumed with knowing the mechanics of everything, how they did it, how it worked. So why is it coming back to you now? What's the grand lesson within the art of partnering, my friend?"

"I was watching lifts, and you told me going up was easy, coming down was hard."

"True."

"And you said Daisy was a generous and forgiving partner."

"Also true."

"And I'm not."

Kees looked him up and down. "You're better than this."

"I don't think I ever got over her," Erik said.

"Of course you didn't. You never finished it. You just left."

"She—"

Kees pointed a long finger at him. "You left," he said again. "You chose to leave. Just sit there and own it."

"You sound like my ex-wife."

"She sounds like a smart lady."

"She's black."

Kees's nostrils flared. "And? What, are we brothers now or something?"

Erik's face burned. "Sorry."

"You are still a kid. Jesus. A mature man would've fixed this with one phone call."

"Hey, I made that call and Opie answered the phone."

"When? Eight, nine years ago? Come on, enough with the excuses, Fish. You were hurt, it's not up for debate. But your marriage fell apart, you look like death on a stick and you're sitting here putting your heart on my plate. I'm not hungry for what went wrong. I want to know what your next move is."

"I don't know what it is. I just know I can't move, period."

"What can't you move on from—the infidelity? Or her?"

"I don't know."

"Well, from what I can put together, she didn't cheat on you because she was an uncaring slut. Or hell, what do I know? She probably was a raving bitch in heat who would fuck anything in pants."

"Jesus, she was n—"

"Forget it. She's a cunt. Don't waste your time."

He flinched. "Knock it off."

Kees pointed at him. "See? That tells me you're willing to dissect the situation. Look, Fish, it sucks when someone cheats on you, but it doesn't necessarily have to be an unforgivable offense. *Certain* mitigating circumstances apply here."

"I know."

"Do you? What are you holding onto? What can you just not let go of?"

"I don't know." He wanted to arm-sweep the bar, send plates and glasses flying out of sheer frustration.

"Do you miss her?"

"Yes."

"What do you miss?"

"I don't know, Kees, I just know I can't find it."

"Bullshit. This is Daisy. You know damn well what it is."

Erik pulled his hands along the crown of his head. "I cannot find the peace I had when I was with Daisy. When I was with her, my *cells* were happy. I miss looking in her eyes and everything else just disappearing. No other woman I've met can look at me and make time stop the way Daisy did. No other woman can talk to me without saying a damn word. Daisy was my soul mate and I miss her."

"What if she were back in your life a little bit? What if she knew where you were and what you were doing and you knew where she was? And you were both just in touch and up to date with each other? Maybe not best friends but friendly."

"I guess," he said. A grudging concession.

"Or is it all or nothing, you sulky infant?" Kees said, smiling.

Erik looked at him, then sank his head into his hands. "God, growing up sucks."

Kees laughed deep in his chest and ruffled Erik's hair. "Do you want to tell her how badly you were hurt? Have her witness it? You know, like it or not, Fish, she's made you the man you are. Do you want to tell her?"

Erik lifted his face out of his palms. "I think I do."

"And when she asks for your forgiveness—and she will—can you give it? Is it forgivable?"

"I don't kn—"

"Goddammit, stop saying that. Tell me what you know. You turned your back on her, now what the fuck do you *want*, man?"

"I want...to turn around."

Kees' hand circled in the air, encouraging him. "Turn around, good. Face her. Confront the issue."

"Yes."

"Not even confront. Have a conversation about it. You can't have the screaming match you were entitled to twelve years ago but you can talk like two adults."

"Yes."

"Do it then." Kees put his hand on Erik's forearm. "What are you waiting for? You of all people know how tenuous life is. Five memorial plaques are hanging backstage, another one for Marie in the lobby. Any one of them could have Daisy's name on it. Or how would you have felt listening to the radio show and hearing Daisy had cancer? What if she died, Fish, and never knew you thought about her all these years? How would a bowl of regret taste to you?"

Erik took a deep breath. "You're right."

"What's the worst that could happen? She tells you 'Hit the road, I couldn't care less what you think of me or how often. It's too late and oh, by the way, I've become a lesbian? I'm married?' What, Fish? What would be the worst thing, tell me."

"Wait. Go back to the lesbian thing?"

Kees balled up his napkin and bounced it off Erik's head. "You are a child. Grow up, Fish. Call her. Call her or I will fucking kill you. There's your motivation. Now finish your damn lunch. Good Lord, when I grab a man's ass I want to feel something."

"I swear, nobody makes me blush like you."

"Shut up and eat."

Dutifully, Erik started eating again. It was cold.

"Bowl of rejection," Kees was saying. "Or bowl of regret. That's what it comes down to, those are your choices. Which will taste worse? You ask me, rejection sucks, but you can choke it down. Regret will give you food poisoning for the rest of your life."

PINK GRANITE

ERIK RETURNED TO NEW YORK with a gnawing, insatiable hunger. A grandmother's delight. He ate all day long, putting on the good kind of weight. Gearing up for a fight.

Miles and Janey Kelly hosted him for Thanksgiving. Not three hours after the feast, he was trawling through the bag of goodies Janey had sent him home with. He was making himself a turkey sandwich, slicing it across when he miscalculated and cut himself.

He hated cutting himself. Even after all these years, the reaction to blood remained a visceral thing. Normally he'd work quickly to staunch and bandage a cut, averting his eyes to just the bare minimum of attention needed, but tonight, for some reason, he didn't. He stood over the sink, bleeding quietly. And watching. He just let it flow. Thought about what was happening microscopically under his skin. The infantry charge of platelets. The ambulance corps of white blood cells. The endorphins coming in on the flank, so actually, no, it didn't really hurt.

What was he so afraid of?

Miles's panting words as they jogged: *At some point you just have to start living the truth of who you are and what you feel.*

Kees's encouraging voice at the bar: *What are you waiting for? What's the worst that could happen?*

Melanie's cry of rage as a plate smashed in pieces on the wall: *You don't fight for anything you love.*

The minutes ticked by. He set down the knife and stared at his finger, at the blood now making small, watery rivulets in the sink. An empty white plate was on the counter, patiently awaiting its snack. He reached toward it, and with the red ink of his wounded finger he began to sketch the letters of his name.

She's made you the man you are.

He looked at the *Erik* written on the plate. He reached his finger again and wrote, just above it, *Byron.*

You did to her what your father did to you.

He zig-zagged through the names until they were just streaks of blood.

All the major events of his life were marked by blood: the blood of gunshot wounds, the blood of Lucky's lost baby, David's blood spraying from under his fists. And one more. A last treasure lay buried back in the fortress of sexual memory. Whole, intact, preserved in golden amber: his name in red letters, written in blood on Daisy's leg.

The night he slid into her body and sealed his fate.

The night he marked her in blood.

"I marked her," he said. "But I didn't fight for her."

You don't fight for anything.

When he fought David, there wasn't a prize. It was punitive damage. He beat him up on principle, just to soothe his wounded pride. He fought for himself, not for Daisy. And then he left.

You chose to leave. Just sit there and own it.

You walk out, shut the door, shut it down and never look back.

You stubborn, vindictive, unforgiving ass.

You spineless victim.

You sulky infant.

"I'm too late," he whispered. "It's got to be too late."

Rejection or regret, that's what it comes down to.

What if it were Daisy with cancer?

What if she died?

He paced the kitchen, his heart pounding. What if Daisy were nowhere? He'd toyed with the idea once, thinking it would make things easier. Now he dug into the image, played it out. Daisy dead. Gone from the earth, erased entirely from existence. A plaque on the wall or a stone in the earth. He saw it then—saw *Marguerite Bianco* chiseled into pink granite, a bouquet of daisies lying beside.

And she never knew you thought about her all these years.

He bandaged up his finger then switched on his PC, searching phone listings. It didn't take long to find Joe and Francine were still in Bird-in-Hand.

He picked up the phone.

His chest felt flayed.

You're a hero, not a victim.

He'd left the lighting booth. When everyone ran away from the stage he left the booth and went toward it. When people screamed, he spoke calmly, calling James's name. And when James held up a gun, Erik held up a penny.

He could do this.

You marked her. Go fight for her.

Because you can't breathe without her.

Slowly he drew air into his aching lungs, distilled the strength from it, then let go what he didn't need back into world. He did it again, filling the reservoir, tossing the ballast overboard.

"I'm not afraid of rejection," he said. "I'm afraid of regret."

Going up is easy. Coming down is the hard part.

You're a hero, not a victim.

He had this.

You're good. Your heart is huge. Your love is amazing.

You are generous and forgiving.

He dialed.

PART SEVEN: DAISY

YOUR CHILI RECIPE

JUST SAY HELLO. Hello, Francine, guess who?

One ring.

Don't be cute. Just say who you are. Talk a little, feel her out, ask if you can have Daisy's number.

Two rings.

She could quite possibly say no, or even hang up on you. In which case go jump off the nearest bridge.

Three.

No, don't jump off a bridge. Fight. Get in your car and drive to Canad—

"Hello?" Her voice was breathless, as if she'd run for the phone.

"Hi," he said, relieved and terrified. "Francine?"

"No, it's Daisy."

He stood up, and his chair fell over behind him.

"Hello?" she said.

"Daisy."

"Yes, it's Daisy. Who is this?"

He filled up his chest. "It's Erik."

"Who?"

He gripped the edge of the desk, steadying himself. "Erik."

A few beats of confused silence. And then, "Fish?"

She still won't say my name, he thought, swallowing against his dry throat. "It's me."

Silence again. He strained his ear, the receiver clutched in a white-knuckled grip.

"Hi," she whispered finally.

"Hi," he said. He felt a little light-headed. He sat on the floor.

"Holy shit."

"Yeah." He lay down. Better.

"Why are... How did you know I was here?"

"I didn't. I was calling your mother to try to find you. It didn't even occur to me you'd be there."

"I'm right here," she said. "I came for Thanksgiving."

"Is this a bad time to call? Are you in the middle of...?"

"No, no, I'm alone. I mean, everyone is passed out. I was just coming downstairs for some pie. And now... This is bizarre, just a minute." Erik heard the scrape of a chair. "I'm sorry, I have to sit down."

"I was sitting. Now I'm lying down."

"Oh my God," Daisy whispered.

He closed his eyes. Imagined her sitting at the long farmhouse table. Pictured the kitchen and its butter-yellow walls. Francine's treasured cast iron skillets, copper pots and pans, brightly colored enamel. The milk glass pendant lights casting a warm glow over it all.

"You ruined my pie," she said absently.

"What kind?" he asked.

"Apple. Mom made it."

"How's your mother?" *What did she make for dinner,* he longed to ask. *Does she ever make pepparkakor? Will you cut down the tree tomorrow?*

"She's fine. She and Pop are fine." Her voice seemed so small. Erik couldn't tell if she was speaking softly out of courtesy for others in the house or if this was all the volume she was going to give him.

"How are you?"

"I'm stunned. Oh, you mean in general." Now her voice rose up into a more conversational range. "I'm good. I'm doing well. Thank you."

He sat up. "I saw the article in *Dance Magazine.*"

"Pardon?"

"The article in *Dance Magazine.* About you and Will and the company, doing your first *Nutcracker.*"

"You saw it? How?"

"Believe it or not, Kees showed it to me."

"You saw Keesja? When?"

"Just last week. I went to Lancaster."

"What for?"

"Because I've never been back and it was time."

"Oh. I went back for the ten-year anniversary."

"I know," he said. "I heard the thing on NPR."

"You did?"

"I heard it when I was driving home from work. I had to sit in the car until it was over."

"What was that like?" she said.

"Surreal."

"It was surreal being there. I hadn't been back since graduation."

"I couldn't believe when Will sent my necklace to me."

"Oh my God. We couldn't believe when they moved the stove and it was underneath. I was so happy to see it. I knew you were heartbroken over losing it."

"I was. I took the earth apart looking."

"Will said you wrote him after. Letting him know you got it. But I guess he was hoping for something more."

A pointed edge to her last words. Erik closed his eyes and took hold of what he owned. "Yeah. See, I was extremely busy being an asshole, so I just sent the bare minimum."

It got him a chuckle. "And what neighborhood of Asshole City are you calling me from tonight?"

"I'm up in Brockport."

"I see. Me, I... Well, I guess if you read the article and heard the thing on the radio, you know what I'm doing."

"It all sounded fantastic. And I loved the picture of Will and Lucky and their kids. Two?"

"Two and number three on the way. Will sneezes and Lucky's knocked up."

Which seemed the perfect point to bail out of the chit-chat. "Dais?"

"Yes?"

"How would you feel about me coming to see you?"

A clink of silverware on china. "Well," she said, "I'm going back to Canada tomorrow."

He smiled. "I didn't mean tomorrow."

"When did you mean then?" she said coolly.

"Whenever it's convenient for me to come out and talk to you and have your undivided attention and—"

"You had my undivided attention for years, Fish. You were the one who disconnected everything."

He bit his lips. "You're right. I should've said I would give you my undivided attention. Finally."

"What makes you think I want it? Finally?"

"This was a bad idea," he whispered.

"What the fuck does that mean?"

"I'm sorry."

"Fish," she said sharply. "This was a really *good* idea. All right? It was a superb idea but it's going to be a shitty conversation. You can't call me out of the blue after twelve years, pick up where we left off and have it just be...like nothing happened. You can't."

"I know."

"I did a terrible thing to you," she said. "I never denied it and I still don't. But you cut me off without even... You just walked out and never gave me a... Oh, Jesus *Christ*." She wasn't crying but her whole voice seemed to collapse in on itself. "I just came downstairs for some pie and all of a sudden it's today."

He could barely push words through his constricted throat. "What do you mean, today?"

"Today. The day you call. You think I haven't been waiting? I haven't been pining my life away but if you think there isn't a part of my heart still wondering if today is going to be the day, you're out of your freakin' mind, Fish." She sighed heavily. "I'm sorry," she said. "I'm a little out of my own mind and like an idiot, I quit smoking a year ago."

"I'm sorry, I caught you off guard," he said. "Honestly, Dais, I was calling your mother. I didn't imagine you'd answer the phone."

"You think about someday, you prepare mentally for someday. But someday is never today. And now it is."

"I know."

"I've imagined this call for twelve years. Now you're on the phone and I'm completely at a loss. I've forgotten all my lines."

"When you imagined this," he said. "What did you have me saying?"

Another heavy exhale, like a small windstorm in his ear.

"Maybe we shouldn't jump right into it," he said quickly.

"Well for fuck's sake, I don't think you called me for my chili recipe. You want to jump into small talk? How's the weather up there? You watch the game today—how about them Broncos?"

He laughed.

"If you don't mind, I think I'll jump immediately into it because you could disappear again."

"I won't."

"Oh, won't you? You're really good at it."

"I know. And I'm sorry, truly sorry it took me this long...to grow up."

An abyss of silence on the other end which he didn't know how to interpret, so he rushed to fill it up with words. "I am not good at disappearing, Dais. I am spectacular at it. I made a conscious choice to shut down and ignore you all these years. The last time you called me—it was the fourth anniversary and I said all of six words and then hung up on you? It was obnoxious. And cowardly. I'm sorry. And I appreciate you not slamming down the phone on me now, because I kind of deserve it. I definitely deserve it."

More silence, then Daisy whispered, "Thank you."

"You're welcome." It felt lame in his mouth, almost pompous. Doing her some kind of favor. It wasn't the tone he wanted to set.

"God, if I can't smoke then I need to make some tea."

"All right."

"So give me your phone number and I will call you back."

He felt a stab of panic at the thought of severing the connection. "No, please don't hang up," he said. "Just put the phone down. I'll wait."

"No," she said. "Fish, I'm glad you called tonight. But all those years without a word... They're kind of hard to just brush aside."

"I'm sorry," he whispered.

"So, I am testing you. May I?"

"You're testing I won't go away?"

"Frankly, yes. I waited twelve years for you to call. Now you can wait while I make a cup of tea and throw up."

He took a deep breath and gave her his number. "That's my home line. 555-0411 is my cell, same area code. And there's a phone booth downstairs. If I jump out the window I'll land right by it so let me give you the number."

She laughed. "Don't jump. I'll come back. I mean, I'll call you back."

"I'm not leaving. I don't care if the house catches fire."

"Holy shit, when did you get so dramatic," she said, the tiniest bit of teasing in her voice. "I'll talk to you in a bit."

Once she hung up, Erik collapsed on his back again, the breath rushing out of his lungs. "What just happened?" he asked the ceiling.

He sat up. She was making tea. Good idea. He pattered into the kitchen, pulled the kettle onto a front burner and lit it, busied himself with mug, teabags and milk. He stared at the blue flames licking the edges of the kettle. He could feel his body on high alert, the minute twitches of his muscles, his stomach skittering and wobbling like a sick gyroscope. And yet. Another sensation. Something out of the past. A more profound rearrangement, somewhere deep in his psyche, the atoms and elements of his being sorting themselves out, shifting into the places where they belonged. He was realigning, the compass of his soul lining up with True North.

I called her.

I heard her voice. We spoke. We will speak again.

It's today.

He was meant to do this. It was today and he was exactly where he was supposed to be.

Living the truth. And being tested.

He sat down, stared at the phone and waited for the water to boil. Waited for Daisy to come back.

HUMAN COCAINE

THE CONVERSATION WAS A LONG and arduous exorcism. Sprawled in bed later, limp and exhausted, his soul rid of demons and his bones drained of their marrow, Erik could keep only a few parts intact and clear in his head. But he remembered what was important.

A strange reluctance gripped him when he faced the opportunity to tell her how she'd hurt him. The time was here, he was ready and she was listening, but still he hesitated. It was a conscious effort to peel his fingers back from the pain he'd clutched tight all these years. A miserly compulsion to continue hoarding and hiding the stash.

Hurt, he remembered, was a habit.

Say it.

His mouth closed up in his hand, he could feel the command of his brain traveling along synapses and nerves, engaging the muscles in his jaw, making his tongue form words and his lungs push air behind them.

Tell her. What are you waiting for?

He dragged his hand away from his mouth. "What happened that day killed me," he said.

"It had to. And I'm so sorry."

"It haunted me. It still does."

"What haunts you, tell me. Please tell me."

He felt his eyes flare as he let the raw impact of the long-ago day back into his heart.

"When I saw you with him," he whispered. He had to be so careful with this grenade he'd been carrying around.

"When I saw him where I was supposed to be. Where only I had been. It was burned in my eyes and it became all I saw."

"God, it must have. I wanted to die. I can only imagine what it was like for you..."

Her voice was calm, humble. Above all, it was receptive. She was an empty cup, beckoning, and he gently let himself tip over and pour into it.

"It was like an earthquake. Inside my head."

"Like a concussion," she murmured.

"It was a concussion. It was shocking on so many levels. Both what it was, and who it was. It's... It shattered me. I truly felt like I was losing my mind."

"I know. I was so ashamed."

"And it broke my heart. I felt useless."

"After everything you did. I'm so sorry. I never stopped regretting it. Not for a minute..."

This wasn't how he thought it would be. He'd imagined a more dramatic disposal of the grenade: pulling the pin with his teeth and lobbing it. Massive pyrotechnics, the earth going up in flames. Instead it was as if a battle-hardened, veteran soldier had approached with quiet authority and held out a rough but wise hand. *Give it here, son.* And as Erik gave it up, he didn't weep, but he put his forehead on the rim of the table and let the moment wash over him.

The battle was over, he'd surrendered his last weapon, and he was hunkered down in his foxhole amidst the smoke and rubble, shaken and spent. He ached all over. His skin hurt. Yet it was a leaching kind of pain, a detox. The poison was finally seeping out of his soul.

At her own kitchen table, four hundred miles away, she waited for him. He could feel her patience like a low current through the receiver. He took his time. The storm passed. The smoke cleared. He picked up his head. "I don't even know if this is a valid question anymore but why did you do it?"

"Of course it's a valid question."

"Probably not easily answered."

"Doesn't dismiss it."

He waited, but she was quiet.

"What happened, Dais?" he said, setting his empty cup on the table in front of her. "Please tell me."

She spoke in disjointed sentences at first. Memories and emotions pried from the vaults of her own mind. She had, as Erik had suspected, gotten high with David.

"I was high, but I was conscious. I knew full well what was transpiring. I could've stopped it. I could've left. But I was done."

"Done," Erik said. "Done with me?"

"With me. To begin with, I was sick of myself. Sick of who I'd become. Sick of my head and my stomach. Sick of nightmares every other night, of anxiety every time you and I tried to make love. Tired of trying to be strong, tired of trying to hold everything together for everyone. I was just done.

"And furthermore," she said, drawing a deep breath. "I was in withdrawal. Not just from drugs but from the shit you and I were freebasing in my bedroom at night. You know what I mean?"

"I do," he said. "You needed the pain."

"I'm sorry," she said. "I wish I had something more justifiable, something deeper or more profound, but I don't. I hit the wall. I didn't care. I was acting out all the dark, weak and ugly things I had in my head. I didn't think about you or the consequences. I didn't think about David and what he was getting from it. It could've been anyone. It wasn't about connection. It wasn't making love. It was human cocaine, and it got me high enough to finally let me be at my lowest."

"I see," he whispered.

She went from human valium to human cocaine.

"I'm sorry," Daisy said. "I'm so sorry, Fish. It was the stupidest thing I've ever done. I broke your trust, I threw us away and it was... When I think of my worst moment, and I don't mean the worst thing that happened to me, but the moment when I was at my worst. My most despicable moment. That was it. I've never topped it."

"You were high."

"So what."

"You were weak."

"Weak is accurate. I was weak."

"And he preyed on it."

"I can't speak for him. I don't know his side of the story and it's irrelevant. I only know what I did, Fish."

Erik was quiet, taking it in, taking her in as well. He knew the difference between *I'm sorry I did it* and *I'm sorry I got caught doing it.* He detected none of the latter here. She was remorseful, but not groveling. Dignity was in her self-awareness, her unflinching ownership of what she'd done and her refusal to blame David for it.

"I can't think what else I can say," she said. "I'm trying to give reasons and not make excuses. I don't know if it helps or just makes it hurt more but I don't think it's much more analyzable."

"I'm just taking it in," he said.

"I understand."

"I imagined conversations with you too, you know."

"Did I follow the script?"

"Dais," he said, sighing. "I'll be honest. Even in my head, in my made-up scenarios, I never addressed the issue."

"What do you mean?"

"I only imagined talking to you. You and me. Just being us. In our little bubble, in our private universe. I'd just imagine the good parts. I never confronted you, not even in my head. We always said David only wanted what he couldn't have. I think I only wanted what came easily. I didn't fight for us, not even in my imagination. I don't fight, Dais. I walk away, shut it down, cut it off, bury it. I threw us away for...for what? I don't know. All I know is twelve years later, you're still in my head and I don't stop thinking about you. I can't stop thinking about you. And I really want to come see you and—"

"You think about me?" Her voice was blurred.

"Of course I think about you."

"I think about you every day. I swear. I'm not trying to be maudlin or dramatic. But not a day goes by I don't think about you one way or another."

"I do too. Every day there's something, some little thing making me remember. It won't stop."

"You see?" Now her voice was dissolving. She was starting to cry. In his ear, across two states, Daisy was crying for him. "I thought you forgot. I mean I just thought you left it. Got over me, moved on and forgot about it. Forgot me."

"I never forgot. I can't. It was the happiest I've ever been in my life and I don't know how to get—"

"I'm sorry, Erik."

There. Finally. His name. He closed his eyes. "I never got over it, Dais," he whispered. "I just left it."

"I'm sorry," she sobbed. "Erik, I'm so sorry."

He started to reply *it's all right,* but he checked himself. It wasn't all right and she wasn't asking to be excused.

She just wanted to be acknowledged.

"I'm sorry." This was her ugly cry. The gut-shredding weep he'd only witnessed a few times. A fevered heat would be filling her face. Her fingers dug into the hair at her temples, her teeth and soul bared.

Hold still, Erik thought. *Just listen. It's all she wants.*

"I'm sorry."

"I know," he said. The full weight of the truth behind the words. He knew as he had never known before.

"I never meant to hurt you. I didn't do it to hurt you, please believe me."

"I know you didn't. I know now, Dais. I know."

"I'm sorry."

"I know. I believe you." He was the old soldier now. *Give it here.* He waited, patient, letting her fill his hands, and holding it carefully. Believing it.

"Are you all right?" he said, when she'd quieted again.

"I'm a mess."

"You need to go get a tissue?"

"No, I have a dishrag."

"I have a beach towel."

She sniffed. "Brilliant."

"I'm sorry, too," he said. "I'm sorry I cut you off. I'm sorry I never gave you a chance. I want the chance. If you tell me it's not too late and there's still a chance, I want to come see you and talk about this."

"It's not too late," she said. "And I'm ready if you are."

A BETTER WAY TO LEAVE

"GIVE ME YOUR DAMN phone number," Erik said before they hung up. "Whatever else happens, I am never not going to have your phone number. Ever again."

"Will you use it?" she asked.

"I will call you tomorrow," he said. "What time will you be back home?"

"By five. Four o'clock your time."

"I will call you tomorrow, four my time."

A pause. "Would you be offended if I didn't hold my breath?"

Erik managed to putter Friday away in a mix of nervous activity and nervous clock-watching. He dialed her number on the meticulous dot of four.

She answered after two rings. "Crisis Hotline."

"This is me always having your phone number," he said. "How does it sound?"

She hung up.

Erik blinked at the dead receiver in his hand until it rang back a few seconds later. "Well-played, Marge," he said.

"I'm sorry," she said, laughing. "I couldn't resist."

"It's all right. I had it coming."

They compared calendars and Erik proposed flying out on Wednesday, the fourteenth of December. "Or we can throw another day at it and I can come out the fifteenth. Your birthday."

A pause shimmered between them, glazed with just a hint of discomfort. Her birthday was shrouded in such sexual connotations. Erik grimaced, hoping he hadn't sent the wrong message.

"Come Wednesday," she said. "And if we're alive for my birthday I'll make a cake. Or a cyanide soufflé or something."

Avoiding any more assumptions or awkward sleeping arrangements, he asked her for the name of a hotel. "Should I rent a car?"

"Yes," she said. "I have a few rehearsals scheduled so you should be free to come and go."

"I'll fly in, drive myself to my hotel and you'll meet me there?"

"Yes. The lobby of a hotel is a good place to meet, don't you think?"

"No crying in the lobby."

"Throwing up is allowed."

Logistics settled, they talked about their days for twenty minutes, then said goodnight.

The next night's conversation lasted two hours. He told her about his marriage. He kept it short, didn't talk about the infertility. Just a simple story. Daisy was quiet, almost ominously silent, neither asking questions nor interjecting.

"I'm sorry," she finally said, her voice airless and tight. "You're going to have to tell me the whole story again when you get here. Frankly, I stopped listening after 'I got married...'" She gave a nervous laugh, which dissolved into a jagged-edged sigh.

He felt his heart contract. "Dais..."

"I'm sorry." She was still trying to laugh it off. "I don't know why I'm... Just give me a minute."

"I was a lousy husband at the end," he said, feeling a strange blend of guilt and apprehension.

"But you were her husband," Daisy whispered. And then she was crying. "I'm sorry."

"It's all right," he said.

"Let me call you back."

"No," he said. "Stay. Cry all you want. Please just stay."

"This is ridiculous. I'm sorry."

"Stop apologizing. Take your time." He let her be, let her ride it out.

"You know, any time you want to get sloppy, feel free." She sniffed with another sigh. "I can't be having all the fun."

"Wait until I get to Canada. I'll need a separate suitcase for my emotional shit. It's going to be embarrassing, trust me."

She put the phone down to splash cold water on her face. When she came back, he said, "I can't believe you're not married."

"Well," she said. "I came close."

"To Opie? I mean John. Sorry."

"Oh, God, he hated that name and no one could stop using it. No, it wasn't him. Someone else. And I'll tell you about it another time."

"Will you tell me about when you were cutting yourself? Not right now. When I see you. It should be a face-to-face conversation but I wanted you to know I knew."

"I'll tell you about it."

"If it's too hard though..."

"I'll share whatever you want to know," Daisy said. "There's no point holding back or avoiding."

"True. But—"

"Erik, listen. Let's not shelter each other. I'm not defining what's going on here. I'm not even assuming we're friends again. And it's kind of liberating, don't you think? Put it all out on the table, there's nothing to lose. I'd rather know everything and be hurt. I hated not knowing where you were. God, it made me crazy..." She trailed off, and the lost years swept through Erik, a biting, gnawing pain of regret for the time he'd thrown away.

"It seemed so important at the time," he said, shaking his head. "So necessary. And now I can't understand how I managed to completely shut down."

It was the only way I knew, he thought. It didn't make him feel any better.

"You're here now," she said. "I still can't believe I'm talking to you."

"I might not ever shut up."

"Say anything then," she said. "I'm not afraid. I want to know everything. I need to have everything so I can figure out what I'm going to do."

"Do with what?"

"Do with you," she said, as if it were obvious.

THEY TALKED NEARLY EVERY NIGHT as the reunion crept closer. Ten days away. Then a week. Two days.

Then tomorrow.

As he packed his bag, Erik called down to Key West and spoke to his mother. "I'm going to Canada tomorrow," he said. "Not sure how long I'll be gone."

"Canada? Why there?"

"I'm going to see Daisy."

A beat of silence. "Well," Christine said. "How did this come about?"

"I went looking for her."

"After all these years. What finally made you decide?"

"It was time. It was time a long time ago. Unfortunately, Mom, my father set a shitty example of how you leave a woman, and even more unfortunately, I followed it. Not knowing there was an alternative. A better way to leave. Or a different way to stay. I know now, and I'm going to Canada to set a better example. Even if I never have a son someday."

"I think that's wonderful, Erik," Christine said.

"I'm slightly terrified."

She laughed. "Because you loved her."

"I did," he said. "Possibly I still do."

"Leaving isn't always the end of loving. Love doesn't give a shit about geography, Erik. It's not a thing you can abandon at will."

He sat on the bed next to his open bag and ran his hand through his hair. "Look, Mom, I never asked you this," he said. "But is there part of you still waiting for him?"

"For your father?"

"Yeah. Waiting for him to call or something."

"Of course there is, honey."

"If he did call...would you hang up or listen?"

He heard her draw her breath in and let it out. "I hope I say this the right way," she said. "I would slam the phone down on the father of my sons. Because I will never forgive him. I would listen to the man I loved. Because part of me needs to hear what he has to say. Am I making any sense, Byron Erik?"

"Perfect sense, ma'am," he said. "And I'm sorry he never came back and set you free."

A soft laugh caressed his ear. "Sometimes people surprise you."

"Or they don't."

He waited. For dismissal of the past. For platitudes or philosophy.

"You know, Erik," she said. "While your father was here, he was a good man. And I see a lot of him in you. The good things. Don't be ashamed of them. Because I also see how you're different from him. Especially right now. You are *suprisingly* different."

If he'd crafted her response it couldn't have been more perfect. Erik swallowed hard, curled up tight into her words. Basking in them, he told her he loved her.

"I love you. And I'm thrilled you're doing this. What you had with Daisy deserves a second chance. You go find out. Listen to each other. And then you'll both be free."

After hanging up, Erik flopped on his back and rolled toward his bedside table. He took out the blue leather case with Joe Bianco's Purple Heart and lifted out the inset. The flattened penny was still there but it wasn't what he wanted. He pried up the postcard of the Metropolitan Opera House, trimmed to fit precisely within the bottom of the case. The last thing Daisy had written to him. The only words of hers he'd kept.

I'm sorry, Fish, I know how important it was to you. I feel terrible it's lost. I hope you find it.

He held the card to his face, inhaling a scent that wasn't there.

MATRYOSHKA

WITH A QUIET HUM, the doors of the hotel slid open, and Daisy walked into the lobby. She wore a camel wool coat over jeans and boots. Her dark hair drawn back, not a tight ballerina bun, but loose and casual, her curls falling over one corner of her sunglasses. Hands in her pockets. Head turning to the right and the left. Anticipation in her shoulders.

Erik had been sitting in a chair by the fireplace. He stood up. His heart expanded until he was nothing but a heart. A giant pounding heart on two shaking legs walking over to her. His own hands thrust deep in his jacket pockets, clenched, holding on to the lining, holding on tight or he would fly out into space and lose her forever.

As he got close she took her sunglasses off, revealing her eyes. Blue-green and bright. Older, a little shadowed, faint lines at the corners. Looking at him.

Trembling all over, he looked at her.

Trembling just as much, she smiled. "Welcome to Canada."

He swallowed. "My new favorite place on earth."

Carefully they moved into each other's arms. Erik held her, paralyzed with feeling. He wanted to crush her to his chest, seize her tight and never let go. He mustn't. Not yet. He held his embrace in check, then worried he was coming across too casual. He couldn't find a compromise. His arms kept starting and stopping. He couldn't take it in.

I am holding her. I haven't touched her in twelve years. She's in my arms. I can smell her. I'm holding her. This is happening.

"I can't believe it," she whispered. One of her hands pressed against the back of his head, then slid away. "I'm shaking."

"No, that's me," he said, trying to still the tremors taking over his legs. Gently he turned his nose into her hair. He felt light-headed. His heart was going to burst right through his chest. "You smell the same," he said, a little stupidly.

She let him go, stepped back and looked him over. He held still and let her.

"You're the same," she said. "I know you're different but you look just the same."

She was beautiful and he couldn't speak. He just stared as she pressed her fingers to her mouth, then curled them into fists beneath her chin while she kept looking him up and down. She reached tentatively, touched his necklace. "I'm so glad we found it."

"Me too," he said.

They hugged again, still carefully, not giving over to it yet. Erik felt himself fall backward in time, coming to rest on a quivering freshman night when he first gathered her against his body. *Thank you,* he thought then. *Thank you,* he thought now.

"Well," she said. "Should we go try to be normal?" She held out her hands, showing him how they shook. "If this is normal."

"The new normal," he said. His shy hand came up to touch her cheek. Not meeting his eyes, she took his fingers, squeezed them as she moved his hand away. She was biting her lips and shaking her head the tiniest bit.

"Are you all right?" he asked.

Now she nodded, still looking past him.

"Nauseous?"

She nodded harder and he laughed. "Me too."

"I'm all right," she said, and let go his hand. "What should we do?"

"Show me where you work," he said. "I'm dying to see."

"We can walk there," she said, putting on her sunglasses. A different flicker of discomfort had passed over her face though, and Erik frowned.

"Should we not go?"

She indicated the doors with her head, and they walked out. It was cold, but not agonizingly so, and the sun was shining. Erik put his own shades on.

"Here's the deal," Daisy said. "I told Will and Lucky we've been talking again."

"What was their reaction?"

"Lucky wants to kill you," she said, smiling up at him. "But Will was neutral. Neither joyous nor indifferent." She stopped and touched his arm. "I didn't tell them you were coming to see me. I'll take you over to the theater but if those guys are there, I'm going to turn us around and leave. All right? I want you to myself today."

Erik nodded. "I have shit to work out with Will but not today. Today is just you, me and the nausea."

They walked along, hands in pockets and occasionally bumping arms. Erik tried to take in his surroundings but he could barely register anything beyond Daisy's presence beside him. Eventually he noticed the theater facade up ahead, and the complex of brick buildings attached to the rear of it.

"The theater is used by a community playhouse," Daisy said, opening one of the doors, "and the Saint John Orchestra. And us. But we have all those adjoining buildings. All the studios and rehearsal spaces connected right to the theater. We only just moved under one roof a year ago. But it's been great. Feels like a home now."

The lobby had red carpet and gold moldings, a ticket window at the far end. Three sets of doors into the theater, the middle set was open. Daisy walked over and put her head in, then looked back at Erik and gave him a thumbs-up.

He exhaled in relief and followed her in. She took him all over the complex, from the storage rooms beneath the stage, to the lighting booth in the balcony. The sun-lit studios. The student lounge. The dressing rooms. He asked questions. She showed and told. Her eyes were bright, her face flushed with pride and accomplishment. She'd found her Plan B. She was doing what she was born to do.

The tour ended at her office. Small and snug with soft brown walls, plants on the windowsill and hanging prints and posters.

"Hey," he said, going toward her desk. He'd spied the Matryoshka—the Russian nesting dolls he'd given her as a birthday present.

"You still have these," he said, amazed.

"Of course I do."

They were un-nested, lined up in size order. He picked up the largest one and something rattled inside. A look of alarm crossed Daisy's face, she stepped and reached as if to snatch it back. Then she dropped her hand and sighed.

"What?" he asked. "What's in here?"

"It's stupid. Don't laugh. All right fine, laugh. It's funny now. I was just a lunatic at the time."

Erik twisted the doll open. Inside was a dollar bill and some change. He looked at her, puzzled.

"Remember when I sent back all your clothes?"

He nodded.

"I went through all the pockets first and I kept whatever was in them. You had a dollar and fourteen cents to your name."

"I was rich back then," he said. He opened the next doll and found two washers, a screw, and a guitar pick. "Seriously?"

"Seriously."

He picked up another and raised his eyebrows.

"Oh yeah," she said, smiling. "It gets worse."

He opened it. Stared a long time. "Lint," he said.

"It was bad."

"You went through all the pockets and kept my lint."

Daisy shrugged.

The next doll held a small lock of hair, scotch-taped. "All right," Erik said, "as a keepsake, this makes sense. How did you get my hair?"

"Lucky gave you a haircut one time and I kept some."

"Why?"

She looked at him with mild disbelief. "Because it's what you do."

As he twisted open the last doll, Daisy turned her lips in, a pinched look around her eyes.

"What's in there is rightfully yours," she said. "I shouldn't have kept it, but I did."

He tipped onto his palm the tiny gold scissors which used to hang with the other charms on his necklace.

"Oh, Dais."

"I know."

"You had the sax."

"I had the sax."

"Where was this? I thought it was lost?"

"I had it. When we first found your necklace, it was missing. But I poked around in the dust and grease and finally found it. It was obvious why your necklace was under the stove, I mean, how it had gotten there. And it seemed symbolic mine was the charm that fell off. So when I found it, I didn't give it to Will to send back to you. I kept it."

Erik looked at her.

Her eyes were far away. "For a while I wore it on a chain around my neck. It made me feel close to you. I thought that... I had a funny idea it would connect us. You'd feel me wearing it. Christ, here I go..." Her voice broke. She stepped back from him, laughing a little, pressing the heel of her hand to her suddenly streaming eyes. "Anyway, after a while I realized it wasn't a good thing to have hanging around my neck," she said. "And I put it inside the dolls with my other little souvenirs. My secret little shrine at the office. The end. Are you hungry?"

"I'm stunned," he said. He looked back to the little scissors on his palm. He cleared his aching throat. "I'm really torn here. I'd like to ask for it back but I love you had it all this time."

"It's yours, it was a gift."

"But you kept it with you. You needed it. I don't know what I'm saying."

She took a deep breath. "How about," she said, her voice trembling, "you put it back in the doll and you'll know where it is now. You'll know it's with me."

"All right." With some reluctance he put the scissors back inside the doll and twisted it closed. "I can't believe you kept my lint," he said.

"I loved you," she said. "And I wanted to save you."

He looked at her. She looked back.

They stared.

It happened.

"I missed this," he said.

"I missed it too."

"But it's still here. We can still do it."

"It's still here. And nobody else does it."

He closed his eyes, gently letting the bubble break.

"Are you hungry?" she asked. "We can go get some dinner."

"A little. But I don't feel like being in a crowd. I just want to sit somewhere quiet with you and talk."

She nodded. "How about we go to my house and I'll cook."

"You will?"

"If you want."

"I want."

"I left my coat in the theater."

She turned out the light and they walked through the dim corridors to the side door leading into the theater. There Daisy stopped short and Erik plowed into the back of her.

Will was sitting in the front row. Busy with notebook and papers, one ankle perched on the opposite knee. When he saw Erik, the pencil he'd been twirling in one hand went flying over his shoulder.

They all stared.

Finally Daisy spoke. "You wouldn't believe what Customs lets into Canada these days."

Will shook his head. "You're right. I wouldn't."

Erik put his hands on Daisy's shoulders. "Give me five minutes?" he whispered.

She nodded, smiling. "Take ten. I'll be back in my office." And she slipped out the door they had come through.

Slowly Erik walked closer to where Will sat.

"So," Will said. "Obviously you've come to suck my cock."

"I have."

"Finally. What took you so long?"

"I would've been here sooner but I ran into Dais on the street and..."

Will smiled. "She told me you called."

"Finally."

"Yeah, you are inexcusably late."

"Am I too late?"

Will sighed and stretched his arms along the seat backs. He tilted his head and stared at the ceiling.

"Even if it is too late," Erik said. "I have to start owning this. What I did was wrong. And I'm sorry. I needed to come in person and say so."

Will was still looking up, his lower jaw moving around. He closed his eyes. "If you don't finish what you start this time," he said. "If you disappear on her again, Fish, so help me God. I will kill you. I won't just bruise you a little. I will bury you by the side of the road and piss on your grave."

"It's not lost on me how you picked up the pieces—"

"Bullshit," Will said, standing up, his papers cascading to the floor. "You have no idea what it was like. For her or me."

"You're right, I don't. Not yet. I didn't come here just to make myself feel better and walk away again. I came to stand still and feel. Feel what I didn't give Dais a chance to feel twelve years ago. Finish what I started."

Will nodded, arms crossed over his chest, fingers working at the material of his shirt. Will didn't fidget unless he was upset. Erik knew that. Knew it like he knew the sky was blue.

"I'm sorry," Erik said.

"It hurt like hell, you know. Your fight with her was your fight with her but to throw me over the side..."

"I know. I ran like hell from everything. It was the only way I knew how to deal. Doesn't make it right or excuse it, but I'm only just figuring out why I did it myself. It's why I called her. It's why I came here. I own this. And I need to feel it. You can bury your pain or avoid it. You can tattoo over it. But you won't be free of it until you feel it. My own father never set my mom free. Never set me free. I came here to set Daisy free. I owe it to her. And I owe you at least one opportunity to punch me in the face and I won't duck. Swing away."

A smile began to curve up Will's mouth. "Well, I'll be fucked," he said.

"I've been fucked for years. Be nice to have some company."

The smiled faded as Will shook his head, looking at the floor. "You're killing me."

"I'm sorry," Erik said. He took the last few steps to close the gap and put his hand on his friend's shoulder. "I said some truly shitty and unforgivable things that last phone call. I didn't mean them. You didn't deserve them. You were a prince to send me back my necklace and I could barely put together a note. But I've done some growing and... I'm owning it. I treated you like shit. You were my best friend. You were like a brother to me and I abandoned you. I'm really sorry, Will."

Will looked up, his eyes brimming. "I swear to God, you are such a fucking crybaby."

Then he seized Erik. Grabbed him in arms and hugged him hard, his hands pummeling and patting until they both landed with a not-so-loving smack on Erik's ass.

"Jesus," Erik said. "I said in the face."

Will pushed him away. "Wanted to do that for years. I best go for it before you disappear again."

"I'm not going anywhere."

Will started unbuckling his belt. "You're going on your knees, asshole."

Erik sprang back, laughing, and headed for the door. "Rain check."

"Yeah, that's right. Run away, Fish."

"It's what I do," Erik said. "Now watch my ass as I run."

"High and tight," Will yelled after him. "Just like a girl's."

BUILD SOMETHING BEAUTIFUL

"IT'S A SWEET LITTLE house," Daisy said, turning the key in her front door, "but I really bought it for the porch."

"Who wouldn't?" Erik said. The porch ran along the whole front of the small house and hugged one side. It was bare now, but he could imagine wicker furniture and flower boxes in spring. Daisy sitting out here with a book and some iced tea. He added himself into the scene, sitting on the steps, playing guitar.

It was too easy.

He was an idiot.

"Come in," Daisy said.

It looked nothing like La Tarasque, and yet the moment Erik stepped inside, he knew every piece of furniture, every cushion and lamp and knick-knack had been chosen and placed to evoke the essence of her parents' house. Right down to the Meyer lemon tree by the window.

She gave him a short tour of the downstairs, ending up in the kitchen.

"It's a carbon copy of your mother's," he said, gazing around at the yellow walls, the red-enameled pots on a shelf. A basket of cloth napkins, a bowl of oranges.

"Not exactly. I don't have her big table."

"I know, but..." It was obvious and yet he couldn't explain. It was all so familiar.

Daisy took two beers from the fridge. "Opener is in the drawer there." She put her head through the loop of a red butcher apron and tied it around her narrow waist.

"What are we having?" Erik said, opening the bottles.

"You kidding? Grilled cheese and tomato soup. The best conversational food out there."

As Erik sat down at the island, a grey cat gracefully jumped up and onto the counter. "Hello," he said, holding his fingers out to be sniffed.

"Bastet. My live-in lover."

Having passed inspection, his palm moved in long, slow arcs over the top of Bastet's head and down her silvery back. Her eyes were powder blue marbles. "She's beautiful."

"She," Daisy said, "is a standoffish bitch. As are most Russian Blues."

As if cued, the cat meowed at her. Daisy leaned in, lips puckered, letting Bastet rub and nudge at her face. "But yes, she is beautiful."

Erik sat and drank his beer, chin resting on his hand between sips. Daisy sliced bread and cheese. Assembled the sandwiches and set them on the hot grill. Warmed up soup. She lit a few candles, turned on some music. His eyes followed her everywhere. He was reminded of their long-ago Thanksgiving, when he'd watched her move around the kitchen with her mother. Blithe and confident and happy. As if she'd never suffered a day in her life.

"Tell me what happened to you," he said. "After I left."

Daisy flipped the four sandwiches on the griddle over. "We tabled this one, didn't we?"

"I needed to be looking at you."

She smiled at him before turning to take some plates and bowls from a cabinet. "After you left, two things were going on. Three. One was mourning you. Two was beating myself up for sleeping with David. The third was dealing with the trauma of the shooting."

"Did it ever come back to you?" he asked. "Anything from the day?"

She slid her spatula beneath the corner of one sandwich, peeked under to see how done it was. "Yes, it did."

He sat a little straighter on his stool. "It did? Really?"

"I'll get to that." She took a pull of her beer. "So, after graduation I got into the corps of the Pennsylvania Ballet. Living the dream, right?

I assume so because I can barely remember a thing from those days. I remember waking up every morning being shocked the sun was up. *I'm alive? Again? I thought surely I'd be dead by now.* I wasn't taking care of myself at all. Not eating, barely sleeping—"

"Were you still doing coke?"

She shook her head. "But I was smoking like a fiend. God, the chain-smoking. I was a shell. Just going through the motions." She flipped the sandwiches onto a cutting board and sliced them on the diagonal. "And I got fired."

"Shut up." Erik passed her one bowl at a time to be filled up with soup.

"I know. Me, right? The smartest girl in ballet? I blew it. I mean, the tactful way to put it is they didn't renew my contract." She rolled one of her shoulders dismissively. "I got fired. Which broke me out of my pity party a little. Unemployment will do that. But dance is a small world, I had some good contacts. I got into the Metropolitan Opera Ballet and I thought it would be good—New York, fresh start. Out of Pennsylvania, away from the memories and the ghosts. This was my second chance. I wasn't going to screw it up. I started caring for myself better—just in terms of eating healthy and not smoking so much and managing my body. And then I ran into Opie one day. I mean John. Dammit."

He laughed. "See?"

"The artist formerly known as Opie. We were going to the same master class and it was totally random, but totally wonderful at the same time. I felt really lonely and it was good to see an old friend. We went for coffee—you know, the four-hour cup of coffee? And we just kept going..." Her voice trailed off. She bit a corner of her lip as she sat down.

"I always liked him," Erik said, wanting to put her at ease.

"He was good to me," Daisy said, stirring her spoon around her bowl. "And he was there when the window broke."

"The window?"

She was in a diner with John, one evening in the hard winter of 1995, when New York City was getting pummeled with its umpteenth snowstorm. As they sat eating in a booth, a sanitation truck came down the street, perhaps a little too fast. The load of snow in its plow flew up against the front of the diner and broke one of the windows.

"Right behind where I was sitting," Daisy said. "So one minute I'm eating an omelette, the next minute I am under the table, curled up in a ball, screaming your name."

She looked at him and he looked back, not making a connection.

"I was screaming your name," she said. "Because of the broken glass."

His spoon clattered into the bowl. "The glass," he said, a hand to his head.

She nodded.

"You saw James shoot the glass of the lighting booth."

She kept nodding. "I've never experienced something so surreal in my life. As soon as the window shattered, it came back to me. Being on the floor of the stage, hearing shots. Knowing I'd been hit. Knowing Will was shot, too. I didn't know it was James. Just someone with a gun was in the theater. I couldn't get up. I pushed on my elbow, twisted my head and looked over my shoulder. I saw him shoot out the windows of the booth. And I screamed your name. Then the memory stops. My brain pauses until I woke up in the hospital the next day and they'd cut my leg."

"Holy shit."

"You remember the nightmares I had? Just vast, dark silence. No people, no sound. Just terrible space?"

"I remember."

"After the day in the diner, the dreams had imagery. They went from being a black cavern to a crazy hall of mirrors." She glanced at him. "Your dreams were filled with blood. Mine were filled with broken glass. And then the real breakdown started."

She took a bite of sandwich and he ate some more of his own dinner. Her silence was thoughtful but she didn't speak.

"Go on," he said. "Please."

"I was obsessed," she said. "With glass. This horrible compulsion to smash mirrors or break windows." She smiled at his raised eyebrows. "I wasn't doing those things. I was just thinking about it. All the time. And then one night I smashed a wine bottle in the sink and..."

She put her forehead in her hand. "God, I haven't talked about this in a while. I cringe telling it now, it sounds really sick."

His heart twisted in his chest. He made his hand gentle on her arm and kept his voice calm as he asked, "What did you do?"

She reached to ladle some more soup into her bowl. "First, I took a piece of the glass and tried to cut my fasciotomy scars open. It wasn't a conscious thought at the time, of course, but later in therapy we talked about how the surgical procedure had been necessary to relieve the pressure building up in my leg. And in a real sense, pressure was building up again in me. My entire body, my entire being was suffering from compartment syndrome. And I tried to release it." She looked at him. "I didn't do a good job. It's harder to cut through scar tissue than you would think. Plus in my line of work, my legs tend to be visible. It wouldn't be something I could keep secret. So I started just making these little cuts. Like on my lower back or along my waist or stomach. And then I'd..." She put her hand to her head again, laughing a little. "This got hard all of a sudden."

"It's all right."

"I'd put straight alcohol on the cuts. Or I'd get this lotion—it was anti-itch and it had menthol in it."

He pulled back, his face screwing up. "Jesus, you'd put that on your cuts?"

"Yeah. Anything to make them sting. The harder the better. I used vodka once. Lemon juice. Salt another time—how about that metaphor?"

"You were really feeding the hurt," he said. "Just like you and I used to do."

"I was in trouble."

"Did John know this was going on?"

"Well, naturally he found out when we went to bed together." She glanced at him and her face colored behind an apprehensive smile. "You got married. I can talk about this."

"I swear I'm a grownup now," he said. "And the statute of limitations on jealousy is long over."

She ran her fingertips beneath her eyes. "It's just... When there's no official breakup, it's hard not to feel every other man is cheat—"

"No," he said. "No. That was David. And we've talked about him. Everything else, everyone else—it was your life after I left. All right?"

Eyes closed, she let her breath out, nodding her head. "Thanks," she whispered. Her shoulders relaxed. "So when John and I started sleeping together, naturally he saw the cuts."

And in spite of his reassurances, a stab of nauseous jealousy hit Erik in the gut. *You left,* he reminded himself. *You chose to leave. Opie picked up the pieces while you fucked your way through Geneseo like a dog, sleeping with other men's wives. Drop your pearls and grow up.*

"He saved my life," Daisy was saying. "He called my parents. They got me into a hospital up in Westchester County. I was there a couple weeks, then I started going to a therapist regularly and..."

"Digging."

"Digging. Learning how to stop scarring and punishing. Hurting myself as much as I hurt you. But I couldn't wait any longer for you to forgive me. I had to forgive myself. I couldn't go anywhere, couldn't grow or evolve until I did."

"And is that when you sent me back my stuff?"

She nodded. "My skin healed. The sun came out and it was spring. I felt better than I had in years. Felt like myself again. John and I were turning a corner into our relationship. He moved in and I still had this box of your stuff. He kind of gave me a soft ultimatum, asked me, 'When are you going to let go of him?' So I packed it up. I called you, just to let the record show I tried one last time."

"I hung up on you."

"And I sent it back. I was fine. I remember sitting in therapy, telling Rita, 'Holy shit, I'm actually *fine.*' A few months passed, I went to Chicago for the *Phantom* auditions and when I came home, John told me you had called."

Erik flopped sideways, putting his forehead into the crook of an elbow. "Could that conversation have been any more awkward?"

She laughed. "Frankly, no."

"I swear. As it dawned on me you were living together, I was just a blithering idiot."

"When he told me you called I was a blithering idiot," she said. "To be fair he sprung it on me the second I walked in the door. Hi, honey. Erik called."

"Erik called. He was looking for a necklace. I think he was stoned."

"I was immediately in tears. Not quietly sneak into the bathroom and cry in a towel. No, right there in the doorway, bag still on my shoulder, bursting into tears. John just walked out of the apartment. He couldn't even watch. And I couldn't blame him." Resting her elbows on the table, Daisy pressed her fingers against her eyelids. "I wanted to kill you," she whispered. "You finally called. And there wasn't a damn thing I could do about it."

"You wrote me the postcard."

"Yeah, with John looking over my shoulder. God, what a mess. We made up but the whole incident put a crack in the relationship. Then I got into the touring production so being separated didn't help things. It was over within three months. A civil breakup as far as breakups go. It had terms. And closure. But I felt terrible. Yet another guy who gave me his all and saved me from the abyss and I broke his heart..."

"I'm sorry the call screwed things up."

She shook her head. "It wasn't about you." She looked at him. "That sounded harsh."

"No, I know what you meant." He reached for another sandwich triangle, pulled it apart and dunked one part in his soup. "Did therapy give you any huge breakthroughs?"

She was in the middle of chewing, so she shook her head, the back of her hand to her mouth. "Lots of little ones," she finally said. "I still hadn't forgiven myself for what I did to you. I figured I would need to dig into why I'd slept with David in the first place. And like I told you, it turned out to be a whole lot of little reasons, not one big one. But no, I had no big revelation about how my inner child had been neglected or any such shit. I was always a pretty self-actualized person. You know my family. You know my relationship with my parents. I don't carry a lot of scars from childhood."

"You don't have my baggage," he said, touching his chest.

She held up her spoon, thinking a moment, then she looked at him. "I did a stupid thing," she said. "I'd never been a stupid kid. I didn't look for trouble. You know me, I looked for stillness. And my ballet teachers, all those Russian women I trained with, each and every one said at one point, 'No stupid girls are in ballet.' And they aren't. You have to be smart or you'll never make it."

Her eyebrows wrinkled, and she stared off at a far wall. "I was always so cerebral. Practical. I had such a thing about not being stupid."

"We all do stupid things," Erik said.

She glanced at him, smiling. "I suppose you can analyze it and say I was having my rebellion moment. After the shooting, I felt like a victim, and I was struggling with the possibility of not being a girl in ballet. Therefore I could now be stupid." She shook her head, and set her spoon down in her empty bowl. "But it doesn't ring true for me. Bottom line, it was an egregious error of judgment. A royal fuck-up. And I needed to stop beating myself up over it."

"As my therapist said, 'Not everything has to be a thing,'" Erik said.

Daisy laughed now. "I cannot believe, after twelve years, we're sitting in my kitchen comparing anecdotes about therapy."

He sighed. "I guess this is what we should have been doing thirteen years ago."

She nodded, and sorrow shimmered in her eyes. He could see the words building up in their depths. An insight she was hesitating to share.

"Tell me," he said.

"I wanted to be strong for you," she said. "Strong and still. But I was so weak after the shooting. Such a wreck inside. I was afraid to let you see me wrecked, so I went and was a mess with David because I didn't care what he thought. I didn't need to be strong for him..."

Erik stared, open-mouthed. "You could've been a wreck with me," he said. But even as the words left his mouth he realized he couldn't think of a single time he'd seen her shattered beyond her ability to pick herself up. His plans went to C and D, minimum, but Daisy's war room left his plans in the dust. She'd been his fortress of stillness and strength and she'd never cracked until the end.

And then I left.

As it dawned on his mind, she looked at him, her gaze still sad, but unblinking. "You only like when people behave the way you expect them to."

He pushed his bowl away and put his forehead into a hand. A long moment of silence passed as her words pierced his skin like needles and their meaning pumped into his veins.

She fucked up, he thought. *She* was *fucked up. She was young and traumatized. Weak and not in her right mind. Or maybe she just did something stupid. Either way, she didn't act the way I expected. And I couldn't forgive her. If it wasn't perfect, it was useless. She cracked and I left.*

She touched his wrist, breaking his thoughts. He rolled it up to her and her fingernail gently traced the daisy.

"I thought you might've gotten rid of it."

"I almost did," he said. "A few times. But I never followed through. I guess I needed it."

"Like the sax."

Staring at his wrist, watching Daisy's fingertips, he thought about her tattoo, how the little red fish had never failed to thrill him. Every time he opened her jeans or slid her underwear down, it caught his eye like a surprise and he would think, *There I am.*

I have set you in my presence forever.

A quiet desire slid arms around his shoulders, gathered him close.

"Do you want tea?" Daisy asked.

He nodded, wanting many things.

She smiled at him, then pushed her kettle onto a burner and lit it. She gathered the soup pot, ladle and spatula, set them in the sink and started running soapy water. She took off the apron and set it on the counter. She was so graceful. Even washing dishes. Relaxed and serene, barely disturbing the air around her. A grown woman at home in her kitchen. At home in the life she had created.

Loving her felt like creating something. A cathedral. Spires and stained glass and bells. But she broke one window and I indiscriminately tore the whole thing down.

"Qu'est-ce qui se passe?" Daisy said, drying her hands and coming to lean on her elbows.

"I hate what I did," he whispered, looking back down at his tattoo.

"I hate what I did, too." Her fingers came around his chin and she turned his face toward her. Tears had collected along her eyelashes. "And I love that we're here."

Her head came closer. She smelled like sugar. Her gaze shone blue-green like the earth. Her lips pressed his, soft and light, and deep in the cathedral of Erik's being, a bell tolled.

Here I am.

He closed his eyes as she drew back.

Nothing man-made was perfect. Not even massive churches. A partnership wasn't about being beautiful and adored in the spotlight, it was about incorporating the mistakes into the architecture and continuing to build something beautiful. Together.

She's a generous, forgiving partner.

I can be one, too.

The bell pealing in his heart and her kiss still thrumming on his mouth, he opened his eyes. Daisy was by the refrigerator, reaching up for a cookie tin on its top. She pried off the lid and set the tin on the counter.

"I didn't make a cake," she said. "But I made these."

He didn't have to look. He'd already smelled the orange zest and the faint overlay of black pepper. Thin rounds in a nest of parchment paper. Flecked with the promise of sweetness and spice. Golden and crisp with memory.

Daisy took one, put it in her palm. "Make a wish."

This, Erik thought, and nodded at her. She pressed her finger down on the cookie's center. A soft crunch. A decision. A truth.

"It broke into five," she said, holding out her hand.

He took one of the pieces. "Means no wishes come true, but we still have cookies."

She smiled. "A broken cookie is still sweet."

They looked at each other a long time.

"I still love that we're here," she whispered.

"I still love us," Erik said. And took a bite of pepparkakor.

ACKNOWLEDGMENTS

I REMEMBER WHEN I was young, listening to my father pick out the chords of "The Man I Love" on the grand piano in our living room. It seems some stories are meant to be written.

I declared my intention to turn this universe of characters into a book in November of 2013. Since that time, so many people have given me their unrelenting support and encouragement. To them I owe my unending thanks and all my love. With you as my friends, anything and everything is possible.

Paul Preston came back to reveal the story, tell me about Meisner technique and show me there's more to a scene than doing what's required. When the emotion is there and the emotion is authentic, the genuine scene ultimately follows. It works onstage. It works on the page. It works in life. You must live the truth of who you are and what you feel.

If this book is my baby, then Ami Harju is my doula. She read the earliest incarnation, separated the few chapters from Erik's point of view and told me, "This." She went on to read every version of The Man I Love, providing sound advice and valuable feedback. We were born to be friends. And I love us.

Stacie Fuss has always been with me, even when we were out of touch. She also read early drafts cover to cover and was a tireless sounding board. Always ready with coffee or baked Alaska. Thank you, sugar.

Jen McPartlin and Julia Bobkoff: my friends since childhood, both creative, visionary and inspiring, and two of the bravest women I know.

Dr. Dan Gingold always informed me about the weather in Los Angeles as he patiently and thoroughly answered every medical question. Likewise Detective Anthony Spennecchia was more than generous with his expertise. Thank you, gentlemen.

Rebecca T. Dickson, editor extraordinaire, was tough, impossible, relentless, demanding, pushy and profane. I thought it would kill me. You only made me stronger. There aren't (oops) sufficient words of thanks. Only four-letter ones.

I thank Desiree Wolfe for her wonderful guidance. And Tracy Kopsachilis for a beautiful cover design.

Ellen Harger is a brilliant writer and my one-woman support group. A dear friend. A needed friend. Best of all: a new friend.

My advance read army: Krista, Francesca, Donna, Kathy, Melissa, Mike, the other Mike, Julie, Mary, Patti, Francie—you are my betas, my behind-the-scenes crew. Without your show, there is no show. (And now I owe you all a dollar.)

I am grateful to my dance teachers and dance partners, past and present. I even thank the wolves. For not all of them come to kill you in the night. Some of them come to inspire.

My brother, Steve, whose plans go to Q, minimum, and who can take anything apart and put it together. My father, Bernie, who gave me a love of words and taught me to curse in six languages. My mother, Carol, who gave me the gift of dance and is my wisest, kindest friend and advocate.

My daughter Julie and my son AJ had to endure late dinners, missed ball games, distractions, outright neglect at times, and the constant sight of the back of my head and shoulders at the computer. And still they cheered me on, knowing what it meant to me. It is a privilege to be your mother.

And JP. The man I love. My soul mate. My partner on the path. My truth. We married in the shadow of Cathedral Rock. And I want no heart but yours to sleep under my hand.

THANK YOU

IF YOU ENJOYED *The Man I Love*, I'd love to hear about it. Please consider leaving a short review on the platform of your choice (Amazon, Goodreads, B&N, etc). Honest reviews are the tip jar of independent authors and each and every one is treasured.

If you subscribe to my Reader Club, you can get a *free* download of my flash fiction collection, *Love and Bravery: Hardcore Acts of Courage:*

BIT.LY/LOVE_BRAVERY.

As a Club member, you'll get firsthand news about future releases, upcoming events where I'll be, and exclusive giveaways.

If you're a Facebooker, join others who enjoyed my books in the Read & Nap Lounge:

BIT.LY/SLQR_LOUNGE.

Stop by my website at

SUANNELAQUEURWRITES.COM,

or tweet me at @Suannelqr.

Wherever you find me, all feels are welcome. And I always have coffee.

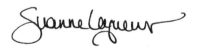

ALSO BY SUANNE LAQUEUR

THE FISH TALES

THE MAN I LOVE

GIVE ME YOUR ANSWER TRUE

HERE TO STAY

THE ONES THAT GOT AWAY

FISH TALES FOUR-BOOK BOX SET

VENERY

AN EXALTATION OF LARKS

A CHARM OF FINCHES

TALES FROM CUSHMAN ROW

FLASH FICTION

(FREE TO READER CLUB MEMBERS)

LOVE AND BRAVERY: HARDCORE ACTS OF COURAGE

ABOUT THE AUTHOR

A FORMER professional dancer and teacher, Suanne Laqueur went from choreographing music to choreographing words. Her work has been described as Therapy Fiction and Emotionally Intelligent Romance. She prefers Contemporary Train Wreck.

Laqueur's novel *An Exaltation of Larks* was the grand prize winner in the 2017 Writer's Digest Book Awards. Her debut novel *The Man I Love* won a gold medal in the 2015 Readers' Favorite Book Awards and was named Best Debut in the Feathered Quill Book Awards. Her follow-up novel, *Give Me Your Answer True,* was also a gold medal winner at the 2016 RFBA.

Laqueur graduated from Alfred University with a double major in dance and theater. She taught at the Carol Bierman School of Ballet Arts in Croton-on-Hudson for ten years. An avid reader, cook and gardener, she started her blog EatsReadsThinks in 2010.

Suanne lives in Westchester County, New York with her husband and two children.

EXCERPT FROM
GIVE ME YOUR ANSWER TRUE

Suanne Laqueur's award-winning debut novel The Man I Love *thrilled readers with its memorable characters and depth of emotion. Erik Fiskare's journey of love, recovery and forgiveness captivated hearts but also left open-ended questions. Now Daisy Bianco has a chance to tell her story and give her answers true...*

"WHY DON'T YOU START from the beginning?"

Daisy stared at the woman sitting across from her. "Because I like starting in the middle."

She felt foolish as soon as the words left her mouth. She was twenty-four years old. Snotting back like a sullen teenager served no purpose.

"Sorry," she said. "I'm so tired. And I don't have much of a filter lately."

The woman tilted her chin, her smile was understanding. She had a head of salt-and-pepper curls, parted on the extreme side and anchored behind her ears. Her glasses looked expensive and trendy but the rest of her looked second-hand thrift. Despite it being January, her feet were bare in worn, scuffed Birkenstocks. The orange toenail polish was chipped.

Her name was Rita Temple. She was Daisy's third therapist in five weeks.

"What happened with the previous two?"

"I couldn't connect," Daisy said. "The first one... He was at the hospital. Maybe it was because he was a man. I don't know. But I walked into his office the first time and it felt horrible. The air in the room was so oppressive. And it had such a clinical smell. It was an office, like this, but it reeked of alcohol and disinfectant. I felt like I was in a gown on the exam table, waiting to get a shot." She shrugged, embarrassment uncomfortably warm along her cheekbones. "I had an instinctive reaction to both the space and him. I gave it a second chance but the same thing happened."

"People have instincts for a reason," Rita said.

"The second therapist, Dr. Reilly, she was nice. I saw her a few times."

"This was also at the hospital?"

"Yeah, but she came to my room. Not that my room was all that great a space, but at least I had some of my things around me. I still felt like I couldn't connect. She was so quiet. And I know..." She held up her hand to stop any verbal traffic. "I know I'm supposed to talk and you're supposed to listen. I think I'm looking for a therapist with a streak of big sister. Someone a little tough."

"Why tough?"

Daisy looked down at her take-out coffee cup. "I don't know." But a little entity within her turned from its prim wooden chair facing the corner, lifted its woebegone face and whispered, *I've been such a bad girl.*

"Sounds like you want to be told off," Rita said. "Or punished."

Daisy rolled her lips in and blinked back the threat of tears. "I fucked up," she said. "I've fucked up my life so bad."

She sniffed hard, scraped her fingernail against a stain on her pant leg then looked around the room. The walls were painted a soft grey, silvery and warm, like sable. She had a weird impulse to run her hand along the surface, sure it would have a nap.

The knick-knacks adorning the end table looked personal and significant. A bowl of sea glass and several small, corked bottles containing sand and labeled with names of beaches. Books lined the shelves like multi-colored bricks, most battered and creased, obviously read and consulted many times.

"See anything you like?" Rita said.

"A lot of children's books stuffed between the professional ones." Daisy pointed. "The *Betsy-Tacy* series. And what looks like every Maurice Sendak book ever written."

"I'm a huge fan."

"And something smells like lemon, and lavender."

"The bowl on the table has both. Does it remind you of something?"

"Home."

"Where is home?"

"My parents' house in Pennsylvania. They have a little farm and orchard. My mother grows herbs. In summer she'll have bunches of lavender hanging all over to dry, lemon verbena and mint. Her family was all perfumers. Except her, she was a dancer. Like me."

"Where do you dance?"

"With the Metropolitan Opera Ballet. I've been on leave since December. When I went into the hospital..."

The silence pulled tight. Daisy reached to the bowl, crushed lavender buds between her fingers and wished for a cigarette.

"While I was out, one of the tenors died," she said. "Richard Versalle. Right onstage during *The Makropulos Case.* He was climbing a ladder, singing the opening aria... Had a heart attack and fell twenty feet to the stage. Dead." She shook her head. "I don't know what any of that has to do with my little breakdown."

"Here's a tip, and this will apply to any therapist you may choose to work with: don't worry about relevance. The first few months of therapy are about spilling your guts. Good, bad, ugly and incoherent. Because you won't know what's relevant or isn't until it's all in front of you."

"More is more," Daisy murmured, not sure how she felt about *months.*

"Exactly. The plan is you spill and I sort. If you decide to stay, that is."

Mulling over the plan, Daisy thought about taking her shoes off and pulling her feet under her. No sooner did she think it when Rita kicked off one of her own sandals and drew that foot up beneath her knee.

"Try to find a beginning," Rita said. "Or just start somewhere. We can go backward or forward, it doesn't matter." She had a marble composition notebook in her lap. She opened it now, clicked the end of her pen.

"I love that sound," Daisy said. "When the spine of a new book cracks."

Rita smiled. "So do I."

"So," Daisy said. "It could start six weeks ago when I started cutting myself."

She paused for a reaction, but Rita only kept writing.

"Or," Daisy said, puzzled, "I could start two weeks prior when a broken window triggered some kind of flashback."

"A flashback to?"

"To when I got shot."

Now she waited for Rita to show a startled expression. To gasp or say "Oh my goodness."

Silence except for the scratch of pen on paper.

"Or maybe I should start the day of the shooting," Daisy said, now throwing whatever she could think of in a careless volley. "Or when I cheated on my boyfriend and destroyed my life. Or when I started doing drugs, because I was high when I cheated on him. But the drugs started after the shooting so it really goes back to then. I guess it has to start with the shooting. But really it starts with Erik."

"Erik was your boyfriend?"

Daisy nodded. "He was my life. My life started with him. And I fucked up and he left and I deserved it. But I can't leave. I can't leave it and it won't leave me and I don't know what to do anymore."

She exhaled and took a sip of coffee. Then sat up choking as hot liquid dribbled over her chin.

"Dammit."

Through the monologue Rita had been taking notes. Her eyebrows went up and down. She gave short, brief nods, sometimes with a twist of her bottom lip. A terse sound of agreement in her throat, or a more lyrical "Hmmm." Now she looked up, pen still poised over the pages.

"This is good," she said.

Daisy's own eyebrows rose. A first. She'd expected more non-verbal invitations, not praise for the mess she'd made of her life.

"Glad you like it," she said, smiling as she ran her singed tongue along the roof of her mouth.

"Basically, you've given me a story in reverse," Rita said. Her smile was broad as she turned her notebook upside-down and squinted at it. "Now how about we turn it around?"

Tears sprang to Daisy's eyes. She could feel her heart press against the inside wall of her chest in a terrible longing to be free. The little penitent gazed hopefully from its chair in the corner.

Please turn it around.

The unexpected simplicity of it stole her breath. The cup trembled in her hands. "I want to turn it around," she said. "I hurt so much and I can't... I've tried everything."

Rita put the end of her pen between her teeth. Behind her glasses, her eyes were kind. But something was mischievous in her expression. "You haven't tried me."

Daisy pressed the back of her hand into one damp eye, then the other. Something in her reached across the expanse of carpet and plugged into Rita Temple's socket. A small current began to thrum in her chest.

"When did you graduate college?" Rita asked.

"Nineteen ninety-three." Nearly three years ago. It felt like two decades.

"From?"

"It was a fine arts school outside Philadelphia." Why was she being coy? Was this the final test to decide if she'd come back again?

Rita intertwined her fingers and set them down on her notebook. "Were you at Lancaster?"

Daisy put her cup down, heeled off her shoes and pulled both feet up. She drew one of the throw pillows into her lap, hugging the chocolate-brown chenille to her stomach.

"Yes," she said.

CPSIA information can be obtained
at www.ICGtesting.com
Printed in the USA
FSHW020509060919
61772FS